Blood is Thicker

I0549577

To Dulcie Zazula,
my fifth and sixth grade teacher.
You started the dream.
And I never forgot it.

Chapter One

"I hate shape shifters!" Ian exclaimed as he cranked the wheel of his beloved truck, sending it drifting around a turn in the gravel road. Daniel had to brace himself against the door to stop from being thrown across the cab, as the headlights cut a new path through the dusk. He checked over his shoulder to make sure Winchester, their German Shepherd, hadn't taken too much of a tumble in the truck bed. He didn't have to check the speedometer, however, to know it was stretching far past that of the recommended speed limit.

"Yeah, and vampires, and lycanthropes, and faeries, and any other Fifth World supernatural race that so much as looked at you the wrong way," Daniel snapped, feeling irritable. He was grasping his right arm, blood seeping through between his fingers. The deep gash stung, and he ground his teeth against the pain.

Ian shot him a glare, pinning him with chilling blue eyes. The dimming light from the receding sun caught his brother's cropped brass coloured hair, lighting up the rare tints of gold in it. Daniel could tell there was an angry retort on his older brother's lips, when Ian suddenly did a double take, seeming to notice Daniel's injury for the first time.

"Hey, *hey*," he said fearfully, all traces of his previous words vanishing on his lips. His hand tightened on the steering wheel, concern flashing across his face. "You're not bleeding to death on me over there are you?"

Daniel exhaled. Tilting his head back against the headrest, he closed his eyes for a moment. He felt completely disheveled from their recent narrow escape. His white t-shirt was ripped along his cut, stained with blood and dirt. The sad thing was, despite it all-- they'd been through worse.

In truth, Daniel knew he wasn't much cut out for this line of duty. Killing the Night Children was a Knocte's responsibility.

The Night Children, a group of Fifth Worlders, were notorious for choosing to live an evil existence. They had little regard for innocent human life, and viewed midnight massacres to be more like parties. Not only that, but their actions had caused a great deal of prejudice to build between even the good Fair

Children of the Fifth World races and the Knoctes. The Knoctes, a race born with reflexes and heightened senses able to rival the abilities of Fifth Worlders, had long ago made it their duty and line of work to protect the naïve victims of the world-- the Innocents. And often times they were willing to take that duty to the extreme. It was what they lived for. What they breathed.

Ian was a Knocte.

Daniel wasn't.

They had never figured out why that was, except to narrow it down to genetics, the same way Ian could have blue eyes, while Daniel himself had brown. Sure he too harbored abilities that were above the norm. He was a walking encyclopedia and god of all things technological. A Scitor-- more commonly known as a Scit. He could read the signs of Night Children activity a mile away, and it was his and every other Scits' job to inform Knoctes of such incidences, prepare them for each case they took.

But Daniel was different than other Scits in one aspect. He went along for the ride. He followed his older brother on duty and watched his back. They had always operated as a team, long before they'd ever known the unwritten rule about Knoctes and Scits operating within professional circumstances only. And though he didn't have his brother's supernatural speed or strength, Daniel was as prepared as any human could be. He had trained in many areas both academically and physically; areas of weaponry and combat were not foreign to him. He offered what he did have in order to try and save lives. It was uncanny and a lot of Knoctes and Scits alike didn't agree with it. As groups only known to interact on a business level, his partnership with his brother was completely unheard of.

Not even Knoctes took cases together.

Having a partner was seen as a liability and a responsibility Knoctes couldn't afford to have on their shoulders. Despite everything, however, no one could argue with results, and Daniel knew he and his brother held one heck of a good track record.

"*Dan?!*"

Ian's brow was still furrowed with worry, and Daniel could see his eyes were flickering uneasily between him and the road.

"I'm fine!" Daniel quickly barked a reassurance. "I'll live."

Ian only gave pause for another moment, and then with a

curt nod, seemed to decide to believe him for the time being.

"Do you think it's still following us?" he asked, returning to business.

Daniel didn't have to check over his shoulder to give an answer.

"Yes," he said resignedly, "it's been following us for three days straight, Ian, it's not likely to quit now."

"Good," Ian said with a mirthless smile, "cause we're here."

Reaching down, he slammed the truck into four-wheel drive, just as it careened off the road. Cutting through the ditch, Ian swerved around the deadly section of road they had made so not two hours ago, having planted IEDs in a hasty, cavalier line.

Fire was only the thing Daniel and his brother knew of that could kill a shifter. Their otherwise moldable, generating bodies, went up like old, long dead, bone-dry Christmas trees. So much as a spark and the creature was sent reeling, becoming nothing more than a pile of ash.

Daniel and his brother, however, had less of a spark in mind… so much as a boom.

Ian swung the truck back up onto the road, and when they were at a safe distance, pulled the emergency brake, swinging the truck back around to face the direction they had come. He killed the headlights, letting it idle.

A quiet, anxious anticipation fell over them.

"Get Winchester inside," Daniel ordered, breaking the silence without turning to look at his brother, his eyes instead fixed on the vacant road ahead of them.

He heard the familiar creak of the truck door as Ian hefted it open, and he must have brought his fingers to his lips, because his sharp, deafening whistle suddenly cut through the air. Winchester obliged, obediently leaping from the truck bed and launching himself into the cab. Usually the tracking dog would trample his way onto Daniel's lap, but as if sensing the tension in the air, he was on full alert. He stood on his hind legs in between them, his front paws propped up and resting on the dashboard. His snout was nearly pressed against the windshield, his eyes watching the curve in the road in front of them expectantly. A low, determined growl rumbled in the back of his throat.

"Easy," Ian mumbled and stroked the dog's head once, but Winchester hardly seemed to notice, his eyes and ears completely trained on his surroundings. "What does it look like?" Ian asked.

"When it swiped me it was a hefty, middle aged, balding man," Daniel said vindictively, "talk about blending in, that's about as generic as they come." He stole another glance down at his arm and pursed his lips. "I'm going to need some gauze sometime soon," he admitted.

Ian's attention left the road.

"Sometime soon?" he repeated in exasperation. He grabbed Daniel's shoulder, forcing him to turn and show him the damage. Grimacing Daniel reluctantly peeled his hand away to show his brother.

Ian swore loudly.

"You mean *now*," he grumbled, "Keep pressure on that."

Daniel laughed sardonically. "What did you think I *was* doing?"

Ian pinned him with an annoyed look. "Just shuddup," he snapped, letting him know he found no humor in the situation. "I know I have gauze around here somewhere."

He'd just turned to search the backseat, when headlights flew around the corner in front of them. Any hope Daniel had of bandages was lost, as the yellow truck sprayed gravel, speeding in their direction. The only thing separating the two vehicles from a head on collision was a short stretch of rural road and one very deadly IED line.

The corner of Daniel's mouth tipped up into an almost smile.

"Or sometime soon," he reiterated.

"Is that the car?" Ian asked, shooting his brother a hasty glance, the oncoming headlights lighting his face. "Is it? I'm not letting no Innocent drive through no line of doom."

"It's the same one that's been following us," Daniel confirmed.

Ian flicked the truck into reverse, but kept his foot on the brake, his eyes fixed pointedly ahead.

"Awesome."

When the other truck grew close enough that its headlights illuminated their dark idling figure, the shape shifter slammed the brakes on, sliding the truck to a gravel crunching stop a few meters in front of them, and a few feet short of the IED line. Ian practically growled in frustration. The cab door to the other truck swung open and long legs stretched towards the ground.

"Oh, come on!" Ian complained as he watched the model tall, blond figure the shape shifter had adopted emerge completely out of the vehicle. "That is *not* fair!"

The creature leaned against the hood of its truck and curved an elegant, nail tipped finger in a beckoning gesture. The clothes it was wearing hadn't ever heard of the word modest. Daniel found his brother's distress almost humorous. Having Devlyn, a long-term girl of his own, Daniel felt no desire towards the unnatural figure poised in front of them.

"Come on, boys. I don't have all day. Come out and play," the shape shifter mocked, her voice raising to reach them, where they still sat idling in their truck. Daniel exchanged an uneasy glance with his brother. Then with a sigh Ian flicked the truck back into park and reached into the back seat for the flare gun. Noticing the preparations, Winchester trampled across his lap to paw at the truck door impatiently. Ian turned to reach for the handle, but stopping short, spun back around to face Daniel.

"Just stay here," he said making a 'lay low' gesture, the gun held firmly in his right hand. Winchester let out a small annoyed whimper. "Find some gauze and try not to die, all right?"

Daniel didn't answer as his brother thrust the door open, letting Winchester leap down onto the road before him. Ian slammed the door shut without a backwards glance and strode towards the battle that awaited him, shoving the gun into the waistband of his jeans as he went.

Ian planted himself just before the IED line, Winchester halting at his side. He gave the appearance of cool indifference, but every muscle in his body was tensed for a fight. He sized up his opponent, making sure to leak just enough emotion into his features to show how unimpressed he felt.

"I know I'm a handsome devil, but is it really necessary to stalk me?" he asked sardonically.

"Ian, always the charmer," the shifter stated with dripping sarcasm.

Her voice was too high, too shrilling, that it just missed the normalcy territory. It grated in Ian's ears and took away some of the creature's otherwise obvious appeal. If you looked hard enough there was always something off, some small unnatural piece, some crack that leaked through a shape shifter's facade.

"You know, I think I liked you better as an old man."

The shifter smiled. "Sorry to mess with your concentration."

Ian smiled, an audacious retort coming naturally to his lips. "It comes back pretty quickly when you know everything you're looking at is ten kinds of fake. Not that it takes a whole lot of brain power to off a shifter…"

"Well," the shifter said, cherry red lips lifting into a smirk, "we'll see about that."

With a twirl of her wrists two daggers seemed to almost materialize in her grip.

It was just like a shifter to be able to hide a weapon anywhere. Ian reached back to unveil his own weapon, as the creature twirled the knives once more in a threatening circle, eyes burning with excitement. Then something else caught her attention and her gaze shifted just over his shoulder.

Ian could practically sense his brother's presence even before he came to stand beside him.

I'm gonna kill him.

Daniel stood with a serious expression on his face. His hair was a tousled mess of brown strands, rich with naturally red highlights, making it a rare auburn, almost mahogany colour. It hung in his eyes; eyes that were so dark and warm they gave a sort of puppy dog appeal to his young face. A shotgun rested erect against his shoulder. No one would have noticed he wasn't a Knocte with how naturally he adopted the pose-- well, except for the fact that he'd brought a shotgun to a shifter showdown, but Ian had long ago learned to trust his brother's Scit logics. Daniel's bad arm was patched with gauze and held on haphazardly with a strip of cloth he'd managed to wrap around and knot.

Blood was already seeping through.

"Oh, good. We've decided to stop cowering," the shifter mocked, her face smug as she eyed the shotgun, her eyes laughing. "How's the arm?"

6

"Bite me," Daniel snapped.

"I can do a lot more damage than that, honey," she promised.

Daniel's mouth twisted with displeasure, and Ian was inclined to believe her.

He wasn't one to underestimate an opponent, though he'd claim just the opposite in a heartbeat. He was watching her every movement carefully, and it didn't escape his notice when her blades stopped twirling, her grip tightening discreetly. He guessed her next move before she even made it. The expression on her face was a familiar one. It was the same one she'd gotten the last time Daniel had entered the equation, and well, that hadn't exactly turned out in their favor.

Ian moved at the same time the Shifter did. He slammed into his brother with unannounced strength as the blade was hurled in his direction. The dagger cart wheeled through the air, just glancing off Ian's shoulder before he and Daniel both crashed in a heap on the ground, eating gravel dust. Winchester's vicious barks rang out beside them, as he danced around the perimeter of the IED line, leaping forward and springing away with bared teeth.

"Boys, boys, boys," she chastised as they scrambled to compose themselves.

Ian shoved himself to his feet, hauling his little brother up after him by the front of his shirt. He attempted to shrug off his injury, as his gaze checked Winchester for movement that might go too far, wishing he could call their small companion back without giving away their plan. The shifter barely acknowledged the dog, however, as she took purposeful strides towards them, a single blade still in hand. The moment before she reached Winchester, she suddenly brought herself up short, freezing mid-step. She eyed the section of road in front of her with contempt, and then glancing right at the brothers, Ian watched the anger grow in her features.

"How stupid do you think I am?!" she demanded, glancing down at their IED line again with distaste, like their amateurish ways were somehow beneath her. With a disbelieving shake of her head, she leapt safely over the line, her eyes transfixed on Daniel. Winchester sprang forward the moment she was within reach, sinking his teeth deep into the flesh of her calf. But just as fast as he'd tare a strip of skin away, it would start to regenerate, blood

7

running down to her ankle. She hardly even seemed to notice, or pay the dog any heed. In fact, she'd hardly given Ian a second glance either, instead showing an unsettling fascination with his brother. The realization flooded Ian's mind with instant concern, his senses snapping to acute attention. Why had his brother become such a singled out target? Why were those hatred-laden eyes boring through Daniel with an intensity that made absolutely no sense, while he was ignored? Ian was the Knocte, and by far the larger threat. He couldn't remember a time when his brother had ever seemed to be a creature's focal point or main concern.

But as if to confirm the uneasy belief, without warning the shifter sprang at Daniel.

Ian had the flare gun up and around before she'd barely left the ground.

"Hey!" he yelled as his finger pulled the trigger.

The fireball shot out with precise aim, and Ian squinted through the sudden flash of light and smoke, as the flare flew towards the creature's chest. She looked over at him if only for a second, a crafty smile pulling up her lips. Ian watched in disbelief, as in a matter of split seconds-- she started to change. The clothes, skin and tissue of her chest sprang apart, like un-meshing wires leaving an open gaping hole, just large enough for a flare to slip through. Ian had just enough time to scream what felt like a slow motioned "No!" before the flare sailed safely through the shifter's person without catching.

Then things were all happening quickly again. She slammed into Daniel with break neck force, flattening him on his back once again on the graveled road. The shotgun tumbled uselessly from his grip and skittered across the rough stones, freeing up his hands to catch the shifter's wrist in time to hold at bay, the knife that came down over his throat.

"Ian!" Daniel grunted as the shifter tried to use her leverage to force the knife into its malicious duty. He gritted his teeth, struggling against her strength. The tip of the blade kissed his neck as Ian dove for the abandoned shotgun. In one swift motion he grabbed it up, and spun, connecting the butt of it with the side of the shifter's head. The force knocked the shifter aside and no sooner than she hit the ground, Winchester was on her, teeth sinking into her neck, her shoulder, her leg, anything to slow her down, give the brothers an edge.

His attempt didn't last long, for as soon as the shifter was able to orientate herself enough, she threw him off effortlessly. The dog hit the crunching gravel, paces away, but Ian was there, swinging the butt of his shotgun again, the moment she got to her feet. Its wood cracked against nose and cheekbone, and she reeled backwards, stumbling towards the IED line. She caught her balance right before it, gripping her knife tighter with one hand and reaching up to wipe at her bloody nose with the other. She pulled her hand away to observe its streaked redness, and laughed.

"What are you going to do with a shotgun?" she leered, "You can hit me all you want"--she spread her arms wide; mockingly-- "But I still have a throwing arm, and I have good enough aim to finish your brother off right now."

Ian felt his Adam's apple working as panic began to set in again. Daniel had pulled himself into a sitting position, and was thumbing away a spot of blood running down his neck. Their gazes met, and he knew in the same way Ian knew, that the threat was not one to be taken lightly. Although Ian might be fast enough to dodge a throw like hers, his brother, a Scitor, would not be. Daniel didn't have the unnatural speed needed, and was set too far from Ian, for him to affectively block her shot in anyway. The shifter's laughter grew higher, louder and more shrilling as she cocked her wrist back. Ian's mouth twitched in anger.

"Ian! Line! Now!" Daniel spat, ordering him from behind.

And Ian understood.

He instantly swung the shotgun around, slipping his finger in against the trigger. He lined up the shot and squeezed. The blast went right between the shifter's legs, ploughing into the IED line.

"Game over. Freak," Ian said between clenched teeth, before the resulting blast threw him off his feet.

He struck the road, hard, several feet away, and laid there, ears ringing, eyes blurring with dust and smoke. Only bits and pieces of the world made it through the confusion at a time. Ringing-- flames enveloping the shifter, licking across skin as if it was made of paper, mouth opened wide in a shriek he couldn't hear-- Winchester's wet tongue against his face and hand-- more ringing-- ash drifting down all around like discolored snow-- Daniel's face above his. And then--

"Ian! Ian, snap out of it!" Daniel's good hand was balled in the fabric of Ian's shirt, trying to shake some sense into him. Ian blinked and then pulled himself into a sitting position, coughing debris from his lungs. Daniel let out a breath and swatted his back, as Winchester trotted a guarding circle around them both.

"Dead?" Ian rasped, looking up at his brother who was crouched in front of him, arms resting on his knees.

Daniel smiled tiredly, shifting his injured arm.

"Very," he assured him. "Unfortunately for us though, there's no way that went unnoticed-- even out here."

"That bad?" Ian asked, and stretched to look over his brother's shoulder, taking in the aftermath. There was no proof that a shifter had ever been present, all evidence of the creature's existence having disappeared into the wind. As for the rest of the scene...

"Well," Daniel shrugged, "we just made the world's biggest pothole.

Chapter Two

The old wooden stairs leading up to the Roadhouse porch creaked under the weight of Ian's sneakers as he ascended. Daniel followed in his wake, still slightly groggy from crashing in the truck on the daylong drive back. He had the hood of his favorite sweater pulled up, casting shadows over his cheekbones. Panting softly after them, Winchester brought up the rear. The bouncer, a guy Ian didn't recognize and who had been leaning against the doorframe immediately stepped forward, hand held palm out for them to halt. Probably in his thirties, the man was dressed undoubtedly clean cut for his position, a white button-down shirt over wrinkle free jeans, his brown hair tidy and cropped short. In reality though, the man was less of a bouncer, and more of a guard, keeping the Innocents from the nightmarish awakening a Knocte home base would be to them. Though on second thought-- Ian knew it could just as well be for the Knoctes' sakes. The Roadhouse to an innocent mind would look like a rowdy, occasionally mournful place, full of weapon wielders swapping conversations and stories that would label them off as madmen.

"Name," the man demanded in a tone that hinted at boredom.

Without hesitation Ian took another step forward, placing himself directly in front of the man. They would have been standing face to face, if Ian weren't easily two heads taller.

"How about just the brass taxes, huh?" he said, and holding his forearm out between them, shoved his sleeve up to show the tattoo imprinted on his skin just below the inside of his elbow. It was a black outline of a shield with a crescent moon and two stars to decorate-- his Dignus. The stamp that labeled him a Knocte, a soldier against nightmares.

The man's eyes slid from verifying Ian's arm over to Daniel. "And him?"

Ian was just about to snap something along the lines of: *he's with me*, when Daniel stepped purposely past him.

"Here," his brother offered, sincere brown eyes half hidden, but still as big as ever, as he dutifully rolled up his sleeve to display his own Dignus. Matching shield, matching moon and stars

11

to Ian's own. Ian shot his brother a look. There weren't very many people who knew Daniel possessed the mark. As a Scitor it should be impossible for him to get one. Instead, Scit's usually carried a form of identification to get them into places. Daniel had said himself, when he was no more than ten years old, that it was so like Scits to use paper and Knoctes to use tattoos.

But the man didn't seem to notice anything amiss, and with a nod of his head, waved them past.

The odor of whisky, leather, and sweat immediately hit Ian as he pushed his way into the Roadhouse alongside his brother. It hung in the dimly lit air like a welcoming cloak. The familiar smells along with its familiar sight, was one of the only true sensations of home Ian knew he and his brother felt. It had been a long drive back, and seeing the place was like greeting an old friend.

Across the room, and stretching the entire length of the farthest wall, sat an illustrious mahogany bar. Its elegant wooden canopy hung with crystal glassware, and its back wall completely made of mirrors, reflected the different bottles and brands of alcohol on the ledge before it. Carvings were crafted in the bar's every surface, images of leafy vines snaking around its perimeter, faces of werewolves, dragons, and those of other various creatures lurked in the wood work, staring back at them, teeth bared.

The sound of clashing balls from the three pool tables at the far right of the Roadhouse added to the acoustics of laughter and jeering belonging to the countless Knoctes around them. A group stood around a mounted TV screen, gesturing animatingly as they watched the latest hockey game, cheers and boos echoing with each goal. A few tracking dogs were play fighting, chasing one another under tables, nipping and biting at heels and ears. Waitresses dressed in short dresses and tight jeans weaved in between both the tables and the leathered booths, their trays held high with liquor filled glasses, the liquid hardly ever displaced under their elegant grace.

But there was only one waitress of the Fair Child race that worked at the Roadhouse, Ian knew, only one faerie that had been his brother's closest and best friend.

Ruby Becker.

And that faerie was now standing directly in front of them both.

"Dan!" she exclaimed, her face alight with excitement, as she beamed up at his brother, uncontrollably grinning ear to ear. The flecks in her grey eyes sparked brightly like stars breaking through a storm cloud, and her dark hair shimmered with natural translucent faerie streaks of blue and gold. She had painted her fingernails to match the colours, alternating them between each finger. The halter knee length dress she wore was slightly ruffled at the bottom, and gave the appearance of a dusk sky, splattered with a gold star burst on her left side. It splayed the shimmering dust across her dress, fading as it reached the right. Ian knew it was probably an article from her own clothing line.

He had no idea where she came up with this kind of crap.

"Hey, Bee," Daniel said, a genuinely warm smile spreading across his face.

Ruby spread her arms wide, like she was going to bombard him with a hug, but caught herself, stopping short just in time.

"All right," she ordered. "List them off."

Ian could recall too many occurrences where she'd tackled him on sight, only to find out a moment later that he was still recovering from unseen injuries. 'Listing' injuries had become a normal precaution.

You'd think I always brought him back in ten pieces...

"Just my arm," Daniel assured, and rolled his shoulder back carefully, but Ruby was already reaching forward, catching it gently between her thin hands. Daniel didn't argue as she pushed up his sleeve to reveal the angry red patch job Ian had witnessed Daniel do in the truck on the way back. It was not a fond memory. Ian could still hear his brother's sharp intakes of breath at every thread the needle made through his skin, and he watched Ruby struggled to hide her grimace as she eyed the result.

"Floss stitching. Nice touch," she said weakly, and anyone could tell that she didn't really mean it. She collected him into a careful hug, her arms wrapping gingerly around his neck to avoid his arm.

Ian flinched in spite of himself, instinct sending an automatic warning shooting through his system. The proximity of a Fifth Worlder that close to his brother, never failed to put him on edge, or send his senses spiking into high alert. Even after all these years of the two being best friends, his feelings had never changed towards the faerie. His eyes continually followed her every movement with a sense of skepticism and distrust. Some would call it discrimination; others understood his bone deep urge to find something wieldable, something iron.

He couldn't help it. It was in the very fabric of his being. Woven through his DNA.

Or at least... that's what he told himself.

Over his brother's shoulder he watched as Ruby peaked up at him. She gave him a tentative smile, as if she could somehow read his thoughts, and wanted to send him a sign of reassurance. But Ian knew it would never work. He'd never be put at ease. Not when Daniel was on the line. Call it paranoia or justified, but either way, it was what kept him and his brother alive, and because of that fact, he could never bring himself to regret it. The only response he gave her was to keep his features cold as he unwaveringly met her gaze. With a dejected sigh, Ruby ducked her head back down to rest on Daniel's shoulder.

The moment Devlyn Morrow saw the Browning brothers weaving their way through the crowd in the Roadhouse, she felt like she could breath easy for the first time in weeks. She leaned over the smooth surface of the bar, her fingers drumming impatiently against its wood, as she waited for them to reach her. She hoped Daniel wouldn't read too much into the wisps and patterns she'd sketched on her skin, curving over her wrists and climbing up her forearm. It was no secret she painted and drew her way through every emotion, the good and the bad, anxiety and worry being two big contenders for causing her fingers to itch towards a writing instrument. Paper or no paper, Daniel's recent absence had been no exception.

She could see Ruby towing Daniel behind her, her hand locked around his in a vice grip. Devlyn understood the need. Daniel was a constant in her life, a foothold, and every trip he took with Ian, every time he went out on duty, there was a chance he wouldn't be coming back. As they drew closer, she could make out most of Daniel's face, even under the shadow his hood cast, it was gentle and boyish in the dim lighting, strands of auburn hair hanging in his eyes. And when those warm, deep, brown eyes met with hers, a tired, but loving smile spread wide across his beautiful face. He carried with him a stronger sense of home, than her small apartment would ever be able to supply her. And following like a silent shadow behind him-- Ian.

The brothers were similar in many ways, from the left cheeked dimple that appeared in their smiles, to their prominent cheekbones, but more than anything, their comparability rested in their every movement. It was as if they were permanently in sync, so that during a fight it was hard to tell where one ended and the other began. They were like magnets. When one moved the other followed, whether it was shifting in their seats, or a round of combat. And to anyone who had ever heard them talk about one another, it was clear that they lived and breathed loyalty like it was the essence of who they were.

But Ian was also so very different from the brother Devlyn had come to love. Where the line of duty had taught Daniel to be compassionate and kind, it had taught Ian to be cold and untrusting. He was all handsome sharp angles and cold, piercing blue eyes. Ian was like the crashing waves and the shifting sand of a beach, while Daniel the solid rock and glowing lighthouse. Both separate elements, and yet completely entwined as a single entity. Where Daniel was steady, passionate, and pensive, Ian was all reckless action and vigilance. Even now his blue eyes swept the Roadhouse, suspicious of everything and everyone, like enemies would leap from the very woodwork around him. As always, he paid careful attention to Ruby as she led Daniel through the throng of people, for if there was one thing Ian was not reckless with-- it was his little brother. Daniel, like he was with many, was his brother's anchor.

"Look who I found!" Ruby announced when they were within reach, and she threw Daniel's arm into the air as if she were proclaiming him the winner of a fight. Winchester barked as if for emphasis, his tail thudding against Daniel's pant leg in his excitement.

Dan, my Daniel, Devlyn thought, but had no need to say it. She knew her eyes and smile would communicate the feelings just as clearly.

Scrambling to get around the bar, and nearly knocking into

the other bartender in the process, she reached out for him. He held open one arm for her, and she instantly knew his other side held an injury. Careful to be gentle, she caught hold of his face and pressed her lips against his, relief flooding through her as his arm closed tightly around her, holding her against his good side. His hood instantly driving her mad, she ripped it down off his head, his deep brown, partly auburn hair springing free, static electricity singing through her fingers as they weaved through the strands, purposely ruffling it further. For a second she thought she could hear Ian give a small amused laugh, but the truth was, Daniel's hair was better this way, all sticking up like he'd run his fingers through it many times. It was a small kind of crazy, sexy chaos. It spoke of long hours consisting of toiling, thinking, and stolen naps. Or maybe it reminded her of the times she'd woken up next to him, turning over to see him propped up on one arm, a happy, lazy smile on his face. Sometimes it seemed there were only two heights to Daniel's hair, in his eyes or in the air.

Breaking away to lean her head against his shoulder and close her eyes, she thought she could feel the tattoo on her left hand, as she breathed in the smell of Daniel's old favorite sweater. Placed just above the wrist between her thumb and the rest of her fingers, the half circle was a symbol of commitment. Sliding her hand over Daniel's heart she knew the other half of the circle rested there, just beneath his shirt. Knoctes didn't have promise rings, didn't have engagements or weddings. Their lives were often too short and uncertain, too nomadic, or too poor for such sentimental privileges. So instead they marked their chosen with a sign of loyalty and of continuing promise. The circle was almost like a ring; only they each got half, half of something both permanent and bonding.

"You okay?" she whispered into Daniel's sweater, her fingers now curling around one of the drawstrings to stop herself from reaching out to his injured side.

"I'm good," he promised, the same as he always did. He pressed his lips to the top of her head, and then leaned down to rest his cheek there. "All good."

"You know," Ruby cut in, breaking Devlyn and Daniel from their own little world and causing them to look over at her suddenly. "I probably have something for your--."

"You know what sounds great?" Ian interrupted, talking over Ruby's attempt at offering one of her ointments. The faerie race was extremely good at mixing organic materials, and her tinkering often came in very handy, especially in the brothers' line of work. Unfortunately, the faeries that belonged to the Night Children used their concoctions as advantages in fights against Knoctes, often to harmful ends, causing Ian, in particular, to have grown very wary of any and all of them. "A beer sounds great."

Side stepping his way around them, Ian made his way over to the bar where he parked himself on one of the leather cracked stools. With a small smile and a roll of her eyes Devlyn followed, Daniel and Ruby behind her, and retook her position behind the bar. Turning to retrieve a couple beers from the mini fridge, she cracked them open, and thunked one down in front of Ian. She handed the other off to Daniel as he slid onto the seat beside his brother. Ian twisted the bottle to the label side, and nodded to the blue mountains approvingly, as Winchester slid to his stomach under Daniel's stool. Ruby disappeared into the back behind the bar, where Devlyn knew she'd be making her way through a labyrinth of rooms.

The Roadhouse was somewhat of a multipurpose building. It didn't just give Knoctes the chance to rest, meet with their Scitors, and hustle a little money off one another, it also had several back rooms stocked with weapons, ready to supply the Knocte masses with anything they could need for a case. There were vaults and safe rooms formed from every metal lethal to Fifth Worlders, all melted down and mixed to create their walls and doors in case of an attack. Not to mention the vending machines, the mini Laundromat and the couple of showers they had separate for public access. All around it was meant to be a safe haven of sorts, a stopping ground, a home base.

And Devlyn meant to keep it that way.

For Knoctes and Scitors alike, even the few trusted Fair Children that had earned their place.

And as if on cue, Ruby re-emerged from the back, a small jar cradled in her hands.

"Be glad I'm looking out for you," she said to Daniel, and Devlyn watched both the brothers swivel to look at the faerie, Ian pausing with his beer halfway to his lips. His eyes grew cold as they locked on the jar, like the ice in his gaze could crack the glass and cause it to shatter.

"He'll be fine," Ian began to protest, as Ruby stepped up to the bar. "He doesn't need--."

"Ian, relax," Daniel muttered reprovingly, and instantly surrendered his arm, laying it on top of the bar. As Ruby reached for his sleeve, Devlyn grabbed for Daniel's free hand, lacing her fingers through his.

Stitched or not, the cut was red, leaky, and angry.

Devlyn swallowed hard, and felt the sudden weight of Ian's eyes on her. She knew what she'd see, if she looked up and caught his gaze, knew what those eyes would say. It would be the same thing they always said, begging her forgiveness. *I'm sorry. I'm so sorry. I did what I could.*

Opening the jar, Ruby dipped her fingers in the substance and spread it over Daniel's wound. As she applied it, he let out a small sigh of relief, for which Devlyn was grateful, despite the fact that Ian was shifting uneasily in his seat nearby. She was just about to say something reassuring to the anxious brother, when another voice spoke over her.

"Well, look whom the cat finally dragged in. Ian, brother, it has been too long!"

The entire party at the bar turned to face the familiar newcomer.

Luke Collings' nearly white blond hair was styled neatly to perfection, his long overcoat crisp and sharp looking. He never had it any other way. He had a clean cut, calm composure-- that fooled no one. It was as deadly as it was serene. Those dark, canny eyes of his took in Devlyn and the others, with an air of cool arrogance, and she found herself scowling.

She wasn't sure she'd ever get used to the way Knoctes called each other family, brothers and sisters. Knowing the Browning brothers as she did, such terms felt empty coming from anyone else, especially tossed out so casually. Even coming from Luke, who she and the brothers had known for years, it struck a wrong cord. Ever since she'd known him, Luke had always found pleasure in stirring up tensions where there weren't any. There was just something about him that set Devlyn's teeth on edge. And she knew she wasn't the only one. Daniel's shoulders had tensed the moment he'd heard Luke's voice, and Ruby had shrank back altogether. As a faerie, she had never been highly regarded in Luke's eyes. In fact-- quite the opposite. Where Ian felt distrust, she knew Luke felt something more sinister.

Ian was the only one who seemed relieved at the man's sudden appearance.

"Luke!" he laughed, a smile spreading across his face for his old friend. He stood up to greet him, extending his hand in an offer of Conexus. It was a display of bond meant to be between two Knoctes. It was only offered if there was a relationship of deep trust and friendship between the one who offered and the accepter. It was not dealt out lightly. And despite the unwritten Knocte-Knocte rule, Devlyn knew Ian swapped Conexus with his brother all the time. Knew he hadn't thought twice about it being any other way.

Devlyn couldn't help but cringe slightly as Luke stepped up to clasp hands with Ian, in a way that looked like they might start a mid-air arm wrestle. At the same time Luke's Belgian Malinois tracking dog, Milo, trotted over to sniff friendly at Winchester, who licked his muzzle in greeting.

"How's the line of duty been treating you?" Ian asked, gesturing for Luke to sit in the empty seat beside him.

Much to everyone else's relief, it was an offer he waved away.

"I have been busy. Very busy. I just recently finished off a couple of faeries, and have a lead on a vampire up in Fort McMurray. Something is starting. Finally starting." Devlyn could see that malicious spark he always got, light his eyes when he talked about his job, like each kill was a savory candy. "I can feel it."

Ruby had taken several steps back, and was just about to quietly retreat, when Daniel glanced over catching her eye. Devlyn could see him searching for something to say.

"Thanks, Bee," he decided simply, and grabbed the small jar of ointment off the bar, holding it up. "Do you mind if I keep this?"

Ruby shook her head, those bright flecked eyes of hers wide in her face, as she glanced over at Luke, uneasy at being brought to his attention. But Devlyn knew what Daniel was doing.

His soft brown eyes were earnest in letting Ruby know that he didn't care who heard him. She was his best friend and he wasn't about to hide it. Not now. Not ever. He used her medicines, they helped, and he wasn't ashamed of it. It was moments like that, which reminded Devlyn just why she loved him so much.

Much to Ruby's probable relief Luke's eyes slid uninterestedly past her to land on Daniel. "My deepest sympathies on the recent news."

Devlyn froze. At the same time Daniel turned to him with a confused look. "The latest news?"

Luke raised an eyebrow and glanced her way. "Devlyn hasn't told you?"

Oh, Luke. She wanted to beg. *Please, please, don't.*

But he didn't give her the chance to say anything. "Jack," he said, and that's all he needed to say.

Daniel spun to face her. "Dev?" he asked at the same time Ian said, "That short nerdy dude with glasses?" Though she knew perfectly well Ian knew exactly whom they were talking about.

She didn't answer Daniel's inquiry, just stared at him with eyes she knew were sad. He deserved to know. But not like this, not with Luke standing over them, and Ian watching intently between them all.

Jack Menford had been Daniel's close and only Scitor friend, until about a month ago when he'd become a lycan, having been infected with lycanthropy through blood-to-blood contact. Since then, it seemed like it was only a matter of time. Scits and Knoctes never usually lasted long being a part of the Fifth World. Suicide was highly common, but so was vengeance. The Night Children took every advantage they could find, and a helpless, confused, ally-less, newly reborn was easy pickings. Devlyn and Daniel had tried to track Jack's whereabouts for as long as they could in the beginning, but he soon slipped under their radar. There hadn't been news for weeks.

Until now.

"Is he…?"

"No, no," she said quickly, realizing what conclusion Daniel was jumping to. She reached out for both his hands. "He's not dead."

"Yet," Luke added casually.

"Luke," she exasperated aloud this time, looking up at him, the 'please' implied in the way she said it. Then she turned back to Daniel. "Jack turned to the Night Children, Dan. There was evidence on the news this morning."

Luke nodded. "I saw it myself. Three Innocents died."

Daniel stood up abruptly, his hands slipping out from under hers. "Jack?" he said in disbelief, looking between them all. "You do know who we're talking about, right?" When no one said anything he emphasized it again. "Jack! The guy who memorizes encyclopedias when he's bored, because he finds it fun. You're trying to tell me he joined forces with the very creatures he's spent his whole life researching to try and stop? That now he suddenly finds fun in running through the streets killing Innocents?"

"I don't know, Dan," Devlyn said helplessly. "Maybe he convinced himself it was the only way. Maybe it was self preservation."

Luke snorted. "Right, because that is the problem we are faced with." And with a sudden whirl of coat, and a disgusted shake of his head, Luke turned and left the way he came, his tracking dog scrambling to follow at his heels.

Devlyn sighed, burying her face in her hands briefly. Ruby had disappeared silently from the group, probably across the Roadhouse somewhere serving patient guests.

"What are the Innocents calling it this time?" Ian asked, watching his friend go.

"A bear attack," she answered tiredly, she had been working for several hours on her feet, and the current conversation was beginning to wear her down in other ways. Daniel still looked like he couldn't believe it, but at her words he flashed her a concerned glance. Whatever he must have seen in her face was enough to temper his indignation.

Ian gave an amused shake of his head, taking another sip of his beer. "Yeah, heard that one before."

It wasn't funny. None of it was funny.

Daniel took his seat. "Dev," he said gently. "We'll figure this out, I promise. But you should go home and catch some rest."

"I'm fine."

He gave her a look. "I know you're off shift. There have been two bartenders on since we got here."

It was true. She'd continued to work, because she knew he'd come in tonight.

"I'm not the only one who could use a couple nap hours, you know," she teased with a half-smile, and ruffled his hair again.

He took her hand. "Go," he urged. "I promise I won't disappear."

"Come visit me later tonight then."

He smiled. "Always."

Ian rolled his eyes.

Ignoring him, Devlyn planted Daniel with a quick kiss and then took off into the back, striping off the apron from around her hips as she did.

She was barely out of earshot before Ian took up the conversation again. Daniel was just glad he'd waited that long. He knew Devlyn worried on a constant basis, and this conversation wasn't something she needed added to her plate.

"I'm starting to think Luke's right, Dan. I mean, Jack lasted a month. *One* month, before he went dark side."

Daniel gripped his beer bottle tighter. "Ian," he warned.

"*And* he was a Scit."

Daniel turned on his brother. "You really think Jack could do something like that?" He raised his eyebrows. "Really?"

The sides of Ian's mouth pulled down in consideration. "Well. Circumstances..."

"It's Jack!"

"It *was* Jack," his brother emphasized and Daniel could feel Ian searching his face, where he knew his frown was deepening. "Oh, come on, man," Ian persisted after a moment, lightening his tone slightly. "Every day one of those things takes a wrong turn, and we're the ones left cleaning up the mess. You"--he pointed an accusing finger at him-- "might be able to sweep it under the rug daily. But me?" He shook his head. "I don't entirely doubt that they all go bad eventually."

"Do you even hear yourself sometimes? We aren't going on a rampage killing innocent people, Ian! Riddling monsters is one thing-- but murder is another. It's on us to know the difference. And it's a choice we have to live with."

Ian stared at him. Then giving a weighted sigh, pinched his

fingers across his tired, sunken eyes. "I know. I know, Danny," he relented. "It's just an interesting theory, that's all."

"Interesting," Daniel repeated quietly, both condemning the word and putting as much acid as he felt into it. Images of Knoctes going after Jack, coming for Ruby, immediately swarmed his mind and he found himself clenching and unclenching his jaw. "Do the world a favor, and let this be one theory we put to rest."

Beside him, Daniel watched Ian cast him a somewhat exasperated sideways glace, then quickly down the rest of his beer, and push up from his seat. His long legs popped with release.

"All right," his brother said sternly, in that big brother voice, Daniel occasionally found patronizing. "Bury it. Dev's right. We could use a few more good hours of rest ourselves. Especially if you two are planning to paint the town red at ungodly hours of the night."

With a knowing nod, Daniel gave in. Abandoning what was left of his beer; he followed Ian and Winchester towards the door. He made sure to catch Ruby's eye one last time and give her a parting smile, before he pushed his way outside.

The sun hung low on the horizon, slowly nestling against the earth. The vast expanse of blue sky stretching out before them was streaked with tinges of pink, marking the beginnings of a sunset. The crisp air and heady earthy smells rushed forward to meet them. Daniel always loved returning home. With the speed at which their lives ran at, sometimes a small, slow paced town was the perfect remedy. Whenever they passed the old, paint chipped welcome sign; Daniel was a little more content.

Ian pulled the keys to his beloved truck out of this jacket pocket. Daniel knew the purr of its engine was Ian's own remedy of contentment.

His brother ran a cherishing hand along the sleek black hood as he felt his way towards the driver's side door.

The truck was a monstrous thing, decked out with everything from LED headlights, custom rims, billet grills and chrome, to off road lighting. It was one unstoppable piece of machine and Daniel didn't even want to imagine how much money they'd put into it over the years.

Ian slid behind the wheel as Daniel lowered the tailgate so

Winchester could jump in.

Ever since he had been old enough to ride in the back, the truck bed had been Winchester's domain and permanent seat for all road trips. Slamming the tailgate shut, Daniel slipped into the passenger's seat, Ian barely giving him enough time to get the door closed, before shifting the truck into reverse and peeling out of the Roadhouse parking lot.

Daniel couldn't help but smile at the goofy grin that always lit his brother's face when he was cruising the streets, feeling more than hearing the roar of the engine. The radio blasted loudly through the cab, and when certain songs played Winchester would howl along from the truck bed, like he knew the words.

Shaking his head in amusement Daniel shifted his gaze to look out the front window, where the string of beads, hanging folded in half over the rear view mirror, caught his attention. It swayed softly back and forth.

He could still remember when Devlyn had given it to him. He had just turned eight and she had proudly dangled it in front of his face, bouncing on her toes with excitement. The beads stringed along it were all different colours and random sizes, a particular order seeming to elude them, but Daniel instantly knew he loved it. It was a perfect representation of the chaos of his life, and it just, well, *fit*. He never looked at them without thinking about her, and absentmindedly his hand moved to his pocket.

Ian reached over and turned the radio down to a less ear splitting level.

"You going to tell me what you've been playing with?" he asked. "I'm not blind. You've been doing it ever since we hit the post office on the way back."

Daniel's hand froze, and for a long moment he didn't say anything, then finally, slowly he removed the letter from his pocket and laid it on the dashboard.

Ian stole glances from the road to peer over at it, his brow knitting in confusion.

"What? You've had a pen pal this whole time, and he's fallen madly in love with you, and you don't have the heart to tell him you're already committed."

Daniel ignored his brother's jab.

"It's an acceptance letter," he said simply, his eyes never

leaving the dashboard. "From a university I applied to."

Ian said nothing, the cab falling silent. Eventually he managed a small jerky nod.

"You know what this means, right?" Daniel asked, turning to take in his brother's ashen face.

Ian did.

It was no secret that Daniel and Devlyn couldn't keep the Knocte-Fifth World lifestyle up forever. She'd spoken plainly about wanting to settle down, eventually start a family. Ian could see how hard it was on both of them to live apart as they did, when they could be together. Stealing nights alone every few weeks, catching up and playing hooky, only to have Daniel run off again, would never be an acceptable life. Devlyn had never complained when Ian stole his brother away, but it registered on her face, the toll of the danger, and the weird hours. The stress for Daniel's safety was something Ian could, all too well, understand.

She hated it.

And he couldn't blame her.

"I know," he sighed. Then his voice took on a warmer tone. "But I'm happy for you, Danny. Really, I am."

And he was.

He would never have wished this life on anyone, never mind his own brother.

Where he knew he probably wouldn't be good for anything else, Daniel could get out of the whole mess, take off with Devlyn. He'd be safe. Well, safer. He'd get to study at a university and become a doctor, or something else as equally impressive. He'd be raking in some real dough, instead of having to hustle pool or play poker to make ends meet. He'd have the white picked fence, the 1.5 kids, and he'd mow the lawn every summer like any average Joe. He would have all the things Ian knew he would never get from life. Daniel would make something of himself, and leave Ian to tramp around the country, fighting the things that go bump in the night by himself.

Being a born Knocte, working alone wasn't something he couldn't manage, he was built physically for the duty after all, but the thought of turning to another Scit for a case, or having an empty passenger seat leering over him, was like a knife in his gut.

Ian knew they'd eventually grow apart living two different lives, it would be inevitable, and it hurt to imagine that he might one day look at his little brother and see a total stranger. The new arrangement would mean tearing him in two, and he only hoped there was enough tape in the world to put him back together.

He kept his face carefully impassive, careful not to reveal any of his thoughts to Daniel. He had to keep his game face on, and at all times think about what was best for his little brother. What Daniel needed was different from what Ian thought he needed. This would be just another bump in the road, another thing he would learn to bury, in order to move on.

"I know you are," Daniel said, a weak smile pulling up the sides of his mouth. "You've always been there, always wanted what's best for me. I'm not expecting that to change now."

"Yeah," Ian said as he felt Daniel's words, and was suddenly glad he had the road as an excuse not to turn and look at his brother.

Keep the game face on.

"And that never will change."

"We'll make it work," Daniel tried to reassure, but his words fell flat, they both knew the separation was going to be a chasm they'd have to learn to bridge.

They pulled up behind the Ray Motel. The R on the red neon sign out front had long ago burnt out, and Daniel had told Jim Ray, the owner, fellow Knocte, and father figure, about it more than once. After years of it going untouched however, he and his brother had started calling it the Ay Motel, and to be truthfully honest, Daniel knew they would both be disappointed if Jim ever did get around to fixing it.

It was one of the things that set their motel apart from the chain of Ray Motels around the country. That, and the concrete parking block that sat out front of their room. Ian had blown a chunk out of it with a shotgun when he was fourteen.

Jim made a good living from his Motel chain, catering to travelers and servicing Knoctes since 1984. Daniel and his brother had come to live under Jim's roof after he'd found them destitute on the street. The man had also quickly discovered Ian to be a Knocte with reasonable skill, even at his young age, and that

Daniel's curiosity and thirst for knowledge ran far deeper than simple nerdiness.

He had taken them under his wing, homeschooled them, and taught them everything he knew about their titles, the Fifth World, and how to fight it. Jim was a genius Knocte himself, and even at the age of fifty-one, he wasn't slowing down any. In fact, the last time Jim had called them, he was on duty up in the Yukon.

Pocketing the letter, Daniel climbed out of the truck after his brother. Ian dug in his pocket for their room key, fishing it out to let it dangle from his index finger, as Winchester leapt from the truck bed to meet them at the door.

Jim had long ago permanently designated one of the rooms to their use, when they'd grown old enough to need a place of their own.

Ian had chosen their room for a number of reasons. It was in the back, hidden from the road, room thirty-three-- Ian's favorite number, and his busted parking block marked the space in front of it. All in all, Ian would say there was a higher power pointing a big neon sign at the motel room practically begging for them to take it. Most importantly, however, the motel room was free, and although small, supplying only the bare necessities, it was a place they could call home for however brief a span they weren't on the road.

The visits were usually so brief, in fact, that Daniel knew he and his brother thought of the truck as their more permanent residence.

Ian opened the door, flicking on the lights to reveal the classic set up. It styled the white walls and two queen beds expected of the establishment, completed with a desk, and a tiny -- whack it to make it work-- television set. A bedside table and lamp was sandwiched between the two queens and a miniature fridge hummed mildly in the corner. The last had been their addition. Ian tossed the keys onto the desk, and Daniel remembered their gratitude when Jim had allowed them to change the locks from the classic motel key cards to something more lock and key secure.

He paused to take his shoes off at the door, nearly tripping over Winchester, while Ian unbothered with such an action, made a beeline for his bed, and flopped down, face first, into his pillow. Daniel often wondered how his brother could even breathe sleeping like that, but Ian's soft snoring filled the motel room before Daniel's head even hit his own pillow.

Chapter Three

Ian was ten years old when he had heard the sound of breaking glass. He was now up out of his bed, with his ear pressed against his bedroom door. For the longest time he heard nothing else, and had just turned around to go back to sleep, when his mother's piercing scream rang out through the darkened house.

He didn't stop to think.

He thrust his bedroom door open, heart hammering a mile a minute in his chest, as he darted down the hallway as fast as he could towards his parents' bedroom. He stopped short when he found the door surprisingly open, and suddenly switched tactics, applying the same stealth technique that always worked to confuse Danny when they played hide-and-go-seek together.

Carefully and quietly he leaned in to look-- and what he saw, he knew would be seared into his brain for the rest of eternity.

David Browning was wielding what looked like a standing lamp, the very one that used to sit in the corner of the room, only now, the lamp shade was shredded, and the light itself had been mangled almost beyond recognition.

And Ian could see why.

David was using it to try and fend off a tall, lanky man, who obviously hadn't stopped by to borrow a cup of sugar; the broken window proof of forced entry, and a confirmation of the shattering glass Ian had heard moments before.

The intruder was hunched forward like he was ready to spring at any moment. Wild black hair and enraged, pale, milky blue eyes gave him a crazed appearance. His upper lip was pulled back in a fierce snarl, revealing amazingly white teeth that seemed to glint like razors even in the darkness. His fingers curled in at the tips like claws, and he seemed to dance around Ian's father as if to test the effectiveness of his lamp stand defense.

David swung at him again and again, each time forcing the intruder to retreat, but the blows seemed to have no lasting effect, and as the intruder circled patiently, Ian could see his father's strength wearing before his eyes.

Frightened as he was, Ian forced himself to swallow his fear. They needed him. He took a determined step into the room--

and froze again.

Another brain stabbing imagery assaulted him as he suddenly noticed his mother, Lilian, half laying on the floor, slumped against the other side of the bed from her husband. She was just opposite where Ian had been peering in the doorway. The bones on one side of her body looked limp, almost like they'd been crushed to the point of never being used again. The side of her face looked like it had been dashed against something hard, and a crescent shaped bite mark seared the skin of her neck and collarbone. An astonishing amount of blood stained her white night gown and matted her blond hair.

Her eyes reeled, somehow managing to land on him, and even then he could tell it took a lot of effort for her to hold them there.

"Ian."

When she said his name, it was barely a movement of her lips. She tried again, a little stronger this time.

"Ian." she rasped, her voice both relieved and yet panic stricken at his appearance. She motioned weakly for him to come over to her with her good hand.

Ian obeyed numbly, stumbling over himself, and collapsing to his knees at her side.

"Mom…" he started, but was unable to finish, his expression unimaginably horrified and gripped with pain.

"Run," she told him, her eyes pleading with him to listen.

He shook his head. "No. I won't. I won't--."

But he was cut off by another crash sounding off from across the bed, this one followed by a cry of pain uttered from his father. Ian's eyes snapped towards the sound, and he was temped to rise up from his knees and check on his dad.

Lilian caught the movement, and guessing his intent, ordered him again.

"No, Ian. Run!"

But he wouldn't listen, stubbornly refusing to leave. His family needed his help, and he couldn't bring himself to abandon them, no matter the icy fear that was racing through his veins, like an unwanted poison.

How many times had his mother watched over him while he was sick and held him in her loving arms?

How many times had his father fixed a scraped elbow of his or a bruised knee?

A lot.

And it was time to repay the favor.

Ian slowly started to rise to his feet, not missing the terror that was evident in his mother's face for her son.

Then she suddenly zeroed in on something behind him, and whatever she had seen, suddenly gave her renewed strength for a moment. She reached out and clutched the collar of Ian's pajama top, forcing him back down to her eye level, keeping him hidden from view and from the mayhem that continued on the other side of the bed.

And that was the moment Daniel appeared at his side.

"Mom! Mom, I'm scared" Daniel said, his voice shaking from sheer terror, his eyes wide with fright and disbelief.

Lilian locked eyes with Ian then. They blazed with as much determination, as they were laced with pain.

"Run, Ian... Take your brother... and run. Whatever you do... don't stop. Don't... look back."

"But, mom--" Ian protested in the same moment Daniel clutched Lilian's nightgown, yet another crash echoing through the room.

"There's nothing...," she had to swallow hard before she could continue, "nothing you can do here"

She spoke hesitantly, and Ian could tell every sentence, every word, was a battle raging inside her. It was one she was managing to win, if only for the short precious moment it took to plead with him. Though her words were sharp, they were barely above a whisper.

Ian felt her really look at him then, like she was peering through him now, into his soul.

"Take care of your brother, Ian," she begged. "Keep him... keep him safe."

Ian looked at his brother then, and Daniel glanced back, his face betraying the questions that lay there. Questions that could only be:

What's happening? We're all going to die aren't we?

Realization hit Ian then, like running full tilt and slamming into a brick wall. He may not be able to save his parents.

But he could save his brother.

And his brother was just as much family, just as important to him as his parents were.

He gave his mother a serious nod, and suddenly he felt like an adult, with the new responsibility laid on his shoulders. An adult with a job to do. A purpose. He turned to look at his brother again.

"Danny, let's go."

The words pained him to say, as much as he knew it needed to be done. He knew his little brother heard the catch in his voice, and Daniel's eyes flashed back to their mother, entirely uncertain, as tears started to streak down his small cheeks. Lilian released her hold on Ian, cherishing her younger son's cheek for a moment.

"Listen... to your brother, Daniel," she said, and her hand slipped from his face involuntarily. She let out an exhausted sigh, one sounding like it weighed heavily on her heart. "I love you, boys... My boys...," she whispered, her voice trailing off.

And then she was starring blankly ahead, unblinking.

Daniel shook her.

"Mom! Mom!" he called, but she didn't move again.

Ian was frozen for a moment, trapped by his mother's dead eyes, and then biting back the scream of anguish he felt building up inside of him, he forced himself to look away.

"Danny, come on," he said, gently prying his little brother's fingers from their mother's nightgown.

A loud snarl tore through the house and Ian heard their father cry out again.

They were running out of time.

Daniel still sat on the floor, looking like he wouldn't ever be able to move from that spot.

Ian grabbed his brother's shoulders, forcing Daniel to look at him.

"Danny, listen to me! We need to get away, we need to run. You're going to have to trust me, okay?"

Daniel blinked, and looked at his older brother like he was seeing him for the first time. After a brief second he finally, shakily, nodded in agreement.

Ian didn't hesitate, except to spare a final glance back at their father, before grabbing hold of Daniel's hand, and starting towards the door. He kept low, being more careful now not to get spotted than he had been coming in. Daniel followed silently, almost numbly, in his footsteps. When they hit the hallway, Ian broke out in a run for the front door, ushering his brother quickly outside and shutting the door tightly behind them.

Instantly, he looked up towards their parents' window, unable to help himself. The curtains were blowing out the busted window, cruel twists of fabric looking like something straight out of a horror movie.

Who was he kidding?

This whole nightmare was pure horror movie material; only it didn't give you the jolting thrill the movies did.

Experiencing it was different.

Experiencing it was unlike anything he'd ever felt, and one look at his brother's face told Ian he would completely agree.

Then Ian caught a movement from his peripheral vision and he spun to face the window again, just in time to see a dark shape drop down and disappear into the bushes beneath. Ian looked around frantically for some place he and his brother could hide, his eyes falling on the family's big, black truck parked in the driveway. With its sturdy durability and its lockable doors, it was their best shot.

He had seen the stranger move, and Ian knew they wouldn't have a hope of out running him on foot.

"Danny, Danny get in the--," he started to tell his brother, when suddenly his feet were taken out from under him.

He ate asphalt, and with a groan rolled onto his back. He heard Daniel calling out his name, but he couldn't focus enough to locate him, wondering how hard he'd hit his head, as dizziness swept over him.

"Get in the truck!" he managed to shout out to his little brother, before a heavy booted kick laid into his shoulder blade, forcing him to roll over onto his stomach. Hard hands clasped the sides of his head, fingers digging into his flesh, cranking his head at a hard angle, trying to break his neck.

Ian grunted trying to kick his assailant, but the stranger had him pinned down on the driveway.

Then suddenly, without warning, the stranger let go of him. The thing whirled around and Ian squirmed to get a view of what had distracted him, half expecting to see his father, but instead just in time to see Daniel deliver another kick.

"Leave him alone!" Daniel yelled angrily in his brother's defense.

A kick from a six year old was hardly enough to do any damage to the stranger, never mind maim him, but it was enough to distract him, shift his focus just long enough.

Ian slammed his fist into the side of the stranger's head just as the thing lunged at his little brother. The stranger's fingers still managed to rake Daniel's chest, but his attack wasn't the deathblow it was intended to be. It was off kilter, dazed, if only for a moment. It gave Ian enough time to get to his feet. He swayed a little, but willed himself to stay focused. He kicked the stranger, trying for the same spot in the ribs that his brother had taken to, then turned, hauling Daniel to his feet, who had been too shocked to scream when taken down, but clutched at his shredded shirt all the same. Without looking back, Ian half dragged, half carried his brother to the truck, where they climbed in. Ian smashed the locks down, and they sat, Ian in the driver's seat, and Daniel in the passenger's. They were both breathing hard and staring with huge, frightened eyes into the darkness around them.

"Y-you, okay?" Ian asked shakily.

When all Daniel gave was an answering whimper, Ian immediately spun round to examine him. Daniel was still clutching his chest, blood seeping through the five shred marks that decorated his shirt, painting his fingers red. Silent tears streaked down his face. Ian reached over and pulled up his shirt, staring at the long gashes. Ian couldn't fathom how the stranger had been able to make scratches that deep. He found himself looking down at his own hand, thinking it impossible. It was almost like the intruder's skin was made of something harder, more durable, and his fingernails made of something more sharp and deadly. Ian knew the gashes were going to need medical attention. He knew from personal experience what cuts looked and felt like when they needed stitches.

He'd fallen out of a tree in their back yard last summer, and a branch had caught him on the way down, but compared to Daniel's injury, his hadn't been half as bad.

Ian racked his brain, trying to remember what his father

had told him to do, and remembered being handed a dishtowel and told to "keep the pressure on."

He immediately ripped his pajama shirt off over his head and handed it to his brother.

"Hold this, okay?" he said, putting it in Daniel's hand and pushing it against his chest. "Like that."

Ian couldn't help thinking that, something that strong, who could tear up his brother with a single swipe, and jump out windows, running faster than humanly possible, wouldn't stay down for long. It hadn't seemed all that bothered by getting a pounding with a lamp... how long would a simple punch in the face and a kick to the ribs last?

Suddenly Ian felt himself grow cold inside.

This wasn't over.

And as if to back him up, there was suddenly a loud metallic crash above them, denting the roof of the truck, and causing Ian to jump in his seat. Turning to his little brother, his voice took on an urgent tone.

"Climb in the back and hide under the seat," he commanded.

Daniel looked at him like he was crazy, still holding the balled up shirt to his chest.

"You can do it!" Ian found himself nearly yelling, his eyes trained on the roof, which had fallen eerily silent again.

Daniel slowly and painfully obeyed, climbing into the back seat and crouching down on the floor, but when he tried to squish under the seat, they found it wasn't possible. In fact there wasn't any space under the bench seat at all.

That was when the driver's side window smashed apart, showering Ian with glass.

His own scream mixed with Daniel's, as he threw himself over into the passenger seat, his arms flying up to shield his face. He could hear Daniel trying to move in the back, shifting around the seat, panicking.

He quickly sat up, trying hastily to brush all the glass away, his eyes never leaving the open window-- when the stranger suddenly appeared.

One minute nothing.

And the next it had caught hold of his leg, nails sinking

35

deep into his skin, making him gasp in pain as it tried to haul him out the window.

Screaming, he grabbed for the headrest, grasping it like a lifeline, his knuckles turning white as he tried to kick his leg free. Daniel called out his name, his hand reaching out.

That was when something fell across his torso. Straining to get a look, Ian craned his neck, and found that a shotgun was now perched there.

Seeing it-- he made an instant decision.

Suddenly releasing his hold on the headrest, the creature dragged him back over into the driver's seat, and he gasped as the shattered glass bit into his back. He braced his free leg against the door, halting his movement, and using the shotgun, clubbed the hand that had its nails imbedded in his other leg.

With a discontented wail, the thing released its hold and Ian scrambled to get back into a more defensible position.

He barely had time to sit upright, when the passenger side window shattered, making a matching set of busted windows. The creature's head came into view, a line of drool dripping from its blinding teeth, as it dangled over the side from the roof. It snarled loudly, a very inhuman like sound.

And that was the moment everything began to move in slow motion for Ian.

The moment he knew, that for as long as he lived, he would never be able to understand or explain what happened, except to say it was pure, raw instinct.

The moment he found himself swinging the gun around, at the same time he flicked off the safety. Pumping it to expel the spent shells and reload the next into the chamber, he then aimed and squeezed the trigger. It happened all as if he'd done it a hundred times before.

And the result was instantaneous.

He'd hit his mark-- the deafening crack imbedding itself into the creature's skull. There was no blood or brain matter, or any indication that he'd struck and killed something human, instead the creature's head exploded like he'd just taken fire at a hunk of cement. The shattered pieces sprayed out and clinked softly to the ground, like a handful of pebbles that had been tossed into the air and had showered back down to the earth like rain.

The rest of the body slid from the roof, hitting the asphalt of the driveway with a dull thud.

The truck cab went silent, completely still for a long minute, as Ian attempted to register what had just happened.

Had he really killed it? Got rid of it forever?

He wasn't really sure how he'd managed to get rid of it forever. He could feel the weight of the shotgun in his hands, and smell the gunpowder in the air, but still found it hard to believe it had actually happened.

Then it occurred to him just how he had gotten a hold of a shotgun in the first place, and he whipped around to look in the backseat. The backseat itself was lifted up like a toddler's toy chest, revealing a mini arsenal, and Daniel was slumped beside it, his half lidded eyes at risk of closing, the front of his shirt soaking through with blood faster than Ian knew how to handle. He felt panic grip him, greater than any he had felt that night, because he knew it was just the two of them now, and if Daniel didn't make it-- he was all alone in the world.

"Hey!" Ian called to him, smacking his cheek a little, until Daniel stirred and opened his eyes again. "Stay awake, okay?" Ian found himself begging.

He had to get Daniel to the hospital. And they lived out of town.

He knew enough to get into town, just not enough to know where the hospital was. But it didn't matter, he tried to tell himself, he'd find it. He reached up and yanked the visor down, glad in that moment that their dad always kept the truck keys there, despite their mother's continual lecturing.

Daniel seemed to have spotted the keys in his hand, because he managed to croak out, "You don't know how to drive, Ian."

Ian couldn't help but shoot him a dark look for a split second, before he jammed the keys in the ignition, starting the truck. "I'm gonna learn!"

He slammed the gearshift into reverse and the truck instantly started to roll backwards. He had to remind himself which peddle was the brake and which one was the gas from the brief lesson his father had given him.

In that single memory, Ian knew his world had been

changed forever. The thought of the afternoon Ian had spent with his father was now a memory that caused a pain deep in his chest, instead of bringing a smile to his face. He once again had to repress the scream building in the back of his throat as he shoved the truck into neutral and then drive. He hit the gas, maybe a little too hard, and the truck peeled out of the driveway.

Ian didn't know what time it was when he reached the hospital, but the sky was starting to get lighter on the horizon. All he did know was that it had taken far too long.

He'd kept talking to Daniel, asking him stupid questions, questions he demanded answers to. He had to know Daniel was awake in the backseat, too afraid to take his eyes off the road to check, even for a second, for fear of killing them both. Taking his eyes off the road to look for the H sign was risky enough by his book.

Daniel's replies had come a little snappy and annoyed at first, but they quickly became tired, sluggish, and eventually he'd stopped answering altogether. During that time the ride had been nearly unbearable, fear and panic leaking into every corner of Ian's small body.

He parked hastily in the first place he could find, extremely crooked, and taking up more than one space, but he was beyond caring about formalities.

He leapt out of the driver's seat, almost forgetting to shove the gearshift up to the P, and pulled his little brother out of the backseat. He carried Daniel's unconscious form towards the bright, large EMERGENCY sign. It shone an eerie red glow into the parking lot, lighting his way as he hastily stumbled up to the doors, burdened by the weight of his brother.

What happened from there was a blur.

He remembered bursting through into the hospital, and having people suddenly surround him, asking him questions in urgent voices that he found he didn't have rational answers to. Daniel was hurriedly removed from his arms, and rolled away on a gurney, surrounded by doctors and nurses in blue scrubs and facemasks. He remembered trying to follow, but had a nurse quickly block his path, telling him he couldn't go any further. He found himself asking her the only question that seemed important

"Is he okay?" and repeating it over and over when he wasn't given a straight answer. Instead she kept looking down at him with a sort of sad expression, explaining that his own injuries weren't as urgent as those of other people in the emergency room, and that he'd have to wait his turn. Her voice was steady, professional and probably meant to be reassuring.

But that just made it all the more infuriating.

His whole world was cascading out of control! He didn't understand how she could possibly be standing in front of him so calmly.

He certainly didn't have the ability anymore. Calm was no longer within his grasp, and he felt all the control, all the self will he'd kept with him for his brother's sake slip away, leaving behind only a raw pain that seemed to burn him up from within, and consume his entire body. The scream he'd worked so hard to keep locked away, ripped free, tearing from his throat without warning. He threw back his head in a full body cry full of anguish, pain, and misery.

Ian woke in a cold sweat, at the exact same spot in the dream he always did. He sat up slowly, the sheets he hadn't bothered to pull over himself, rumpled and disturbed beneath him. With an irritated sound, he wiped the perspiration from his face with the back of his hand. He couldn't help remembering the shocked silence the emergency room had fallen into after his outburst. So still and silent, it was like no one was breathing. Everyone's eyes had been fixed on him, stunned like they could actually feel the pain he had emanated out to them and they didn't know how to deal with it.

"Haven't had that one in awhile," he mused to himself, then instantly glanced over at his brother's bed to see if he'd heard, but only Winchester's balled up form lay snoozing on the covers.

Right, Daniel had to be with Devlyn by now.

He couldn't help wondering what they were doing as he turned to look out the window, finding the sky was still dark.

His brother couldn't have left that long ago.

He groaned.

He was never going to get a decent good night's sleep, was he? He got up out of bed, dumping his shoes by the door, before heading over to the desk, where a coffee maker sat waiting for him. He started a pot, and pulled his mug out of a desk drawer, the one with the local country station printed across it. Sitting in the swivel desk chair, he fiddled with it mindlessly, as he listened to the coffee maker groan, like it wasn't very happy to be up this late.

"Well, you and me both," he muttered under his breath, when suddenly his cell phone was blaring annoyingly into his tired and groggy atmosphere, interrupting his thoughts.

"Who in the h--," Ian started, fishing for the phone in his jacket pocket, but cut himself off when he pulled it out and read the number. With a spreading smile, he flipped it open.

"Well, if it isn't Jimmy, alive and well!"

"Call me Jimmy again boy, and the next time you see me, it might be your last," Jim's gruff voice chastised.

"I'm deeply frightened-- truly. Quaking in my socks actually," he deadpanned. "But I think I deserve some leniency. I mean, what time is it exactly?"

"Don't smart mouth me. I know you weren't sleeping."

"Ominous," Ian noted. "You still after that lycanthrope? How's the Yukon? Seen any polar bears yet?"

"It's summer here too, Ian," Jim informed.

"So… no polar bears then."

The man sighed. "I finished the lycan off a few days ago. The thing's a doornail."

"A true knight in shining armor," Ian remarked, using the shoulder technique to hold the phone to his ear, while he poured himself some coffee. "Heading back home anytime soon?"

"Yeah. You might say that," Jim said, a mischievous note Ian hadn't missed leaking into his voice.

"Meaning?"

An answering knock echoed suddenly through the motel room, and Winchester's head snapped up on the alert.

Jim's laugh thundered over the phone.

"A little aged for these kind of games aren't you, old man?" Ian quipped.

Jim chose to ignore the comment, barking out orders instead. "Answer the door, boy. May as well bring a cold beer with you when you do too."

Smiling and shaking his head, Ian snapped the phone shut.

Only Jim Ray.

Chapter Four

Daniel's sneakers clomped, and rang against the black metal of the fire escape as he zigzagged his way up to Devlyn's living room window. It was on the second floor, and in all honesty-- quite easy to break into. Crouching in front of the window, he reached into the pocket of his favorite sweatshirt for his knife. He flicked the blade open with one swift movement of his wrist when he found it. With his hood up he felt like some sort of cat burglar. He jammed the knife between the sliding panes of the window so it was against the old fashioned latch, which sat positioned in the middle of the window frame. Adding pressure, he forced the latch to flip open, returned the knife to his pocket, and then hoisted the window up. Knowing he only had a minute he ducked through, stepping over the sill, and bolted through the living room and kitchen to the security box hanging beside the front door. Devlyn almost always turned her alarm on when she went to bed, and often forgot to turn it off again when she awoke. Tonight was no exception. It flashed the seconds as he tried out passwords. He discovered the correct one on his third attempt, and breathed a sigh of relief as it beeped and delivered a final flash of green.

He stepped back satisfied, and glanced around the apartment. It was its usual colourful and painted self. No wall left blank. In fact, the walls of Devlyn's apartment changed colour on a day-to-day basis. Murals painted on top of murals. There were a few masterpieces that stayed. The painting of a ladder 'propped' beside the front door was one of them. A small, blond, curly haired girl, he'd always thought of as Devlyn, was depicted having climbed to the top. She had a hand stretched out over the top of the doorframe, a lantern dangling from her grip. Rays of light shown from it, radiating down on top of the door frame, stretching to the wall's corners, and piercing towards the ceiling.

The light to bring him home.

A promise that she'd always leave the light on for him.

As he made his way back through the apartment he noticed the new additions. One positioned next to the fridge, he recognized as the taillights of his and Ian's truck, speeding off down a road. It left a cloud of dust in its wake, painted in a billowing, artful swirl.

He ventured into the bedroom, following the smell of fresh paint, Devlyn's signature breadcrumb trail, and stopped in the doorway. With a spreading smile he leaned against the frame, enjoying the view. She was standing in front of another newly muraled wall; her head tilted back as she looked up at it, blond curls streaming down her back. A paintbrush stuck out of the back pocket of her jeans, forgotten like it always was when she got inspired and lost in her own head.

Another one was tucked behind her ear.

"I do have a front door," she scolded, without turning to face him. "And you have a key."

"Where's the challenge in that?" He grinned, and then remembering the password, "Guernica? Really?"

"There's nothing wrong with Picasso," she stated distractedly.

Stepping up behind her, he encircled her waist with his arms, looking over her shoulder to get a better view of the mural.

"I think I remember this."

She leaned back against him, her reply coming slower this time, like it always did when she was lost in the world of colour and memory.

"Yeah. I've been thinking about it a lot lately for some reason."

Painted on the wall in front of them was a scene from the drawing room at Jim's place, the ever present, and hideous orange striped couch front and center. Six bodies had crammed themselves on and around it, however, like it was the comfiest and oldest of friends. Daniel could see a slightly younger version of himself sitting on the right side of the couch, with Devlyn stretched across his lap. His hand rested on the faded denim of her jeans, and he leaned in to whisper something in her ear, his face just touching her hair, as she turned in to listen to him. As a result, she was smiling, eyes shining at whatever he was sharing, her arm looped loosely around his neck. Her fingers played in his hair, which stuck up at all angles in a way he knew she found alluring. Ruby perched on the armrest beside them, her legs tucked up neatly against her chest, translucent blue and gold tinted dark hair hanging sleek over one shoulder. She stared tranquilly ahead at the viewer of the mural, as if watching a TV that should be there. On Daniel's other side, Ian took up the middle of the couch. He had his leg crossed over one knee, and an arm stretching out along the back of the couch. With his other he was trying to hand off the remote to the younger Daniel, who was preoccupied and not paying attention. On the floor in front of them, Jack sat with his legs crossed campfire style, and his arms wrapped around a bowl of popcorn resting in his lap. His black rectangular glasses looked too big for his small, thin face, and he held his chin slightly up in the air, as if he was trying to keep them from sliding off his nose. On the far left of the couch sat Luke, back straight, feet flat. His elbow rested on the armrest, and his face leaned into the palm of his hand, as he watched everyone with a look almost like distant curiosity.

"Every expression," he marvelled. "How do you remember it all like this?" He reached out from her side as if to touch the wall, but her hand immediately snapped up to grab his wrist.

"It's not dry," she hastily informed.

"Sorry."

They both stared at it a second time, Devlyn growing thoughtful again. "I dunno. When I start painting… it all just sort of rushes back." She looked over at him. "Don't you remember it all?"

He shook his head slightly. "Not in so much detail. I remember us. You playing with my hair, your laugh. But that doesn't mean I was memorizing the rest of my surroundings quite so thoroughly…"

"It was the first day all of us met together at the same time."

Daniel nodded. He remember that much.

"Why does Luke look like he wants to eat us?" he asked, expecting her to laugh at the question. Instead she offered up a shrug. It wasn't the kind of shrug, however, that meant she was clueless to the matter-- he knew better than that, she put far too much of herself into each painting --just that she didn't know quite how to express it as words.

"He always looks like that," she reasoned. "As if he has a stick shoved where the sun don't shine."

"Like a scarecrow. Yeah."

"Hmm," she said absentmindedly, her head tilting to the side. She took a step closer to the painting, and he let her. One of her arms wrapped around her waist where his had been a second ago, the other lightly touched her face. Her eyes squinted at Luke almost like she could imagine it.

"But that," Daniel added, gesturing to the mural. "That's, uh…"

"Creepy?" she supplied, dropping her arms and turning to face him. There was paint smeared across the curve of her collarbone.

"Very," he agreed.

"But it's how I remember it." She looked back over her shoulder. "I glanced at him during the show, and there was this… I dunno. Hunger? --I guess. He was taking everything in, us, the movie, but in this greedy short of detached way, like he found both scenarios odd. And no matter how hard he wanted to--" her voice grew thoughtful, confused "--he couldn't understand it."

But Luke had always been that way.

Once when they were younger, Daniel and Ian had found a sparrow fallen from its nest in Jim's back yard. The mother wouldn't take it back after they'd handled it, so Jim had let them adopt. They kept it in a cage, feeding it with an eyedropper and some wet rice.

When Luke came around, however, he couldn't imagine why they'd want to do such a thing.

"It's just a bird," he'd said, and had actually gotten angry with them whenever they took time away to care for it. After he'd left the house that day, Ian had found the bird dead, its neck broken. He'd kept saying it must have been an accident, but he wouldn't meet Daniel's eye. They both knew. It had been Luke.

"Luke doesn't see relationships or feel connections with people the way most do," Daniel said, reiterating his thoughts. "It's always been that way. Ian told me that Luke didn't have the best childhood growing up."

Suddenly she turned, stretching up onto her tiptoes so she was closer to his height. She dragged his hood away from his face with gentle hands, letting it fall back against his shoulder blades.

"Then he doesn't know what he's missing."

Her dark blue eyes glinted, and Daniel knew he was grinning like an idiot. He pressed his forehead against hers, relishing in the rare moment they had to just be with one another.

"I love you, you know that?" he said with absolute sincerity. "Let's get changed. I owe you a night out."

Ian and Jim clanked the necks of their beer bottles together before settling on the end of Ian's bed. Jim was wearing a button-down shirt that was once white, but had now turned grey from mixed washing, and a pair of old ripped blue jeans. He was subconsciously scrubbing at his stubbly salt and pepper beard.

Jim still had a full head of hair, which he had always been quite proud of, though he claimed it was a miracle with the amount of stress he'd had to endure raising Ian and his brother.

They'd still managed to whiten it a great deal.

But while they'd aged him, the line of duty had not. Yes, he bore the scars of the job like they all did. In fact, a small white one had cut through his right eyebrow for as long as Ian could remember, but Jim was also incredibly fit for a man of his age. Years of hard work demanded nothing less, and while he could still hold his height against Daniel, Ian had dwarfed him years ago.

"We really need to get you boys a table around here," Jim noted as he stretched his sore legs, cramped from hours of driving. He groaned, the bags under his fatherly grey eyes displaying to Ian just how many restless hours he'd drove. "Next time I'm flying."

Ian took a swig of his beer, his still half full mug of coffee sat on the desk forgotten. "You say that every time."

"Yeah, well, this time I'm serious," Jim said defiantly.

Ian smiled to himself.

The old man said that every time too.

Jim took another long pull of his beer before speaking again. "Well let's have it."

"Have what?" Ian paused, beer bottle halfway to his lips, to give him a questioning look.

"You don't fool me," Jim said gruffly. "I've noticed something's been off with you from the moment I walked in that door. So spill."

With a reluctant sigh Ian leaned forward, elbows resting on his knees. He pinched the bridge of his nose between his fingers, closing his eyes like he could already feel a headache coming on.

"Dan's uh…," Ian started and had to retry. "He's out with Dev."

"That's not exactly unusual," Jim pried. "They did sort of dedicate their lives to each other."

Ian gave another sigh, this one running bone deep. "He got accepted into university," he said abruptly. "And it sounds like he's going."

Jim was silent for a minute.

"Well, I'll be," he said finally, leaning back as if a surprise blow had hit him. "I thought I'd die twice and hell'd freeze over before that boy got up the nerve."

The attempt at a joke was lost on Ian.

"Why?" Ian asked suddenly turning to look at him. "We both knew it was coming sooner or later. Dan and Dev have to settle eventually, start the whole steady job, family thing, and there isn't a college or university on this planet that could refuse my brother."

"Yes," Jim agreed, "but it wasn't just a matter of going off to school, Ian. You know that. This is about him giving up the life he has here, the life he's always known with us-- particularly his brother."

Ian was quiet for a long moment, lost in his own head. "But he's smart enough to know it's what's best for him. For both of them."

"Just not what's best for you," Jim said sympathetically. "Am I right? The kid's a genius, Ian, and a technological whiz. University is going to be a walk in the park for him. He's going to have a life he'd never imagined for himself, but he's a born Scitor and there's always going to be some part of his heart that's drawn back to this field, part of him that belongs here with you, fighting by your side. There's no doubt in my mind that together Dan and Dev could stand up to hell and win, but that's also what the two of you have been doing your whole lives. This isn't going to be easy. Not for Dan. Not for anyone."

Ian felt Jim's steady gaze trained on him and returned it without blinking.

"I want what's best for my little brother, just like you do," he said immediately. "You don't think I sit here and tell myself that where I end up doesn't matter?" He paused, his lips pressing together in a tight line, before he could continue. "But I don't see it going anywhere good. Not after this. He's all I've got left, Jim.

47

And if I lose him…" He trailed off at the thought, not willing to fully register it. "I don't think I can go this one alone. It's always been us. Just me and my little brother. I'm responsible for him, and it's my job to keep him safe. How am I supposed to do that when I'm not around? When he's miles away? I can't go through life day-by-day playing pen pals, and wondering how he's actually doing. "

Reaching over Jim placed a strong hand on Ian's shoulder.

"Daniel's not the six year old kid he used to be, Ian. You've done your job. And don't you dare think for an instant that you're in this thing alone. If you haven't forgotten-- I'm right here. This family's bigger than you make it out to be."

"That was horrible!" Devlyn said, throwing her head back in a carefree laugh.

They were sitting side by side in the truck bed, their legs crossed over one another's at the ankles. They'd parked the truck at the edge of Macy's Golf Course. Nine holes and completely deserted, not a soul around at the current time of night, only the crickets with their disjointed symphony. She had a container of ice cream resting in her lap, just one of the assorted goods they'd picked up after their late night restaurant endeavour had failed. It was rainbow flavoured, she'd picked it out both for its colours, and the fact that she'd always wanted to know what a rainbow tasted like.

Daniel was giving her a withering look.

"What?" she shrugged. "Someone had to say it."

"It wasn't that bad…" he muttered, his words trailing off disheartened.

"Dan, you looked at the wine list like it was an alien species. And you're a brilliant man-- my brilliant man, but you've never eaten a lobster before in your life."

"I was figuring it out."

Now it was her turn to give a withering look. "You were stabbing at it."

"*I* was making progress. You…," he started laughing, that wonderful, carefree, boyish laughter, and had to start over. "When the waiter put it down in front of you-- I thought you'd lose it. 'Dan, I think it's staring at me!'" he mimicked, his eyes dancing with amusement.

She smacked him hard. "Shut up!"

But she was grinning.

"And when you came back from the restroom," he tugged lightly on the hem of her white cotton dress, "this was practically see through."

She felt her jaw drop open. "It was not!" she exclaimed, horrified. She sat up abruptly, switching the ice cream to her left hand so she could point a stern finger at him. "And no bathroom sink should have that amount of water pressure!"

"I dunno," he smirked, "you definitely attracted some attention."

"Daniel. James. Browning." She scolded, frowning.

He chuckled lightly, leaning over to press his lips against her temple. His breath played through her curls, not saying anything for a long minute.

"I have something to show you," he said finally, breaking the silence.

She hummed her curiosity, and then sensing a sudden shift in his emotion, she pulled back so she could see his face. It had quickly grown serious.

"Dan, what is it?" she asked warily, searching his features.

He seemed wary himself, giving her a shy smile. "Dev, it's all right. It's good news."

But she wasn't inclined to believe him.

He fished in the inside pocket of his suit jacket and pulled out a piece of paper, the folds in it so deep she knew he'd read it multiple times. He held it out for her between two fingers, and setting aside the ice cream on the edge of the truck bed, she snatched it from him, unfolding it hastily.

She smoothed it out over her knee, expecting to extract a small smile from Daniel, but he just watched her cautiously, and her uneasiness grew as she glanced down at the page.

Scanning it, her eyes widening. "Dan..."

He sat up beside her suddenly, their shoulders touching. "It's what I want."

"No." She shook her head. "No, it's not."

She was starring down at an acceptance letter.

University.

A place that would appreciate every ounce of his intellectual ability.

A place that would lock him away behind walls and pages, where he'd be both bored and unsatisfied.

"I want this," he repeated. "I want a life with you."

"You have a life with me," she countered.

"Sporadically," he sighed. "We're going to need a house eventually, Dev, a place for us. Soon. And what if we have kids someday?" he questioned. "The line of duty doesn't pay-- you know that." His brown eyes pleaded. "I love you. I want a life with you-- and I know that means I can't keep doing this gig I call a job forever."

Wordlessly, she reached for his hand where it rested in his lap. His fingers tightened around hers.

"But you love what you do, Dan," she whispered.

"I love *you*."

"Every case you take with your brother, you come alive. I've seen it."

"And leave you to worry after me, alone for weeks at a time."

"Yes, I worry, and that probably won't ever change," she admitted, "but so do the families of police officers and firefighters, who put themselves at risk to save the lives of others. You *protect* people, Dan."

He wasn't listening, his expression growing farther away from her. "I don't want my life with you to suffer."

She sighed.

Speaking of family…

"And Ian?" she whispered, her voice barely audible.

Daniel's eyes darkened, the weighted question immediately grounding him, just like she knew it would.

He said nothing for a long minute, staring out at the manicured lawn of the golf course.

"We'll get through it," he said finally, adamantly. "We always do."

But she couldn't see it. The Browning brothers were fitted puzzle pieces, and she knew better than to try and separate them.

"You and Ian," she said slowly, reasoning, "you get through things *together,* Dan, by working as a single unit-- as true brothers. Not as two people related that occasionally send one another postcards."

She saw the pain flash across Daniel's face, and he closed his eyes for a second, forcing it down.

"Look," he said, opening them again to regard her. "I know our past has left my brother and I--."

"Largely co-dependant on each other," she interrupted him. "Yes, Dan, I know."

Actually-- it went without speaking. It was like each brother had gained a sixth sense of the other, built up from years of side-by-side work.

"And that's also why I know this John Doe lifestyle you're talking about isn't going to work."

"So what am I supposed to do, Dev?" he pleaded, his brown eyes so big in his young face. "I have to do *something*. I can't keep being the nomad that wanders through your life all the time. I've devoted my life to you. It's time I started acting like it."

"Daniel," she said disapprovingly. She set aside the letter, reaching out to touch his chest, where she knew both his tattoo and scars laid beneath. "It's not always going to be a walk in the park. The line of duty is something you're called to do, it's in your very fabric, and you love it."

"Everyone has to give up the motorcycle eventually."

"You known this isn't a motorcycle, Dan," she said firmly. "It's a way of life."

"I just--."

But she didn't let him finish, leaning forward to lightly press her lips to his.

He blinked. "What was that for?"

"For loving me. For being my genius, who can get accepted into any university he desires. For the heart behind this gesture," she said, reaching for and holding up the acceptance letter again, "but mostly just to get you to shut up." She smirked.

He gave her a small, unsure smile.

Suddenly the sprinklers sprang to life around the golf course, shooting above the border lining trees in high arcs. Looking out at them, she watched with captivated fascination as they made their wide turns, spouting water like an airborne waterfall.

51

She didn't remember starting to laugh, but suddenly Daniel had joined her in her childlike outburst.

"Do you smell that?" she exclaimed. "The smell of wet earth and freshly cut grass? There's nothing else like it." She could hear the awe in her own voice.

Glancing over at Daniel, she could see that his eyes shone, his lips twitching up into an amused smile. She loved seeing him like this, relaxed, all rich browns.

And he was hers.

"We could get a little closer you know," she mused.

His deep eyes turned to her, suddenly perplexed. "You mean the sprinklers? Run through them?"

"Well... yes actually."

He suddenly got that intrigued, pensive look, when his Scitor abilities sparked his curiosity and perspicacious nature.

"I've never run through a sprinkler before," he admitted.

She felt a moment of fleeting shock.

How could she have known him for so long, and still have little admissions like this surprise her?

She hastily clamoured to her feet.

"Well there's a first for everything, Mr. Browning." She beamed, and then turned and leapt off the tailgate.

He didn't move from his position. "You won't get far you know," he teased lightly. "Not in those shoes."

Okay-- true. She'd borrowed her heels from Ruby. They were bright blue and about three inches too high.

Easily rendered though.

Stooping she fought with the straps of her heels, only just managing to get them free, before Daniel had lurched to his feet. She took a moment to admire him, all adorable tussled hair, hanging across his forehead, and sun darkened skin stretched over hard muscles.

Then she turned and ran.

Even without her shoes she didn't make it far. She'd only reached the first sprinkler, when Daniel caught up with her, shoes and socks abandoned alongside hers back at the truck.

She put the sprinkler between them, pivoting at pace with it, just out of its reach, and his. Daniel was doing the same from the other side, stalking like a well-versed jungle cat.

Finally he lunged, and as an immediate reaction, she shoved her hand into the sprinkler. Disrupting the spray in his direction, she squinted through the unruly shower of water, getting herself about as badly drenched as her intended target.

With a call of surprise Daniel gave into his sopping state, leaping quickly through the sprinkler towards her. Spinning on her heels, she beat a hasty retreat for the next one, her bare feet squishing in the waterlogged grass.

But he caught her, strong arms scooping her right off her feet and against his chest. His stride never faltering as he charged the path true.

She screamed joyously, head thrown back, as the second sprinkler hit them. Arms wrapped tightly around Daniel's neck and knotted in his tangled hair, she could feel her own curls now dripping with water droplets, falling heavily around her shoulders.

She felt more than heard Daniel's laughter over the sound of shooting water, and he hit the ground, sprawling and rolling with her, until they both lay on their backs, breathing heavily.

Small fits of giggles escaped her lips as she stretched her arms out, letting her fingers run through short blades of grass. She turned her face to look at him.

His eyes were closed, his lips pulling up a smile both pleased and amused. His auburn hair dripped water, plastering it to his face, and his sodden clothes clung to his familiar frame. She could see his scars through his shirt, five parallel slash marks. Every time she saw them, she got the urge to curl up at his side.

And she did.

Sliding over and resting her head on his shoulder, she stretched an arm across his chest, holding him like the fragile human being he was, and would never see himself.

Sighing contentedly, he shifted, winding his own arm around her automatically, hugging her close.

They stared up at the night sky.

"There are so many of them," she remarked quietly. Daniel understood, nodding. He was watching the stars too. "My grandma used to tell me when I was little, that God made a new star every time someone came home to live with him."

She glanced at him with a shy smile, but he continued to say nothing, staring up at the night sky. She watched his face grow pensive, his fingers skimming distractedly up and down her arm.

Oh, Dan. She sighed inwardly. *Can't you put your clockwork mind to rest for one night?*

Time became an unimportant factor of the universe as they lay there together.

Only when they caught themselves shivering, did they find the motivation to make their way back to the truck, retrieving their discarded shoes along the way, though not bothering to put them back on. Once inside the cab, Devlyn promptly blasted the heat, attempting to dry her drenched curls. Combing it through with her fingers in front of the vents, she caught Daniel shooting her amused looks, and quickly dubbed it a fruitless effort.

Leaning back instead, she propped her feet up, toenails painted a brilliant lime green against the dashboard.

They exchanged a Cheshire cat's conspirators look, revelling in the forbiddance of it.

If Ian found out she was doing such a thing-- he'd blow a gasket.

"Can I open my eyes yet?"

Daniel guided Devlyn down the hallway, his hands on her hips behind her.

"No," he said firmly.

"I know we're in my apartment building."

He frowned, peering over her shoulder to check for any sign that she was peeking.

"Dan, I know my own house," she said in annoyance, as if she could sense his actions, but there was amusement in her voice as well.

They stopped in front of room two hundred and twenty one.

"Just trust me," he whispered. "You love surprises."

Even standing behind her, he could sense her smile.

"Like the time my eighteen year old, brown eyed boy, took me on a midnight swim and told me he had an inclination for a certain tattoo?" she reflected warmly. "Yeah. I do."

"You were beautiful that night."

"Yeah, yeah," she said dismissively, all retrospect lost, and if her eyes were open he was sure she would have rolled them.

"We were both gorgeous people bathed in moonlight. Now don't you dare leave me in suspense!"

Daniel chuckled. "All right, all right." Reaching forward, he used her key to unlocked the door, pushing it open. "There."

She stepped forward automatically, slipping from his grip. He hung back, watching her silently, until she'd passed the entranceway.

"Open your eyes," he prompted softly.

And though he couldn't see her obey, he knew she had by her sudden intake of breath.

Stepping into the doorframe after her, Daniel flipped the light switch, illuminating what she was seeing in a 100W glow.

"Surprise."

There were yellow lilies everywhere. Placed elegantly on counters and tables in tall glass vases, they were wound around handles, window frames, and tucked in every nook and cranny available, their heady aroma consuming the apartment.

Devlyn's eyes were shining. Venturing farther into the room, she stepped cautiously, like one wrong move would make everything disappear. She took it all in with a slow turn, her wet curls sticking to her forehead and cheeks. Her soaked dress clung to her form, leaving puddles around her feet on the lament wood flooring.

"How could--? How did you--?" she rambled off, unable to finish either sentence. Her wide, dark blue eyes roamed the room, her fingers skimming over the surface of the entranceway table.

Daniel shoved his hands in his pockets where he leaned against the doorframe, and shrugged modestly. "I have friends in high places."

She spun to face him. "Ruby!" she exclaimed, understanding immediately lighting her face. "It had to be!"

Daniel smiled guiltily. There was indeed only one person he knew who could take flowers and work them into the very fabric of a room. "Okay, so I have artistically inclined designer friends who I may have loaned at key."

She shook her head in amused awe, and with two long strides, she was suddenly in front of him again. Fingertips that could make even the smallest details beautiful with a paintbrush pushed through his hair, her forehead pressing against his.

"Thank you," she whispered with utter sincerity, her eyes wandering his face. "How did I ever get so lucky?"

"As I recall, it *was* you who found me."

She laughed lightly. "So it was." And crushed her lips to his.

He deepened the kiss and her body pressed closer, a perfect match for his. He stepped forward, meaning to back her up against the wall, and instead collided them both into the entranceway table. Devlyn gasped as one of the glass vases rocked violently, and fumbling for it, Daniel only just managed to stop it from crashing to the floor.

Panting, his wet hair in disarray, Devlyn laughed uncontrollably beneath him. Her hands curled against the nape of his neck, and the belt loop of his dress pants, were the only things keeping her from falling back onto the table.

He'd successfully turned their apartment into a China shop.

Kissing her forehead he swept her up into his arms instead, padding his way to their bedroom, where he tossed her lightly, laughing, onto the bed. She pulled him down beside her, and lying on their backs, they stared up at the ceiling.

Painted like the night sky, it was a startling replica of the one they'd been admiring earlier. Lighter paint wisped across as the Milky Way, and he could pick out The Big Dipper, Orion, and Ratatosk. It was counted as one of the master pieces in the apartment that was ever present, and Daniel knew that once the lights were off, the stars would continue to glow softly, aided by the luminous paint they were created from.

Without a word, Devlyn's fingers played with the dog tag necklace around his neck, eventually finding the buttons of his shirt, and making deft work of them. Her fingertips brushed over his bare skin, tracing the five parallel scars that slashed diagonally across his chest.

Shivering he drew her into his arms, his face buried against her collarbone. She smelt of green apple body wash and herself.

That night Daniel dreamt of sprinklers.

He was running through Macy's Golf Course, chasing after Devlyn. For some reason, the sight of her dark half circle tattoo on the pale skin of her hand was the only thing keeping her within his

*sight. He'd just ducked around another sprinkler in his continued
pursuit, when another figure had suddenly joined the scene behind
him, a flashlight bobbing in the darkness. The newcomer called out
his name and Daniel couldn't help looking back over his shoulder,
the voice one he recognized and knew well.*

Ian.

*His brother was heading in the other direction, calling for
him to join, his flashlight waving impatiently.*

*Daniel halted his advance immediately, skidding to a stop,
as he planted his feet in the earth.*

*He felt stuck, looking forward towards Devlyn, then back at
Ian, then to Devlyn again.*

*Devlyn disappeared behind the next sprinkler and he
instantly took a step in her direction, only to hear his brother's
calls become more insistent, laced with urgency.*

*He took a step back, his eyes still glued to the spot where
he'd lost sight of Devlyn, half of him begging to follow, the other
half compelled to turn around.*

*All the while Ian continued to call his name, over and over,
in only the way that he could, breaking apart the* Da *and the* nny *so
the last half sounded more like* nay *than* nee, *shouting each like
they were their own word, yet somehow meant to be together.*

Da-nay!

Danny!

A loud bang jolted Daniel from sleep, the bedroom door
flying inward.

Devlyn screamed, sitting bolt upright, and Daniel threw
himself in front of her. He blocked her from view, pressing her
back against the headboard, his arms spreading protectively.

"Relax!" The intruder barked sharply. "It's me!"

"Ian?!" Daniel gasped, relaxing his stance. Behind him
Devlyn groaned loudly, her forehead dropping to press against the
back of his shoulder.

His brother was hovering in the doorway, an anxious look
on his face.

"I don't know the code."

"The what?" Daniel asked disbelievingly.

"The code!" Ian repeated impatiently. "The code for the

freaken alarm system that's about to go off."

"I have a door," Devlyn mumbled quietly to no one in particular.

"It's Guernica," Daniel replied hurriedly.

"Right," his brother nodded and disappeared from the doorframe-- only to immediately reappear. "How do you spell that?"

With a sigh Daniel rattled off the letters in order and Ian vanished again.

"Good morning to you too, brother," Daniel muttered to the empty air, and Devlyn groaned again.

"What's he doing here?"

"Probably itching for a case. I mean, we only just got back from our last one yesterday," Daniel muttered bitterly.

She sighed. "I love your brother-- really, but some days…" she trailed off.

Daniel spun so he was facing her.

"Please don't leave me, because my family's insane," he pleaded lightly, tucking a stray lock behind her ear. "I promise I'll try and teach him boundaries."

Suddenly there was a loud bark as Winchester bolted into the room. Without pause he leapt onto the bed and drowned them in wet kisses, shaking and whining with excitement.

"And what about him?" Devlyn laughed, trying to push the dog down. "You going to teach him boundaries too?"

Daniel just smiled, scratching Winchester behind the ears, as his tail thumped against their legs.

"We should get dressed before any other unannounced visitors bust in."

Leaning around the dog, she kissed his cheek, her fingers brushing briefly over his scars again. "Okay."

"Really guys, I can make breakfast," Devlyn offered, not for the first time, as Daniel and his brother struggled around a wriggling Winchester to put their shoes on at the door.

She was leaning against the wall of the entranceway, a housecoat now wrapped loosely around her frame. Her bed-ridden hair was twisted listlessly up into a knot.

Beside him, Ian was shaking his head. "Jim will be waiting

for us back at the Ay. I told him we'd meet up again this morning."

"Jim's back?" both Daniel and Devlyn tried to clarify at the same time, their fondness for the man evident in their voices. But Daniel knew it was true. Being the owner and having a key, Jim had a bad habit of letting himself into their room unannounced.

"He showed up last night," Ian said, and then looked briefly between them. "You were busy."

Devlyn and Daniel exchanged a conspirators' glance.

"Anyway," Ian continued, "he's waiting on us-- and food. Plus I'd like to borrow my Scit for some, you know-- *Sciting*."

Daniel made sure to shoot Devlyn an 'I told you so' look, which she answered with a roll off her eyes, and stepped towards him.

"Just be careful, all right," she pleaded. "When you come back I want you in one piece."

She glanced meaningfully at Ian, who nodded solemnly.

His wellbeing was never a joking matter when it came to the two of them.

She stretched up on her tiptoes to kiss him earnestly. "When you leave here, don't forget why you came."

He smiled warmly with recognition at her usual parting words. "Leave the light on for me."

Ian made a gagging noise, and forcefully wrenched the door open behind him.

Daniel turned, annoyed. "How'd you even get here anyway?"

His brother shrugged. "Walked."

Daniel repressed a sigh. The trek wouldn't have been a short one, and he found himself wondering, once again, if Ian had slept any.

"And *you'll* be walking back if you don't start moving," his brother promised.

Turning the door handle to motel room thirty-three, Daniel walked in balancing a cardboard tray of coffees, and a take out bag in one hand. Ian followed in after, kicking the door shut behind him. The moment they stepped over the threshold, they were immediately bombarded by Jim. Ian swapped Conexus, pulling the old man in to swat his back warmly, and then watched with amusement as Jim crushed Daniel in a bear hug, his brother having to raise their coffee and lunch above his head in rescue.

With a small laugh, Ian perched himself on the bed beside the bottle of solvent he'd left in place alongside the guns he had been cleaning. They laid dismembered on the bed, fanned out around him on towels, and by habit he immediately lifted the nearest one and resumed cleaning. With Jim looking over his shoulder and talk of a new case, he thought he'd better finish the job before he got a lecture. Jim had always been very adamant about gun care. "They've saved your lives more than once," he'd always said. "Give them some love and care once in awhile."

Winchester came next, barking excitedly and leaping at Jim in welcome. It nearly knocked the old man over in the process.

"Down," Ian reprimanded automatically, as he inspected the barrel of a gun through one eye.

Winchester obeyed, instantly dropping back to all fours, and followed behind Daniel as he walked to the desk. When he passed him, Ian grabbed a coffee out of the tray. He didn't need to look. He knew they'd all be the same-- black the way all three of them liked it. Daniel handed the second off to Jim and then dumped the rest of his load on the desk next to his laptop. Digging around in the to-go bag, he came up with the four burgers wrapped in tissue paper.

"They weren't serving lunch yet, but we managed to pull some strings," Daniel informed Jim with a triumphant smile, and then held up the first candidate. "All right," he said on quick inspection, "we got ourselves a bacon cheese burger, hold the pickles--"

Ian held his hand up to receive a toss, and it arched across the room, Winchester bolting after it, convinced it was a game. Ian snatched it gracefully out of the air, just in time to foil the tracking dog, who let out a disappointed whine as Ian set the supposed ball aside for another sip of coffee.

"A hamburger with extra onions and mustard--," his brother continued with a grimace, and tossed it in Jim's direction. Jim caught it, only to have Winchester in his lap a split second later.

"It's got flavor," The man claimed, pushing the dog down.

"Every time you say that," Daniel said with a laugh. "And every time, it gets no closer to becoming true."

Ian smiled in amusement around the lid of his cup, and raised his hand to bump air fists with his brother. Jim immediately started grumbling something about 'bringing out the flavor', which Ian missed most of, as Daniel pulled out the next order and crouched down, arms resting on his knees. He carefully unwrapped a small burger, and whistled for Winchester.

"Don't think we forgot about you," Daniel said, and ruffled the dog's ears. Winchester only sniffed at it momentarily, before taking it in his mouth and quickly retreating into a corner of the room to devour it.

"That's going to get all over the carpet," Jim deduced, eyeing up the dog as, sure enough, Winchester slid onto his belly, and started ripping the treat apart with his teeth, holding it steady between his front paws.

Ian shrugged at the same time his brother did, and Daniel carried the last burger, with identical toppings to his, Ian knew, over to the bed. Brushing some of the guns lightly aside, Daniel parked himself next to him. Ian could feel Jim watching them both as they unwrapped the tissue paper to their burgers and took an appreciative moment to look at their meals. Both their heads tilted at the same angle as they took a large bite, and then together they wiped their mouths with the back of their sleeves. Ian hadn't even been aware they had done it simultaneously, until Jim spoke.

"You boys weird me out sometimes," he said honestly, still staring.

"What?" Ian demanded at the same time his brother did.

Jim just gave them a knowing smile around a mouthful of food, and shook his head. "Nothing, forget it."

They managed to get lost in conversation, polishing off the rest of their food with a brush of their fingers. Ian could tell Jim was waiting impatiently for Daniel to bring up anything to do with his thoughts on university, but as always, his brother was a master at manipulating the conversation.

Instead Jim ended up relaying a story about his last case in the Yukon, reiterating his stakeouts, describing annoying people he'd met along the way, and eventually the desired shotgun to the head, leaving the vampire a hunk of dried up concrete on the sidewalk.

In no less time than it took Jim to finish his story, Ian had lost all patience on the old man's behalf.

"Okay," he implored, turning to face his brother. "We've been polite long enough."

Daniel's brow furrowed. "What's that supposed to mean?"

"Meaning," Jim clarified, "I've been over here yammering on about killing some stunt vampire number three, and you haven't even bothered to tell me about getting accepted into college yet."

"Oh," his brother answered in what seemed like genuine surprise. "Right. University though, not college." Then Ian received an accusing glance.

He looked away guiltily and took a sip of his coffee.

"Yes, yes, university," Jim said waving away the blunder. "So, you've decided then? You're going?"

Ian watched his brother's eyes drop to his hands. "Well, it was the next logical step…"

And that's all he said, his forehead pinching together as he receded into that pensive backdoor in his brain.

"It is," Jim agreed gently, "and you're going to do great, son."

The man gave his brother a sort of loving, understanding look that was very fatherly in nature.

Because it was true.

And Ian knew he couldn't hold on to his little brother forever.

A pang echoed in his chest, and suddenly he was searching for a subject change. Any subject change.

"Tell Jim about the flowers."

Jim and Daniel both turned to give him an odd look.

"I nearly drowned to death in them when I walked into Dev's place," he clarified. "I mean, I've heard about guys getting in touch with their feminine side, but…"

"I was going for romantic," Daniel informed. "Flowers kind of come with the territory."

"Did the territory really need a tropically scented jungle?"

Daniel cracked a smile. "Eat me, Ian."

"Gross. You still smell like tulips."

"Lilies."

"Whatever, Danielle."

Jim shook his head. "I swear it's like listening to a couple of seven year olds trying to have an adult conversation."

Ian and his brother turned to give him a look, and Jim raised his eyebrows in an unrelenting 'What? It's true' gesture.

Ian was the first one to break.

"Okay!" he said throwing up his arms. "It's time we hit the road. I need a case. Stat." He snapped his fingers towards the laptop where it rested on the desk. "Danny, time to play Scit for awhile."

Daniel stood, obediently crossing the room to take his place in the swivel chair behind the desk. He flipped open the laptop, wiggling the touch pad. "What? No leave?"

Ian smirked. "I'm sure you and Dev had quite the excellent layover last night-- now it's work time."

Chapter Five

They said goodbye to Jim, all back slapping hugs and staying safe promises. Daniel had found them a case in less than an hour, making sure to also research one up for Jim, sending him to Halifax to deal with a rogue faerie on some sort of twisted poison rampage.

Daniel hadn't give out much about their case yet, except to tell Ian it was in Toronto, and not to worry, that he would get to blast some vamp's head off.

Ian knew that when Daniel didn't go into great detail, it was because he was still mulling a lot of it over. He didn't always know how his brother did it, but Daniel never failed to have a game plan set in motion by the time they reached their destination. Even if he was, at the very moment, zonked out in the passenger seat. His head rested against the window, bobbing with each dip in the road, and his hair was already starting to stick up at odd angles.

It had taken them just over a day to reach the Ontario border. Ian knew he had his lead foot to thank for that, but it had since started raining, and with no indication of letting up. They'd already pulled over to haul Winchester into the truck cab, which now reeked of wet dog, the blasting heater only amplifying the smell. Their small companion lay with his head on Daniel's lap, and tail across Ian's. Passed out like his brother, his paws twitched with whatever dream filled his head.

Ian didn't mind being the only one conscious. The rhythm of the windshield wipers, and the steady rumble of the engine were enough to keep him company for the time being. He wondered briefly if this was what it was like to travel alone all the time, all quiet, except for the truck and his own thoughts. Sure, sometimes he welcomed the peace of mind, but most of the time he lived for distractions, anything to keep selective memories from resurfacing.

And what was a better distraction than a pain in the crapper little brother?

As the rain pounded harder, Ian found himself squinting at the road signs. They were nearly to the city and Ian knew they were as good as lost the moment they were.

His directional skills were zero.

Highway driving was his domain, but anything beyond a straight slab of pavement to follow-- was trouble. He had nearly made out a sign, when the green traffic light ahead turned straight to red. As they flew through the intersection, he caught a glimpse of the little red light camera peering down at him.

He swore under his breath, turning to give his brother a rough smack.

"Eh! Get up!"

Daniel groaned loudly in protest, his eyes remaining closed.

"I ran a red light," Ian informed him impatiently.

"Again?" Daniel complained, his voice groggy with sleep. His eyes popped open to regard him with annoyance. "Really, Ian?"

With a sigh Daniel sat up straight, disturbing Winchester who shifted away from him with a huff, and curled up to resume sleeping.

"There was no one around for miles," Ian retorted in his defense. Perks of bad weather.

"You're going to get us both killed one of these days."

Ian knew his brother didn't really believe it.

Sure, he had his rough spots, but he was an excellent driver. He could control a vehicle like it was his own person. In the line of duty, that's what really mattered.

"Where are we?"

"I dunno," Ian grumbled back. "You try reading one of these signs."

"Never mind," Daniel sighed, "I'll just GPS it."

Fishing in his jacket pocket, he pulled out his phone. It took him a moment to assess the location of the red light camera Ian had ran, and then Daniel flipped open his laptop to hack into the Toronto police data base. The weather apparently hadn't effected any of the wireless connections. He was able to erase all evidence of the infraction before losing the unsecured signal he'd piggybacked.

But just barely.

"Hey, Ian?"

"Yeah?" Ian asked, shooting him a questioning glance.

He could tell Daniel was about to rebuke him for the red light again, but at the last minute he seemed to decide against it.

There was no point really.

If it came down to it-- Ian would do it again.

Daniel exhaled sharply, letting it go. "Take your next left," he said instead.

Ian nodded, flicking on his signal light, and easing the truck into the turning lane. "But I need to know what I'm walking into here."

Daniel clicked around on his computer again for another moment, bringing up information Ian knew he'd saved before they'd left.

"Several people have gone missing from a local subway station," Daniel began, looking up to make sure he had his brother's attention. "All at the same time of night, and all found a few days later at random platform locations. The police haven't released this, but I did some digging, and all the victims were completely drained of blood and had 'crescent bite marks all over their bodies,'" Daniel quoted.

"So... what? Vamp's just camping out in the subway tunnels and chewing on the frequent commuters?" Ian asked in disgust.

"The *three a.m.* frequent commuters, pretty much, yeah."

"So we're going to have to search the subway tunnels?"

"Yup," Daniel said, giving his brother a humorless smile.

"With trains coming at us?"

"Yup."

Ian groaned, his voice dripping with sarcasm. "Fan-freaken-tastic."

Marley stumbled down the steps to the subway platform, holding the collar of her worn leather jacket up against the cold. She was completely drenched from head to toe, the storm outside practically biblical. Her silver grey Weimaraner hound, Lady, shook out her coat in the same way Marley shook out her long bright red hair, causing it to cling to her face with wetness. It was in desperate need of trimming. Her bangs kept hanging down into her eyes and she found herself brushing them back far too often. At three in the morning, the train station was fairly deserted, only a few homeless people were scattered here and there, seeking shelter from the storm.

She kept to the shadowed parts as she made her way around to the tunnel opening, her sawed-off shotgun bumping against her side where it lay tucked in her jacket. Lady padded softly at her side, the only sound the dog's soft panting. She was busy looking for security camera locations-- when she froze.

Two figures filled the darkness under a dead spot of a camera.

The shorter one was crouched down in front of a pipe, a German Shepherd standing by his side and nudging impatiently at him with his nose, while he made some small racket. The taller one stood in front of him, doing a poor job of concealing his partner and the tail wagging K-9. She wouldn't have given it much thought really, if the shorter one hadn't shifted his weight in that moment, causing the dim light to glint off the metal of a revolver he had tucked in the waistband of his jeans. She instinctively moved closer, reaching into her jacket to rest a hand on the sawed-off. She was just beginning to pull it out, when the tall one turned his head enough, that the low lighting caught his features, icy blue eyes reflecting back. It took her a moment to place his face, but when she did she couldn't believe it.

Ian Browning.

Which made the shorter one Daniel. Jim's boys. Although she'd never introduced herself, she'd heard a boatload about them. The Knocte and Scit that worked together. The brothers. She had a vague recollection of glimpsing them once before in a Knocte tattoo shop, but it had been years ago. Normally she'd be stark, raving mad that some other Knocte had picked up on the same case she'd been given and beat her to the punch, but curiosity was quickly getting the better of her.

How exactly did they operate? How'd a Scit manage to tag along without the Knocte tripping over him every step of the way?

Confident they wouldn't recognize her, she stepped from the shadows and took a seat against a nearby wall, roll playing just another person seeking shelter from the storm. Grabbing Lady's chain collar, she pulled the dog down to sit with her. From the new angle she got a better look at what they were doing.

Daniel had drilled a hole through the pipe and was feeding another line into it, as Ian pulled a laptop out from under his jacket and handed it over to him. It took Daniel another moment to get the cord situated and then he accepted the device, flipping it open, and balancing it precariously on his knee. He went to work at the keypad, the screen out of her sight, until he turned it towards his brother in show.

No way.

Video of every camera in the subway station stared back at Ian through the computer screen. Somehow he never ceased to be surprised by his brother's computing capabilities.

"As fascinating as this is, Danny, how exactly is it useful?"

Daniel sighed, a patient sigh Ian was almost positive was reserved especially for him. "What if I told you I could control the cameras?"

"Okay. So… what? You're going to point them at the wall, so the security guards don't come running their heft down here, when they see us jump ditch into the subway tunnel?"

"No," Daniel frowned. "Not unless you want to send up a major red flag shouting 'hey, I'm hacking your system'. Plus they'd just move the cameras back. No, what I'm going to do is use the cameras to take pictures of the subway station like it is now, and then set that as the camera screens, making us the invisible duo."

Ian nodded his approval. "And Hackle and Jackal, the security freaks, aren't going to notice nothing's moving?"

Daniel laughed. "Look around Ian," he said gesturing around him at the nearly vacant subway station. "No one's here, and those who are, are crashed out till next Tuesday."

"All right, all right, point made. Can we get to shooting this thing?"

Daniel hastily finished up what he'd suggested. He tucked his laptop and revolver into their duffle bag, exchanging it for their shotguns. Ian quickly found a hiding spot for the bag, and then he and his brother leapt down onto the train tracks, Winchester following. Wielding their shotguns, they pulled their flashlights out of their coat pockets. Holding and managing the two together, was something the brothers had come to master years ago. They moved in long practiced formation, Ian taking the lead with Winchester focused at his side, and Daniel bringing up the rear, following his brother into the darkness. The flashlight beams cut through the blackness, revealing the subway tunnel to be an ancient mouse hole shaped piece of architecture, the walls lined every half meter or so with square pillars part way protruding out of the grey stone walls. They would create an almost mesmerizing pattern, as they flew by a zooming train window.

"Hey, you didn't happen to check the train schedule did you?" Ian asked, his voice amplifying as it echoed off the dank walls. They were coming up to a curve and they'd paused just before it, keeping tight to the inside wall.

Daniel suppressed a laugh. Only Ian would think to ask such a question after already jumping head first into the situation.

"Of course I did," he tried to sound appalled. "What kind of Scit would I be if I hadn't? We got about a half an hour, give or take."

Ian spun around to shine his flashlight into his younger brother's face.

"Give or take?" he demanded.

Daniel's brow furrowed with irritation, as much as it did against the onslaught of light, but his expression quickly went slack, when he saw the shape looming around the corner in Ian's shadow. Winchester had caught sight of it first, barking like mad. With Ian's flashlight still shining in his face, illuminating it like day, Daniel knew it was easy for his brother to read his expression change, and know exactly what it meant.

"It's behind me isn't it?" Ian asked gravely, but didn't bother to wait for an answer as he spun around with surprising speed, and nicked the vampire in the neck with the butt of his gun. The creature barely seemed to notice as it dodged away, raking Ian's arm in the process. His brother leapt back, just as Daniel's shot rang out, imbedding itself in the vampire's chest. It staggered backwards, the only result of his quick action, aside from gaining its attention.

Daniel had little time to react as the vampire turned and sprang at him, hissing with disapproval. They collided, knocking Daniel backwards, flattening him onto the railway tracks. He managed to grasp his shotgun with both hands, making it a bar in between them as the edge of the railway track bit into his back. The flashlight he'd dropped in the process landed nearby, rolling. Every full circle it made illuminated the vampire's face for a short instant.

It was the first time Daniel had been able to make out the creature's appearance. He was a Caucasian male, about early thirties, with a thick goatee, and heavyset eyebrows. His short brown hair was disarrayed, and his eye colour pale and washed out, like every vampire they'd ever encountered. He'd probably had a family once, Daniel knew, but it was hard to imagine such a thing with the creature's drool dripping down its facial hair and onto Daniel's face, as he tried to hold it at bay.

"Rip. Tear. Drink, " the vampire hissed, milky eyes crazed and ablaze with excitement. Then it chuckled madly, and snapped its teeth at him. "Drink! Drink! Drink to death," it chanted.

"You think so?!" Daniel heard Ian's voice yell, his brother's light suddenly very bright in their direction. The vampire turned, only to find himself starring down the length of Ian's double-barreled shotgun. "I don't!"

He pulled the trigger.

Daniel managed to throw his arms over his face, before being pelted with shards of vampire head. The body teetered for a moment on the spot, before falling over like a ridged statue-- crushing him with its weight. Appalled he hastily shoved it aside.

"You good?" Ian asked, his flashlight once again shining in Daniel's face.

"Yeah," Daniel panted. He wiped the drool off his face using the back of his sleeve, a look of disgust crossing his face. He couldn't help the sarcasm that leaked into his voice when he answered. "Just great."

With a grim expression, Ian extended a hand, pulling him to his feet.

"Where's Winchester?" Daniel demanded, bending down to retrieve his fallen flashlight and swinging it around to search through the darkness.

Pressing his thumb and forefinger to his lips, Ian gave a sharp blast.

Winchester's single answering bark carried back to them through echoes, a sound from deep within the tunnel.

Daniel frowned.

"What's gotten into him?" Ian asked with irritation, as he started off in the dog's direction.

70

Daniel pressed his lips into a thin line, falling in step behind his brother. A good tracking dog never wandered off for no reason. And Winchester happened to be an excellent one. They both held their guns steady, neither one of them letting down their guard for an instant. A feeling that they'd bitten off more than they could chew suddenly pricked at Daniel.

They rounded the next corner-- and stopped dead in their tracks.

Ian swore sharply.

Standing in front of them, arms crossed and waiting in mock formation, was a circle of five vampires. The ringleader, dark skinned and dark haired, stood with an air of superiority, looking completely bored with the whole situation in its entirety. Two females flanked him on either side, one a petite blond and the other a dark brunette from Asian decent, both in possession of heavy attitudes. The vampires standing at the back, however, were the ones that set Daniel's radar off. The two short haired men, one tall and lanky, the other short and burly, both had expressions that promised violence. Clearly these were the protectors and enforcers of the small clan. In the center of them all, an uneasy Winchester crouched, trapped, ears pinned back, fur bristling. His eyes flitting about, trying to keep track of all five vampires at once. A low steady growl rumbled deep in his throat.

Ian's shotgun immediately flew up, leveling with the front vampire's head. "Let him go!"

The leader merely tilted his head back and laughed loudly.

"Ah, isn't this just *rich*? Two ox brains walk into our den like they own the place, come to find they are completely out numbered, and still have the gall to think they can order us about."

"Do it!" Ian spat, his voice like ice. "Now!"

"Sorry, darling," Blondie snapped back, "but Wonder Boy heroism isn't going to win you any points here."

While his brother was covering the hothead role, Daniel's Scit instincts had sky rocketed to full force, his mind whirling like clockwork. It was true they were largely out numbered. Their best line of defense, he knew, would be to tuck tail and run, but with Winchester boxed in, they were out of options.

He made a decision and raised his gun to match his brother's.

"You heard him," Daniel said with indignation.

The ringleader looked back at his small clan with a roll of his eyes, clearly meaning it to be a mocking gesture, but it was exactly the opening Daniel had been looking for, and he could tell Ian saw it too. He signaled his waiting brother with a tiny inclination of his head, and they acted with practiced ease, swinging their shotguns in separate directions from their currently shared target. They pulled their triggers, dispatching two of the flanking clan members. It was a simple maneuver they'd come up with, so they'd never waste a shot on the same target. Whichever side they were on, that's who they were responsible for picking off. Daniel pegged Blondie with little trouble. Just because he didn't have crazy speed and reflexes like his brother, didn't mean he couldn't shoot a stationary object with perfect aim.

Ian beheaded the burly vampire with strategic intention, a trickier shot, Daniel knew, but with generous pay off. It was a dramatic, yet effective way, to announce they planned to stand and fight.

With three remaining vampires, however, now alert, ready, and fully aware of his and his brother's intentions, things were about to get ugly. With a short blanch at his fallen comrade, the lanky vampire made a move in Ian's direction, revenge clearly stamped on his face. This brother raised his shotgun in challenge, when the leader suddenly blurted out: "No, you dolt! The other one-- Daniel. Kill *him*!"

How'd he know my name?

Was the first thought that popped into Daniel's head, as he shot his brother a stunned look. Ian was already starring back at him, surprise and panic written across his usually placid features.

Their exchange was short lived. The vampire changed course obediently, immediately lunging in Daniel's direction. Pumping his gun, Ian spun, getting a shot off before the other two were on top of him. The shot nicked the vampire's shoulder, but he continued to charge on regardless, with barely a stumble to his name. Daniel quickly expelled his shells, before lining up and taking a shot of his own. The creature dove out of the way, the bullets instead colliding with the stone wall of the tunnel behind him. Before Daniel had time to reload, he was knocked off his feet, sending his flashlight once again tumbling across the floor, but he maintained a death grip on his weapon and lifeline, as he went down.

The vampire leered over him for a moment, the faint light from the distant flashlight casting eerie shadows across his face.

Then the first of the fists began to fly.

Daniel blocked the first blow with his shotgun, but in the next instant, the creature had gripped it and wrenched it involuntarily from his grasp, delivering the second one. Daniel caught it across his cheekbone and was about to receive another, when he got his legs beneath his assailant and kicked out, sending the vampire toppling backwards. The effort only gained him enough time to pull himself into a sitting position, however, before Mr. Tall and Lanky was back in front of him again. The vampire thrust his hand out, gripping Daniel's throat, and cutting off his air supply. Lifting him off the ground, the vampire slid him up against one of the indentations between the half pillars of the tunnel wall.

"Eliminate you?" the creature snarled, his lips pulling back from his razor white teeth. "Easiest orders I've ever been given. "

"Orders?" Daniel gasped, his toes stretching longingly for the floor. "I don't--" he struggled for another intake of breath "--don't understand."

"And why would you?" the vampire scoffed. "Poor, poor, Daniel. Just the sacrificial piece to take down the larger game."

"Larg--?" Daniel tried, but the vampire didn't let him finish.

"Let's end this game." And then with a swoop of his arm, he sent Daniel flying clear across the subway tunnel.

Ian had just dropped kicked the clan leader in the gut, sending him to eat floor dust, when he saw Daniel collide with the edge of a pillar just off to his right. His brother collapsed to the ground, automatically struggling to regain his feet, but even Daniel's attempt to prop himself up by his elbows failed, when one immediately gave out on him.

Ian could already tell his shoulder was out. Weaponless and injured, his brother was deemed helpless.

"Danny!" Ian called, and had already taken a step in his direction, when something hard slammed into him. He was sent sprawling to the ground, and before he even had time to gain his

73

bearings, he felt long sharp fingernails penetrating his chest, tearing right through his shirt and into his flesh. He yelled defiantly in pain, as long dark hair swayed above his head. He came to realize in that moment, that it was the young Asian girl trying to rip his heart clean out of his chest.

He rolled sharply, catching her across the temporal lobe with the butt of his shotgun, and successfully managed to reverse their positions. He straddled her torso, pinning her down. He made sure to reload the gun dramatically before he took aim and fired, squinting his eyes against the resulting debris. He didn't miss a beat as he leapt to his feet and spun toward his brother. His flashlight, luckily still in his possession, first caught Winchester's illuminating eyes as he crouched in front of Daniel; having been freed, he'd come to his master's rescue, and then secondly, the body guard of a vampire himself, hunched over to face the snarling K-9.

Ian had never figured out why dog teeth had such an effect on vampire skin. Usually you could only get a vampire to bleed if you nicked the underside of their forearm, their Achilles' heal as it were, but dog teeth, or teeth in general, although Ian had never bitten a vampire to properly test that theory, could rip apart their skin like no one's business. With Winchester no longer outnumbered, and only one vampire to attend with, he actually stood a fighting chance, but Ian was beyond letting it go that far. Anyone who dared mess with his brother had him to contend with. All he needed was a better angle. The shot was one he wasn't at liberty to miss.

Pain flaring through his shoulder, Daniel forced himself onto his knees, reaching for the knife he always kept tucked in his sock. It would do little against his adversary, but there was always the rare chance he'd cut the main artery on the creature's forearm, even if it would take ages for the vampire to bleed out.

The vampire advanced, and Winchester lunged forward, clasping his jaws around the guard's leg. Howling the vampire kicked frantically in an attempt to free himself, but when the dog's will proved too great, he reached down as if to try and tear him free.

Daniel knew he needed to act fast-- and now.

If the vampire did manage to get its claws on the dog, it would think nothing of ripping their beloved pet in two. Grasping his knife tightly, he took aim, and threw with practiced skill. Although he wasn't as quick on the draw as a Knocte would have been, he'd learned to compensate. Pitch it a little farther ahead than his hindered eyes thought he should, and voila-- contact.

The knife imbedded itself hilt deep in the vampire's outstretched forearm.

Perfect.

He hardly had time for that one simple word of self-congratulations, before the vampire, hissing his rage, had the knife removed, slipping the now crimson blade free of his skin using his uninjured hand. With a cruel smile, seemingly out of character for his current predicament, the vampire gave a final kick, dislodging Winchester from his leg and sending him sliding across the tunnel, nails clicking as he slipped against the stone floor. The creature then passed the blade off skillfully between his fingers, before cocking his wrist back, about to deliver a throw Daniel knew, given the range, he wouldn't have the speed to avoid. He cursed internally, his mind whirling-- just as a sudden, thunderous gun crack echoed off the stone walls. The vampire before Daniel was instantly headless. The lifeless body toppled onto the floor-- revealing Ian, gun still held out stretched with one arm, barrel smoking.

"Brawns, but no brain," Ian mocked, before stepping over the corpse and hauling his little brother to his feet by his good arm.

Up close Ian could see the extent of the damage. Bruises were already beginning to bloom along Daniel's cheekbone, his lip was split, and a small stream of blood trickled from his nose.

"You look like you got hit by a bus."

Winchester appeared then, bounding back to Daniel's side. Ignoring the comment, Daniel gave a sigh of relief, and scratched the dog behind the ears with his good hand.

"Did you get them all?" Daniel asked, scrunching his face against his pain, as he continued to favor his left shoulder.

Suddenly remembering the leader, Ian spun around, his flashlight searching through the darkness for any sign of him. He came across nothing, cursing internally. The last he'd seen of the vampire, he'd merely thrust him to the ground.

"Their fearless leader apparently jumped ship, but everyone else is down for the count."

"Great," Daniel said sarcastically.

Their case wasn't closed if there was still a murderous creature lurking about. It meant they'd have to come back again tomorrow.

"Would you mind?"

Ian turned back to his brother, who was indicating his shoulder meaningfully.

"Right," Ian said, flicking on the safely of his shotgun. He awkwardly sandwiched it and the flashlight between his arm and his side, then gripped his brother's shoulder. "Ready…"

"Yeah."

"And…"

Daniel braced himself for the inevitable, but when nothing followed, he sighed heavily. "Are you going--?"

With a sharp jerk, Ian popped his shoulder back into place, and Daniel cut himself off as he cried out tersely in pain, breaking away from him.

"Trust me, Danny," Ian said honestly, telling his brother what he probably already knew. "It hurts a lot less later if your muscles are relaxed."

Breathing heavily, Daniel rolled his shoulder back, testing it. "Right," he said tersely. "You're still a jerk."

Giving him an indifferent shrug, Ian walked over to retrieve Daniel's long lost gun and flashlight, returning to shove them both into his hands.

"We need to break up the bodies we scattered all over the track," Ian ordered, referring to the way they used their shotguns repeatedly to turn the bodies into concrete dust. The bodies became more vulnerable when their heads were absent, an old, lifeless crumbly wall, instead of a solid rock formation. Yet still harmful. "Or the next train that comes through here is going to meet some serious friction."

Daniel nodded. Again Ian was telling his brother what he already knew. Although they usually broke up the bodies to hide all evidence of their work, large concrete like chunks in the way of a speeding subway, was also a cause for concern.

They split up, sweeping their flashlights across the track, finding and reducing all remains to rubble and clearing it to the side. After listening to Ian reload and fire off several shots, finishing off what he counted as the fourth body, Daniel couldn't help but let out a laugh.

"You'd think someone would hear all this."

Ian's flashlight swiveled into Daniel's eyes as he commented.

"What's it matter? Who'd be stupid enough to come in after us anyway?"

And as if to challenge that statement, a sudden rumbling shook the tunnel.

"Uh… Dan," Ian asked, his eyes flitting around the tunnel uneasily. "How long did you say we had until the next train came?"

"Half an hour."

The track was gradually shaking harder beneath their feet, and Winchester began to bark hysterically with uneasiness, the sound reverberating against the walls. Daniel saw Ian look over his shoulder deeper into the tunnel and then turn back to face him.

"Time's up."

Daniel felt panic start to rise.

"There's still a body on this track, Ian," he reminded thinking of the first vampire they'd dispatched, even as he'd already begun his frantic search. He was glad when Ian didn't waste time replying.

With sharp, flitting eyes, it took them only a minute to catch a glimpse of it in their frantically flying flashlight beams.

"Ian, there!" Daniel yelled as he quickly brought his shotgun around and started firing at it.

His brother, instantly turning in his tracks, ran toward the now breaking up heap, getting his own shots off as he went. He reached it with barely enough time to brush the remaining chunks aside with his boot, when he looked up, suddenly staring into the subway train's headlights, as they flew blindingly around the corner.

His brother lurched forward into a run, motioning frantically with his hands. *"Move, move, RUN!"*

Daniel didn't need to be told twice. Whistling sharply for Winchester to follow along, he sprang forward into a dead run. The three figures, silhouetted against the severe headlights, found themselves in a deadly race-- man against machine.

Daniel could hear the wheels scraping on the tracks with no indication of it letting up, or slowing down, for the next stop. The sound was growing steadily closer, causing the hairs on the back of his neck to stand on end. Then he spotted the dim station lights at the end of the tunnel. Pumping his legs harder, he breached the darkness of the tunnel. He stooped mid run to scoop up Winchester, and threw him, along with his gun, unceremoniously up onto the safety of the platform. The motion wasn't exactly a smooth one, and Daniel had to grit his teeth against the pain that shot through his still tender shoulder. He knew the action had taken up valuable time, and jumping, he hurled himself onto the platform after the dog, rolling to the side, just as the subway train streamed by. Its metal shrieked angrily, protesting his escape, and Daniel's head snapped up instinctively on the look out for this brother.

"Ian?" he called, but his voice hardly carried above the noise of the station, as the train continued to fly past him at an impressive rate. Quickly realizing his brother was nowhere in sight, panic seized his chest, and he shoved himself hastily to his feet.

"Ian?!" he yelled for his brother again, the horror of the situation crashing in on him.

"*IAN!*"

Ian had been following behind his brother step for step, fully aware of the danger that was quickly looming up behind him.

What he'd missed was the danger lurking above him.

The clan leader squatted up high, clutching to an imbedded pillar of the tunnel, awaiting the moment when Ian would make his exit. The moment he was in position, the vampire swooped down, landing directly on his back, its claws sinking deeply into his shoulders, attaching itself to its newfound perch.

Giving a startled cry, Ian staggered backwards, placing himself even closer to the direct line of the oncoming train. Struggling profusely, he tried to dislodge the creature, but the vampire's strength proved too great, and unable to use his shotgun, he was nothing but a worm on a hook.

He was in trouble and he knew it.

He found himself nearly completely blinded by the headlights, the train mere seconds away. A concrete vampire may be able to withstand a head on collision-- but he certainly wouldn't.

Making a last minute decision, he flung himself to the side, flattening himself between two of the pillars, as the train surged past, stirring up the tunnel like a whirlwind.

The leader, still clinging to his back, made a discontented hissing sound, and Ian felt the sharp sting of vampire teeth sink into the skin at the base of his throat, as easy as a steel blade would cut through butter. All traces of Ian's tenacious scream vanished in the roar of the subway train, but he didn't need to hear his own consuming rage to feel it pumping through his veins. Making a completely irrational decision, he thrust his back out towards the moving train, the ear splitting sound of grating immediately joining the sound of squealing train wheels.

And Ian could feel the impact it made almost immediately.

Taken off guard, the creature flung his head back, howling in disapproval, but Ian got his desired effect. The pressure of the vampire's slicing fingertips lessened from his shoulder, its immediate attention drawn to the sparks emanating from its own backside grinding against the speeding train cars. Dealing with extremely tight quarters Ian wasn't able to throw the vampire off him, and across the room as he would have liked, but he was able to maneuver his way around in order to meet his opponent face to face.

Surprised by the change, the leader bared his teeth, both sharp and unusually white, but Ian was already in action. He shoved the creature hard into the train. Holding his shotgun horizontally, he used it to pin the vampire down, his free hand pressing the creature's face into the side of the train. Although the train may have had no lasting effect on the tough skin of the vampire's back, its face instantly began to shave away into little grains of sand.

"Why?!" he found himself yelling, shouting it forcefully above the noise. "Why, Dan?!" He let up only enough so the creature could talk, but it just hissed and tried to struggle free.

"That's *my brother*!" he thundered.

"*That's the point!*" the vampire suddenly spat, emphasizing each word.

Ian slammed his face back into the moving train.

The sound of wretched suffering immediately mingled with Ian's own cries for death, and by the time the train had passed-- the vampire was nothing but a headless corpse.

Ian shoved it forcefully to the ground, and leaned exhaustedly against one of the pillars, blood streaming from his neck. It made a slow trail down his collarbone and into his shirt. With the receding train, he could hear his brother's calls, finally able to reach his ears, as Daniel's frantic voice echoed down through the tunnel to him.

He was going to wake the whole freaken neighborhood!

Needing to finish the job, Ian ignored the increasing pain that laced his neck and spread down to his chest. He hoped the sound of his shotgun fires, as he broke up the body, would be enough to convince his brother he hadn't become a bloody smear on the subway tracks.

Winchester was growing increasingly antsy-- and Daniel knew he was to blame.

The dog had picked up on the worrisome quarrel he was having with himself. He'd heard the several rounds of firing, and knew them to be a good sign, but when the train had passed, it was all he could do not to jump back down.

Winchester had injured his paw somewhere amongst the mayhem, and Daniel figured they'd all been either too worked up to notice, or it had happened when he'd thrown the dog hastily up onto the platform. In either case, if he went after his brother, there was no way Winchester wouldn't try to follow.

So instead, Daniel paced, and Winchester limped back and forth across the ledge of the platform, until Ian finally emerged from the blackness of the tunnel.

Daniel felt all tension drain from his system the moment he did.

Ian's eyes had lost that fiery intensity that raged during a fight, when adrenaline pumped heady through his system. Now he just looked beaten and worn, and as Daniel reached down with his good arm to give him a hand up, it was easy to see why. Ian's fresh wounds looked angry, bloody, and with time-- dangerous.

"Here I thought the general idea was to run *away* from the oncoming train-- not pick a fight with it," Daniel said, though even by his own ears, his sarcasm fell flat.

Ian gave him a look that was both cross and tried.

"I offed the Leader," he informed, then added, "You're welcome," as he brushed the powdery remains of the vampire from his pants. "Vamp thought it was an ingenious idea to jump me." He pressed a hand against the bite mark on the side of his neck, pulling it back in examination. He frowned at the blood dripping between his fingers, before he met Daniel's gaze again. "Did you know you can kill a vampire by grinding its head off with a moving train?"

Daniel cracked a smile. "Fascinating. I'll keep it in mind."

Ian shook his head. "I wouldn't recommend it," he warned.

Daniel glanced up at the nearest camera. "We should get going. They're going to notice sooner or later that the train never showed passing the station."

He bent to scoop up Winchester. When he faltered his first try, his shoulder still giving him trouble, Ian pushed him aside to take over the job, seeming unsurprised to find the dog had gotten injured during the fight. He handed over his shotgun for Daniel to carry instead.

Daniel frowned, not entirely sure Ian himself was in any condition to be lifting anything, but followed in his brother's wake anyway, knowing nothing he said would change Ian's mind.

They retrieved the laptop, carefully stashed behind an old, dirty water fountain, and packed the guns back into the duffle bag. Brushing the computer off with a shake of his head, Daniel pried it open using his good arm. He made quick work of returning the cameras back to working condition, quite aware of Ian looming behind him. Burdened with Winchester's weight, his brother's wounds still bled at less than a healthy rate.

He clicked around for a minute more, and then snapped the laptop shut, looking up. When he did, his eyes caught those of a young woman's sitting with her back against the wall a few feet from them. A thin sleek Weimaraner was parked at her side. Her green eyes locked with his for only a fleeting moment, before she looked sharply away.

But it was too late.

She'd caught his attention.

He'd seen the flash of interest in her eyes, and looking closely he noticed her kept jeans, and leather buckled boots that reached to the tops of her calves. Her intense red hair hung in her face, almost like she meant to shield it from him. Daniel instantly knew that a subway tunnel this early in the morning, was completely out of character for her. She had to be here for a specific purpose.

"Ian," Daniel said softly, gaining his brother's attention. "I think we're being watched."

"Come again?" Ian demanded, his eyes flitting around the station on full alert. "Where? How do you know?"

"I may not have your eyes, but I pay attention to what I do see. Dead ahead," he said, inclining his head discretely. "Over by the wall."

Zeroing in on the girl, his brother carefully set Winchester down. He'd only taken a few steps in her direction, when she got to her feet and tried to hurriedly stride away.

Daniel shot a nervous glance up at the camera, which was now back in working order, poised and monitoring. He knew exactly what his brother's next move would be.

"Ian," he hissed in disapproval. But he was too late.

Ian had stepped in front of her, shoving her hard against the wall, his one arm pinning her there. Her dog erupted into frenzied barking, unsure of what to make of her owner's assailant. He sincerely hoped Ian wasn't planning on making another move, because the barks, although a warning for now, were quickly verging on something malicious.

Surprisingly though, she didn't resist.

"Easy," she smirked instead. Daniel wasn't sure whether she was talking to Ian or the dog, but nothing in her voice betrayed any sort of worry over her situation.

"Who are you?" Ian demanded.

Standing this close to Ian Browning, Marley realized just how tall he actually was. It was a rare occurrence that she ever measured up shorter than anyone, especially wearing heels. The fact that Ian could glower down at her with his icy blue eyes and hard-set face was somewhat fascinating. He wasn't a bulky or gangly, awkward kind of tall either. He had filled out every inch of his frame with hard lean muscle. He had on a sharp cologne, mingled with the sweet, metallic scent of sweat, dirt, and blood. The smell of a fight. She found his stance to be solid, despite the amount of blood she could tell he'd lost and was still losing. He looked rather like he'd been used as someone's chew toy, or perhaps a mob of adoring women had gotten a hold of him. The arm he was using to pin her was still bleeding, as was his chest, his shirt soaked through with the evidence. She hadn't missed the bite mark that marred the side of his throat either.

Something about the whole thing sent a shiver up her spine.

Daniel appeared behind them, placing a restraining hand on his brother's shoulder. He looked nearly as disheveled as Ian, his hair in disarray, matted with his own blood in parts, and clinging to his face, which was already turning a deep violet on his left side. His lip was split.

She wrestled with the decision to tell them the truth.

"No one of consequence," she found herself saying. Her vague answer only seeming to stir more interest in the boys. Daniel tilted his head to the side, examining her closer, and then realization seemed to dawn on his face.

"You're a Knocte," he said, sounding unsurprised by the fact, as if he should have realized it immediately. Ian shoved her sleeve up with his free hand, so they could see her Dignus. One shield, one crescent moon, three stars.

She jerked her arm back, craning her neck past Ian to meet Daniel's gaze.

"Well done, brain boy," she snapped, though she was unsettled with how easily he was able to read her. Scits with their intent gazes, and ticking minds, often left her uneasy. She watched his jaw clench, and shifting his weight, he dropped his gaze from hers.

She wasn't the only one who disliked her identity being so obviously found out.

"What do you want with us?" Ian barked right back, any remaining trace of friendliness wiped from his face with the crack at his younger brother.

Whoops...

Marley wasn't exactly sure how she'd expected the brothers to react when they found out she was a Knocte. For Ian to drop his hold? Appear flummoxed? Beg for her forgiveness? She certainly hadn't expected for the vital tidbit to have absolutely no impression on him, as he continued to glare heavily at her, his chilled eyes remaining cold and untrusting.

Knoctes had a tight network; it was practically an unwritten rule that they all considered one another family. Knoctes never messed with each other unless they had a death wish. A 'you mess with one of us, you mess with all of us' sort of system.

She'd heard the Browning brothers didn't think highly of Knocte protocol, but she was finally seeing it lived out for herself. Ian's impulsiveness seemed to prove the rumor easily enough, and somehow she found it struck a defensive nerve in her.

With an unprecedented swift movement she knocked his arm away, but equally as fast he caught hold of her again with his other. Her tracking dog, Lady, stalked forward, but the German Shepherd let out a low protective growl that was enough to give her companion pause. Despite injury, the Shepherd was clearly still loyal to the end.

Narrowing her eyes, Marley glared darkly at Ian.

He didn't so much as blink in response.

"Please." she scoffed, "Don't flatter yourself. What reason would I have to run into you? My Scit caught wind of the same case. Imagine my surprise when I got here, and you two had already set up shop."

She let the accusation seep into her voice, as she made another attempt to shove past Ian. This time he let her, taking a grudging step backwards. Lady instantly wedged herself between them, eyeing Ian with suspicion. Marley reached down to scratch the dog behind the ears.

"You're lucky we did," Ian chided, his untrusting eyes still following her every move.

"What's that supposed to mean?" she demanded. "You may not be able to handle a simple vampire without nearly getting each other killed, but don't assume I haven't taken care of my fair share."

The brothers went silent for a moment, exchanging a brief

look that neither of them seemed to have any trouble interpreting, even if she did.

It gave her the creeps.

"She didn't know either." Daniel let out a humorless laugh.

"Know what?" Marley found herself asking despite her better judgment.

"It wasn't *a* vampire. Yeah, we would be so lucky…" Ian grumbled. "It was a freaken clan of them."

Marley bade her expression to remain neutral. A clan?

She felt Knocte instinct take her over.

"How many?"

"Six," Daniel answered automatically, and then glanced over at his brother. "And they knew who we were."

Another silent exchange passed between them, Ian's face creasing with worry. She'd never felt more like a third wheel in her life.

"Well you boys do make your way around the Knocte network. I only need one guess. Ian and Daniel, right?" she inquired. "No use lying. We all know I'm right." In fact their names may as well have been written on every wall of every Knocte home base. To say that their reputations preceded them-- would be a vast understatement. "Let's face it. A Knocte and a Scit working a case together-- not exactly a common occurrence."

Ian leveled her with a practiced glare. "Well you better thank God you saw it today, or you'd be a vampire chew toy."

"Ian," Daniel rebuked, as he shifted in agitation.

His brother ignored him.

"Just don't expect me to return any favors," she warned. "I work alone."

"And that, my good friend, *is* what you see every day. The Knocte M.O. And exactly the kind of crap thanks I'd expect from someone like you anyway," Ian scorned.

Daniel looked mortified.

"Remind me, and I'll bake you a batch of cookies next time," she muttered harshly, feeling her blood boil. "But until then…"

Then before she could say anything else that would get her in trouble, she turned on her heels, and stalked off, Lady springing forth to follow her.

She pretended not to notice the way Ian's façade dropped the moment she did. Stiffly, he bent to take their tracking dog back into his arms. He did it in such a gentle fashion, anyone would have deemed it incapable of the man he had been not moments before.

The rain the brothers had encountered reaching Ontario let up with their returning journey, the sun finally peaking out from behind the clouds. It wasn't much, but it was enough for Ian to feel the warmth of it against his skin, as he stood outside a small town Stop-n-Go, pumping the truck full with gas. Glancing up, he could see through its front plate glass window into the convenience store. Daniel was still waiting in line for the single, unisex restroom, talking away on his cell phone to someone who could only be Devlyn. Again.

With reassurance that his brother was well preoccupied, Ian reached into his pocket. Removing his own cell phone, he speed dialed Jim-- who picked up on the second ring.

"Is this important, Ian? I'm on duty."

Always the charmer.

Putting the gas nozzle in its holster, Ian leaned back against the truck. Winchester came up behind him in the truck bed to hang over his shoulder and exhale doggy breath into his face.

"Uh… yeah. Yeah, I think it might be."

Jim's voice instantly flipped, changing from dismissive to concerned, his tone softening. "What's wrong, son?"

"We're stopped right now about a couple of hours from the Ay. Dan felt the need to call Dev for the umpteenth time this trip and--"

"Please tell me you didn't just call to whine about your brother," Jim cut in impatiently. "Or is there something else?"

Ian let his answering silence linger, as he shifted his weight, and pressed his lips together into a thin line.

He had been avoiding the subject with Daniel for nearly the entire drive now, but even so it had been gnawing away at the back of his mind. He knew he needed to voice his concern, no matter how much realer it would cause it to seem. This wasn't a subject he would talk about with his kid brother. No, this was one reserved for Jim, who was waiting patiently on the other end of the line for him to pull himself together.

"Do you remember a month or so back, when you were on a case and you overheard Dan's name being mentioned between two lycans?" Ian said finally, breaking the silence.

"Yeah," Jim answered slowly. "That's not something I'm inclined to forget. Why?"

Ian pinched the bridge of his nose.

"While we were on duty last night, we ran into a vampire clan-- and they knew him, Jim. And I mean they carried a full hate-on for him. Made a pretty valid attempt on his life too. I pinned one of them down and tried a little Q and A, but I didn't get much out of him." He paused, feeling his anger starting to surface, until he was rushing through the rest of his speech. "Well, anyway, trouble's flooding in with a capital T, and I feel like I have to watch the kid's every step, like freaken Night Children are going to pop out of bushes with machetes, and chase him down the street the moment I turn my back. The last shifter we took care of went after him too. Like, what in the--?"

"Language, boy," Jim reminded him tersely, and then went silent on the other end, his wheels turning, trying to pull the pieces together. He eventually let out a long sigh. "You're right though, this sounds like something nasty's brewing. Twice is a coincidence, but three times…"

"But why him, Jim?" Ian asked out of frustration, almost like he couldn't help it. "I just don't get it! All he ever tries to do is good, and somehow it always manages to get shoved back in his face." He shook his head disdainfully. "He deserves better."

"Daniel doesn't do the things he does for the sake of pleasing others, Ian," Jim said. "However… he's walking a thin line, and even though I hate to be the one to come out and say this-- I think it's time you start giving your undoubtful approval of this whole university idea he's got."

Feeling disgruntled, Ian slouched farther down against the truck. "So he's just going to have to run, is that it?"

"No, Ian," Jim said patiently. "He's got Devlyn. He's going to slow his pace down, settle, have a normal life. Think of it this way: we're hiding him, allowing him to blend into a mundane life. You think he deserves better? You want to protect him? This is how you're going to do it."

Ian made a frustrated sound in the back of his throat.

"Don't. You know I'm right. I'll call you when I'm back in town." Then the line went dead.

"Yeah. Good talk," Ian said bitterly to no one, and then removing the phone from his ear, hit the end button as if it mattered, and returned it to his pocket.

Daniel came around the truck, just in time to see the tail end of the action.

"Who was that?" he asked offhandedly. His arms were loaded down with a gas receipt, a couple bags of ice, and two cups of coffee. Their thermos supply had run out long ago, and they hadn't bothered with a motel to give them a chance to replenish. Daniel rested them on the rim of the truck bed, and pulled his coffee free of the cardboard tray.

Ian looked lovingly at the bags of ice.

His injuries still smarted, and the hastily done gauze patchwork was becoming annoyingly itchy.

"Dev," he mocked. "She wanted to make sure you made it from the store to the truck okay. You know, without her sensei guidance via telephone."

"Hilarious," Daniel muttered, his sarcasm purposely dull, and his tone unimpressed.

Reaching over, his brother tossed him a bag of ice a little harder than necessary, and Ian caught it up against his chest, letting out a pained grunt as it connected with his wounds.

"Jerk."

Daniel raised his eyebrows around a sip of coffee, and shrugged unrelentingly.

"You didn't tell Dev we were going to be back in town tonight did you?" Ian asked, pressing the ice bag against his neck. "Because if she sees you like this-- she's going to freak right out."

Even though Daniel had bothered to change his shirt and wash his face, there was still blood dried in his brother's hair. His face also displayed heavy evidence of the fight they'd been through. A bluish bruise had formed along his cheek, giving him a partial black eye.

"No," Daniel said, but avoided his brother's gaze as he opened the truck's driver door and leaned in to pack their new supplies away. Ian knew how much his brother hated lying to

Devlyn. How much the guilt ate at him.

"Cheer up, Danny," he said helpfully. "At least you didn't break anything. You'll see her soon."

Chapter Six

Daniel smacked the vending machine that stood outside the Ay motel, as punishment for eating his toonie. They'd gotten home late last night, or rather earlier this morning, and had been fresh out of coffee-- yet again. So any form of a caffeinated drink, Daniel figured could do him some good. He'd hardly gotten a couple of hours sleep, when Winchester, who'd slept almost the entire trip back, had woken up begging to be let outside. Ian was busy, having already claimed the shower. He'd either gotten up way too early, or as Daniel suspected-- hadn't slept at all. Again.

So that had left him to drag his hide out of bed. With Winchester's leg still giving him trouble, Daniel had made sure to wrap it for good measure, before letting the dog outside, where he now half bounded, half limped, straight into the dew filled grass close by.

Daniel smacked the machine again, hitting the money return button impatiently.

A shrill ringing from his pocket nearly caused him to jump out of his skin, and without bothering to check the caller ID, he hit the answer key and held it up to his ear, still preoccupied with the vending machine.

"Yeah," he answered, distractedly.

"Hello, Daniel," came the reply. "It's been awhile."

Halting all activity, an instant light flew on in his brain.

"Jack?" he sputtered. "Is that you, man?"

"Affirmative."

Lost pocket change entirely forgotten, Daniel found himself doing a quick scan of his surroundings, suddenly worried about their conversation being overheard.

"I thought you--."

"Would be pushing up the daisies by now? Not yet, my friend. I'm afraid there's a lot you don't know. But that's why I called."

Leaning forward, Daniel braced himself with one arm against the vending machine. "What is it?" he asked, his voice automatically dropping to a lower tone.

There was a pause on the other end of the line.

"Jack," Daniel said slowly, knowing his friend too well. "If you're worried about the phone being bugged, now's really not the time..."

"Meet me at the city park in ten minutes. I'll try to explain everything there."

Daniel sighed. "Jack, I--"

But Jack must have picked up on the apology/excuse in formation, because he quickly cut him off.

"I haven't changed, Daniel. You know me."

Then the line went dead.

Daniel weighed the phone in his hand, the same way he was weighing the options in his mind.

Bringing Ian along was out. As far as Ian was concerned, Jack was only target practice now. It would be shoot first and ask questions later. And Daniel wanted answers.

Yet going alone was a terrible idea by anyone's standards. He could very well be walking straight into a trap, and even if he did make it back alive, Ian would tear a strip off him.

But... if there was something else going on behind the scenes, Daniel had to know, especially if that something proved his friend's innocence. He was suddenly faced with the chance that the alleged accusations against Jack had all been a mistake-- and that made the risk worth taking.

Resolved, Daniel whistled in Winchester from where he pounced back and forth under the nearest pine tree, barking excitedly as angry squirrel chatter emanated back at him. Daniel had to hand it to the dog; his injury wasn't slowing him down all that much. He'd be back in the circuit in no time.

Winchester joined his side and they slid back into the motel room, where Daniel snagged the truck keys off the desk, knowingly muttering "I'm going to regret this" under his breath even as he did so.

He uttered a quick apology to Winchester as he left him trapped in their room, and then slid behind the wheel of the truck.

Please God, he thought as he backed out of their parking space, *don't let this be a mistake.*

He stepped on the gas as he rounded the corner out of the Ay Motel's parking lot. Devlyn's beads clinked softly against each other as he did, offering some small morsel of hope and reassurance.

Stepping out of the truck, Daniel swung around to open the back door, throwing the seat up to unveil their arsenal. As discretely as possible, he grabbed a pistol, checking to make sure it was loaded with silver bullets, before tucking it into the waist band of his jeans at the small of this back. He also pulled out a silver knife stashing it in the sock of his right shoe. Letting the seat back down, Daniel locked the doors and cautiously made his way across the street and onto the city park grounds.

A lazy paved path wound its way around the park, flooded with early morning joggers and cyclists. A well-trimmed lawn lay behind the border, a perfect middle ground for picnics and Frisbee chasing dogs. What lay beyond that, however, was the city's surrounding forest, hiking territory, and uncharted wilderness alike. Doing a quick scan of the park he came across nothing but families throwing baseballs, and walking their dogs. An elderly couple sat on one of the benches, sipping their coffees.

Nothing jumped out at Daniel as out of place, nothing screamed 'potential secret meeting' in the back of his mind. He shifted his gaze towards the rough shadowy tree line. Taking in the possibility for the need of seclusion, he sighed.

Naturally.

Nothing shady ever happened in an endearingly open, sunlit local. Daniel weaved his way casually through the crowd, checking to make sure his shirt carefully concealed his weapon. The last thing he needed was someone to see it, and cause a massive panic. Breaching the tree line, he wandered aimlessly, having mixed feelings about his distance from the surrounding world. With each step he took, the families were safer, but with each step the risk to himself increased. The hum of humanity eventually faded to nothing, and Daniel's eyes scanned the forest, trying to take in everything at once, not trusting the growing silence for an instant. When he reached a clearing, and there was still nothing but swaying grass and looming trees, he stopped.

He wasn't about to wander forever.

"All right, Jack!" He shouted, spreading him arms wide and spinning a small circle to view his surroundings in their entirety. "I'm here! I thought we were going to talk!"

"And indeed we are."

Daniel turned, spotting Jack. He was casually leaning against a nearby pine tree at the edge of the clearing, as if he'd been there all along. Upon seeing him, Daniel had to remind himself that this Jack might not be the one he remembered.

He still found the concept hard to imagine.

Even in shadow, moving with unearthly silence, Jack just didn't have the cold-blooded ambience. He had intelligent green eyes, half hidden under a mop of blond hair, and black, rectangular rimmed glasses. They were smart looking, but for all intents and purposes, completely unneeded now, and most likely sporting ordinary, non-prescription lenses. Jack's eyesight would've become crystal the moment he changed. Sharper than ever before even. His glasses had always been a part of him, however, and he still wore them faithfully, even if they did have a bad habit of sliding down the bridge of his nose. It was long ago that he'd adopted the compensative habit of pushing them back up again, and it was comforting to see some things didn't change. Jack's scrawny physique promised minimal threat, and his neon yellow sneakers were anything but menacing.

"What'd you need to tell me?" Daniel asked. Neither of them risked a step forward.

"I haven't murdered anyone, Daniel," Jack said slowly, crucially.

"Luke is pretty set on the idea that you did. If fact, he's spreading rumors all about it. Says he saw the whole thing."

"Of course," Jack said resignedly. "I am a liability to his theory if I stay clean. Those 'human murders', that he so conveniently pinned on my shoulders, were actually members of a pack he shot down in cold blood."

Daniel's eyebrows shot up of their own accord. "But if you didn't turn to the Night Children, then how are you doing it? How are you slipping all the revenge driven mongrels out there?"

Jack offered a small smile. "Well, I joined a pack of my own, strange as that may be. The very same one actually."

Daniel gauged his next words carefully. "Why'd they accept you so easily? What did you have to give them? What did you do?"

"I merely offered some helpful information, and in return,

they watch my back. Protect me."

It was then that dark shapes started to melt out of the forest, different earthy shades of wolves, numerous enough to completely surround him in the clearing. They padded in fluid silence, without so much as disturbing the foliage on which they trod. They appeared like ghosts, materializing before him, following him with eerie glowing eyes.

Then the silence was broken by deep, throaty warning growls, reverberating from all sides. Daniel's reaction was instant as he reached for his gun, whipping it out to hold in front of him. The movement was so routine he hadn't thought twice about it, but as the weapon came into view, he instantly knew his action had been a mistake. Warning growls erupted into something real, more menacing. Lips pulled back over teeth, ears flattened, and fur bristled. This, Daniel quickly realized, was a deadly game, and he was walking a thin line.

"Daniel," Jack's voice cut through the noise. His tone was cautious, but Daniel could see the panic in his friend's eyes. "Put the gun down."

Daniel held fast to the only lifeline he had, fearing things would take a turn for the worse. A Knocte never abandoned a weapon. It was a clear violation of years of training.

Around him claws embraced earth, and wolves hunched into crouches, preparing to spring.

"Drop it!" Jack ordered. "Now!" He'd inched his way towards Daniel, trying to place himself in some of the wolves' paths, blocking their shot at him.

This man was no murderer. Never was.

And Daniel wasn't a Knocte.

He gave in with a sigh.

"Okay!" he yelled, throwing his hands in the air, the gun hanging uselessly from his fingers. "All right!"

He tossed the weapon towards Jack. It skidded on the ground, coming to rest at his feet, half buried in the leaves. If there was going to be an attack, at least he was giving his friend a chance. Would Jack's newfound pack turn on him for helping an outsider? He remembered the small knife he'd tucked into his shoe, but with the wolves' numbers, it was rendered a poor defense.

As it turned out, his precautions were unneeded.

The moment the gun left his hand, the snarls cut off abruptly in unison, the silence as sudden as an explosion, like the entire pack was in complete harmony with each and every one of its members. Some relaxed their stance, with an almost enigmatic satisfaction, while others still crouched dubious and untrusting. Dozens of watchful eyes studied him intently. They hadn't anticipated his move, Daniel realized. They'd been expecting a fight today and nothing else. Then he'd turned around and done the unexpected-- he'd given in. And Knocte's never gave in. A Scit might, but then again, they didn't carry around guns either.

Daniel shot Jack a look, to find his friend looking almost... proud?

"Daniel, would you be so kind as to show everyone the underside of your left arm?"

"Jack," he warned.

His friend's eyes were soft. "Please."

With a regretful sigh, Daniel extended his arm, knuckles downward. The Dignus displayed on his tanned skin, made him feel both wary and exposed. An inhuman rumble passed amongst the onlookers, and he quickly dropped his arm back down.

"Explain," he demanded.

A few glowing eyes shifted to settle on Jack, a silent highlighter to the importance of the next few words. It was like this strange gathering was just as much of an enigma to some of the wolves, as it was to Daniel himself.

"You're a man with many faces, Daniel," Jack stated outright. "And we could use your help."

"My help?" he said incredulously. "I don't understand. What could you possibly need with a renegade Scit?"

"Luke's theory is steadily becoming a reality," Jack said gravely. "If he gets his way, we're facing a full scale war. Most Knoctes wouldn't think twice about which side they'd stand for-- but you're not like the others, Daniel. You'd think twice."

Daniel ran a hand through his hair. "You're right. I'm not like the other Knoctes. I'm a Scit, Jack. Like you."

"That's not what your Dignus says."

"Jack," he said in exasperation. "The real Knoctes? They hate every last one of my guts. You know what it's like. If you think for one minute they're going to listen to a single thing I have

95

to say-- you're wrong."

"*Think*, Daniel," Jack insisted, nearly shouting. "Ian, Jim-- you have ties to the Knocte network. Now more than ever is the time to use them. You may be what prevents this war. And if you had that chance-- wouldn't you take it?"

"I...," but whatever train of thought Daniel had, abruptly ended.

Jack had suddenly fallen to all fours, knees and palms pressing into the earth, finger's curling around decomposing leaves.

"Jack!" he called in alarm, and immediately closed the distance between them, dropping to his knees, and grasping his friend's shoulders. He could feel Jack's body shuddering beneath his touch, and then it suddenly clicked into place. Realizing what was happening, Daniel quickly dropped his hold, and took a hasty step back.

In the next instant Jack's bones started to shift under his skin. He cried out continuously, shouting in pain over and over, as his current body betrayed him. Agonizing minutes went by, and then with a last snap, Daniel was nose to nose with a large pale wolf.

The wolf had black coloring outlining its eyes, much like the glasses that had once sat on the nose of its human counterpart. The rest of Jack's clothes had disappeared as well, lost in the change, replaced by fur.

The wolves had moved too.

Daniel hadn't even realized it, until they were suddenly surrounding Jack, flanking him on his sides, and clustering in behind him. Even as they enveloped Jack in their numbers, Daniel found all eyes glued on him, any hostility that had been present lost. The wolves' shoulders were relaxed, their eyes soft, staring at him with meaningful patience. He found himself meeting every pair of eyes one by one, all glowing different colours, all filled with a passion that was too intense to be wolf, but too wild to be human. Almost without his own permission, he was nodding.

"I'll see what I can do."

His answer seemed to be enough. Without a sound, the wolves turned and vanished back into the forest one by one, not so much as a whisper to mark their leave. The Jack-wolf gave a quick departing bob of his head, and then took off after the others, a streak of pale fur against green vegetation, almost too fast to see.

Winchester snapped his head up on the alert, hearing Daniel's approach in the same instant Ian did. Ian could recognize his truck's engine a mile off, the sound permanently ingrained into his mind.

He was standing near the door, arms crossed tightly over his chest, brow heavily set, when his brother strolled casually back into the motel room, nonchalantly tossing the truck keys onto the desk.

Winchester was lying on the bed behind Ian, a low whine escaping his throat as he licked his lips in gleeful impatience. He'd normally be the first one to the door, greeting Daniel, but the dog was smart, and picking up on Ian's mood, knew someone was in serious trouble. He was still shaking with pent up energy, when Daniel turned, looking up from removing his shoes to acknowledge his brother's presence.

"Hey."

Hey? Ian raised an eyebrow. *Hey?!*

He was going to kill him.

"Hey?" he echoed disbelievingly. "You've been gone the entire morning, and all you've got to say is-- *hey*?!"

Daniel shrugged unrelentingly. "I can't go for a drive if I want to?"

Ian's anger boiled over.

"Oh, yes-- you can! But I've lived my whole life with you, and you don't just *decide* to go for a drive. Also, you're the biggest tech nerd I've ever met, which means you don't just become allergic to answering your phone!"

"Okay, okay," Daniel said, raising his hands in surrender. "I had an..." --he seemed to weigh his words carefully-- "appointment."

Ian merely fixed him with a diminishing glare.

Daniel exhaled a heavy sigh, and pushing his auburn hair out of his eyes, walked over to drop onto his bed. Across from him, Winchester let out another whine.

"Jack called," he admitted. "Wanted me to meet him."

Ian couldn't bring himself to believe what he'd just heard.

97

"Jack? Furry, fangy, on Luke's hit list, Jack?"

Daniel nodded mutely.

"And he wasn't six feet under?"

"No."

He searched his brother's face. "Is he now?"

Daniel's eyes snapped up to meet his, expression hard. His answer was crisp, spoken through clenched teeth. "No."

"Well what?" he demanded. "You sip lemonades together?"

"He wanted my help, Ian."

Ian took a couple steps towards his brother until he was looming over him. "Of course he wanted your help. He has a target on his back the size of freaken Texas! The point, Dan, is that he's a murderer. Don't you get that? A murderer!"

Daniel stood abruptly, causing Ian to rock back on his heels. Although Daniel barely leveled above his shoulder, in that instant, it hardly seemed to matter.

"What?" Daniel snapped. "Because Luke says so? Because a Knocte's so incapable of lying? It wasn't just Jack, Ian, the pack was there too. They *all* asked for my help. Those people that Jack supposedly killed? They were all pack members. *Luke* was the one who murdered them!"

Ian heard every word Daniel said, but only one thing was coming to register.

"The whole pack was there?!" He swore loudly, turning away to run his fingers through his hair. He clenched it so tightly, he thought he'd pull it out by its roots. "What were you *thinking?!*" he raged. "You walked right into that! Every Fifth Worlder we've met lately has been trying to get its claws into you, and you're suddenly like: 'this time will be different.' I thought you were supposed to be the smart one! You could have gotten yourself killed!"

"But I didn't," his brother answered calmly. "They needed me-- need *us*. We have to talk to Luke. We need to throw some water on his fire, before he causes all hell to break loose."

Ian spun back around, unable to prevent himself from pinning Daniel with a dark look.

"Why would Luke lie? He's a Knocte-- he wouldn't kill anything that wasn't asking for it."

"You're so sure? I've known him just as long as you have," Daniel reminded him.

"Yeah, but you're--," he began, and immediately cut himself off, biting his tongue. He couldn't say it.

Daniel shook his head in exasperation.

"A Scit?" he finished for him. "Yeah, Ian-- I am. And you're the Knocte. Which gives you just as much of a biased opinion." Ian watched him take a deep breath, trying to cool some of his anger long enough to bring the conversation to some sort of point. "Look," he sighed, "I need you to back me up on this, okay? I just want to talk to him. The whole thing doesn't have to go sour."

"But that's exactly what's going to happen anyway," Ian mumbled quietly, and then raised his voice to include his brother. "Well. We need to go to the Roadhouse anyway… our cash supply is hitting a dangerous low. Plus," he added sheepishly, "it's already out of the bag that we're back in town." He sighed. "I called Dev after you disappeared, thought you might have taken off to go see her."

Daniel was still brooding, but as the last few words sank in, the prospect of seeing Devlyn was slowly winning out over his stirring anger, and a smile slowly began playing at the corners of his mouth.

"All right, let's go," Daniel said with finality, and made like he was going to retrieve the truck keys again.

Winchester saw this as an invitation to bound over and scratch excitedly at the door, while Ian quickly rushed to snatch the keys up first, jumping over the beds like he was five years old. He made a show of gripping them tightly, shooting his brother a warning look.

Daniel smirked. "Sorry I played with your toy, Junior. It's a wonder you ever passed kindergarten."

"Bite me," Ian said pointing a 'watch yourself' finger at his brother. "And don't get too excited, you still look like you got seriously worked over. Seeing Dev isn't going to be all bubbles and sunshine."

A knowing smile spread across Daniel's features. "Says you."

Chapter Seven

The smell of liquor and smoke hit Daniel and his brother the instant they pushed their way into the Roadhouse, Winchester trotting along at their side. Daniel picked out Devlyn immediately. Wearing dark jeans and white tank top, she was weaving between tables and tightly packed bodies. She was collecting empty beer bottles, adding them to the collection she had neatly piled atop a tray, balanced in her right hand.

Almost as if she could feel the weight of Daniel's gaze, she glanced his way, and their eyes met, her face instantly spreading into a broad grin. Setting the tray aside, she broke into a run for his direction, dodging her way through groups of Knoctes, her blond curls flowing behind her, until she slammed to a sudden halt in front of him. Her eyes seemed to assess his appearance, raking him up and down for any indication of injury. He knew she noticed his bruises, the moment her face fell, but with a 'don't worry about it' shake of his head, Daniel caught her up in his arms anyway, lifting her right off her feet. His bad shoulder protested, but he didn't let it show. Out of the corner of his eye, however, he watched Ian make the wincing gesture for him. Devlyn buried herself in his embrace and Daniel felt the last traces of pain and worry he'd been carrying with him slip away. He pressed his lips to her forehead and set her back on her feet. She took a step back, looking up at him again. She reached up to trace the bruise around his eye, and then her fingers moved down his face to his busted lip.

"What about the other guy?" she asked, her voice uneven, as she tried at a smile, but her fear wasn't far beneath. She exchanged a brief glace with Ian, who looked away guiltily.

Daniel pretended to contemplate his answer. "Not great…"

"Very dead actually," Ian said with finality, stepping forward. "Come on, we got work to do. Choose your battle ground."

Daniel rolled his eyes. "Poker."

He was always the one who played poker. Being a Scit he had a knack for reading people.

That left Ian to hustle pool, his game of choice anyway, and with a departing nod and a mock salute, he sauntered off towards the tables, Winchester following closely at his heels.

Daniel still remembered the first time Winchester realized he had grown tall enough to reach over the pool table by standing on his hind legs. He'd relieved the cue ball from the game and took off running with it. Daniel and Ian had chased him through the Roadhouse for ten minutes before they finally got it back. Winchester had gotten in so much trouble that day; he'd never done it again. That didn't stop him from continuously standing tableside though, and following the balls' every movements each time they played.

"You're just in time. A Texas hold 'em tournament starts in five. Buy-in's three hundred." Devlyn informed, drawing his attention back to her. "I'm the lucky bartender in charge."

She held out her hand in between them, wriggling her fingers.

Daniel smiled warmly, pulling out his wallet from his back pocket and slapping three hundred dollars worth of bills into her open palm. It was very nearly all he had.

"Challenge accepted."

Daniel studied the Knocte across from him with interest. It was down to the two of them. Everyone else had been forced to drop out, their lost money represented in clay chips. The clay chips sat stacked, either in front of Daniel, in the other Knocte's depleting pile, or in the hefty pot that piled high in the center of the table. The players still all kept their seats, however, curious as to how the remainder of the game would play out.

Daniel watched the Knocte as he fiddled with what was left of his chips, using an absentminded hand to expertly stack and fold them into each other. Daniel could tell it was purely out of habit. The Knocte had brown hair, too short to hide his eyes, and wore an old, beat up baseball cap to compensate for it. Despite the hat, Daniel had caught glimpses of the guy's face from under the rim. Not that it really mattered, for his pale blue eyes were always carefully impassive. There was one thing though, Daniel had found to be drastically helpful.

The Knocte was thoughtfully chewing a toothpick, and Daniel had instinctively zeroed in on it. Throughout the game he'd noticed the little quirks that would easily go unnoticed to the untrained eye. When the Knocte was bluffing he tended to clench the toothpick with his teeth, a sort of anxious, anticipatory habit, but when he had a good hand, he liked to wiggle it with assured arrogance. The toothpick was wiggling now; he wasn't bluffing, but the movement lacked vigor, and Daniel watched a small muscle twitch in the man's cheek, as the tempo in the stacking and folding of his chips increased. He was nervous. Not completely positive he had the upper hand.

"All in," the Knocte finally decided, pushing the remainder of his chips into the pile.

Daniel could feel Devlyn watching him from where she'd perched herself, sitting backwards on a chair, her forearms resting gingerly on the backrest. He called, tossing a matching number of chips into the pot.

The Knocte up ended his cards with a smirk to reveal two jacks, and in this case, Daniel discovered, the suits didn't matter. He blew out a breath. The flop before them consisted of two queens and a four. The turn was a jack and the river a three. The Knocte, content with his full house, started to reach for the mound of chips, when Daniel tossed his hand out for him to see, and the Knocte froze, finding himself face to face with Daniel's two queens and the weight of his four of a kind.

Devlyn's delighted laugh mingled in with the exclamations from the other players around the table. She clapped him on the shoulder --luckily his good one-- and he allowed himself to grin openly for the first time since he'd started playing.

The Knocte, suddenly furious, shot to his feet.

"What do *you* even need the money for, *Scit*?!" He sneered the last word, his tone clearly implying the title was something beneath that of a bug he might find on the underside of his shoe. Daniel stiffened as a few murmured agreements went around the table. Beside him Devlyn scowled heavily. It was so unlike her usually soft expressions and delicate features.

Daniel said nothing, pushing up from the table.

The Knocte, like the rest at the table, was well aware that he took cases with his brother. That was information he knew everyone was privy too. He also knew the Knocte's question came loaded with an underlining meaning, he really didn't wish to get into.

Devlyn shot to her feet beside him.

"Good game, gentlemen," she said, her tone clipped as she dismissed them all. She then lowered her voice to include only him. "Come on. I'll cash you out."

Nodding to her, Daniel met the eyes of every Knocte at the table one at a time.

"It's been a pleasure," he said with an audible air of sarcasm, and reached for Devlyn's hand. She curled her fingers around his gratefully, as she tugged him away.

"I should kick them out of this bar," she muttered as soon as they were out of earshot, all hushed rage. "All of them."

And at her tone, Daniel couldn't help but chuckle.

Ruby looked about the same as she always did, glamour up to perfection, poised behind the bar. Her black tank top, covered in sequins, sparkled in the foggy light of the Roadhouse, as she leaned over to pass a couple of beers to their recipients. Her fitted skinny jeans and tall high heels weren't out of character either. The lack of her carefree demeanor, however, was. Daniel could tell something was troubling her, even before he'd reached the bar. He also knew he wasn't the only one, when Devlyn immediately broke off from his side to take the faerie's place.

"Take a break, Ruby," she said apologetically. "Thanks for covering for me."

"Grab us a couple of beers, and we can go watch my brother play," Daniel suggested, tipping his head in the direction of the pool table.

Ruby smiled, none too convincingly, and ducked to open the mini bar fridge.

"Don't have too much fun without me, now." Devlyn smiled, leaning closer to him over the bar.

"Wouldn't dream of it," Daniel promised, planting a quick kiss at the corner of her mouth, as Ruby started towards the pool tables, beers in hand, and luminous hair swishing behind her.

Daniel turned to follow.

"Uh... Dan?"

He spun back around. "Yeah."

"You wanting this?" she asked innocently, holding up an impressive wad of cash.

"Oh, right," he said grabbing hold of it. But she held on.

"And try not to get anymore black eyes, please."

With a guilty smile, he agreed, pocketing the cash gratefully, and heading after Ruby.

She had already found a spot, sitting cross-legged on an unused pool table next to the one Ian was now leaning over, carefully aiming out another shot. She handed Daniel a beer and the bottle opener, as he parked himself next to her. He wasted no time in cracking it open and taking a long pull.

"So you want to tell me what's wrong?" He cut to the chase, without taking his eyes off the game. Ian had finally let fly, and one of his solids met a corner pocket. Daniel could tell he was just toying with his opponent, a big, bulky, bald guy, with more tattoos than unmarked skin.

She looked down, fingering the lip of her beer bottle. "Knoctes are growing less lenient about a faerie working at their precious Roadhouse. Today one even went as far as to pull a gun" - -Daniel flinched immediately at her words-- "and tell me that if I ever went near him again-- he'd kill me, because he didn't want the poison I was serving."

Daniel shook his head scornfully, feeling anger course through him. He turned to look at her, and whatever brutal retort he had on his lips in her defense, instantly vanished, as she gave a small sniff. Her eyes were beginning to water, as she looked down at her toes, purposely avoiding his gaze. Daniel felt his features soften immediately, as he set his beer down to reach a comforting arm around her, letting her rest her head on his shoulder. She buried her face in his t-shirt and he pulled her in, tucking her protectively under his chin. .

"Hey," he said soothingly, running a gentle hand up and down her arm. "I've been meaning to talk to Luke."

"Do you ever feel like we're fighting a losing battle, Dan?" she asked, turning her head to look up at him. "That everything we're trying to do, trying to stand up for, isn't getting through? That it means absolutely nothing to everyone else?"

Daniel was quiet for a moment, as he watched the game with a pensive expression.

"I think," he said finally, quietly, "that anything that requires you to fight for it, isn't supposed to be easy. Does it mean you can't win? That you always drown trying to swim up stream?" He smiled thoughtfully. "I don't think so." He shook her shoulder gently. "We can do this, Bee. It never was easy."

"No, it wasn't," she laughed lightly, shakily. And then after a moment, "How did I get so lucky? To have a best friend like you?" She gave him an appreciative smile, wiping at her eyes with the back of her hand. "You were always smart, Dan. You trust your own eyes and aren't influenced by rumors. You see things in people that no one else does, the good and bad, and you don't deserve all the flak you get. But you can still get out while you can. Dev told me about university. You can do it, you know. Take her and disappear, start a real life together. You have that option, and the chance to do it before it's too late.

Daniel was quiet for a minute. "I know," he said finally. "And I want that. I want every bit of that life with Dev-- but I can't stop thinking of the consequences. My brother. What will become of him? I keep wondering if he'll turn to Luke, and the thought scares me, really shakes me. And this fight, the one I've had a place in for nearly my whole life… is my part really over? Especially when it feels like it's barely begun? And, of course, Dev has her own opinions on the matter. The whole thing has started to make me wonder if it doesn't have to be one or the other. Maybe I can try and find a way of settling with Dev that doesn't mean us dropping off the face of the earth. Just today I had someone ask me to help."

"Ah, yes, the lycanthropes. I heard about that." When Daniel shot her a surprised glance, she shrugged. "I'm a Fair Child. You know that. Or have you forgotten I'm a part of that circle?"

He gave a light laugh. "Hard to forget, when you walk around like a constant disco ball."

She looked down at herself with a pleased smile, a smile she only got when she wore things she'd designed herself.

"I milk it for all it's worth," she admitted, "but seriously, Dan, I've been hearing your name come up far too often, and I'm worried. I'm not exactly sure what it's going to mean for you."

Daniel thought about mentioning the encounter he and Ian had had with the vampire clan, but before he could reply Winchester let out a high pitched whine. Daniel looked up just in time to see that Ian's opponent had taken a bad shot, and balls were rolling aimlessly and torturously around the table under the dog's nose. The other thing he happened to notice in the background was the Roadhouse door swinging open.

"Look who finally decided to join the party," Daniel muttered as Luke strode through the crowd, and found an empty table to inhabit. "Care to tag along? It wouldn't hurt to have back up."

Ruby gave a dismal laugh. "I really don't think I'll be helping your case any."

"I'm not exactly helping my case either."

He shot her a rueful smile and stood up, instantly earning his brother's attention. He inclined his head in Luke's direction and Ian seemed to get the message. In his next shot he managed to sink his remaining two balls at once, then just as quickly followed suit with the eight ball. He left a dubious Tattoo Haven to contemplate where he'd gone wrong, while Ian himself snagged the cash pile from the tableside, and shoved it deep into his pocket.

"Fine," Ruby said, sliding off the table to her feet beside him. "I'll come." She watched Ian approach warily, and offered up an 'I'm going to regret this' sigh as he joined them, Winchester trotting along at his side. "But just to be clear," she added quietly, stepping slightly behind Daniel. "I'm here for moral support only."

"She's coming?" Ian asked, having heard, and not bothering to hide his discontent with the idea. Daniel felt Ruby shrink under his brother's gaze, the way she always did, and made a displeased face as he pushed passed his brother. He made sure to clip Ian's shoulder as he did.

"Can it, Ian."

Luke sat contentedly in his chair, his usual overcoat hanging open over a black shirt and dark jeans. He had his leg crossed over his knee, and was spinning a glass of red wine with one hand, while wielding a newspaper with the other. Ian pushed his way to the front, his raised eyebrows daring his brother to object.

Daniel didn't bother.

"The newspaper, Luke? I thought you had better taste than that," Ian joked, greeting his friend with a lighthearted grin. "You know they only ever get it half right."

Luke let the paper fall to the table, revealing the amused smile he wore. "Ian! Good to see you again, brother. What do I owe the pleasure?"

Hands shoved in his pockets, Ian leaned back, over exaggerating his consideration of the question. His mouth dragging down at the edges with the false impression of thought.

"Nothing," he said after a moment and then gestured to himself. "This charm's completely free."

Luke laughed loudly. "Lucky me."

Ian grinned. "Why do I suddenly need an excuse to talk to an old friend?"

"Well, call me crazy," Luke said leaning around Ian to steal a glance at Daniel and Ruby, "but this smells like an intervention to me."

Ruby crossed her arms over her chest and averted her gaze.

"We just need to talk to you for a minute," Daniel said stepping up. "One minute."

Ian sank into the chair next to Luke, and gave him an apologetic smile.

Luke shot him a knowing look. "Called it."

Daniel didn't plan to waste time. "It's about your theory," he said, taking the third seat. Ruby pulled a chair over and settled herself beside him.

"It's always about my theory, Daniel," Luke said calmly, taking an unhurried sip of his wine. "What about it?"

"For one. It's going to cause the death of thousands of innocent people."

"Your definition of innocent and mine are very different."

Daniel clasped and unclasped his hands for a minute, in an effort to keep his voice calm.

"So I've noticed," he said, and leaned forward across the table. He was about to add to the thought, when suddenly the absence of Luke's tracking dog dawned on him. "Where's Milo?"

Luke seemed to give the floor a pitying look before answering. "Fell behind."

Daniel blanched. "You're kidding, right?"

Ian attempted to say something, sensing the layers of tension stacking themselves higher with each word spoken, but he didn't so much as get a breath in.

"You cannot become too attached to the things of this life, Daniel."

"You son of a--!"

"Hey!" Ian exploded cutting him off. "Cool it!"

Daniel ignored him.

"He was nothing but loyal to you, Luke! He didn't deserve to go out like that. You'll never change, you know that? Milo didn't deserve your abandonment, and the Fair Children sure don't deserve your kind of treatment. They haven't actually *done* anything yet, Luke. Can you honestly justify killing them? Killing their children even? Especially when all you're really doing, is making supremacist genocide sound like it's okay? If I have to throw a thousand textbooks onto this table to remind you how that story ends, I will."

At that last bit Luke leveled him with a serious look over the rim of his wine glass. "While we're on the topic" --he set his glass gently back on the table-- "let me put it to you this way. If you lived back in the 1890s and you were walking down a street and you happened to glance over and see little Hitler playing in his backyard alone, with what you knew today, would you honestly walk away? No, you would take him out right then and there-- wouldn't even about it."

Daniel's mind flashed back to earlier that day, in the park. *You're not like the others, Daniel.* Jack had said. *You'd think twice.*

"Yeah, except," Ian interjected. "Slight problem. See, our DeLorean kind of ran out of plutonium…"

Daniel didn't have enough patience for both Luke, and Ian's smart remarks.

"No," he said roughly, "the problem is that we can't be sure every Fair Child is going to choose to go dark. We don't really *know* anything. Your theory is exactly that-- a theory!" He could hear his voice escalating at a rapid pace and tried to bring it down a notch. "Come on, Luke. Please. It's too equivocal. You can't be encouraging Knoctes to act on this. Not when the grounds are based on speculation."

Luke considered Daniel for a long moment, stroking his upper lip with an index finger. "You use the word *we* very flippantly, for a Scit unnecessarily concerning himself with Knocte business."

Ian stiffened in his seat, the first signs of support Daniel had seen from his brother since the conversation's beginning.

Luke continued, "You know, Daniel, us Knoctes can fight our whole lives to kill each and every Fifth Worlder that sticks its nose in the wrong direction, until we are killed off ourselves, or die of old age, and the job will still not be finished. It is never finished. There will always be more. Always another creature lurking in the dark, killing the truly innocent of this world. It is a never ending cycle, and a meaningless life I do not wish to live. If we are to get the job done, the job we have been born, bred and designed to do, true action needs to be taken. All I have been suggesting is to go back to the source, cut off the head of the snake. All Fifth Worlders are, are disease stricken Innocents, who then decided it was a brilliant idea to spread uncontrollably. Get rid of the disease, and you get rid of the problem. Unfortunately there is no cure, so what options are we left with? Is it not the most plausible solution to eliminate the carriers? It is basic science."

An unsettling silence fell over the table.

Daniel wasn't sure about the rest, but he was having trouble finding words that would suit his sudden urge to grab hold of Luke by the front of his shirt, and smash the living day lights out of his face. He was shocked when Ruby was the first to break the silence.

"What did I ever do to you?" she demanded.

At the uncharacteristic forcefulness of her voice, Daniel almost smiled. Luke could get the better of both of them.

"It is not about what you have done, faerie. It is about what you will one day do. How are we to know, that at this very moment, you are not working at the Roadhouse to learn and gather information about us? We certainly did not anticipate that Jack, who used to be our ally and a trusted Scit, would turn against us. In truth, I do not know whether you have done anything to me, but when so many of your kind have, it leaves no room for trust between us."

Glancing over, Daniel could see Ruby's fist clenched at her side, her fingernails digging half moons into her palm. She looked like she wanted to bolt, like she regretted her interjection.

"You know," Daniel said stepping in, purposely rescuing her from having to give any sort of reply. "I'm still having a hard time picturing Jack killing anyone-- unless he was clubbing them over the head with an encyclopedia."

Luke merely threw him a pitying look.

"What I think my brother is trying to say," Ian offered up, "is that we heard a different version of the Jack story. One that doesn't involve him turning into a psycho killing nut bag."

"And what version would that be?" Luke asked blithely, but his expression was letting Ian know that he didn't appreciate being ganged up on.

"The version where you can't kill Jack," Daniel snapped instantly, "because he has his very own impenetrable furry shield protecting him. The version where he's actually innocent, while you-- you're the one who's responsible for the deaths. They weren't Innocents at all, were they, Luke? They were lycans. Lycanthropes you claimed were ignorant victims, in order to pin the whole ordeal on Jack, making your theory appear plausible. But now you're floundering, because Jack's untouchable, and it's probably due in part to the fact that you royally ticked off a lycanthrope pack."

"And where precisely," Luke asked slowly, "did you come across such a preposterous story?"

Daniel felt a muscle in his cheek twitch in irritation, and he found himself rising to his feet. He leaned out over the table, palms flattened against its surface. He got right in Luke's face. "Believe it or not, some of us actually care about what the Fair Children have to say, and listen to their grievances!"

"Oh, and I commend you on that," Luke said, his sarcasm laid on thick. He rose to match Daniel's height. "But not all of us have the time to poke and prod around the blurry edges of our own denial."

Daniel knew his rage was written clearly in his features, and he could tell Luke was having a hard time controlling his own emotions. For a moment, Daniel watched him struggle to keep his composure, until his face finally settled into a picture of cool malice.

Ian, not incredulous about the direction of the situation, sprang up in between them, placing a firm hand on both their chests.

"Throw some water on it, guys," he ordered, his eyes like daggers as he took turns pinning them with equally lethal looks.

His gaze held on Luke. "Listen, my brother almost got himself killed digging up this info, and it's got a pretty solid basis to it. We're looking into it, so from now on we're going to deal with Jack. You got that? Not you. Us. Take on a case that isn't swathed in so many shades of grey."

Luke's face was a hard mask, as he took in Ian's words, but he gave a reluctant stiff nod. Ian had left no room for contention. "Fair enough," Luke said tersely. "But keep in mind, if a war breaks out, no one will be safe."

Daniel pressed against his brother's hand, but Ian clenched Daniel's shirt, his fist balling in the fabric just below the collar, and his restraining force held true. "Luke, please," Daniel begged. "Just-- reconsider."

Luke sat down, nestling back into his seat, and retrieved his wine. He didn't even give Daniel a second glance as he sloshed the crimson liquid around the glass. Ruby's hand twitched ever so slightly, like she wanted to swat the refined piece of glassware right out of his grip, and send it smashing against the hardwood of the floor.

"I believe you have worn out your welcome at this table," Luke said, waving dismissively in his direction.

Daniel began to say something else, when Ian used his leveraged hand to shove him forcefully in the direction of the door, causing him to stumble backwards a few steps. Ruby must have seen his expression deflate, because she unhitched herself from her chair, moving to stand next to him, as Ian gave his departing words to Luke.

"It's all right," she said with a rueful smile, her voice barely pitched above a whisper, so as only to include him. "You tried, right?" She pulled something out of her jean pocket and pressed it into his hand. Daniel could feel the shape of a smooth, glass jar, cool to the touch. "For that eye of yours," she explained. "It should help with the bruising."

"Thanks, Bee," he said, his mouth tipping up into a small smile.

She reached out to tousle his hair, and he pulled her into a brief hug-- an affectionate gesture from an old friend, before she slipped into the crowd in the direction of the bar. He glanced back at the table to find their exchange hadn't gone unnoticed. Even as he tuned back into the conversation, Luke was watching him with a reproving expression. His eyes gleamed in a way that stirred a sudden protective nature in Daniel, and he found himself shifting to block Ruby's retreat from Luke's view.

"--and Ian," Luke was saying, his voice seemingly apologetic. "I'll buy you a beer sometime when you're not otherwise" --his eyes flickered back to Daniel-- "engaged."

Ian smiled flatly as he turned his back on his childhood friend, and shoving Daniel along, walked none too attentively away.

Chapter Eight

Ian could feel the fine sand shifting under his feet, as he made his way across the thin beach bordering the Hudson Bay, in Churchill Manitoba. He pressed his lips in a thin line, and slit his eyes against the cold wind that tore across the open water. It hurtled onto the beach, bringing waves that lapped against the beach front, like the caressing paws of a cat. At least the waves had the decency to be gentle if not the wind. The few scattered trees and smaller arbitrary vegetation was bending to its forceful will, as he tried to catch up to his brother, who had already picked his way farther along the beach. Daniel was closer to the wooden dock, a dock that was perched over the waterfront, looking solid, but worn. Evidence of its struggle against the relentless waves marred its appearance. Large wooden posts, spotted in some places with bird excrement, staked it into the earth, nestling it comfortably into position. A couple of tires clung to the dock's edge, padding for the boats that docked there. At the moment there weren't any. Ian could guess why. He was wearing only a pair of beat up ripped jeans and his usual scuffed sneakers, and he wondered, not for the first time, why, as he felt like he could shiver right out of his own skin.

The grey mass of clouds that stretched out above him was doing little in way of improving the situation, as it blocked the already descending sun from his view. At least Winchester was warm in the truck, sitting the case out because of his injury.

Lucky dog.

"Hey, Dan!" he called out ahead of him. "Remind me again, why we're practically naked out here?"

Daniel turned to face him, the icy wind tossing his hair across his forehead and into his eyes. The fading light glinted dimly off the dog tag that hung around his neck, a matching one to his own. Ian wondered if Daniel could feel the stinging coldness of it against the base of his throat, much in the same way he could.

"Water dragons see in thermal heat radiation, like an infrared camera," Daniel yelled back. "The colder we are, the more likely we're to go undetected."

"Naturally," Ian muttered, the instant heating pads

weighing down his jean pockets, finally starting to make some sense.

He was lazily swinging the machete he was wielding around in his grip. At least he knew how to kill it. A blade through the heart. It didn't even have to be a special type of metal. It made for an easy weapon choice, however, it didn't necessarily promise an easy kill. Sure, as Daniel would put it, dragons lacked grey matter, and as Ian would put it, had little in way of lights upstairs as a fish does feathers, but they could rely on their heavily armored skin and their brute strength. It also made it harder to anticipate their next move, when they weren't rationally making one. They were unpredictable, ill tempered, tenacious and all around dangerous.

"There's a boat out there!" Daniel called, concern clouding his tone as he gestured out across the water.

Ian halted his walking, and followed his brother's line of sight. Sure enough, a small aluminum fishing boat, with a motor that couldn't be packing more than twenty horsepower, loomed up out of the water, rocking rhythmically back and forth atop the waves. Ian could just make out the silhouettes of the three passengers, who looked to be a father out with his two anxious daughters.

Heck of a time to go out for a sunset troll. Ian thought glumly, but he only gave his brother a shrug.

"We need something as bait," Ian admitted grimly. "If the thing can't see us, it's never going to show up."

Daniel looked at him bleakly.

Ian stared right back. "Just saying."

With a shake of his head, Daniel turned his gaze back towards the vacillating family, and Ian knew he wouldn't be letting them out of his sight for an instant.

"They should be all right." Daniel was reassuring himself. "The dragon shouldn't be able to see them through the boat."

Ian stooped to select a flat, smooth, elongated rock, and with a flick of his wrist, sent it skimming across the water's surface. It skipped five times before sinking from sight.

A wave of fatigue washed over him, and he realized all the nights of lost sleep were catching up with him. It wasn't that he hadn't had ample opportunity to catch a few winks in the past few days, but that his mind was too restless to let him. It constantly thundered out concern, worrying about Daniel and worrying about the future. It was a never ending troubling stream of 'what if?' scenarios, that Ian wished he could silence.

And if it wasn't his relentless mind, it was the dreams that followed. They were scenes from his past, playing over and over again in his mind, like a broken record, as if they held some significance he had yet to figure out. The whole thing was infuriating. Sooner or later he realized, he'd have to face them, otherwise he didn't know how much longer he would be able to stay erect. Once in awhile though he mused, not sleeping came in handy. On the ride here, he'd swapped driving shifts with Daniel and had stretched himself out in the passenger seat about as far as his long legs would allow, and pretended, for both his and Daniel's benefit, that he was asleep. During that time he'd heard Daniel pull out his cell phone and make a call. He'd automatically assumed it was Devlyn, but after three more tries and no one picking up, Daniel left a voicemail.

He remembered every word.

"Hey, Jack, it's Dan. I cornered Luke in the Roadhouse and tried to talk sense into him-- but he's not listening. I'm about as high up on his friends list as you are. Ian managed to get him to remove the target off your back, but if this war breaks out, I realize it's not going to mean a whole lot..." He'd sighed wearily then. *"Listen, I'm sorry, man. I don't know what else to do here. I called Jim and convinced him to give it a try, but he doesn't seem to think it'll do much good. According to him, Luke's only interested in spreading his new theory, and isn't going to stop to listen to the traditional beliefs of an old man. He's looking towards a new generation. Some help I was, eh? No one's going to listen to me, Jack. No one ever does."*

Ian still wasn't sure what he thought about all that.

"Ian," Daniel's voice suddenly broke through his reverie. It was laden with that careful drawl of building panic. Ian's eyes shifted immediately back towards the boat, knowing the safety of the family would be the only thing to stir such unease in his brother.

One of the girls, the older one, was hanging out over the water, gripping the metal edge of the boat tightly in one hand, and pointing vigorously at something just off the starboard bow with the other. Just as the two other figures leaned forward, curiously, to get a better look at whatever she'd spotted, something shot out of the water behind them. It sent up a pelting spray of water as it upended the boat, dumping its contents unceremoniously into the water, with a fit of fearful screaming. The scene playing out so quickly, Ian had a hard time catching a glimpse of what was responsible. It looked almost suspiciously like a… tail.

Ian whirled on his brother.

"Danny--!" he called, knowing exactly what his brother's next move was going to be.

But it was too late.

Daniel was already bolting recklessly down the beach, his machete throwing light. Ian took chase, stopping short only when Daniel stormed onto the dock. His brother tossed his machete aside as he dove headlong into the shiver inducing bay waters.

Ian swore loudly.

Naturally Daniel would be more concerned about bringing ruthless weaponry around an Innocent family, than fending off a lurking sea monster. Ian hoped his brother had another knife on him somewhere, but what he really needed was a distraction-- and fast.

Ian turned, splashing recklessly into the bay, not stopping until he was waist deep in icy water.

"Hey, you overgrown fish! You want a free lunch? Come and get it! I taste good!" he hollered into the dusk, but aside from the initial episode of aggression, the bay had once again fallen into a still calm. A scary calm, in which Ian had no intention of trusting.

The only sign of a disturbance was coming from where Daniel was gently encouraging the family in the direction of the dock. One of the girls had her arms wrapped securely around his neck, and he was carefully pulling her along as he swam. The smaller of the two was attached to her father, and Ian could hear her wails from where he stood.

They were still drawing way more attention than he was.

He fumbled a small handful of the instant heating pads out of his pocket. They were plastic, and thus water applicable. Filled with liquid, they would crystalize and harden as they heated. All it took was a snap from an inwardly floating, flexible metal clasp. He snapped as many as he had in his hand and then tossed them a short distance in front of him. They floated for a minute before starting to sink, being swallowed up by the depths of the water one by one. Using the machete he started smacking and slashing pointlessly at the water, all the time he never stopped shouting. A string of haughty insults filling the night air around him, as he desperately tried to draw the attention of the indiscernible sea monster.

Just when he thought maybe they'd gotten lucky and the creature had become uninterested-- it breeched the surface a few meters in front of him.

He nearly laughed.

When did they ever get lucky?

The creature barely made a ripple as its face broke the surface first, a broad scaly face, with eyes positioned high on the sides of its head, like a rabbit's. They appeared almost milky, filmy as if a waterproof lens was covering them. Estimating its angle of sight, Ian quickly came to realize that the creature could probably be both watching him, and keeping tabs on everything Daniel and the small family were doing behind it.

Great. Just great.

Ian could also see the creature's top incisors, sharp, and long enough to extend down over its bottom lip. A pink forked tongue flicked none too hesitantly in and out as if tasting the air. It had two large fin like pieces of skin that lay flat against its neck just behind its jaw. The beast had an extensively long neck, which came next, curling over in the shape of a question mark, as the monster now rose to loom up high above Ian's head. Its black, slickly scaled, snake like body followed, with four legs reaching up higher than its spine like a spider's. A similar thing was occurring with the claws protruding out of the ends of its feet, only they were slightly webbed, bridging the gap between each of them. Its tail was so vastly long, Ian lost sight of the end of it, but he could make out some of its glistening tail spikes. They seemed to slide in and out from amongst the scales, gliding with relative ease. A sound like a sharpening knife or an unsheathing sword accompanied the motion.

Then they stilled, fully and aggressively out of its skin.

There was complete silence for a moment as the creature stood in all its glory before Ian. It had its head tilted slightly at an angle as if sizing him up. It was something Ian would imagine an eagle doing, and probably had something to do with the small blind spot he suspected the creature had dead center in its vision.

When it seemed to be satisfied that it had come across something worth perusing, the fins that had once lay flat against its neck, flew outwards, expanding like that of an Australian frilled lizard, making it appear as if the creature had grown massive thorn tipped, almost papery thin ears. In the same instant, it opened its mighty saliva dripping jaws, exposing the rest of its sharp teeth. These were uneven, like jagged pieces of glass. A grating, ear splitting hiss emanated from the beast, trembling the waters in front of it, as the sound was sent echoing across the shore. It sent the same shiver inducing sensation down Ian's spine, as the sound of nails on a chalkboard. Its hot breath smelt like fish and rotting corpses, as it stirred Ian's short hair, tousling it around with more force than the howling wind surrounding them.

"This," Ian decided, "is a situation."

Gripping the edge of the dock with one hand, Daniel waited for the father to pull himself up onto it. The younger daughter, a tiny blond thing, no older than four, was reduced to a blubbering mess at the separation from her dad. She bobbed up and down in her yellow life jacket next to Daniel. The older of the girls, Daniel estimated to be about six or seven, still had her arms wrapped securely around his neck, her red, braided hair hanging soaked over one shoulder. She made a few teeth chattering attempts to quiet her little sister down, but then gave into her shivering, and just hung numbly, probably listening to Ian's superficial ranting in the distance.

The father managed to pull himself up, and had turned so his face was now poking over the side, his short blond hair alight with water droplets. He was trying to be brave and resolved, as he soothed his younger daughter with comforting words, his arms extending down to reach for her, but Daniel could see the anxiety and panic in his eyes. The father caught hold of the handle hanging off the back of her lifejacket and Daniel helped push her up from below with his free hand. It took another minute to lift the red haired girl up, and no sooner than he had, the sea creature had emerged off to their right. Daniel took one exasperated look at it, and sprang up onto the dock after them.

"Head for shore!" Daniel ordered, and they all started to run.

A tree trunk sized tail lifted out of the water behind them, and swaying to the side, crashed into the end of the dock, causing Daniel and the rest of the fleeing party to lurch forward and lose their footing. Knowing they had to move faster, Daniel scooped the red haired girl into his arms before he'd even fully gotten back to his feet. The father followed suit with his blond girl, and they where tearing down the dock's length. The dragon was faster this time, the tail suddenly losing its leisurely, lumbering sway, and gaining a more whip like agility. Daniel saw the incoming strike, and only had enough time to turn away from it, using himself as a shield to protect the girl. The spikes came hard, slicing across his back; the impact knocked him forward, and off his feet. The girl gave a small shriek as they fell. Tucking her tightly against him, Daniel rolled gracefully out of it, preventing himself from landing on her. He bit back the obscene language that threatened to escape his lips, as pain seared across his shoulder blades.

He instantly released the girl, giving her a firm, but gentle, shove towards her very pale-faced father, where he stood at the edge of the dock, right before it gave way to sand. At least Daniel was certain he'd be attracting more attention now, if anything was stronger than a water dragon's infrared sight, it was its sense of smell. A sense of smell that happened to pick up the coppery sent of blood, with as much intensity and precision as a shark's would. Knowing he was in desperate need for a weapon now, Daniel's eyes fell on his discarded machete a few feet away. He dove for it, just as the tail came back for more. He barely had time to curl his fingers around its cool hilt before spikes descended.

Audrey didn't know what had changed her mind. Maybe it was the way he'd dove in after that family without a single thought for himself. Maybe it was the instant trust the girl seemed to find in him, the moment he collected her into the safe circle of his arms. Or the way he threw himself in between her and the dragon, but suddenly-- she didn't want to kill Daniel Browning anymore.

It was crazy.

Absolutely nuts, that she found herself actually racing to the guy's aid. She felt the sand between her toes as she bolted onto the beach, and out of the border lining vegetation. Who needed shoes when you had feet as hard as concrete? She met up with the family first, as they scrambled across the sand, dividing their party for a moment as she barreled headlong through them. They stopped a moment, turning back, as their eyes followed her, with an almost curious fascination that she'd dare run in the polar opposite direction of their retreat. And yes, she had had a poorly concealed, archaically curved dagger clutched in one hand. She thought she heard the man muttering something about how dragons hadn't been crazy enough.

"Go! Go! Get out of here!" she barked over her shoulder, not looking back to see if they'd actually listened.

She watched Daniel dive for the machete, quickly rolling onto his back to block the blow, and only semi-succeeding as a tail spike slashed across one of his arms. It snaked away and he gave a grunt, hastily jumping back to his feet.

Audrey reached the dock, and upon hearing her, Daniel looked up in surprise, clearly not expecting anyone to be around who would openly rush into the situation. That slight distraction was just enough to make him lose his focus, and suddenly the end of the tail wrapped around one of his ankles.

"Watch--," she tried to warn him, but it was already too late, as his feet were ripped out from under him.

He hit the dock hard, his shoulder slamming into the wood. Audrey made a grab for his arm, but missed, and the creature started dragging him towards the water. Daniel grunted painfully, and in a show of force he lifted his machete above his head and drove it deep into the dock's worn surface. It jerked him to an obviously painful stop, the lean muscles of his shoulders straining with the effort to hold himself there.

Catching up, and wasting no time, Audrey leapt over him, throwing herself against the thicker part of the tail. She grit her teeth, willfully forcing the tail to turn over and expose the scale deprived, vulnerable underside. The spikes maliciously shot in and out, scraping against her hard skin, but the sound it created was worse than the actual result. She was built to last. She had to admit, that if it wasn't for shotguns, her kind would probably have the world in their back pockets by now.

Using her dagger, with a swift fluid motion, Audrey sliced a deep gash across the underside of the tail. It dropped its hold on Daniel's ankle, the tail skidding across the dock, and retreating back into the water.

Still lying on his stomach, Daniel immediately twisted to face her.

Breathing heavily, Audrey could clearly read the shock written across his features. She knew what he was seeing, as his warm brown eyes locked onto her. A very pale girl, kneeling at the end of the dock, with shoulder length dark hair, and hazel eyes too washed out to be human. She knew she might as well have had Twilight stamped on her forehead. He didn't need to feel her tough, smooth skin, to know what she was.

Vampire.

Ian couldn't help being grateful dragons were easily distracted.

He couldn't see what Daniel was doing on the dock, the dragon effectively blocking his view, but his brother had somehow managed to gain the majority of the dragon's attention for a moment. Its overly large head swung away from him to hiss in Daniel's direction, but with one fluid swipe of machete against hard scales --bam!-- Ian was the center of attention again.

The head snapped back around, and another frilled hiss was emitted in his direction. Its neck coiled up like a snake's, striking forward, its jaws snapping menacingly in his direction. He barely had time to throw himself to the side, before the creature's face struck the water in the very spot he'd been only a moment before.

The very same sort of attack had been going on for a while, and Ian had managed to lure the dragon closer to the shore's edge, quickly realizing it was easier to move out of the way, when he wasn't waist deep in water. He still hadn't come anywhere close enough, however, to get a decent shot at its underside, and his mind began to spin, trying to think of ways to better the situation. He came up short. The dragon appeared set in its ways, content just to continue snapping at him over and over. He was beginning to wonder if it would grow tired of the whole ordeal and slither back into the water's depths.

Then the dragon struck out once again, and Ian leapt to the side, bringing the machete around with enough speed to catch the creature across the eye, a kink in its protective armor. It drew back with a bone chilling screech of displeasure, and what came next, happened so fast that he didn't have time to react.

Almost as if the dragon's action had been linked to some sort of reflex arc, one of its clawed feet shot out, swatting him aside in agitation. Ian hit the water and before he had time to catch his footing and push himself back to the surface, the foot came down on top of him, pressing him into the silt covered bottom of the bay. His head was pinned between two talons, coming to rest just above his shoulders, and digging deeply into the sand.

Forcing himself not to panic, Ian attempted to squeeze the rest of his body through the talons, but it was like trying to squeeze through the bars of a jail cell. He stretched his hand, reaching for his fallen machete, but managed only a handful of seaweed. He was wasting his breath.

Somehow though, through the water and his struggles, he could hear his brother calling his name.

Just like that she was completely forgotten.

The moment Daniel watched his brother go down, it was like a light switch flipped on. She was all but a phantom in his single-minded world.

The dragon was looking around stupidly, with those jerky bird-like movements, clearly confused as to Ian's sudden disappearance. With his body heat concealed underfoot, it had no idea it had just smothered its prey.

"Ian!" Daniel cried, taking the scene in and leaping to his feet.

When his brother didn't resurface immediately, he didn't even hesitate, spinning back towards her, and ripping the dagger out of her hand. She barely had time to protest, before he'd aimed and thrown. She grabbed his arm angrily, and he flinched slightly, but otherwise hardly seemed to notice, as he watched the dagger cartwheel through the air. It lacked the fluid motion of a Knocte's toss, but managed to hit its mark all the same, imbedding itself hilt deep. It stuck in the dragon's throat, just behind the creature's jawline, and pinned one of the flaps down in the process. The water beast gave a feral shriek, staggering as it shook its head vigorously from side to side trying to dislodge the painful nuisance.

The heavy air of anxiety that hung in a cloud around Daniel only dispersed as Ian broke the surface, gasping for air. Audrey thought she could visibly see the tension leaving Daniel's shoulders, as his brother dragged himself, sputtering, onto the shore.

"I liked that dagger," she admitted with a sigh, while the dragon switched tactics, using one of its hind legs to scratch at the weapon, much in the way a dog would soothe an itch behind one of its ears.

To her surprise-- Daniel actually turned to regard her ruefully. "Sorry."

Had he just apologized? A Knocte to a Fifth Worlder? She quickly corrected herself. Not Knocte-- Scit, but still, she could tell he meant it, those deep brown eyes sincere. It was such a rarity, that she felt like she'd just stumbled upon a diamond while rummaging through a trashcan.

Unbelievable.

But suddenly they had bigger problems than a lost dagger.

The dragon had given up on the lodged weapon.

The water beast could have came to the solution of ripping it free with its tail, much in the same manner of precision it had wrapped it around Daniel's ankle, but instead the creature opted for a different course of action, turning instead on the source of its discomfort-- namely Daniel.

The dragon struck out with a scaled foot, and without hesitation she felt Daniel grab her and throw her out of the way. She staggered to keep her footing, and he barely had enough time to free his machete and leap out of harms way himself, before sharp claws tore into the side of the dock, splintering wood, and tearing through supports. Audrey threw her hands up to fend off the debris, as a large section of the dock became victim to the water. The gesture wasn't exactly necessary with her vampire build, but still a habit nevertheless.

"Are you crazy?!" she found herself yelling at the Knocte-- Scit-- whatever. "It can't see me! I don't give off body heat. *You*

123

do! Worry about yourself!"

Daniel gave her an incredulous look for a moment. Then nodded. "Just stay down."

There was actual concern in his voice. Strange times.

The tail swooped towards them, and Daniel instantly deflected it with his machete. The second time he wasn't so lucky as the backswing came too quickly, slamming into him. He skidded across the dock, nearly falling victim to its recent vandalism. Grabbing one of the remaining support pillars he managed to prevent himself from toppling headlong into the water. His weapon hadn't been so lucky, however. Audrey heard the splash at the same time Daniel did, and she watched as his face fell. Despite the disappointment he didn't waste time in getting to his feet.

Unfortunately the dragon was already in for another attack.

"Duck!" she screamed, and threw herself in front of him. Luckily he didn't question it, and immediately hit the deck.

She managed to hide enough of his body heat, that the confused dragon's tail swung wide. She sighed in relief.

Daniel straightened meeting her gaze. "So much for laying low," he muttered, but his eyes were full of questions; questions he couldn't seem to hold back any longer. "Why are you helping me?"

Audrey wasn't sure now was a great time to be chatting. "Why'd you help me?"

He didn't accept the whole answering a question with a question thing. "Every other vampire we've run into lately has tired to kill me. So I'm just supposed to believe you're being helpful? Explain. What's your end game? What does it have to do with me?"

Audrey gave a wistful smile, opting to answer only one of his questions. "My end game is the same as everyone else's. Live. Survive."

"And running into a situation like this--." He cut himself off, seeing the tail before she did. Ducking, he reached out to push her down by her shoulders along with him.

It sailed over their heads.

Audrey knew she wasn't doing a good enough job of hiding Daniel, and it was only a matter of time before the dragon caught on. She wasn't nearly large enough to shadow out all of that male muscle.

"--isn't nearly as detrimental to my health as it is to yours," she finished for him. Her face was inches from his, where they crouched in front of one another, so she knew he could read her expression clearly when she spoke her next words. "But I might be more helpful than you expect. Especially when it comes to your vampire problems."

She watched surprise and confusion flit across his features for a brief second, before she was unexpectedly, and unceremoniously ripped away, tossed aside as if she weighed nothing. She caught herself before she toppled from the dock, instantly trying to scramble to her feet-- but froze when a shadow fell over her. It hadn't been the dragon who'd tried to dispatch her, or even Daniel who'd only been inches away.

"Get. Back."

The voice belonged to Ian, his words and expression equally colder than she would have thought possible, or so she thought, until she met his eyes. Hard. Frigid. Down right scary.

This was a Knocte. And staring up at him from ground level, it was hard not to be intimidated. His actions had been smooth, graceful, and oh so fast. Perhaps faster than any other Knocte she'd ever had to contend with. She would have found it impressive really, if she hadn't been on the receiving end of it. Ian Browning was not someone you messed with. She'd often warned her own kind away from any confrontation with him.

He took another step towards her, and she cringed internally at her lack of a weapon-- but Daniel was there, pulling his brother back.

"Easy. She's not here to pick a fight."

Audrey used the opportunity to rise, and gain a solid fighting stance. She could pack quite a kick herself, if the opportunity presented itself.

Ian's eyebrows rose almost mockingly. "Oh, yeah? Then why is she here?"

Silence met his question. Daniel still didn't know why she was here, and if she was being honest with herself, she didn't really know either-- indecisive as always.

Ian started in her direction again, but Daniel wedged

125

himself between them, placing a restraining hand on his brother's shoulder. His back was to her, and by the look on Ian's face, he didn't like that much at all. She could practically see him silently chastising his brother for being so recklessly trusting.

"Back off," Daniel warned. "We're not turning this into some stupid Luke--."

It happened too fast.

They'd been so worried about each other that they'd forgotten about their real enemy. The dragon whipped its tail out again, this time its prey clearly lit up like a neon sign, and wrapped it around Daniel's neck, cutting off his air supply. It pulled him down hard, ripping him from his feet. He hit the dock with an audibly painful thud, and the tail began slithering back into the water, quickly taking Daniel with it. Audrey hadn't even had enough time to fully comprehend the situation-- when Ian was already in motion.

"*Danny!*" he cried, leaping ahead of his brother, who, despite having dug his heels into the dock's wooden surface, was still sliding uncontrollably towards the water's edge.

Ian didn't waste time in using his machete.

All those swipes at the dragon earlier and she could tell he hadn't even come close to penetrating the scales, but suddenly, so consumed with fury he looked like he was practically burning with it, he found enough force to drive the machete right through the tail and pin it securely to the dock.

There was no time to look surprised.

Daniel had stopped sliding, yes, but the tail stayed locked in its death grip around his neck. His hands were futilely trying to pry it off, fingers grasping at slippery scales. She watched Ian immediately drop to his knees at his brother's side, ignoring the shrieks the dragon was emanating off.

She reached them just as Ian curled his fingers around the strangle hold, trying to lend his strength. He hadn't seemed to register her presence, as she searched for some way to be useful.

"Danny," Ian begged. "Danny!" A vein strained in his neck with the effort of trying to wrench the tail away, and for a moment, he unintelligibly voiced his struggle, before reverting back to hastily muttered reassurances. "It's okay, it's okay. I got you!"

The Knocte's sullen eyes were now full of something other

than bleak coldness. Audrey saw there something else, a raw panic that was consuming him from the inside out. His brother gasped beneath him, trying in vain to find some sort of airflow, his face pinched in pained determination, and his sneakers scraping uselessly against the dock's surface.

Audrey caught movement out of the corner of her eye, and turned horrified. The dragon was coiling its neck back for another one of those cobra-like strikes.

"It's--!" was as far as she got in her warning, before it struck.

Ian twisted with unnatural speed, connecting a kick with the beast's jaw just as it reached him. It did little in way of phasing the creature, but it had enough force to knock its head, along with the sharp teeth, off to the side and out of harming distance. In the same motion, Ian reached for the hilt of her knife where it was still imbedded deep in the dragon's throat and swiftly yanked it free. He spun back towards Daniel then, and Audrey could almost see the gears in his mind turning. He knocked her aside, when she moved to lean over his brother and immediately started digging in Daniel's jean pockets. She thought she saw his eyes light up a little when he pulled out what looked like small heating packs. He started cracking them before he even had them all in his hands.

Then he did the unexpected, turning to face her, he grabbed her shirt at the collar and threw her back over Daniel.

"You want to help?! Help!"

She silently resented him for that, but she didn't argue as she took over his position tugging at the tail. Daniel's gasps were becoming less frequent and his own attempts to free himself were growing feeble. She wasn't as strong as Ian had been, vampire or not, and she couldn't help morbidly thinking that they might lose him. The thought caught her off guard. They? Had she just grouped herself in with these people? Daniel, okay, he was worth saving for the moment-- but Ian? He wanted nothing better than to see her kind wiped off the face of the earth. And she hated him for it.

Distantly she watched the dragon track Ian as he started moving away from them. The creature's front feet climbed up onto the dock after him, claws biting into the wooden edge. It struck again and Ian hurled the heating packs right into its face. Alarmed and overwhelmed the dragon recoiled, rearing back on its hind legs, wailing in protest. Ian didn't waste the opportunity. Sliding on his knees right under the beast, he thrust the dagger upwards. It pierced through the vulnerable skin and Audrey hoped beyond hope he knew where the sweet spot was, the spot where the creature's heart kept. To her relief, it appeared as though he did, as a shower of gore came down on him. The dragon gave such a hissing screech, that with her vampire hearing Audrey had to resist the urge to cringe in a ball and cover her ears. The dragon swayed, its claws trying to regrip the dock to regain some semblance of balance.

At the same time its tail loosened its hold and Audrey immediately clawed it off of Daniel, who choked a couple of times before he was sent into a gasping, coughing fit for the precious oxygen he'd been so deprived of.

Ian tried to back track, wiping blood from his eyes, and really only accomplishing to smear it more thoroughly across his face. The dragon tumbled to the side, taking more of the dock with it, as it went down, a splash the size of a tidal wave exploding upwards and rained down around them. A piece of splintering wood caught Ian in the back of the head, but he managed to maintain his grip on the dock.

For a few moments everything went still. The water settled back into its rhythmic waves, and the dragon floated still and lifeless on the surface, then slowly Ian got to his feet. Making his way over, he stumbled slightly, and Audrey couldn't picture the man she'd seen in action only moments ago ever being so unsteady. She realized that if she ever had a shot at killing him, the time would be now. But for some reason, when he collapsed at his brother's side next to her, and gently helped Daniel into a sitting position, she did nothing but watch. Blood streamed down the back of Ian's neck, blood that was too light to belong to the dragon, but the head injury seemed nothing but a trifle to him.

"You good?" Ian asked his brother breathlessly, a steadying hand still on Daniel's shoulder.

"Awesome," Daniel rasped quietly, flinching at the sound of his own grated voice.

Ignoring the sarcasm Ian extended his hand, and as Daniel accepted the Conexus he pulled his brother into a fierce hug, causing Daniel to wince. Audrey used the opportunity to slowly back away. Retreating into the shadows, she convinced herself that Ian wasn't worth her time or energy. Not today.

"I don't think a place could get more buckets of crazy," Ian mused.

Daniel didn't altogether disagree with him.

They were in a backwards, roadside diner, in the middle of nowhere. It was the kind with a gas station nestled in beside it. A gas station that sported a warning sign, stating it was the last one for miles-- so fill up. The diner walls, interspersed with abstract pictures of grain silos, all twisted and warped, were enough to make Picasso proud. They were even painted with bright, out of place colours. To make things even stranger, there were also rustic bull skulls and wheel spokes hanging in between the artwork. The contrast between the two choices of decoration was truly comical, a clash of the archaic and the obscenely modern. The material covering of their booth was decorated with small pictures of cows, and a few minutes earlier a couple of men had stormed in, hauling the dead deer they'd killed nearby, and flaunting it in front of everyone. Everyone being Daniel and Ian's table, plus one other. The only up side, was that no one even batted an eye at the presence of Winchester, where he camped out beneath their table. Compared to a deer corpse, a dog was nothing of consequence.

Winchester whined as he scratched at Daniel's pant leg, rolling over onto his back expectantly with his paws twitching in the air. Feeling an amused smile play across his lips, Daniel rubbed the tracking dog's underbelly with the sole of his shoe. Winchester wriggled around gleefully, his tongue lolling out of his mouth.

Ian had resorted back to massaging his temples, still nursing his headache from the blow he'd taken during the case. Daniel had refused to let him rest, denying him sleep in case of a concussion. Despite how often his brother claimed to be fine, Daniel hadn't missed the depleting number of pain pills.

"So I've been trying to figure something out," Ian spoke again.

Daniel smiled. "There's a long list of those somethings, Ian. Care to elaborate?"

Ian didn't even blink at the condescending words. "I'm serious," he said unamused. "When did vampires become pro

129

Dan?"

Daniel shrugged. "Change of heart?" He didn't even know what he'd done to make them hate him in the first place.

"So it was just vampire 'be a good neighbour' day? I don't think so. Even if they're not trying to kill us, we're not exactly on their Christmas list. So why the sudden leaping into battle to try and save our hides?"

"I don't know," Daniel said wearily, slouching down in his seat and tilting his head back for a moment to stare up at the ceiling. The vampire's words playing over in his mind: *But I might be more helpful than you expect. Especially when it comes to your vampire problems.* "Nothing's really making sense anymore."

"Tell me about it," Ian grumbled, grabbing up the pepper shaker. Sliding it across the table, he began passing it from hand to hand.

Ian often had habits like that. His brother hated not being in some sort of motion, though Daniel couldn't help wondering if now, it was just meant as some menial activity to keep him awake. Probably a little of each. They were both so completely and utterly exhausted, it was a wonder they could even have a coherent conversation at all.

Dragon kills weren't easy to cover up. Last night had been solid enough evidence of that. They had dragged the water beast's body onto shore-- in pieces because it was so long and heavy. That had been another grueling task altogether, a lot of hacking and sawing on their part, waist deep in shiver inducing water. Once they'd finally lugged all the pieces ashore, they'd piled them high, and with a little help from a can of gasoline in the truck bed, they set the mound ablaze. The scales hadn't burned of course, but those could pass as rocks in the end. Someone might even find them to be a useful skipping tool one day-- Ian sure had. The rest of the charred remains, namely bones and teeth, that hadn't disintegrated into ash, they had buried farther in the brush, away from the beach.

And that wasn't even including the part where they'd had to seal his slit back with a hot iron poker from their arsenal.

Needless to say-- it had been one long night.

Daniel hadn't even realized his mind had gone retrospect on it, until he'd tuned back in to find Ian still contemplating aloud.

"...vampires are trying to kill you. Some vampires are

trying to *save* you. Lycanthropes are trying to use you-- I mean, in what universe do those add up?" he mused.

"I have no idea," Daniel sighed mirthlessly. "There's definitely some piece to the puzzle we're not seeing here."

That was when he spotted their waitress making her way across the diner, her hands weighed down with their food. Ian still found time to fit in a snarky --"No, you think?"-- before she reached their table.

Setting their plates down in front of them, she gave them a more than friendly smile. Ian hardly seemed to notice, as his eyes instantly glued themselves to his meal. Daniel could understand the feeling. He was beyond starving too.

"Can I get you two anything else?" she asked, tossing her blond hair over her shoulder.

Daniel couldn't help thinking it was the wrong shade of blond. The waitress-- or Carmen as her nametag so proclaimed, had hair that was clearly dyed. Her dark roots were showing through at the top, and her hair had that dull colour that came from too much bleaching, and too many dates with a straightening iron. Daniel immediately missed Devlyn and her naturally soft, blond curls.

Ian reached over to grab the ketchup bottle that sat at the end of their table, and held it up for her to see. "I'm covered, thanks."

Daniel gave an agreeing nod, but she must have noticed his earlier scrutiny, because she leaned in closer to them, placing her palms flat on the table. It reminded Daniel of the threatening pose he'd adopted when talking to Luke, only she came across with an exact opposite appeal, as she took turns meeting their eyes, with her incredibly dark brown ones.

"You boys sure?" she asked smoothly. She had pitched her voice low, but the double meaning behind her words may as well have been shouted across the diner.

Ian's eyebrows shot up in surprise. He gave Daniel a quizzical look, before turning towards Carmen, his expression melting into a dangerous smile.

"We'll wave you over if anything comes to mind, okay sweetheart?" he replied easily, and threw in a last minute wink, before the waitress gave him a knowing smile, and sauntered off.

When she was out of earshot Ian turned back towards Daniel, shaking his head in disbelief. "Lest I reiterate: this town is nuts."

"Yeah," Daniel agreed. "Anyone that interested in you-- has to be on something."

Ian's gaze had involuntarily wandered down towards his plate again, but instantly shot up at the quip, pinning him with a haughty look.

"I meant the burger you idiot," he said, scooping it off his plate, where it had sat next to a still steaming mountain of crispy fries. He waved it in front of Daniel's face. "What kind of diner doesn't have a bacon cheeseburger? A regular hamburger is just insulting. It's freaken naked."

He eyed it with an air of disgust, before dropping it back unceremoniously onto his plate. He ripped the top bun off, and grabbing up the ketchup bottle, started to try and coax the substance out of the difficult glass container. He was still in the process of slapping it encouragingly when Daniel's phone went off. Scavenging it out of his pocket to check the number with one hand, Daniel used his other to quickly scrape a couple of fries off the top of his own yellow mountain. He dropped them to Winchester, who gobbled them up greedily.

The call display read that it was Jim.

Daniel had been expecting the call, having sent the man a few texts earlier during the drive. Jim didn't get along well with technology, and it made texting in and of itself a struggle, so it was perfectly normal for Jim to seek out a more direct line of communication. Sometimes it seemed like Ian had even worse luck with electronics. Maybe it was a Knocte thing?

Pushing up from the table, he held up a finger, motioning for Ian --who was giving him an expectant look-- to wait. He headed towards the door and just barely heard Ian commanding Winchester to stay, as he hit the answer key.

"Hey, Jim," Daniel greeted as he pulled open the door to stand outside.

"Good to hear from you, boy," came Jim's warm and familiar husky voice.

"Yeah, you too. Did you get my messages?"

"Most of them I reckon."

Daniel rolled his eyes, letting out a light laugh. "Sounds

about right. Got everything set for tonight?"

"Well sure," Jim drawled, "but don't you think he's going to be even a little bit suspicious?"

Daniel glanced back over his shoulder, through the glass door, to where Ian was still sitting at the booth. He was chewing thoughtfully on a fry, eyes carefully following the waitress as she flitted about the diner.

"Nah," he said. "I think he lost track of what day it was some time ago now. It happens when you're on the road."

"Yeah, maybe if you're Ian," Jim said amused, "but I'd bet my left shoe you know what day it is."

"Of course I do," Daniel grinned. "I'm planning this thing remember?"

"I'm aware. Just make sure you remember your own plan. Ditch that brother of yours, and go round up Dev."

"That," Daniel said with a satisfied smile, "I can handle."

"Who was that?" Ian asked his brother, when Daniel finally slid back into the booth across from him. "Dev? You'd think by now, she'd have figured out she doesn't need to keep pining for your love."

"Hilarious," Daniel deadpanned, and then rolled his eyes. "It was Jim. He was just checking in to-- hey! Did you--? Did you eat my fries?" he asked, giving his seemingly smaller pile a quizzical look.

Ian looked away. "No," he denied, even though it was, in fact, exactly what he had been doing in his brother's absence.

Daniel's eyes flickered up to give him a skeptical look.

"Get it packed up," he said, trying to wave the suspicion away. He pointedly ignored Daniel's gaze, as he searched out the waitress. "I want to get back on the road."

He could feel Winchester pacing restlessly under the table, brushing his legs with every circling. Ian himself had already polished off his meal, regular old hamburger or not, a combination of restlessness, and post battle exhaustion, had made his appetite even more impressive than usual. He watched Daniel glance down at his meal longingly, probably experiencing similar pangs, before he finally gave a smirk.

"What? Scared this place is going to rub off on you?"

Ian gave him an incredulous look, and then stabbed a finger at the upholstery they were sitting on.

"Little cows, Dan," he said with revulsion. "Little cows!" He spun his finger around his right ear, to emphasize just how crazy he found it. He also gave the suiting, and accompanying whistle to go along with it.

They finally flagged down Carmen, and she took Daniel's food away. His brother looked after it yearningly, until it was out of his sight. Ian looked after the waitress for other reasons.

Turning back to the table, Daniel said, "So, I've been doing some research…"

It was Ian's turn to smirk. "Shocker there," he said distractedly.

Fingers suddenly snapped in front of his face.

"Hey!" His brother was frowning. "This is serious. I've been checking in at home and some major red flags are popping up."

That gained Ian's full attention. "What do you mean 'red flags'?"

"I mean the town's lighting up like a Christmas tree with Fifth Worlder activity. There are calls flying in to Fish and Wildlife about wolf sightings near residential areas, and local pets are going missing." The frown deepened. "Fifth Worlders don't usual flock around such a Knocte location. Just doesn't make any *sense*…" he trailed off.

"Kind of like everything else lately? I'm starting to see a pattern. It's getting annoying. I don't like it," Ian decided, watching Daniel's concerned expression. Any worries of his brother's, were worries of his.

Carmen showed up then, interrupting them with a Styrofoam to-go box and their bill. She set them on the table, and turned away, shooting them both a winning smile over her shoulder as she did. Ian pulled the bill out from under the two mint candies, and smiled. He flashed it towards his brother. There was a phone number scrawled across the top.

"I've always had a thing for blonds."

Daniel heaved a tired sigh, as he protectively pulled his to-go box closer to himself. "It's fake."

"What is?"

"Her hair colour. It's fake."

"Well it's a good thing I have a thing for brunettes too."

Daniel mumbled something inaudible under his breath and then stood up. "Come on Romeo, let's go home."

Ian slapped a couple of bills on the table and joined him. "Agreed. I'm about ready to say goodbye to this tumbleweed of a town."

Daniel didn't pause as he strode from the building, Winchester at his heels. The dog's nails clicked on the tile with determined strides, but Ian stopped at the door to give the rustic diner one last look. Then before he followed his brother, he tossed the graffitied bill into the nearest waste bin.

Chapter Nine

Ian was sipping on a beer, propped against a wall at the Roadhouse. Daniel had ditched out on him the moment he'd learned Devlyn wasn't working, and was no where to be seen.

He tried not to let that bother him, as he watched the pool game a short distance away. He noted every amateur mistake the players made with a disdainful shake of his head. His fingers itched irritably towards the pool cues, but he ignored the longing, allowing his eyes another lazy, habitual scan of his surroundings.

It was then that he spotted her, her brilliant red hair like a giant arrow, flashing out her location.

He frowned, suspicious. What was she doing here? It dawned on him then, that he didn't even know her name. She had her nose buried in a book, and her feet propped and crossed at the ankles up on a table.

He was already moving towards her, ready to demand an explanation, before he even fully realized what he was doing. He abandoned his empty beer bottle on the way, setting it down loudly on the edge of the pool table, and earning some less than friendly looks. She was wearing knee high boots, with sharp heels, just like the last time he had seen her. Her leather jacket was hanging off the back of her chair, and her Weimaraner tracking dog was swatting it with her tail, head resting in her owner's lap. The young woman stroked the dog almost subconsciously.

He slowed his step as he walked by the table, one hand shoved in his jean pocket, the other reaching out to rap his knuckles knowingly against the tabletop. Her dog's head snapped up, eyeing him suspiciously.

She ignored him.

"And I'm supposed to believe you aren't watching us," he said, stopping so his tall shadow loomed over her.

She didn't seem in the least intimidated.

"Can I help you?" she asked without looking up from her book, her tone bored, a little annoyed.

Ian didn't like being ignored. He sank down into the seat across from her, and with a sweep of his arm knocked her legs off the table. Her heeled boots clanked loudly as they connected with the wooden floor. Her tracking dog let out a low warning growl.

"Dick," she spat unimpressed, green eyes flickering up scornfully for a brief moment before drifting back down to the pages.

Ian doubted the book was that good, but when he reached out dramatically with two fingers, and pushed it down towards the table, she seemed generally irritated, as it lowered to reveal her expression. The binding hit the table surface with a dull thud. Ian had caught a glimpse of the cover before he'd reached out, and deemed it some sort of mystery novel. He could see the pages now, split open like a dissection in front of her. They were dog-eared, worn, and stained like they'd been read a hundred times or more. Possibly had.

They stared each other down for a moment, icy blue eyes meeting emerald green.

Then she sighed heavily, leaning forward to rub her temples, as if he was giving her a headache. "I'm not following you. I already told you: I have better things to do with my life, than stalk a couple of 'out of the box' thinkers like you and your brother."

"Well, this" --he whirled a finger around in the air to implicate the Roadhouse and the general area-- "happens to be where I'm from. I notice who passes through-- you've never been one of them."

She leaned in further, and he saw the tone she was going to use written all over her face, even before she spoke. Her eyes narrowed dangerously. "This place has never been a hot spot for Fifth Worlder activity before," Her voice was snarky, even a little malicious. "For some reason they're all flocking here like someone painted a giant red 'X' on a map over this town. Do you have any explanations? Because if you do-- I'm all ears. If not: leave me alone, get out of my way, and let me work my case."

She snapped her book shut loudly, and swept it from the table. Ian worked to hide his reaction, as his mind flashed back to the conversation he and Daniel had had in the diner. Standing abruptly, she grabbed her jacket off the back of her chair. In the same motion, she swung it on over her head, one arm sliding in smoothly after the other.

"Where'd you get your info?" he demanded.

She laughed. "A Scit, Ian. Same way you do." She jerked her messenger bag onto her shoulder from under her seat. "No, wait. I think this time an angel might have appeared and pointed shouting 'lookie, lookie!'"

Ian didn't appreciate the sarcasm. "Who?" he asked between clenched teeth.

She just shook her head, giving a slight roll of her eyes. Spinning on her heels, she tried to walk away without so much as a backwards glance. Her heels echoed rhythmically against the floor.

But Ian was already out of his chair and behind her.

"What? You won't tell me? You really think I'm in the market for a new Scit?" He laughed at the absurdity of the idea, but she didn't turn around to acknowledge his presence. She pushed her way out of the Roadhouse, Ian right behind her. He swatted the door out of his way, when it slammed back on him after her.

"Hey!" he yelled impatiently when she strode over to a 1969 Camaro. It was painted an astonishingly bright lime green colour, with two white racing stripes running up and over the hood. "It's an easy question!"

She sighed. It seemed to be becoming a habit, and drummed her fingers on the roof of the vehicle. "It's not actually. Not when it comes to you."

What was that supposed to mean?

Ian didn't allow his confusion to show, as she hefted her car door open, allowing her tracking dog to hop over to the passenger seat. She watched the small companion settle for a moment, and then turned, regarding him almost ruefully. It was the first time she'd really looked at him the whole conversation.

"And Ian?" she said, the corner of her mouth twitching with what might have been a smile. "Get some sleep will you? You look like crap."

With that, she got in her car and sped away, leaving Ian standing alone on the Roadhouse porch, hands jammed in his jean pockets, with more questions than answers. As she drifted around the corner, out of the parking lot, the car sent up a shower of gravel, and he realized, once again, that he'd missed her name.

Devlyn was leaning against her counter mixing a cup of flour into the dry ingredients bowl of her cookie dough recipe. She had the radio on, blasting a country station through the small apartment kitchen. Her blond ringlets where tied up in a loose bun, and she wore a baggy t-shirt over a pair of well-loved jeans. She barely heard the sound of a pebble smacking against the window over her sink, with the volume so ear splittingly high. Abandoning her baking, and toning down the music, she went over to pry her window open and lean outside. Daniel was two stories below, head tilted back to stare up at her, a pleased smile adorning his adorably boyish face.

Winchester stalked in the distance, pouncing at gophers.

She leaned back against the sill, amused.

"'O Romeo, Romeo! Wherefore art though Romeo?'"

"'Did my heart love till now? Forswear it, sight! For I ne'er saw true beauty till this night,'" Daniel called the next few lines of Shakespeare back up to her.

She smiled. "What? No B&E this time?"

He shrugged. "Variety is the spice of life."

"Right. Of course. How silly of me," she said with a shake of her head. Turning away from the sill, she called back down over her shoulder. "I'll let you in."

She went over to her wall-mounted phone, and waited for a moment, giving him enough time to make it around to the front door, before she buzzed him through.

Then she went back to her mixing bowl.

"What're you doing?" came Daniel's curious voice, a couple minutes later, as he entered the kitchen.

"Making chocolate chip cookies for your brother's birthday," she said, whirling around to look at him, mixing spoon still in hand.

He took a seat on one of the dining room chairs, and instantly pulled his t-shirt off over his head, letting it drop to the floor.

She raised her eyebrows.

"What are *you* doing?" she countered, as Winchester began scouring the floor for dropped food at her feet.

"Nothing," he said sheepishly. "It's just a cut that's been rubbing."

"Cut?"

Taking a good look at him now, she saw the faint ringed

bruising around his neck, the red line marking his arm, and the tense shoulders and pinched forehead, that were both clear indicators of his discomfort. She dropped the spoon dismissively back into the bowl, and wiping her hands clean on her jeans, went over to him, her gentle fingers coaxing him to turn around. 'Cut' was an understatement. The gash slashed clear across his shoulder blades, and although the wound was sealed shut, it looked angry, almost like a burn.

"Do I want to know how you closed this?" she asked.

She watched Daniel's face darken with whatever memory flashed through his mind. He shook his head abruptly.

"Probably not," he admitted.

Yeah, definitely not.

"Where'd you leave Ian?" she asked instead, hoisting herself up to sit on the table behind him. She started to massage his shoulders, careful to avoid painful looking areas. Her legs wound their way around his chair to rest in his lap.

He leaned into them, his brow creasing.

"The Roadhouse. I didn't see Ruby though. What's going on?"

"She's...," Devlyn bit her lip, choosing her words carefully, "cutting back her hours. It's getting more difficult, Dan."

He shook his head solemnly.

"Hey," she said leaning down to kiss him comfortingly on the cheek. "I'm watching out for her, and I know you are too."

"Of course I am. I'm the one who got her on the 'put up a stand, and do the unexpected' bandwagon, remember?" He let out a sigh. "Do you think we're crazy?"

She shook her head slowly.

"No. Not crazy. You care, Dan. And despite what you might think, you're not the only one who wants to see a change."

He went quiet, and she knew he was mulling something over, some idea, some thought.

"You don't have to act brave around me," she promised him, leaning forward to rest her temple on his shoulder. "I know Luke's theory scares you, and I know you're worried. So am I. Just tell me where your head's at."

He let out a breath. "The way some of the Knoctes abuse their power...," he trailed off. "Half the time I think they kill more innocent people than they save. Sometimes I wonder if we do any good at all."

"A few of the people you rescue from day to day, may have an opinion on that." She closed her eyes. "I guess sometimes you got to have a little faith. Believe that there are still good intentions out there."

He turned his head to look at her, a hint of a smirk on his face. "Yeah, and the road paved with good intentions leads…"

She frowned at him, and then gave a dismal laugh. "Good people, then. You have to believe there are good people," then added, "Like you."

Daniel nodded, getting that distant, distracted look he always got whenever he grew pensive. The clockwork again.

"Come on," she said sitting up and sliding off the table. She grabbed his hand, warm and calloused against her own. "Help me make cookies. I just need to add the chocolate chips and then you can start rolling the dough."

He let her tug him to his feet, and Devlyn hoped that for a little while, they could just be themselves, two normal people enjoying one another's company, without problems and unspoken worries eating them up on the inside.

Chapter Ten

Ian parked the truck in front of the Ay Motel, slamming the door shut behind him. Recent conversations and events ran through his head endlessly, as if just by thinking hard enough he could somehow put the pieces together. It was futile though-- he knew that. He could no sooner solve the puzzle tired and brain dead as he was, than he could stare down a puzzle and make it put itself together.

He wasn't paying close attention to much of anything, as he dug out his keys and turned the lock to the room, lost in his own head. It wasn't until he hit the lights and nothing happened, that he snapped to attention. He was just reaching for the handgun in the waistband of his jeans, when the lamp flew on across the room, and someone yelled: "Light it!"

It sounded like Devlyn, and as soon as his eyes adjusted, he confirmed it. Crowded in the little motel room was not only Devlyn-- but Jim, Winchester, and Daniel. The last of whom, was frantically trying to send a sparkler ablaze with his lighter. Stacked beside his brother on the desk was a case of beer, with a large, still steaming pizza box balanced on top of it. Jim was lounging on a fold up chair that hadn't been there before, and there was another propped open beside him in what tiny space the room supplied.

"What's going on?" he demanded.

Daniel paused in his attempt, and they all gave him a funny look.

"You'd think a boy would know his own birthday when it came around," Jim grumbled.

Ian blinked. It was his birthday?

"Told you," Daniel smirked, and then with another flick of his lighter the sparkler caught, and he jammed it into the top of the pizza box. It sparked and danced, casting shadows across his face.

"Fine, I'll be the first one to say it," Devlyn said, jumping to her feet off the desk, where she'd been sitting, her legs folded under her. "Happy birthday!"

"And you can stand there as long as you'd like, with that blank expression on your face-- I'm not singing," Jim told him.

Slowly comprehension came, and Ian felt a small smile

spread across his face. "Buzz kill much?"

He watched the sparkler fizz itself down on top of the pyramid of beer and pizza. It was the best makeshift 'cake' he'd ever seen. His stomach growled audibly, and he laughed. "What? No dessert?"

"Catch!" Devlyn yelled and threw something at him. He instinctually snatched it out of the air. Looking down at his open palm, he found a baggie full of cookies-- chocolate chip.

He grinned.

They wasted no time in breaking into the pizza. Daniel passed the pepperoni slices out to everyone, while Jim cracked open beers with his teeth. No one bothered with either plates or mugs.

Ian settled his tall frame in the empty folding chair, crossing one leg over his knee, while Daniel claimed the old fashioned wood and leather desk chair. Devlyn sat perched on its armrest, wrestling with the never ending stringy cheese covering her pizza. Daniel was watching her, his face a mixture of amusement and affection, as he propped his feet on the desk, and slid further down in his seat.

Ian tossed Winchester his crust, as he watched his family with a sense of pride and protectiveness. Jim said something, and Devlyn leaned into Daniel laughing. If anything mattered most to Ian in this world, it was the people with him right now. He could avoid his nightmares and handle his past, as long as he had that one thing. He knew he wasn't the most stable individual ever recorded, but he believed he could be happy, if they were always by his side, and watching his back. They gave him hope for the future, and the feeling of moving forward. And sometimes-- that was all he needed from life.

"Ever come across a girl, with like long, bright red hair and a Weimaraner?" Ian asked Jim, the thought suddenly coming to his mind. Jim stopped his conversation to look over at him curiously.

Daniel dropped his feet from the desk, to sit forward in his chair. "The one from the subway tunnel?"

"Yeah, that one. I ran into her again at the Roadhouse. Seems like she's sticking around." He looked back over at Jim. "Know her?"

Jim scrubbed a hand over his stubbly beard. "Sounds like

Marley Shray, I reckon. Lady's her dog." He shot a look at Ian. "Don't ever make fun of her name by the way. That gal's quite a pistol when she wants to be."

This Ian knew.

"She trust worthy?" he asked.

Jim nodded. "I'd say so, long line of Knoctes that family."

"Who's her Scit?"

"Ain't got a clue. What's with the Q and A?"

Ian tilted his head back against his chair. "Nothing, never mind."

Silence fell over them, and Ian's eyelids were just starting to droop, when Devlyn eyed up the remaining bottles of beer.

"Anyone up for a little beer pong? I brought plastic cups."

As it turned out, Devlyn could be very persuasive, as they cleared and set up the desk. In the end Ian and Daniel ended up going head to head as undefeated champs. Devlyn had never really stood a chance, and Ian's insane, uncanny aim ousted even Jim's Knocte abilities. It was Daniel who finally gave him pause, with his calculating mind, and in depth knowledge of physics. Where Ian knew he had deadly aim, Daniel had infallible equations. It began to look like whoever started the game would finish it off first, and it wasn't long before Jim fell asleep, slumped down in his chair, chin resting on his chest. Devlyn managed it, watching dedicatedly through the games, nibbling on a cookie, and rubbing Winchester's belly with her feet, until he started to drool on the carpet.

Ian was the first one to call it quits, as the red cups started to blur together in his tired vision. He estimated that he'd gone about a week without more than a handful of hours of sleep, and now that he was home, he wasn't sure there was anything in the world that could keep him awake anymore. Not even caffeine, slathered in caffeine, topped with caffeine. It was exactly as Jim had always lectured them, that nothing beat a good night's rest. Coffee was only a temporary cure, like fixing something with duct tape, it wasn't meant to last, not for the long term.

As Ian collapsed wearily onto his bed, the last thing he remembered hearing was incoherent whisperings from Devlyn and Daniel's soft-spoken conversation.

He woke a few hours later with a gasp, the same nightmare that haunted him so unceasingly, fresh in his mind. Disgruntled and annoyed, he stared up at the ceiling. Light patterns danced there, and he frowned in inquiry. His eyes drifted down and across the room to where the TV was turned on and playing some late night infomercial. The sound was muted. He glanced over to Daniel's bed. He was asleep, slouched against the headboard, Devlyn tucked under his chin. Her head resting against his chest, a splash of blond curls, and her body folded into his side. A possessive arm wrapped around his torso. His brother held her to him, one arm slung around her shoulder, while the other held the remote limply at his side. Winchester was curled up at their feet, sound asleep. None of them had bothered to get under the covers before crashing.

Reaching across the small space separating the beds, Ian snatched the remote free. Turning off the TV, he threw the remote aside and fell back into sleep.

Ian didn't wake again until morning; the sound of Devlyn's exuberant screaming jolting him from sleep. He shot abruptly into a sitting position, then clocked that Daniel's bed was empty, and the shower was running.

Jim was gone too.

Groaning he flopped back down and listened to the squeal of the shower, interspersed with Daniel and Devlyn's mixed laughter. Two pairs of feet squeaked against the porcelain bottom of the tub. Winchester barked.

They brought the dog in there?

Ian wondered if it was possible to feel more tired after finally getting a decent amount of sleep. It was like as soon as his body got a little taste after being so deprived, it just couldn't get enough. He forced himself out of bed and found the coffee maker, which had been cleared onto the floor after last night's events. He plugged it in, and started a pot. Sinking into the desk chair, he stared the machine down, until it started making the good stuff.

He was just pouring himself a cup when Daniel and Devlyn stumbled out of the bathroom. Daniel had on a pair of dark jeans, and Devlyn was wrapped in a white housecoat. Ian couldn't remember if she'd left it in the room before, or if she'd brought it with her last night, but in any case, it was cinched tightly around her waist, and her hair was steadily dripping onto it. Winchester barreled between them both into the center of the room, and screeching to a halt, shook his coat out, sending a spray of droplets in every direction. Devlyn threw up her hands to fend them off, screeching with laughter.

Ian couldn't bring himself to care enough to do the same, as he was pelted with water.

"I didn't know showering was a communal event. Why wasn't I invited?" he asked taking a sip of his coffee, and staring at his brother over the rim.

Daniel shot him a dark look, but otherwise ignored him, as he wiped water off his face with the back of his hand. He sat down on the end off his bed, while Devlyn scooped her over sized purse off the floor at his feet, and started rummaging through it. His brother's hair was plastered to his forehead, the auburness of it more evident while wet. Despite his fading bruises, he looked better rested.

Devlyn found whatever she was looking for and sat behind him, her legs bent and straddled around him. Ian saw what she had then, as she dipped her fingers into it and began spreading it across the wound on his bare shoulders-- one of Ruby's concoctions.

He scowled into his coffee.

"Where's Jim?" he asked, sounding about as grumpy as he felt.

"I found him a case this morning, and he took off to grab supplies from his house, before he left on duty," Daniel answered, and then winced, glancing over his shoulder.

Stupid faerie, Ian thought. "Well he's one for goodbyes."

Daniel smiled. "Always has been," he said, and then seemed to remember something. "Hey, I was looking into one for us too, and it looks like there's a faerie out killing wealthy men. Everyone she's ever married has either ended up in the nut house, gone missing, or died. I'm guessing there's some potion at work. But you never know… It could just be a crap ton of bad luck, earning her a boat load of cash." But the shake of his head told Ian otherwise. "Either way it's worth checking into. It's just north of here."

Ian nodded, and then Jim's words drifted back to him. *I*

think it's time you start giving your undoubtful approval of this whole university idea...

"Yeah, uh…," he began, knowing even as he said his next words, it would kill him inside. "I can go this one alone. You can go to church tomorrow-- or whatever it is Dev really does on Sundays."

Normally that would have earned him a patronizing look from Devlyn, but the two of them were staring at him so incredulously, that there didn't seem to be room for much of anything other than shock.

"You're sure?" Daniel asked at last. And even though it was what Daniel claimed he wanted, Ian thought he could detect just a trace of hurt in his brother's voice.

"Dude, I'm like twenty-three now," he pushed vehemently. "I don't need a babysitter."

"Okay, all right," Daniel said, instantly backing down, and smiled uneasily. "Whatever you say."

Devlyn looked like she was seriously considering jumping in to do some damage control, but as her wide eyes regarded them both, he knew she would ultimately leave the decision with them.

"Just let me take Dev home first," Daniel said. "She has to work tonight."

Chapter Eleven

"You got your lunch? Remember your phone number?"

"You're not funny, Dan," Ian informed him.

The truck was idling in the parking lot of the Ay Motel. Daniel had one arm draped across the open window. He had to be standing on the side step, otherwise it would have been quite the stretch. Ian already had the truck flicked into reverse, the only thing keeping him from rolling away, was his foot on the brake, and he was tempted to lift it.

"Sorry," Daniel said, although Ian knew he wasn't really sorry. "Feels like I'm sending you off to school all by yourself for the first time."

So tempted.

"Bite me," Ian said with a scowl. "And what'd you do to my truck?"

He glanced over to once again eye the small screen stuck to his dashboard, and Daniel got that irritated, desperately trying to be patient look.

"It's a GPS, Ian. You hit the green button to turn it on."

"Awesome," Ian said sarcastically. "What's it doing in my truck?"

Daniel sighed. "Look. I figured since *I'm* not going to be there to be your guide and personal GPS, I'd get you a real one."

Ian did not consider the piece of plastic in front of his face, by any means a 'real one'.

"Plus you sure aren't going to kill anything if you can't find it."

Ian stared hard at the GPS, and then grudgingly stabbed his finger at the green button.

"Hello, Ian." came the halted female voice.

Ian blinked. "It knows my *name*?"

Daniel was suddenly amused. "I put it in the system."

"Right, of course you did," Ian said, with a touch of annoyance. Then something occurred to him. "Oh! Can you give her a hot accent? Like British?" He smacked the wheel suddenly. "No, wait! Australian!"

Daniel shrugged, appearing unsurprised by Ian's apparent

revelations.

"I guess." He leaned through the window to point out more buttons. "Just go to Settings, then Text to Speech, then Language."

Ian tried to follow Daniel's show-and-tell with the new toy for about two seconds, before giving up.

"Yeah, I didn't get more than half of that," he admitted, making Daniel repeat it-- several times. Partly because he needed it, but mostly just to get back at his brother for his continual insistence on the contraption. Daniel punched in the destination, and they fiddled and fought with the gadget for a few more minutes, until Ian was satisfied with the results.

"You good?" Daniel asked him, leaning back towards the truck bed, and giving Winchester a final scratch behind the ears, before he stepped down to the asphalt of the parking lot.

Ian nodded.

"Good," he agreed, and let the truck roll backwards.

"And Ian?"

He hit the brake. "Yeah?"

"See you around."

Ian struggled to put a smile on his face, as Daniel stood outside, hair hanging in his shadowed eyes.

"Be seeing you, brother."

Then he backed the truck away, feeling like somehow he was experiencing both an end and a beginning.

Daniel knocked on Ruby's front door. He usually just walked right in, but this time he'd found it locked-- which worried him. The house was a quaint little place, with a small front porch, and blue shutters over the windows. It was about the size of a town house, because that's what it was, but in the present neighborhood, its white siding and clean-cut appearance stuck out like a sore thumb. There were even baskets of flowers spinning in the breeze above his head. You had to hand it to the faerie though-- she knew how to stand out. In the run down old factory district of town, her little white house didn't go unnoticed.

Daniel knocked again. "Ruby? Come on, Bee. Open the--."

The door swung open, and Ruby was standing with a surprised and nearly panicked expression on her face. She was wearing a pencil skirt, and a loosely fitted shirt made of shiny red fabric that caused her lips to stand out.

"Dan?" She grabbed the front of his shirt, and pulled him over the threshold into the house. Slamming the door behind them, she twisted the lock. "What are you doing here?"

"Well, the last time I checked, we were still best friends."

"Yeah, but if you've been tracking the Fifth World activity lately, and I know you have, that Scitor skull of yours lives for that kind of thing, then you know this area of town is at record breaking highs."

"So what if I do?"

She made a frustrated noise in the back of her throat.

"Sit," she said, practically shoving him down into the nearest chair, a big cushy black thing with white throw pillows. Unlike the outside of her house, the inside wasn't quaint at all. Instead, it was more like modern interior design heaven. Everything was black and white with hardwood flooring. There were little splashes of colour, a red vase here, a blue picture frame there, but it was all too orderly and untouched to look lived in. Even the magazines lying around on the glass coffee table, looked strategically placed.

"What did I say to you the last time we were together?" she demanded.

Daniel sighed. "You told me you've been hearing Fifth Worlders talking about me, and that I should take Dev and run, but come on Bee, people talk about my brother and I. That's not exactly new."

Suddenly her hands clamped down on either armrest beside him, as she leaned in, inches from his face. She started talking so quickly that her words almost seemed to blur together.

"No, Dan, listen to me! It's not like before, okay? Before they would jeer loudly, making sure I heard. Now I hear your name and walk closer to investigate, and conversations stop mid-sentence. Something is wrong. I don't want you anywhere near them, all right? They're up to something, I just know it, and it's looking more and more like you're a target. You could get hurt, or worse. Just--!"

Hey, hey, hey" Daniel hurriedly cutting in, trying to ease her frantic ramblings. "I came here to make sure *you're* okay. Dev told me about cutting back your hours. So. *Are* you doing okay?"

She stared at him silently for a moment. "I'm fine."

Daniel raised an eyebrow. "Fine?"

"Okay, worried. Definitely worried," she admitted, "but I'm not just cutting back hours because of Luke's crew, I've been doing more investigating on the Fifth World side of things."

Part of him wondered if she was lying.

"Listen, Bee, you don't have to keep working at the Roadhouse. We both know that was my stupid idea, and it's only putting you in danger now. Maybe it'd be for the best if you quit, just got out of there. You're making plenty of money designing clothes, and selling faerie stuff. It'll be all right, you'll see."

Silently Ruby sank down, sitting on the footstool in front of him, and rubbed her face with her hands. "I don't really want to though-- quit I mean. The place *is* really quite beautiful. I'd miss it. Remember when we carved our initials into the side of the bar?"-- Daniel smiled. He did-- "You told me that, in a way, it made it so they could never take away our right to be there, that it was a statement announcing that we were here to stay. It's the little things like that that make it all worthwhile. There's a part of me that'd hate to walk away from all that."

Daniel pinched the bridge of his nose. He couldn't help the concern that sprang up inside him. "Just-- promise me you'll be careful."

Ruby looked him straight in the eye. He wasn't sure he'd ever seen the faerie so serious before.

"*You* be careful." She reached out and grabbed both his hands in hers. "Dan, just please, please, watch your back for me, and for Dev, and for your brother. We need you."

It was Sunday morning and Ian was lost. The good for nothing GPS kept telling him to "turn left, turn left." But all that was on either side of him was farmer's field, after farmer's field.

"Turn left, turn left!"

"Shuddup!" Ian barked. "There's nowhere *to* turn left. You want me to start cruising the fields? Is that what you want? To do some off-roading? I can show you off-roading!"

Yes, he was starting to talk to inanimate objects. Here he was, day two, and he was already going crazy. It was also likely that anyone would go crazy listening to that automated grainy voice. He hated it, and he hated that Daniel thought he could replace himself with a piece of machinery.

"You just missed your turn! Make your next legal U-turn."

"Oh, that is *it*!"

Ian rolled the window down, and angrily pried the GPS right off its perch on the dashboard, ripping the holster and everything free. He slammed the gas pedal to the floor, and watched the speedometer reach an impressive number, before pitching the gadget, with great arm strength, out the window. It bounced forcefully down the gravel road, spinning and spewing small parts. He watched the trailing wires tangle around it in the rear view mirror. The vehicle behind him swerved out of the way, and then flipped him off.

But Ian didn't care, the driver had no idea just how good that had felt.

A couple of minutes later though, when the silence started to drag on, Ian felt the smugness and self-satisfaction begin to fade. A few minutes after that, and he slammed on the brakes, sliding the truck to a stop on the side of the road. He dragged Winchester inside to sit in the passenger seat, but the dog was restless. He turned around and around in the seat, like he couldn't get comfortable, discontent with its emptiness. Eventually he dropped into it with a high-pitched whine. He exhaled heavily, his head resting on his paws, and stared up at Ian with big puppy dog eyes, that reminded Ian of the seat's usual occupant.

"I know," Ian agreed. "Worst road trip ever."

"Everything all right?" Devlyn whispered as she watched Daniel shake his head down at his phone.

"It's Ian. He's lost."

They were sitting side by side on a pew, their legs touching, as people filed in past them. The worship team played background music, all piano, drums, and guitars, as everyone tried to find a place. The church had a high ceiling, and a spreading cross that took up most of the far end behind the pulpit. The walls were painted a bright white, and the floor was laid with beige carpet. The building had brilliant stain glass windows towering on either side, giving a classic look to the otherwise modern interior. Banners hung between them, filling every inch of the place. They displayed messages like 'King of Kings' and 'Lord of Lords'. Some were just kids' handprints in different colours of paint, with their names scrawled underneath. He could tell Devlyn loved them by the way her eyes lingered.

"Want happened to the GPS you said you were going to pick up for him?" she asked.

Daniel sighed as he scrolled back up through the conversation with his thumb. "He said, and I quote: 'It died an unfortunate and very horrible death.'" Then almost as an after thought. "He *is* getting better at texting though."

"Leave it to Ian to-- hey," Devlyn started, and then paused, catching a glimpse of his face. She reached up to try and smooth the wrinkles between his eyebrows. Daniel wasn't sure if she realized she'd just made some of her own. "He's fine, Dan. Have a little faith, okay?"

Daniel snorted. "Right."

Devlyn sighed, and leaned against Daniel, her blond curls tickling his neck.

"I pray every day that you'll make it home safely, you know. Sometimes it takes longer than others, but He hasn't let me down yet. You're here, with me, right now."

He smiled slowly and brushed his lips against the top of her head. "Where I belong."

That was when the music started, and taking his hand, Devlyn pulled him to his feet beside her. Daniel closed his eyes for a moment and let it wash over him. The dips and rises. The band would begin a song, a chorus of instruments, fingers cherishing piano keys, guitar picks plucking at strings, the low thuds and high clashes of the drums. It crept in volume, sped until it was soaring high, filling every corner, a bursting release, a swelling cry. It would descend into slow vulnerable moments, raw and real, where everywhere he could here rising prayers, both in whispers and exclamations. There were moments when the front stage, band and lead alike, would stop all at once, just so you could hear the congregation ring out all on their own, filling the building with a collective song that sent shivers racing over his skin. It was all voices, young and old, every tone mixing, husky reverberation and operatic ringing, baritone and soprano. It was a choir of the great, the good, the bad, and the worse, but together it could be nothing else but pure rejoicing, a resounding voice of agreement and surrender that could only come from the very depths of the soul. Devlyn had raised a hand high above her head, stretching out to the God he knew she loved so much. Her eyes were closed, her long, fair lashes skimming her cheeks.

Beautiful.

The pastor talked of love, the need for, how it could grow and learn to open, or just as easily turn cold and hard if shut away, its rewards, and the sacrifice it sometimes required. Devlyn kicked off her flip-flops, and tucked her legs under herself as she listened.

Fingers intertwined, Daniel ran a thumb across the back of her hand. Memories of sprinklers and Macy's Golf Course danced in his mind.

And he couldn't help but smile.

Chapter Twelve

Ian splashed cold water on his face. It was running from a grimy gas station sink. Looking in the fingerprinted mirror, he wiped a streak of blood from his cheek. Winchester was drinking from his bowl, the one he and Daniel always packed on their travels for him, and the one Ian had filled with bottled water just minutes before.

He splashed water up his arms and gave his hands another thorough scrub, before turning off the taps, and drying his face with his sleeve. He'd managed to find the faerie, mostly out of dumb luck, and Winchester's supreme sense of smell, than anything else. After that the case had been relatively easy. He might be horrible with directions, but he was great with the delivery. It hadn't taken him long to take her down, though the kill had been a little more messy than he had originally planned.

He leaned back against the wall and its white painted bricks, that were more a dingy grey than white now, and just breathed for a few moments. It was the only sound other than Winchester's lapping, and the dull humming of the lights above his head. He found himself mulling over the latest case and whether or not he'd somehow made it more personal than it had been, when his cell phone went off. Winchester's head snapped up and he let out a small bark.

"Yes, thank you, I know," Ian said digging in his pockets. He didn't bother to check the number before he answered it. Anyone who called this late at night-- or early in the morning as it were, he hoped had a good reason. "Yeah?"

"Ian?! Ian, where's Daniel?!" came the reply. It was a jumble of hasty, frenzied words.

Ian unhitched himself from the wall, his posture straightening. He could tell the caller was female. A dog started barking in the background. Familiarity buzzed in the back of his mind. "Who is this?" he hissed. "How did you get this number?"

The voice came much slower this time, and more clearly. "Is your brother with you?"

Then it clicked. "Marley?" Ian asked.

There was silence for a brief second.

"Marley, I don't have time for games. Stay away from Dan and stay away from me!"

He hung up the phone abruptly, but before he could even re-pocket it, it was ringing again, loud and insistent. He swore. Answered.

"Ian, just liste--," she started.

"No. Shove off. The last time I talked to you, you told me to hit the road, and let you work your case. So work your case, Marley! And leave us out of it."

"This *is* my job!" she screamed into his ear, before he could hang up again. "You know that giant red 'X' I was talking about? I was wrong. It's not over the town, Ian, it's painted on Daniel's forehead."

Ian nearly dropped the phone. "What--?"

She made a frustrated noise in the back of her throat. "You don't have time for me to explain! If he's with you, don't let him out of your sight, if he's not-- find him! Find him right now!"

And then she hung up.

Ian was out of the bathroom and in the truck with Winchester, before he'd even fully thought about it. He hit Daniel's speed dial and waited impatiently while it rang, as he flew out of the gas station and onto the highway. The truck's rear swung out behind them, the tires skidding against pavement. The phone continued to ring uselessly.

"Come on, Dan. Answer the phone!"

Daniel's voicemail kicked in. Feeling his heart start to slam against his chest, Ian tried again.

"Come on, come on, come on."

No answer.

Slamming the dashboard with his hand, he punched in Devlyn's number. She picked up on the third ring.

"Hello?" Her voice sounded groggy, sleepy.

Ian had forgotten what time it was.

"Dev, is Dan with you?"

She yawned. "No. He walked me to work after church, but I haven't been with him since. Why? What's going on?"

Ian's throat tightened. "Nothing," he forced out. "Sorry I woke you."

"Ian, wait--."

He hung up, and tried Daniel again. Devlyn beeped in halfway, but he ignored her call. He had twenty minutes before he'd reach The Ay-- and it was going to be the longest drive of his life.

He pulled into the parking lot, slamming on the brakes in front of his busted cement parking block. The first thing he noticed was that their window had been cracked. The glass spider webbed out, distorting his reflection. He could see a light on inside, as he threw the truck door open.

"*Dan!*"

The motel room door hung slightly ajar. Winchester blew past him, shoving his way into the room, barking frantically. Ian bolted through the doorway after him-- and froze.

The place had been completely destroyed. The lamps and coffee pot were smashed. The desk was upside-down, it's legs in the air like a dead spider's, while the chair looked as though it had been swatted out of someone's way. The blinds had taken a great deal of beating, and hung crooked and dented from the one window. And these were the simpler things, the things anyone could have done. The next set of vandalism, was something not everyone could have. There were three or four parallel slashes torn through the drywall, in several locations. Claw marks. The mattress of one bed had been stood up, almost like a shield. Claw marks shredded the material of one side, exposing the springs. A bloody handprint marked the other. And covering almost every inch of the floor was a mass chaos of overlapping muddy paw prints. More claw marks dragged through the carpet. Winchester was adding more, as he ran crazed circles around the room, his barks reaching vicious and hysterical levels.

"Dan?" Ian whispered, his voice barely a breath. He stumbled into the room, shoving pieces of furniture out of his way. But no one was there. Not a soul was left to tell of what happened. He stared at the destruction around him with something like disbelief, the panic building slowly in his chest, like a spreading disease. Turning, he burst his way back outside. There wasn't a single car anywhere else in the parking lot. All he could hear was the sound of his own heartbeat in his ears, his frantic breathing, as his eyes strained to search the darkness. The rest of the world was quiet, the night still. A streetlamp on the other side of the road flickered out.

His brother was gone.

Gone.

"Dan!" he called again, his chest feeling so weighed down, that he had to fight for every breath. Regardless he forced his voice to lift, to rip through the night sky. "*DANNY!*"

Chapter Thirteen

Ruby was running. She could hear the heavy footsteps echoing after her, as she turned down a back alley. She nearly fell when her foot sank ankle deep into a puddle of water, but she pushed herself forward as the taunting voice grew louder and closer. He was after her, and he wasn't the merciful type, she knew. They were never the merciful type, the type to stop and listen to a faerie's side of the story. He was a Knocte.

She hadn't done it! She swore she hadn't done it! She hadn't even heard about that girl's death, until she'd been accused of it. But it didn't matter-- didn't matter, she was going down for it. And there was no escape. She'd reached a brick wall. A dead end. Panicked, she slapped it with all her force and all her anger. It did little good. Feeling the tears prick her eyes and run down her face, Ruby turned to face her attacker, her back pressing against the wall that blocked her freedom. His silhouette filled the entrance. He hadn't had time to acquire iron bullets, but he did carry an iron bladed knife, a malicious extension to his right arm.

She shook her head frantically. "It wasn't me! You gotta believe--."

Out of nowhere a figure dropped from the roof on one side of the alley.

He landed hard on a nearby dumpster, resting against the alley wall. His shoes hit the lid with an ear splitting metallic crash. Ruby screamed and threw herself against the opposite wall. The Knocte at the end of the alley seemed just as surprised by the intrusion as she was, his head snapping over to assess the third party. The figure rolled off the dumpster and onto his feet with a groan. He shook his head as if to clear it, and started towards Ruby. She slid down the wall to cower on the wet pavement. Her lips were quivering and she couldn't stop her hands from shaking.

"Hey!" the Knocte shouted. "The case's taken."

The stranger ignored him, as he stopped in front of her, blocking the view of the other. His hands were shoved in his pockets. "You okay?" he asked.

It took Ruby a minute to realize he meant her. Too shocked and stunned to speak, she managed a jerky nod. Standing as close as he was now, she could see his face for the first time. He looked about the same age as her, around fourteen, and had a shaggy mop of hair that hung in his eyes, which were a warm chocolate brown colour. He'd just started to extend a hand down towards her, when someone jerked him back by his shoulder, spinning him around.

"I'm talking to you," the Knocte said angrily, his face cast in shadows. "I said this case is taken."

"There's been a mistake," the stranger explained. "My brother and I-- we killed the thing that got that other girl. This one's innocent."

The Knocte frowned. "She was the only faerie around."

"She wasn't."

The frown deepened. "And I'm supposed to believe you?" he growled, his eyes running briefly up and down the intruder. "You're not a Knocte, I can tell. You have no business here. Stand aside."

The stranger shook his head and took a step back, so his heels just touched the toes of her shoes. His arms spread slightly from his sides as if to make himself a shield between her and the Knocte.

"Can't do that."

The Knocte made a malevolent noise in the back of his throat, as he sized up the situation. "I'm warning you."

The stranger stiffened slightly, lean muscles pulling taunt across his shoulders. He set his jaw, saying nothing.

Without further words the Knocte lunged, and the stranger moved to meet him. The knife slid across the stranger's upper arm, and he cried out, managing to shove the Knocte roughly to the side, as he did. A trail of blood trickled its way down his arm and he took an unsteady step backwards, almost falling over her. Ruby shot her arm out for support. He was barely steady before the Knocte came back, slamming into him again. This time they both hit the alley floor, sending up a spray of puddle water, while the knife clattered uselessly to the side. The Knocte grabbed the front of the stranger's shirt, raising a fist, but the stranger had manoeuvred enough under him that, much to the Knocte's chagrin, was able to reverse the hold. The stranger barely got a shot off, however, before the Knocte's fist connected with his jaw and he was sent splashing sideways. It quickly became clear who the stronger party was, as the Knocte pinned his opponent against the ground. He hit the stranger over and over, fist against face, again and again. Ruby could hear herself shouting, screaming, gasping through the rain.

"Stop it! Stop it!"

But no one was listening.

It wasn't until a gunshot went off, ripping into the brick wall above the Knocte's head, that all action came to screeching halt.

"That's enough!" A voice boomed.

A tall figure stood in the entrance to the alleyway, shotgun still smoking in hand. The cold superiority in his voice was enough to give the Knocte pause, and the two broke apart. The stranger looked up, recognition flickering over his bloodied face.

"You!" the voice shouted again, in a tone that was completely ice, as he stabbed the shotgun towards the Knocte, and then jerked it back over his shoulder. "Take a hike. Now. And if you ever touch my little brother again, next time --and I promise you this-- I won't miss."

The Knocte swore under his breath, and picking himself up without another word, he slid past the shotgun wielder and back into the night, retreating under the boy's heavy gaze. The tall figure watched him go for a minute, and then hastily strode over to the stranger, kicking the discarded knife out of his way in disgust as he did. The tall figure's brother, her stranger, had slid back to sit against the wall beside her. Ruby had grabbed his hand.

She didn't remember doing that.

The tall one, who she could see clearly now, and had short, brass coloured hair with blue eyes like frost, immediately clocked his brother's injury. He didn't even hesitate as he ripped a strip off the bottom of his shirt, to tie around the wounded arm. His brother winced as he received the bandage, and Ruby squeezed his hand harder. Then the older one grabbed his brother's chin, turning her stranger's face to examine the further damage.

"You idiot," he was saying. "I told you to go around."

The younger, smaller one of the two, grinned painfully, but otherwise ignored the reprimand.

Ruby watched them together for a minute, and then almost as if she couldn't help herself, asked, "Who are you?"

161

The older brother seemed to have forgotten she was there, dabbing at the younger brother's face, but her stranger turned to look at her, his head tilted back against the wall, so she could see his Adam's apple move, when he swallowed. Those gentle brown eyes of his gazed back at her.

"I'm Daniel," he said through a split lip, "and this is my brother Ian."

Ruby woke, her eyes flying open to stare at the ceiling above her head. It had been a week since Daniel's disappearance, and things were only getting worse. Devlyn was a wreck, Ian hadn't been seen since, she'd heard rumors about Jim trying to round up a Knocte search party, and she'd broke down more times than she cared to admit. The memory hit hard, making the ache deep. Daniel still had that scar on his arm, and every time she saw it, she knew she wouldn't be alive if it hadn't been for him.

And now she was failing him.

She'd tried to dig up information, tried all the connections she could think of. No one was saying anything. The lycanthropes were as quiet as ever, and she wasn't getting anywhere close to finding him. Curling on her side, she buried her head in her pillow. She felt sad. She felt useless. She only hoped the others had had more progress than she did.

Chapter Fourteen

Ian punched the dashboard. He punched it until his knuckles bled. He hadn't slept in nearly a week, his nerves were a bunch of live wires, and he'd exhausted every resource he could think of. He just needed an outlet for his fury. He hadn't stopped driving the streets, looking for Daniel, looking for a clue, looking for *anything*, and twice already he'd run himself out of gas because he hadn't been thinking about it. He couldn't convey his annoyance at having to hike to the nearest gas station with a jerry can in one hand. But what was worse, as if things could possibly get worse, were the memories invading his mind, like Daniel's disappearance had broke whatever dam they were stored behind. Scenes from their past uncontrollably flooded to the surface, seemingly drowning him as they pulled him under.

Daniel was adapting better than he was. His brother had always been the one to a quick smile, and a friendly introduction. Daniel had made friends. Ian hadn't. He didn't want to share his problems, and he didn't want to get close to anyone who was going to leave him.

As it turned out, they had no other family members that anyone had ever heard of, that could take them in after their parents' deaths. So they found themselves in a foster home.

A foster home.

It was like something out of a movie, as if they were a couple of poor, unloved boys shipped away to an orphanage, and left like trash. It was something you'd never image for yourself, something make-believe. But now it was a reality for them. And the one thing Ian hadn't been expecting was how un-lonely it was. It really did feel like an orphanage, with kids of various ages spilling everywhere. Running. Screaming. It was clear their foster family had grown accustomed to taking on others; it was a never ending flow of kids coming, and kids going. There was no time for individuals, Ian and his brother were just another couple of faces, probably just passing through. The whole experience could have been passed off as some sort of nightmarish summer camp really.

New kids almost seemed to find it fun at first, with so many others like them running rampant, but the place quickly stopped being amusing, and started feeling like a prison. You were reminded that no one you knew would ever be coming to take you home. Ever. You realized the life you knew was dead, and because of it, there was a lot of crying at night. Ian could hear it clearly through the walls of the room he and Daniel shared, like it was surrounding him. During the day you could forget, the busyness and the general hum of the place enough to get lost in, but at night when all was quiet and you were alone with your thoughts, it all came crashing back. Daniel used to be one of them. Ian would stay up all night, just staring into the dark, and listening to his little brother sniffle into his pillow, a slow spreading numbness trying to take him over with every hour passing.

Until one night, Daniel padded over and crawled onto the bed next to him. They laid side by side, barely fitting on the single bed together, as they stared up at the cracked ceiling, and started to tell stories. Anything they could remember of their parents. Anything at all.

For awhile it gave them both a small sense of peace-- until they found themselves repeating stories, having run through both their parents' existences as they could remember them.

Things grew hard again after that. Until one day, an off-duty officer, with a crisp collared shirt, walked into their foster home and singled them out.

"You Lilian and David's boys?" He asked crouching down in front of them.

They nodded mutely.

"Then I have something for you." He reached into his breast pocket and recovered two chains, each with a dog tag hanging from it. A hole cut out in the shape of a cross, was stamped right through each one. "I was given the impression that your parents wore these all the time." He held the necklaces out so they hung between him and them.

Daniel nodded, his eyes following the necklaces' gentle swing.

"Yes, sir," Ian found himself replying softly.

"After they were released from the evidence locker, I figured you might want them."

Daniel reached out and grabbed them first. Splitting the

164

two apart, he handed one to Ian carefully, like it was made of gold instead of stainless steel. Ian let him drop it into his open palm. It weighed more than it looked like it should, as if it carried more than just itself with it. Ducking their heads, they both simultaneously draped them around their necks. They glanced at each other, and in the short exchange, a silent promise passed between them, to never, ever, take them off.

"Thank you," Ian said. And he meant it.

Ian shook his head, trying to clear the memory that sent barbs of pain into his chest, but he found another scene quickly following, his mind a runaway train he couldn't seem to stop.

He was staring up at the ceiling fan of his new room. Singling out one blade, he followed it as it spun round and round. He couldn't get the image of Daniel's face out of his mind. The sheer horror that'd been written all over it.

Ian knew he was a horrible brother.

How could he have let this happen? How could he let the system split them up like this? He thought it'd been the right thing, the thing that was best for both of them. But now? Now he wasn't so sure. At the time, he'd thought that what they needed was a new, permanent family-- an adoptive family. He'd thought that even if it meant they would be apart, it would somehow fix things to have a mom and a dad again. Real ones. Ones who had time for them. That it would somehow fill the hole they both felt inside of them. But the truth was...

It wasn't fixing anything.

There was a constant jittery feeling in his gut, a worry that he couldn't soothe, and closed in by the blank beige walls of his new room, he thought he understood the cause. He didn't need new parents; he didn't need a new house, or a new life. He needed his brother. The only real family he had left. He was a fool. An idiot. And he promised himself that he would never let Daniel down like that again. Ever, ever.

He sat up on the bed, still made perfectly with crisp sheets under him, and moved to stand in front of the desk across the room. A single stationary note pad sat on it, complete with pen, like he was in a hotel, or perhaps maybe the good people living in this house knew all along, knew what was coming next. He took up the pen, and wrote a short message. A message of apology, and a message of thanks. Then he grabbed his backpack, and dismantling the screen to his window, slipped out.

The black truck sat in the driveway, towed from the hospital, and finally released from the city impound lot to be inherited by him. He pulled the keys out of his pocket. He'd never let them go. Even when the authorities and his adoptive parents had questioned him about them, he'd lied and said he'd lost them. In truth, however, they had somehow become a lifeline to everything he used to know. To him it seemed worth all the towing bills the adults kept fussing over.

When he started the engine up, he remembered the steps to get it moving, and by the time the light in his adoptive parents' window turned on, he was already backed out of the driveway. He hit the gas. And never looked back.

It took him a day. A day and part of the next night to find it-- the house that adopted Daniel. After he and his brother had been split up, both them and their adoptive parents had been given a slip of paper with the other's addresses on it, and told they could still visit, when they had the chance. Ian had folded his up carefully, and never once let it out of his sight.

Now he stood in front of the place, with its light blue siding and soccer mom mini van parked in the driveway. For the briefest of fleeting moments-- he considered turning back. But he couldn't. He just couldn't. He wasn't sure if it was courage, or selfishness that drove him towards the door, or raised his fist to knock, but he did, and it happened. The parents answered and Ian was almost taken aback, when they didn't seem surprised to see him, their faces expectant.

But of course they weren't surprised, they would have been the first place his own adoptive family would have contacted after he'd run away. What was really surprising was that they seemed relieved. Not in the 'oh good, you're safe' kind of way, but in some way personal, like a weight had been lifted.

"Ian?" The woman asked. There was a tiredness in her face that Ian thought he knew. She didn't look anything like their mother had. She had dark eyes and short black hair. It hugged her face and one half of it looked like it'd been slept on. Considering

the time of night, Ian realized it was quite possible it had been. He stepped into the doorway and out of the porch lights.

"I want to see Dan," he told them, and craned his neck to try and see over them and into the house.

The man and women exchanged glances, and Ian picked up on the uneasiness. His stomach knotted.

"What's wrong? He's okay, right? He's okay?" He shoved his way past them and into the house. They parted for him as his eyes perused his surroundings for any sign of his brother.

The woman cleared her throat, as if uncomfortable with her answering words. "He's not... good."

Ian snapped his attention back to her. "Where? Where is he?"

She hugged her arms around herself, and her husband, a thin greying man with piano fingers, reached over to draw her closer. They were nearly the same height, so their faces touched, as he rubbed her shoulder.

"Upstairs," he answered.

Ian didn't wait for further directions, as he bolted up the first set of stairs he spotted, taking them two at a time. It led to a hallway with several doors. Only one stood slightly ajar. Ian pushed it all the way open, and the door swung back, filling the dark room with enough hallway light to make out its insides.

He recognized Daniel right away.

He sat, his back ramrod straight on the end of the bed, like he didn't quite belong there, with his legs crossed campfire style in front of him. His expression was-- blank. He didn't move, didn't react, though his hair was hanging in his eyes, and someone had just busted into his bedroom. He just stared straight forward at the wall. Stared and stared. Ian felt a sickness wash over him. A deep twisting pain that had him stumbling forward into the room, without conscious thought. He fell on his knees in front of his brother.

Ian swallowed. "Dan?" he choked out.

His brother didn't even blink.

"He doesn't talk," came the woman's voice behind him, back in the doorway. Ian should have known both the adults would follow him up the stairs. "Hasn't since the moment he left the foster home. Daniel's shut himself off, to us, to the world, and I

167

just don't know what else to do." There was something like a strangled sob caught in her throat.

Ian barely even looked her way. But he got it now. They thought he could help. He was their last option.

"Danny?" he asked cautiously. Daniel's glazed over eyes haunted him, stirred something like hysteria inside him. "Hey! It's me, okay. I'm back. I'm here." He reached out, grabbing his brother's knees, and shook them gently.

Nothing.

"You remember me, don't you?" He waited for an answer. When he didn't receive one, he tried again. "Who am I, Danny?" he asked, and found himself shaking Daniel harder. "Who am I?! Come on, you know this!"

Silence.

Ian felt utter panic seize him. His breath started coming in shorter, harder gasps. No, no, no! *His mind started reeling, he was still a kid, and he didn't know much, but he did know this: He couldn't lose his brother. Not him too. Ian's head spun, searching for anything that might be enough to reach Daniel, to draw him back.*

"Remember that night? You know the one. That thing came into our house. You and me beat it! Remember that? The windows in the truck exploded." Ian was searching again. "It got you. Right here." He placed a hand over Daniel's shirt, exactly where the scars would lie beneath. He could feel his brother's shallow breathing, steady under his hand. "Danny..." his voice trained off in a whisper that was almost a whimper.

For a long moment nothing happened.

Then Daniel's finger twitched.

Ian's heart pounded. "Danny? I know you're in there! It's Ian-- your brother. You know that! Ian! Ian! Ian! Ian!"

Daniel blinked. And Ian jumped on it. He sprang up, putting his face right into Daniel's. He grabbed his brother's shoulders and shook him so hard, that Daniel's head rocked back and forth.

Someone grabbed him from behind.

"Son, I don't think--," came the man's voice, but Ian threw him off, jerking free. He didn't understand. Everything was on the line. Everything.

"Danny! I can't do this alone! I get it now, okay! I get what you're feeling! But no more! I'm not going to let it happen again! I'm here now! And I promise I won't ever, ever leave again! I promise! Ian promises!"

Ian crushed his little brother in a hug, wrapping both his arms around him. He didn't let go, just held him. Held him for a long time.

Slowly something started to happen, started to change, and Daniel's eyes began to focus, catching up with the present. Then barely a whisper, barely a crack of his lips. "Ian?"

The man and woman jumped like they'd been shot.

Ian felt like crying his relief. "Yes! Yes, it's--," he started to say, quickly degrading into a mess, as Daniel snapped to life.

His younger brother threw his arms around him so fast, hugging him back so fiercely, that it was like being trapped in a vice. Daniel's grip was so hard, so firm, and desperate, that it didn't feel like it could have belonged to the boy that was him, not two seconds ago. His fingers dug into Ian's shirt, like they would tear right through.

Ian found himself saying the same words again and again. "I'm sorry. I'm sorry. I'm so sorry."

"Ian," Daniel cried into his shoulder. "You found me."

"I'm so sorry."

Ian was getting them out of here. They'd run. He didn't know how they'd do it, had no idea how they were going to survive on their own, but he was going to get them out. All that was important was that they be together again. All they would ever need was each other. If they had that, if they had that one small thing, then everything else would be all right. Because nothing else could compare.

"I'll always find you," Ian promised. "Got that? Always."

Devlyn rapped on the truck's passenger side window. She could see Ian sitting inside, his forehead pressed against the steering wheel, his eyes shut. It took him a long time to lift his head and notice her. He looked at her for the span of several seconds before hitting the unlock button. She pulled the door open and settled quietly beside him. She could see Winchester sleeping stretched out in the back seat, one of his legs hung in the air twitching. Silence stretched out between them.

"Any luck?" Devlyn asked into the stillness. She had to know if he knew something.

Ian sighed, all the air seeming to leave him at once. He gave a stiff shake of his head.

Devlyn kicked off her shoes and pulled her legs up against her chest on the seat. Feeling small, she wrapped her arms around them, resting her cheek against her knee. "Me neither. I only managed to find you, and I'd hoped… I mean I thought maybe…" she let her expectations trail off lifelessly.

More silence followed. Ian's eyes started to droop, only managing to stay at half-mast. He reached forward, fumbling for the thermos that lay across the top of the dashboard. A muscle worked in his jaw, as he screwed off the top. He went to fill the mug sitting in the cup holder, but when he upended the thermos over it, nothing came out. He closed his eyes in defeat, and then just let the thermos drop from his fingers to the floor. It rolled into the passenger's side, where her feet should have been, and he pinched the bridge of his nose briefly in a show of frustration.

"You move like him you know," Devlyn found herself saying, realizing she'd been watching him intently, watching him for any little bit of Daniel he could give her. "Or maybe he moves like you, I honestly don't know anymore."

She didn't think she could leave Ian now, not until Daniel was back, not until they found him. She was like an addict that needed her fix.

Ian turned and just looked at her, like his face was too tired to make an expression.

"I told him that once. He laughed it off, but it's true." She sighed, and looked up towards the roof of the cab. "I keep having these dreams about us. Me and him. Before." Her words came out a little more strangled than she meant them to. "About the day I gave him those." She pointed to the string of beads folded over and dangling from the rear view mirror. "Our first official date. Sprinklers."

"Don't," Ian suddenly snapped. "Don't do this."

Devlyn gave him a cautious, but questioning look. Really she was just glad he had said anything at all.

"Don't talk about him like he's already dead."

His words were like a slap in the face. She pressed the heels of her hands against her eyelids, willing to stay in control of herself. Her bottom lip started to quiver, and she bit it to make it stop.

"I'm trying. I'm trying not to think-- I'm hoping, and praying, with every ounce of me. And I'd do anything, *give* anything--." Her words choked off.

"Yeah," Ian said. "Trust me. I get it."

Chapter Fifteen

Marley's heels echoed off the sidewalk as she wandered around the old factory district of town. She was tired. Tired of being ignored and tired of having her calls go unanswered. Lady trotted along at her side, looking up at her every so often, as if wondering where they were going, wondering about a course of action. But there wasn't one. There was no plan.

Except find trouble.

"Just tell me where he is!"

These days it didn't take long.

Marley pulled a gun out of her boot, and kept it close as she rounded the corner into an alley. There were two faeries standing toe to toe. She could tell what they were by the translucent streaks in their hair. One was a short female, with dark hair streaked blue and gold, her eyes a stormy grey that seemed to be turning in an angry torrent. The other was a tall male, with a lanky build, and a deep translucent gold tinting his otherwise sandy blond hair. The girl had her hands balled in the front of his shirt, and he was pressed against the wall of a building. It had been her voice Marley had heard.

"Forget it. You're too close to this, Ruby," the man replied.

"Exactly! He's a person, Lou-- my best friend. He's not some toy you can just--."

That was when they noticed her.

Ruby took a hurried step back, dropping her hold on Lou and folding her hands behind her back, almost like she was ashamed of her actions.

"Well, well what's all the fuss about here?" Marley asked, and then watched Ruby's expression fall, clearly realizing she was in the presence of a Knocte, and not a friendly one.

"She's just sore about Daniel Browning's disappearance," the one called Lou smirked. He said it like a joke, and for most Knocte's, Marley realized, it probably would have been funny. Too bad he'd picked the wrong Knocte, one who didn't appreciate his kind of humor.

She gave him a heated glare. "Really? Well, I happen to be *Ian* Browning's friend" --okay, she had to admit that was a stretch, but it was worth it to watch the smirk die on his face-- "so I think I understand, just a little, where faerie girl here is coming from." She pulled her gun up, suddenly leveling it with Lou's head. "So you're going to answer her question. Where is he, Lou?" She made a point of sneering his name, like it left a filthy taste in her mouth.

Ruby's hands had fallen to her sides, her lips parted in surprise. Silence followed, as Lou seemed to deliberate Marley's intentions. His eyes held on hers, searching, and she tried to keep all emotion off her face, preventing him from reading into anything. But he saw it. The one thing she'd hoped he wouldn't. If she was team Daniel, then she wasn't on Luke's band wagon, and if she wasn't on Luke's band wagon...

"I don't know," Lou said carefully, deciding his answer. His hands were slightly raised in a falsity of surrender. "And you won't kill me-- because you can't prove it otherwise."

It really was, internally painful sometimes, being on the good side.

Slowly Marley lowered the gun, shaking her head with irritation.

"He's right," she said regrettably, glancing at Ruby, who was looking about as deflated as a dead party balloon.

Lou let his hands drop to his sides, the smirk quickly beginning to make its way back onto his face. He'd just begun to say something, just begun to open his unhelpful mouth, when she spun around and brained him with the butt of her handgun. She'd moved so fast, he hadn't seen it coming. She felt it connect with his skull, and he stumbled back against the wall, falling clumsily to the sidewalk, where he lay blinking in surprise. Marley blew red hair out of her eyes, and kicked his leg out of the way, as she moved to crouch down in front of him. He stared at her in shock, as she slowly, mockingly, fixed his lapels one by one. As she smoothed them out, Lady leaned over her shoulder and growled into his face. Saliva dripped onto his cheek.

"For the record," she said, "exploiting character weaknesses in the good guys, is never a genius plan, if your sorry hide is ever in need of saving one day." She patted his cheek a little harder than necessary, and then straightened, turning to face Ruby. With every seriousness she said, "I think we need to talk."

They waited while Lou picked himself up. Then cringing

under the belittling look that was all Marley, he staggered out of sight. The moment he was out of view, Marley turned to Ruby again.

"He's a dick," she informed her, tucking her handgun away into the back of her jeans.

Ruby almost smiled. "Always has been."

Marley cut to the chase. "I'm going to take a leap of faith here, and assume that if I told you I have a way of finding Daniel, you'd want in on it."

Ruby paused, bemusement leaking into her features. She gave a slow, untrusting nod, but her eyes gave away her interest and her desperation, the little specks of light in them shining through the grey.

"Being a faerie, you're good at that sort of hocus-pocus crap, right?" She didn't wait for an answer to that. "Well how do you feel about truth serum? Think you could swing it?"

Ruby's shoulders took a noticeable slump. "You're talking chemistry." Then half to Marley, and half just muttering to herself, she said, "Why does everyone think just because I'm a faerie that means I've got a degree in science? I have more of what people call an artistic eye for detail."

Marley frowned. "Don't you make--?"

But the faerie cut her off. "Organic ointments do not involve test tubes and beakers," she said angrily, and then took a wary step back, seemingly worried that her sudden burst of frustrated abrasiveness would draw anger. When it didn't, she continued. "I dabble more in plant leaves and certain choice oils-- and even then most of my knowledge comes from old recipe journals passed down to me by my mother and grandmother."

"You're saying I've wasted my time?"

"I'm saying," the faerie sighed, and ran her fingers through her translucent hair, "that I would need a recipe as well as access to whatever ingredients are necessary."

"We need a stocked lab."

Ruby gave a humoring shrug. "If that were possible then we might have something to talk about. One thing faeries *are* good at is tweaking recipes we do get our hands on. Once I have a general idea of what I'm doing, I might be able to lend one or two things of my own."

"It's a start," Marley decided. "Don't happen to know any chemist faeries do you?"

"A couple," Ruby admitted, then shook her head. "But I can't get a peep out of anyone lately, never mind access to a laboratory." They both stood pondering silently for minute. "How about you?" the faerie ventured. "Any Scitor chemists you have contact with?"

"No," Marley found herself answering somewhat bitterly. "Unfortunately, my best guy only returns my calls when he feels the need to drop enigmatic hints or give ominous warnings." She waved the thought away. "But it doesn't matter, he's been off the professional chessboard for sometime now." Pensively she reached down to scratch behind Lady's ear. "We're going to have to get creative."

"Creative... how?" Ruby implored.

"Nice joint," Marley noted as she stepped into the medical research laboratory. The room was incredibly white; white worktables, white cupboards, white machines, like they had something to prove about their sterile nature. "Looks... clean."

Glen slipped in behind her, taking a moment to look down the hall they'd come from both ways, before closing the door securely behind them. He turned to look at her then, running a hand through his side-swept brown hair, and offered up a shrug. "Sure. I wouldn't put a UV light to it though."

Marley let out a laugh, and smoothed out her green dress. It was a form-fitting thing with a steep 'V' neckline. The straps stretched over her shoulders and followed her spine down, ending in a bow at her lower back. It was short—dangerously so. And although it wasn't consistent with her usual attire, desperate times were calling.

"So, what brought you to Albion?" Glen asked, catching up to her. Marley had learned both Glen's name and his helpful medical background at the little Knocte bar called Albion he'd spoke of. She'd scoured out many locations like it over the last several days, but finally in Vancouver she'd stumbled upon the jackpot.

"Business," she said elusively.

He nodded. "Looking for a case? Or already on the job?"

175

"Umm," she blew strands of red hair out of her eyes, and made a noncommittal gesture. "It's actually…" *What? A mission to procure ingredients? Hopefully from you?* She suddenly felt the conversation was delving into a dangerous topic and made a split second decision. She stepped up to him, and draped her arms around his neck, "personal business."

Glen's eyebrows nearly shot up to his hairline. "I see," he said unevenly. "A little time off then?"

Marley leaned in closer, purposely putting their lips in dangerous proximity. "Something like that," she said in a low voice, and then broke away. "So," she continued, as if she hadn't just baited him, "Are you going to give me the tour? You promised you'd show me around."

His brown eyes followed her as she moved backwards, and he had to clear his throat before answering.

Hook, line, and sinker.

"Right, yes, the laboratory," he said, and hurriedly stepped after her.

He gave her a brief run down of the place, including the machines they used and the layout. She pretended to absorb the information with interest, but it wasn't until he pointed out a particularly large storage closet that she really began to take note. She couldn't help noticing it was securely locked. A brief scan of the room told her that the key wasn't just hanging from a peg on the wall either. She wondered if Glen had one on his person somewhere, and was just trying to remember if he had other keys on his keychain besides the one used to get them into the room, when Glen's voice broke through.

"Marley?"

"Hmm?" she said, and then noticing his inquisitive face, quickly tried to catch up with the present. What was the last thing she remembered him saying? "Sorry, I was just thinking about the…" she pointed vaguely at the machine that now sat across the room from them, "Magnetic… Spectro…"

"The Nuclear Magnetic Resonance Spectrometer?" Glen said helpfully.

She snapped her fingers at him. "Yes! That. Fascinating."

His brow furrowed slightly in puzzlement. "Yes, it is rather good for determining the structure and properties of--."

"Yes, I know," Marley broke in dismissively, even though it was a complete lie, and before he even had time to process it, she was continuing, "but I have a question about something else actually."

He blinked. "Okay…"

"Do you happen to know anything about truth serum? Say, a recipe?"

He laughed. A near snorting, scoffing laugh that subsided quickly when he realized she wasn't joking. He forced his face into a more stoic expression before repeating: "Truth serum?"

"Yeah, you know, like Pinocchio's nose, but more effective."

He crossed his arms and leaned back against the island lab table. "I'm not sure any truth serum would be more effective. What are we talking about here? Scopolamine? Sodium amytal? Sodium Pentothal?"

Marley didn't miss a beat. "Whichever is better."

He rubbed the back of his neck. "They're basically all barbiturates meant for sedation or hypnotics. We're likely to have some Sodium Pentothal around here, though its use as a general anesthesia has become rather dated. As for a recipe… we probably have a product information sheet for it-- but why?"

Marley shrugged. "Just a thought for futures cases."

"I wouldn't really suggest it," he said truthfully. "It's not the most reliable of techniques-- if it's a working technique at all. Unless you have some sort of magical fix-all."

Marley smiled. *I have a faerie. Close enough.* "You'd be surprised what I have up my sleeve."

"That," he said somewhat coyly, "I can believe." He took an adventurous step closer, and it was then that she noticed the split ring of his keychain poking out of the pocket of his jeans.

Taking hold of the collar of his blue button-down shirt, she yanked him roughly towards her, crushing their lips together. He was so startled at the abrupt nature of the act that he stood awkwardly for a moment, with his hands slightly lifted in surprise. She could almost hear the click when his brain finally kicked into comprehension, and his hands went around her waist. He tried to pull her towards him, but she dragged him back towards the island lab table instead, where he lifted her onto it. She felt his fingers run up her legs, as she let hers venture lower, brushing the keychain in his pocket. She'd just hooked her finger around the split ring, when he took a sudden step back, breaking the lip action. The motion pulled the keys free, and they stood staring at each other-- Marley with his set of keys and Glen with her pocket pistol.

She cursed herself inwardly, suddenly regretting her choice to wear a thigh holster.

Glen looked down at the small pistol in his palm, back up at her, and then narrowed in on the keys in her hand. "Why do I get the feeling you might have ulterior motives for wanting to see the laboratory?"

She considered trying to lie her way out of the situation for only a split second before dropping the act. "Oh, please, like you didn't have any."

He was visibly taken aback, and she could see him attempt to compose himself before answering. "There are security cameras." He warned, seeming to remember that she was a Knocte, and he a Scitor. "And I have your gun."

She gave him a condescending look. "I could have that gun out of your hand before you figured out how to turn the safety off. And call me crazy, but something about our late night lab visit has me assuming that we're not actually supposed to be here. You're not sweating it too hard though," she observed. She slid off the table, carefully moving to stand in front of him again. "Scits are good with computers. Something tells me you had every intention of fixing the little security camera problem, and perhaps the computer login record while you were at it." She stretched her hand out in between them, silently asking for the gun.

He didn't surrender it right away.

She stared him down. "If I was here to kill you. I would have done it already."

With a sigh that moved his shoulders he put one hand up in a sign of good will as he slowly passed off the pistol to her.

"Thank you," she said, not unpleasantly, as she returned it to the thigh holster.

His hands dropped to his sides, and she thought she could see his initial panic begin to give way to a Scitor's curiosity. "So why *are* you here?"

"I told you. Truth serum. It doesn't supply itself."

"So you thought you'd sucker me into just handing it over?"

"More or less."

That seemed to strike a nerve. "Great. Just perfect," he muttered with evident sarcasm. She watched as be began to pace slightly. "My job's not exactly easy, you know. I get called in to observe autopsies from some of the 'weird' bodies-- the question mark cases, so I can help determine cause of death. And, I mean, you try to keep your job with the Government Division of the Supernatural breathing down your neck, ordering you to conceal the truth, even as you're supposed to be searching for it. The G.D.S agents are not exactly the kind of people you want on your tail all the time. I should have a degree in lying not medicine. Not that anyone would believe me if I really told them how half the people I'm called in to see really died—I'd end up losing my job anyway."

Marley wasn't interested. "Your job's rough, I get it. But it's your real job, you know, the *Scitor* one that I'm more interested in. You have a Knocte in front of you who needs all the help she can get."

"So far you've toyed with me *and* tried to rob me. Why would I help you?"

"Because…" The conversation wasn't going anywhere, and she silently resigned herself to the need of a little confession. "A friend of mine's gone missing, and I need to find him."

Glen wasn't moved. "Knoctes disappear for days at a time. He or she is probably on a case that's taking longer than anticipated. That hardly warrants the necessity of truth serum."

"He's a Scit actually. And believe me, I know one or two people he would never keep in the dark. About anything."

Glen looked skeptical. "A Scitor?"

"Yes," she snapped impatiently. "And I crossed a province, over mountainous terrain, to be standing this close to someone who can help me. I'm not leaving without what I came for."

Glen was still hung up on something else she'd said. "All this trouble… for a Scitor? If you don't mind my asking… You're a Knocte. Why do you care so much?"

She weighed her options for a minute before she spoke carefully. It was possible she could use his curiosity to her advantage. "If I tell you, you'll agree to help me?"

Just as she'd weighed her options, she felt his brown eyes studying her, measuring her for what her information might be worth.

"All right," he agreed at last, and taking a step back, crossed his arms over his chest. "Why the concern then?"

Despite her offer, she spoke rigidly. "I'm repaying a debt to an old friend. Finding a missing buddy of his seems like a small price to pay."

"That must be some debt."

She gave a short humorless laugh. "You have no idea. And I pay my debts. But truth is… for him, well, for him I'd have helped anyways. Some things you do, you owe as favors, others you do because you find the person's worthy of your help."

She thought he'd press the topic further, but instead he said, "And this missing Scit, your buddy's friend. Who is he?"

She stiffened. "It's not my name to give out."

He scowled. "I'll tell you another thing about Truth Serum. The working stuff is not only hard to come by, but it's not free either."

"Daniel," she said reluctantly, but twirled his keys around her finger as a small reminder that she still possessed them. "Daniel Browning."

His eyes widened. "Like the Browning brothers, Daniel Browning?" She frowned, and as if guessing her silent inquiry Glen said, "Their reputation does precede them. If one of them has gone missing, they're leaving an awfully large shoe to be filled."

The key twirling stopped. "Yeah, well, he can refill it himself when we get him back."

"We?"

She stepped closer so he felt the weight of her gaze looking down on him. "Enough. The goods. Now, please."

He seemed to debate with himself over whether or not to push her for further information, but in the end he simply held out his hand and said, "Keys."

She didn't hesitate as she slapped them back into his palm.

"Thank you," she said genuinely, as he moved towards the supply closet.

His back was to her, so she couldn't read his face as he

turned the key in the lock and said, "I heard there was talk of a war against Fifth Worlders…"

"A little more than talk I think."

He disappeared into the closet, but his voice carried back to her. "Any idea what side the Brownings are on? When you succeed in your rescue mission that is."

"Depends on which brother you ask."

Wordlessly, he reemerged from the closet, a container of yellow powder in one hand, and a sheet of paper that looked like it had been torn out of something in the other.

"And you?" She asked, hurriedly taking the spoils from him. "If you had to pick a side."

Glen hesitated, just long enough for her to notice his sudden caution, before he proceeded. "I'm a Scitor," he stated as if it was an answer in itself, then must have felt the need to elaborate when she showed no comprehension, because he continued. "If Knoctes start thinking they can go after whoever they want, then soon they start thinking maybe they don't need a Scit anymore. Why hire someone who's going to take time being choosy about the targets they research." He seemed to begin to say something more, then stopped.

She waved him on encouragingly.

Spit it out, brain boy.

He complied but not before rubbing a hand against the back of his neck. "I've been heavily engaged with a research project recently involving Fifth Worlders, or rather newly changed Fifth Worlders, and more specifically their memories. And from what we've come to find, there *are* instances where Fifth Worlders never regain any memory of who they were before they were changed. This is where the lines might get blurred, because as a result, these creatures run on pure instinct, the raw energy of wolf or vampire, or whatever. But the ones that do remember-- they're no different than you and me… cognitively. They're perfectly rational beings. It's true some still choose the life of a Night Child, but for the same reasons an Innocent might choose a life of crime. The only difference being, one race is supernaturally charged to do a lot more damage. But academically speaking, there is no evidence supporting that all Fifth Worlders become Night Children, in fact, quite the contrary."

"It does explain why some of the Fifth Worlders we come across are slobbering disasters and others want to have philosophical debates," Marley mused, susceptibly.

Glen's smile was pleased. "Precisely. And succinctly put."

The information was definitely something she could find useful, and she carefully filed it away, but she hoped it wasn't the only useful information she'd walk away with. She held up the piece of paper he'd given her. "These the instructions?"

He nodded. "The powder's hygroscopic so keep it dry and store it at room temperature. The sheet let's you know the solubility and dosage as well, for when you're ready to use it."

She gave the page a once over, flipped it to insure there was nothing hiding on the back, and then nodded her approval. "Thank you." He gave her a half-hearted smile in return, jamming his hands in his pockets. "I guess this is where I take my leave."

"Yes, I guess so."

Marley found herself hesitating in awkward silence for a moment, and then moved past Glen in the direction of the door. Before she'd taken more than three steps, he called after her.

"Marley." She turned back around to see Glen pulling his wallet out of his back pocket. He retrieved what looked like a business card, and held it out to her. "If you're ever in the area again and need a case..."

"Thanks, but I have a Scit," she said automatically, but she reached out to take his contact information anyway.

"You never know."

"No," she admitted, "I guess not."

On a whim she stepped up and gave him the briefest of grateful pecks on the cheek. Then without further ado, she exited the way she came, leaving him to his erasing duties. She stored the card in her bra as she headed towards new prospects, and a change of clothes.

It had taken her three long, sleepless days, but Ruby was sure she'd gotten it right this time. She filled a syringe with the yellow tinted liquid and gave it a flick. She'd hardly believed it the day she'd answered her door to find Marley on the doorstep, leaning against the frame, a cocky smile on her face. The leather clad Knocte had waved their newest hope flauntingly under Ruby's nose. From there, Ruby had dug deep to make this thing work, pulling up old family journals and taking advantage of multiple search engines, until she'd found confidence enough to make an attempt. She hadn't wanted to risk wasting their entire product in trials.

Her eyes went to where Marley was lounging nearby, stretched out on the loveseat in the drawing room. Her long legs dangled over the armrest and the throw pillows had been tossed out of her way, littering the floor around her. Lady pushed and chased them around on the hardwood floor, whining enthusiastically. Marley was so engrossed in her book that she barely seemed to notice Ruby as she came up beside her.

"It's ready," she said fingering the needle again. "It's going to work this time. I'm sure of it."

Marley said nothing, her eyes never leaving the page of her book, as she swept her brilliant red hair over one shoulder, and tilted her neck to the side, exposing its bareness. Swallowing hard, Ruby tried to ignore the three other puncture marks there, now left to bruise, as she quickly cleansed a spot next to them. Marley did little more than blink in reaction, as the needle slid into her skin.

Ruby hated being rushed like this, it was an absolute law of hers, that she never tested on a human unless she was one hundred percent certain of the outcome. Circumstances had changed, however, and they were quickly running out of time. They both knew it.

Ruby set the emptied syringe aside, and Marley retreated her legs to make room for her on her own sofa. Only when Ruby was settled, did Marley put her book down.

"How do you feel?" Ruby asked.

Marley shrugged.

"Okay…" Ruby sighed uneasily. "Ready?"

Another shrug. Lady plopped a throw pillow on Marley's lap and Ruby watched her toss it idly over her shoulder. It skidded into the kitchen, and Lady went bounding after it.

"Are you really friends with Ian?"

Marley gave her a curious look, as if reading into any hidden reasons behind the question. "No," she said finally, and gave a harsh laugh, "but I do know him-- sorta."

"How'd you meet?"

"What is this? An interrogation?" Marley asked unpleasantly. Ruby said nothing, just waited. Marley sighed heavily. "Him and Daniel" --to her credit, she didn't even pause on the name-- "intercepted one of my cases. They basically job blocked me, tried to push me around, and then saved my life by preventing me from walking into a whole clan of vampires." Her speech had been fluent enough, but after she'd answered, she blinked in surprise, and then frowned, like she hadn't quite meant to phrase it that way.

They were getting closer.

"What's your name?"

Marley gave her a patronizing look. "You think I'm going to lie about my name?"

"Try," Ruby prompted. "We can't test if this works, unless I know whether you're lying."

"Fine," Marley said tiredly. "Ca-- Li-- T-- …Marley."

Bingo.

They looked at each other with wide eyes, and then Marley, calm and collect, like she hadn't doubted the outcome the entire time: "We got it."

Chapter Sixteen

Refusing to waste anymore time, they left immediately, Marley only taking a few minutes to stock up on what she considered necessary supplies. Those of which contained mostly weapons. The sheeting rain that now crashed down around them, hardly seemed to matter with the weight of the new discovery they carried. Lady snapped at the droplets disdainfully, as the threesome lurked their way through the streets of the old factory district.

After only a couple minutes of this, Ruby couldn't help scorning her choice of attire. She was wearing her red sparkly flats, the ones that made her feel like Dorothy from the Wizard of Oz, and they kept filling with water, every step she took. It was warm enough that she didn't need a jacket, but her clothes were so completely soaked, that they clung to her form, restricting her every movement. She found herself jealous of Marley's heeled boots and leather jacket, which sent the rain peeling and sliding neatly off of it. Their hair, at least, was in the same unfortunate state, plastered to their face and dripping under the weight of the water.

A noise, like the sound of a tin can being kicked into the gutter, brought Ruby out of her compare and contrast session. Looking ahead, she knew Marley had heard it too. She'd stopped walking, standing perfectly still and silent, a hand reaching into the pocket of her jacket. Lady's ears were pricked forward at her side, one twitching slightly as if to catch the noise again. That was when they heard the sound of laughter, echoing off abandoned buildings, and mingling with the soft patter of falling rain. Marley made a motion for Ruby to wait, as she crept closer, flattening herself against the wall of the alley they'd been walking down. Two figures passed by on the main street, their shadows briefly falling over Marley, though their eyes never once noticing her. Even from where she was, Ruby could tell none of them were Lou, and her hopes instantly died. For all she could tell, they were just a group of Innocents. Marley let them walk by, and Ruby thought she'd had similar notions, until she pulled something out of her jacket. A sling shot. She dug in her pocket for its counterpart and came up with a handful of what looked like little silver balls. Curious despite herself, Ruby ventured forward enough that she could see, as Marley took aim and let one fly. What, in fact, *was* a real silver ball connected perfectly with the back of one of the figure's heads and slid down his shirt collar. He jumped like he'd been shot. Giving a hoarse scream, he danced on the sidewalk, tearing at his clothes like they were burning him alive, until the silver ball fell free and rolled pathetically into the gutter. Ruby instantly glanced back over at Marley, who nodded knowingly and mouthed the word *lycan*.

The lycanthrope whirled around, and Marley's arm instantly shot out, sweeping Ruby forcefully against the wall beside her, and out of the light of the nearest streetlamp. The lycanthrope hastily searched his surroundings for a tense minute, finding nothing. He gave one of his companions a nudge, and the team moved away more quickly, casting anxious looks over their shoulders. They knew, right well, that they were being watched.

Marley turned to look at her, holding up a finger. One. They only needed one of them. Then she tore down the street after them, a deadly, silent streak of red hair. Lady went with her, her paws padding lightly on the concrete of the sidewalk.

Using what speed she was given as a faerie, Ruby raced after them, pushing to try and keep up. She had to fight to keep her flats on her feet. Why she wore the stupid shoes anyway, she still didn't know. Runners would have been the practical choice-- though she'd never really been the practical type had she? Ahead, the lycans broke apart, and Marley stayed the course, following the one she'd hit with her sling shot earlier. Watching them turn down a back road, Ruby veered off. She knew this part of town better than anyone, and she knew where that road headed. She planned to head him off, and as she'd expected, she beat him to the end. He was a couple of strides away from freedom, when Ruby threw herself out in front of him, her arms thrust out ahead of her.

"Stop!" she screamed.

The lycan started, and planted his feet so fast that he skidded forward and tripped onto his hands and knees. He didn't try and get up. Ruby could see Marley closing in, her leather jacket flapping out behind her as she ran. Then a cracking sound, like the snapping of dry twigs, brought her attention back down to their victim. His face was gritted in pain, and the bones of his shoulders jerked under his skin. Ruby immediately realized what was happening.

"Marley!" she yelled in a panic. "Marley, he's trying to shift!"

"Lady!" came Marley's responding command, cutting through the night.

The dog leaped forward, colliding with the lycan, her teeth sinking into shirt and skin. He gave a cry of surprise, as he rolled onto his back, his arms thrown up to protect his face. He wasn't trying to shift anymore, his instincts forbidding it. While he was shifting, he was helpless, and being under attack didn't leave him much room for vulnerability.

Then Marley was there, holding a silver bladed knife over his throat with one hand, and digging in her pocket for the needle with the other. She found it and pulled off the protective rubber stopper with her teeth. She motioned for Lady to get out of her way, and then tilting his head up with the flat of her blade, plunged the syringe viciously into his neck. Ruby could hear the knife hiss against his skin. He gave a gurgling sound and Marley pulled back, getting to her feet. She stood over him, her shadow casting him in the dark.

"Looks like it's your lucky day," she told him, a thrilled, adrenaline filled smile on her face. "You just became our new Pinocchio."

He coughed and pulled himself into a sitting position, dislodging rain droplets from his dark hair as he did. "I don't know what you mean."

"No," Marley said shooting Ruby an amused smile, "I suppose you don't."

Ruby couldn't hold back any longer. Wrapping her arms around herself she stepped forward into his line of sight.

"Please," she begged him, "where's Dan? I mean Daniel, Daniel Browning. Where is he?"

"Who?" the lycan asked innocently.

"I highly suggest against playing coy with us," Marley said flatly. "You'll come to find, very shortly, it won't work all that well."

He gave her a heated look, and propped one arm over his knee. "I don't know where they're leaving him," he said finally.

Ruby and Marley exchanged glances, and then Ruby was right in front of him, crouching down, hunched over against the rain.

"Leave him? What do you mean *leaving* him?"

He didn't answer. Pressing his lips together, he strained against the invasive liquid inside him.

"Talk," Marley ordered, her silver knife twirling menacingly over her fingers. "Or I'll find the right puppet strings to pull, and make you talk."

He cried out in a sudden burst of frustration. "Look! All I know is that they were going to drop him off somewhere where he would be found. Somewhere around here, close to someone who knows him."

The knife stopped twirling. "Then what was the point of all this?" Marley demanded. "What was the point of this whole charade, if you're only going to let him go?" Her eyes narrowed. "What did you do?"

He clenched his teeth together so tightly, Ruby could hear them grinding. "We--." He clutched his head, gripping his hair in an effort to remain silent.

Marley had just taken a threatening step forward, when he sprang unexpectedly to his feet, and made a break for it. He moved so fast, they weren't left with much time to react. Marley shot forward, about to tear after him again, but Ruby scrambled to grab her jacket before she got too far.

"Let him go," she said. "I'm the only friend Dan has in this area, Marley. It has to be me! He has to be close to my house somewhere!"

Marley's eyes snapped back to regard her briefly, and then shifted to follow the lycan's retreating figure once more. "He knows something he's not telling us. We should follow him."

"We know where Dan is!" Ruby protested. "I don't know about you, but the reason I went to all this trouble was to find *him*. I'm not about to put that off! For anything! So with or without you…" She spun on her heels and took off in the direction of home.

It wasn't long before her pace quickened, and then as if she couldn't help it, she was running again. But this time it was different. It wasn't like before, when she'd been trying to keep up with Marley. This time she tore through the streets blind to everything except one thought. Daniel. He was within reach. She just had to push a little harder, search within the parameters of her house, and she could do it, she could find him. Every slap of her feet that brought her back closer to her house, was like a healing remedy, every labored breath that drew her closer, was hope. She could feel the relief starting to build inside her, getting ahead of itself, as she looked down alley after alley. She wiped the dirt off old factory windows to peer inside at their dank, musty insides. She felt like she was checking things off a list, and at every turn it neared its end. It wasn't until she paused in front of an alleyway a block from where she lived-- did all those feelings come crashing down through the floor.

Lying crumpled and unmoving in a puddle of muddy water, was a body-- but a body she'd know anywhere. She felt rooted to the spot. A strand of wet hair hung in her face, but she couldn't bring herself to brush it back. She hadn't realized Marley had been following her, until she was at her side, staring down at the still form with her. After all their searching, Ruby couldn't even bring herself to move another step further. Fear had dug its claws in so completely. She didn't want to see. She didn't. But she couldn't look away.

Knowing it was up to her to make the next move, Marley pulled her phone out of her pocket and dialed a recently familiar number. She stood shifting her weight, while it rang-- then it hit voicemail.

"Hang it all, Ian!" she muttered loudly in frustration. She hadn't been able to reach him since the day Daniel went missing. Now was no exception.

"What's Devlyn's number?" she asked Ruby.

Ruby wasn't listening. She'd spaced out. Marley snapped her fingers in front of the faerie's face, and Ruby slowly turned to regard her, pale and ashen. Marley repeated the question. It took another couple of tries, but she finally pulled out the answer she needed, and dialed that number too.

Devlyn picked up on the second ring.

"Hello?" Funny how one word could be so quiet and broken.

189

"We found him."

Marley was leaning against the corner of the alley, not quite inside of it, but not quite outside of it either. She couldn't see much in the dim, old and worn street lamps but shadows, until the truck's headlights suddenly flew around the corner. The turn was taken at such a high speed that the tail end swung out, and the truck drifted. Marley could smell burning rubber as it slammed to a jerking halt at the side of the street. She couldn't see anything for the onslaught of headlights, and she found herself squinting against their brightness. Blinded to everything else, she tried to focus on the voices. In the desolate street they carried themselves a fair distance.

"Ian! Ian let me out!" came what could only be Devlyn's voice from the truck cab, panic ridden and frantic.

"Stay in the truck, Dev," Ian replied roughly.

"What?! No, I--!" she started to protest.

"I said"--something about the slow, deathly calm tone Ian's voice came in, sent the hairs at the back of Marley's neck prickling. She could only imagine what Devlyn was experiencing-- "stay in the truck."

A moment later the truck door slammed, Winchester streamed past, and Ian was in front of her. He hadn't put his hood up, and his brass coloured hair was already drenched. The rain dripped down his face, collecting on his eyelashes. His heavy gaze held on her, hard and intent.

"Is he...?"

Marley knew what he was asking. She could see that same dangerous, deathly quiet that she'd heard in his voice, echoed in his chilling eyes and his overall stillness. She couldn't give him his answer. "I-- I don't..."

Something in her simple words, and the vastness they couldn't seem to cover, broke whatever wall he'd slammed up in defense of it all. For a second his eyes flickered, the ice cracked, and something moved. Some emotion she had thought was too far down to be reached. Something she wasn't sure she'd ever quite understand as long as she lived. And then it was gone. And he was gone. Down the alley and to his brother.

Still, muddy, and grime covered, his brother lay at his feet. And with him, the faerie. She had Daniel's head cradled in her lap, keeping it from the flooded ground. She hunched protectively over him, trying to keep the rain off, as she clutched one of his hands against her so tightly, her knuckles were white. Daniel's other lay limply over his chest.

Ian felt his legs give out, and he fell to his knees in front of them. He could see her face then, a mess of tears and clinging soaked hair. Every inch of her shook, trembling so hard, Ian thought she'd leave her skin behind. She was more disheveled, more *human*, than he'd ever seen her before. A terrible numbness began to creep through him.

This was why he hadn't let Devlyn come. This was the reason people walked around with scars marring their very insides. Ian would know. He had enough of them already.

"Danny?" His voice felt thin, a sliver of string tied to nothing.

He brushed his brother's hair away from his face. Checked for a pulse. The moment he found it, blood pumping beneath his fingers, he laughed. A tired and grateful laugh that caught in his throat.

"That's it, little brother," he said gutturally. "That's it. We're here. I got you."

Chapter Seventeen

Daniel was surrounded by white. It wasn't a room; there were no walls and no ceiling, just a vast expanse of white, as far as the eye could see. He wandered it aimlessly, not sure why he was there, not having a clue where he was going, or if he could even go anywhere in a place like this. Wherever he went, it was just more of the same. More white.

That was, until a man came into view, sitting on a chair like he'd always been there. Examining his fingernails, he had sandy blond hair, sea green eyes, and when he looked up at Daniel, a crooked smile.

"'Ello!" He called with a British accent. He stood up and the chair under him vanished in a plume of drifting smoke.

"I'm dead aren't I?" Daniel asked. "This is heaven?"

The man made a face. "You think this is heaven? Way to set your sights high, mate." He shook his head. "No, you're not dead-- thank goodness. If you were, well then all my fantastic hard work would have gone to waste."

Daniel regarded the man. Shoving his hands in his pant pockets, he realized he was also wearing completely all white clothes.

"What hard work?"

The man gave a lopsided grin. "The dreams, of course! Those are my bit of handiwork. I've been working on all your mates. Throw in some nightmares here, a little nostalgia there. A dash of retrospect when needed."

"You've been... giving everyone I know weird dreams?"

"Not just dreams!" he said aghast. "Memories. Moments from the past. Almost drove me barking mad, digging and sorting through it all, but it's been brilliant."

Daniel felt a frown crease his forehead, a sinking feeling beginning to form in his stomach. "Sorry, you did what?" he asked. Images of his brother's tired and lined face flashed to the forefront of his mind.

"Memories! Dreams!" the man exclaimed, and then made a gesture of interlocking his fingers to prove the point.

Daniel's jaw clenched. "You've been digging through our

minds?! Going through our *thoughts*?!" He took a threatening step forward and the man shrank back.

"Well... yes," he said. A sheepish note, that wasn't there before creeping into his voice.

"Who are you?" Daniel snapped angrily.

"Name's Reid," he said. Daniel stared him down, drawing on the man, until he felt the need to explain himself further. "I'm an Artifex Animi."

"An Artist of the Mind? Really?"

"Ah, you know your Latin then."

Daniel felt his patience withering. "Stop it, all right! Whatever you're doing. Whatever *this is*. The dreams. Everything. My *'mates'* go through enough crap. They don't need every painful memory slammed back in their face!"

"They're not all bad," Reid said defensively.

"Just," Daniel spoke slowly, "get me out of here."

"I'm not the one keeping you, mate," Reid said. "We're in your head after all."

"You're lucky you found him when you did. Poor kid was soaked clean through to the bone."

Ian was only half listening to Jim, as he held up the doorframe to Jim's spare bedroom. Daniel lay on the bed inside. He was in dry clothes at least, but still unconscious. On either side of him, were Devlyn and Ruby. Devlyn was lying beside him, her yellow head resting on his chest, as she stared up at the ceiling. Ruby had fallen asleep in her bedside chair, her forehead pressed against Daniel's shoulder. Winchester slept curled up at his feet.

Ian took a sip of his beer, and just watched them, the slow rise and fall of their chests. He wasn't sure how a scene could look so whole, yet feel so desolate all at once.

Jim gave him a nudge. "Did anyone tell you, you look like death recently?"

Ian's mouth formed a hard line, but he said nothing.

"You got to take care of yourself, son," Jim said, piercing him with his fatherly grey eyes. His forehead was etched with worry wrinkles. "Daniel's home now, there's no sense in having the both of you out of commission. You got me?"

Ian dipped him a half-hearted nod. Jim studied him for a

minute longer and then turned away, retreating back towards the kitchen with a shake of his head. He muttered as he went. Ian caught bits of it. "…never listens… sandwich."

Marley took his place. Her fiery hair was still damp, hanging over her shoulders in tendrils. It looked like she'd just stepped out of a shower.

"He's right you know." She'd acquired a beer of her own. It hung loosely out of one hand, as she crossed her arms over her chest, and leaned back against the doorframe, her green eyes thoughtful. "I think I prescribed you something for that already. What was it now? Oh, I dunno-- *sleep* maybe?"

Ian grunted at the sarcasm. "What're you still doing here?"

She gestured grandly into the room, and towards the four figures. "Relishing in a job well done." She tipped her beer bottle towards him and then took a swig.

Ian looked straight ahead at his brother's relaxed and seemingly lifeless features. "He's not awake yet."

Out of his peripheral, he saw Marley give him a sidelong look. When she didn't seem to find whatever it was she was looking for in his face, she sighed, sloshing her beer around the edge of her bottle in a slow circle. "Do you always default to douche bag?"

Ian said nothing, just turned away from her, having a sudden desire to follow Jim's trek to the kitchen. He felt the need to be moving, the need to be doing something-- even if it meant making a sandwich.

Over his shoulder, from where he'd left her, he heard Marley mumble, "No need to thank me or anything."

The moment Daniel realized the truth about the situation, the truth about who was really in charge-- everything changed.

It was instant.

Suddenly he was wearing jeans and a red t-shirt, they were standing in the parking lot of the Ay Motel, and Reid was thrown backwards away from him, flattened on the pavement by an invisible force of Daniel's making. He could feel the air humming around him, like it was restless, begging for any whimsical change. Here in his mind, all was possible, and nothing was real.

He flexed his hands.

"Bloody hell..." Reid grumbled, sitting up painfully. Then he gave a few slow claps. "Impressive though. Most impressive. You know most people never figure that one out? But I guess you aren't most people. You're brilliant, you are!"

Suddenly without barely a thought, Daniel was directly in front of Reid, moved as if nothing had changed. He towered over him.

"Blimey!" Reid exclaimed in surprise, scrambling back and onto his feet. "But we're on the same side you and me!"

"Then why are you screwing with our heads? You had no right to our past!"

The lights shining through the windows of the motel rooms behind them began flickering spasmodically on and off.

"I'm not '*screwing*' with you. I'm cheering you on."

Daniel raised skeptical eyebrows.

"I did what I did for a reason, all right? You had to remember why you came together in the first place. Why it's important you *stay* together. I'm not mental; I know you and your mates are the only chance any of us have against Luke's crew. I'm just trying to keep you together."

Daniel regarded the man sternly. "If you're really on our side"--Reid nodded at this-- "then show a little *faith*, man. We were in this together, long before you showed up and started poking around in our private lives. We aren't going to fall apart, because we're not constantly being reminded of what we have."

"You went missing, Daniel."

It was such an out of place statement that Daniel blinked, taken aback by it. "What...?"

"They're in it together, because of *you*, mate You're the sticky gooey stuff that holds everyone together. Without you..." He made an exploding gesture with his hands, accompanied by sound effects of pieces spinning to the ground. He seemed to enjoy talking with his hands.

Daniel was shaking his head.

"What? Don't believe me?"

Daniel glared.

"All right then, I'll show you. We'll 'It's a Wonderful Life' it up."

He raised a hand above his head and snapped his fingers.

The sound was so deafening it seemed to scare their current scenery out of its place. The Ay Motel whooshed away in a blur of colours, seeming to freeze on the peripheral. Then without warning, it snapped back as something completely different.

Devlyn was at the Roadhouse, Daniel could see her sitting on top of the bar, her feet resting gingerly on a bar stool. Luke was there, striding through the building that was all but vacant except for them. He flipped the open sign to close and strode back towards her.

"You could not let it go, could you?" Luke said with a pitying shake of his head.

Devlyn held her chin high, everything about her posture screamed defiance, but her eyes followed Luke warily. He was pacing the floor in front of her, like a circling vulture.

"Everyone gave in. Everyone faced the truth. Everyone except you."

"*Your* truth," spat Devlyn, her eyes flashing. "Not *the* truth."

Daniel wasn't sure he'd ever seen her so angry.

Luke stopped pacing, coming to a halt in front of her. "See, that is where you would be wrong my dear Devlyn." He reached out, his fingers trailing slowly along her jawline. With a repulsed shiver, she jerked back from his touch.

Daniel found his hands clenched into fists at his sides, red-hot fury taking him over.

"You see, all you have to do is tell a big enough lie. Repeat that lie often enough, and that is all it takes for people to eventually come to believe it. As soon as they believe it, it *becomes* truth."

"You can't override the truth, Luke," Devlyn said. "The real truth is unremitting. It will always be there to fight back."

"Is that what you are doing then? Fighting back?" Luke asked. "Oh, little naive Devlyn." He reached into his jacket pocket pulling out a silver handgun. He leveled it with her chest. "This battle has already been won."

"*No!*" Daniel exploded, throwing himself between them, just as the gun sounded off.

It all happened too fast. The bullet flew through Daniel, like he was a phantom and nothing else. He spun around just in time to watch it slam into Devlyn. Her lips parted in surprise. He reached for her too late, and watched the light go out of her eyes, as she toppled backwards off the bar. A waterfall of blond curls.

Marley was staring at the wallpaper in Daniel's room. It was horrendous really, the kind you'd only expect to see in an old farmhouse like Jim's. It was an ugly pale yellow colour that reminded her of a short story she'd read once. The main character had gone crazy from staring at it. Marley was beginning to think she'd become victim to the same fate-- but she didn't blame the wallpaper.

"He's getting worse," Ian said, his hands locked behind his head. He was pacing the room. He had been doing so for hours. Back and forth and back and forth and--.

"I know," Devlyn snapped, which was uncharacteristic coming from her, but even her enduring patience was beginning to wane. "I'm trying here, okay?"

Devlyn was still lying beside Daniel. Marley watched as she handed off a cloth to Jim, who dipped it in a basin of cold water and passed it back. She resumed pressing it to Daniel's forehead. Her curls dangled off one shoulder, skimming his chest. He'd broken out in a cold sweat overnight. Shivers racked his entire body and he jerked, tossing and turning in his sleep.

He'd yet to open his eyes, and come back to them.

Maddening silence followed again, filled only by Ian's footsteps. Marley found herself counting each one. It took him five strides to make it from one side of the room to the other. She'd just finished counting her fourth set of five, when Daniel jerked in his sleep again, moaning in the back of his throat.

"Come on! That's not normal!" Ian complained.

Then very quietly from the far corner of the room: "I think I know what's going on here."

Four pairs of eyes turned to regard Ruby. She was sitting on one of the numerous wooden kitchen chairs that'd accumulated in the room. She hadn't said anything in a long while.

"You do?" Devlyn asked at the same time Ian barked an accusing: "*What?*"

"I think he may be riding an after effect," she said quietly.

Something Marley's Scit had said to her once nudged at the back of her mind, but it was Jim who spoke first.

"She may be right you know," he said, his face thoughtful as he mulled it over. He ran a hand through his salt and pepper hair. It was a mess, sticking up at odd angles.

"Come again?" Ian asked irritably.

"An after effect usually happens after a complicated, really powerful, or ill-prepared potion has been used. It's like a blowback, or a withdrawal," Ruby explained.

"So we're talking faerie mojo?"

Ruby nodded.

"Perfect," Ian spat sarcastically, throwing his hands in the air. He was getting more erratic with each passing minute. He really needed to get some sleep. It wasn't normal for a person to go so long without it. "So the Fifth World groups are tag teaming now? The lycanthropes kidnap Dan, and the faeries drug him up. I have half a mind to storm into the nearest vampire clan and demand what they contributed."

"Son," Jim said with an ever-patient sigh, "you're rambling."

Ian closed his eyes, tilting his head back towards the ceiling, then resumed pacing.

Jim looked to Ruby. "Anything we can do?"

"You--."

"Ian!" Marley exploded, unable to control herself anymore. Oh, yeah-- she was going crazy. "Sit. Down. You're giving me a headache."

If she'd been expecting a smart remark in response --and she had been-- she never got it. Instead he sank silently into the nearest free kitchen chair. Marley noted, however, that he never really stopped moving, even while straddling a chair backwards. His fingers twitched over his lips thoughtfully, his muscles jumped at the back of his shoulder blades, and his foot bounced against the floor. The only thing unmoving about him, were his eyes, their icy blue stillness trained on his brother.

Ruby gave her a wary look and then tried again. "You can't do anything. You just wait it out." She looked away, almost guiltily. "And hope it's not more than he can handle."

The scene retreated. Halted for a moment as if calculating, and then rushed back again as something different.

Ruby was sitting on a stool spinning her cocktail around by the stem of its glass, in an empty bar Daniel had never seen before. Right away Daniel knew something was wrong. For one, the outfit Ruby was wearing was in no way showy. There were no sparkles, no sequins, and no vibrant colours. She was wearing a plain jacket over a sleek black dress, classic and boring. Secondly, as she flirted with the bartender, the only other person in the room except for himself, her laugh was-- off. It was high-pitched, flippant, and absent of all warmth. Daniel didn't know why this would set off his internal alarm, like it did. No one would even notice anything strange, if they hadn't known her as long as he had.

Ruby convinced the bartender to have a drink with her. He poured a shot of something in a glass, and then turned to grab another bottle from behind. The moment his back was to her, Ruby's hand shot out, and Daniel just caught a glimpse of her dashing a few drops of some clear liquid into his drink, before she pulled back, like nothing had happened. She'd used her faerie speed. A speed she'd had so little use for in the past.

"What are you doing, Bee?" Daniel found himself wondering aloud.

He took the stool beside her, trying to catch her eye, but it was like he didn't exist. He did notice another change though. Her eyes seemed darker somehow, as if the storm in them had taken over, clouding what sparks of light there had been there.

She raised her glass for a toast, and the bartended complied. Daniel swallowed uncomfortably, as the man started lifting his glass to his lips.

"I don't think you want to--," Daniel started, and then realizing he was being ignored, made a grab for the glass.

His hand went right through it.

What was this? A Christmas Carol?

Daniel balled his hand into a fist as the bartender threw his drink back. Ruby took a small sip of her own, and then calmly set it back on the bar, and just watched.

It took mere seconds. Suddenly the bartender was choking, clutching at his throat. He stared at her with wide eyes. Ruby took another sip of her cocktail.

"Ruby!" Daniel yelled at her.

The bartender collapsed onto the floor, convulsing. White

foam slid out of his mouth. Then slowly, twitchingly, he grew still. Daniel looked away disgusted, anger surging through him. He glared at his best friend.

"I hope he was a really evil son of a--."

The door to the bar chimed, cutting him off as another faerie walked in. Daniel had seen him before, but couldn't fit a name to the face. The faerie took one look at the dead body, one look at Ruby-- and sighed.

"You sure that was justifiable?" he asked her. "The guy was just a weapon supplier."

Ruby slid off her stool, and fixed the cuffs of her jacket like their imperfection was the worst thing that had happened to her all day.

"Probably not," she admitted. "But he was arming our enemies. We can't afford much more of that."

The other faerie shook his head. "You used to be the best of us, Ruby."

"Yeah, Ruby," Daniel found himself snapping.

"The best of us died out a long time ago, Lou," Ruby said simply. "There's no more 'get out of jail free' cards left in the deck. This game's all about survival now."

Retreat. Halt. Rush.

Daniel was standing in an open field, tall grass bending in the wind, grabbing at his pant legs. He was in between two lines of a good old-fashioned war front. On one side of him were countless Fair Children, a huddled crowd of murmuring voices. He caught sight of Ruby and Jack somewhere in the middle and his chest tightened. They were all in a flurry, planning battle strategies, saying goodbyes. There was backslapping and hugging, some shifted uneasily or started pulling out weapons. He saw two vampires pound fists, and a grey wolf nuzzled a light brown one.

Then he turned to look over his shoulder. On his other side, stood row upon straight row of Knoctes. None of them spoke, or moved, they just stood with guns at the ready, staring straight ahead. And at the front-- stood Ian. His face was blank, his eyes fixed ahead of him, and there seemed to be nothing left in him. He was a stone statue with only ridged animations of life.

"Ian...?" Daniel said, not quite believing what he was seeing.

He had taken a step in his brother's direction, when the Fair Children suddenly sprang forward, moving past him with blurring speed. The Knoctes moved in formation to meet them, and the two sides collided.

Daniel called his brother's name, spinning around on the spot in an attempt to relocate him.

Then he spotted him, marching forward, loading his shotgun, with a distinctive: *Click. Click.* Daniel yelled out his brother's name again, as Ian leveled the gun and blew out the first Fair Child to cross his path. He didn't hesitate. Didn't blink.

Daniel tried to grab his shoulder, but it was like trying to get a grip on a handful of air. Cursing internally, he strove to keep up with Ian's purposeful strides.

"Ian," Daniel begged desperately. "Don't do this. Don't *be* this."

Ian took out another. This time a wolf, as he pulled a handgun out of the waistband of his jeans. The creature collapsed in a furry heap, its front paw still twitching.

"Snap out of it, man! This isn't you!"

Ian wasn't listening. It was like he was deaf-- deaf and blind to the pain and the cries that filled the air around him. It was chaos. Daniel felt each death around him, like a physical blow. He found himself stumbling, his breathing ragged.

Then Ian paused. Daniel turned to see what had caught his attention, and in front of him a little ways ahead-- was Ruby.

"No."

She stood with her back pressed against Jack's, who she shouted over her shoulder to. As attackers drew close, she sprayed them with liquid, flinging it in every direction. It burnt flesh like acid and caused Knoctes to stagger backwards.

Ian reloaded his handgun, inserting iron bullets. Daniel tried to step in between them, but suddenly he couldn't stand anymore. He crumpled to his knees.

Ian took aim, leveling out a shot.

"No," Daniel croaked, his hands fisting in the grass. "Ian, please. Don't let this happen."

Ian's finger played over the trigger. He hesitated. Daniel tried to get up-- and couldn't.

"You have to stop it. All of it," he begged, "These are good people."

Suddenly a hand grasped Ian's shoulder, giving it a comforting squeeze.

Luke stepped into view.

"It is all right, Ian," he encouraged. "You are one of us now."

Ian still stood, weapon lifted, unmoving, but Daniel could almost feel Luke's poison seeping into him-- its malice working.

Daniel hunched over, fighting against something he couldn't quite explain. He felt it heavily, a dark presence, pressing in on him, squeezing out his every breath. He kept hearing himself saying the same words, like it was all he could remember to say, all that could escape his lips, "...good people... good people."

"Pull the trigger," Luke urged.

"...good people."

Ian's finger stilled over its place.

"...not you."

Daniel's forehead was pressed against the ground now, he felt the earth choking with blood, cool against his face. He closed his eyes.

Ian pulled the trigger.

Retreat. Halt. Rush.

Reid stood before him. Daniel was slumped against a wall, unable to hold himself upright anymore. His head hung limply, heavy as lead.

"Whether you want to believe it or not, mate," Reid was saying, "a happy ending rests on your shoulders."

Daniel tried to look at him, but his eyelids felt weighted. He fought to channel his mind, and managed to convince the scene around them to change into a starry night sky, manipulating the wall at his back into becoming a thick tree.

That seemed to catch Reid's attention. He frowned and glanced down, finally registering Daniel's condition.

"But I've kept you too long," he said suddenly, ruefully. "You just needed to know what was at stake."

Daniel felt a remark stir his mind, but fatigue ripped it away, before it could become words.

"This faerie stuff is nasty business," Reid continued. "A little push though, I think-- and you'll come around." He crouched down in front of Daniel and pressed a palm to his forehead. "Good luck, Daniel. See you on the other side."

Then a force like a brick wall slammed into Daniel.

Devlyn knew Daniel was struggling. His chest no longer rose and fell in a steady rhythm. His breaths came in broken hitches, each one growing farther from the last. She smoothed his hair away from his forehead, anxiously.

"Come on, Dan," she whispered.

She'd been trying to drown out all the fighting and bickering for hours. She didn't want to listen-- to any of it. Not the false hopes, or the worst outcomes. They just needed a little faith. It was what she held on to so tightly. What kept her going.

But their voices had climbed so high, they'd become impossible to ignore.

"Absolutely not!" Ian was shouting.

"But if you just give me a chance--," Ruby begged. Her voice quivered. "I think I could--."

"No!" Ian roared. He was standing behind a chair, gripping the back of it so tightly, Devlyn was surprised it didn't splinter into a million pieces. "It was faerie junk like that that hurt him in the first place! If you think I'm going to let *anything* like that near him again--."

"We're running out of options, boy," Jim piped up. "We need to try something."

Ian shot him an unpleasant look. "Well try something else."

"Oh, come off it, Ian. It's not like she uses anything harmful," Marley said suddenly, surprisingly coming to Ruby's aid. "You could give it a fair shot."

"And what," Ian said, shifting his cold gaze to her, "suddenly makes you an expert?"

Marley sighed. She stared at the ceiling for a span of several seconds, then slowly, with a slightly regretful shake of her head, pulled her hair over one shoulder. The bare skin of her neck, exposed little bruised needle marks. Devlyn gave a small gasp in spite of herself.

"Still breathing, Ian," Marley said irritably. "Still here enough to be annoyed with your stubborn, headstrong character."

Ian was so shocked, he didn't say anything for a long

minute. Ruby groaned, burying her face deeply in her hands. She took a few retreating steps back. This seemed to trigger Ian, his eyes suddenly snapped up to follow her. They were so intently menacing, that Ruby's next step faltered.

"You--!" He was so angry he could hardly get words out. As if guessing his next course of action, Marley immediately sprang in between them. She was just in time to head off his advance. "You're experimenting on *people*?!"

"Hey--!" Marley started, and watched Ian's body tense. As if fearing he was going to do something drastic, Marley's hands shot out, gripping his shoulders. Her fingers curled fists in his jacket, like she could physically hold him in place. The image of someone trying to hold back a very enormous dog by its collar, flooded into Devlyn's mind.

Daniel's breathing faltered beneath her again, and she hurriedly glanced back down at him.

"Guys…" she said fearfully, but her plea went unheard. The only beings in the room who seemed to notice her distress, were Winchester and Lady. Sprawled out on the floor, their ears twitched in her direction.

"You're no different from anything else I've ever killed!" Ian continued to accuse. A vein stood out in his neck.

Ruby had turned a ghastly pale colour.

"Ian, Ian! It was *my* idea, all right?" Marley tired to reason. "Mine, not hers. It was my decision. *I* asked her to do it. *I* let it happen."

It was that moment, Daniel stopped breathing.

Devlyn's heart seemed to slam to a stop.

"Guys!" she begged. "Not breathing! *HE'S NOT BREATHING*!"

Suddenly Ian was beside her, as if the space between them hadn't existed. Jim was looking over his shoulder a second later, all previous conversation forgotten.

"*WHAT HAPPENED?!*" Ian demanded.

It was a question Devlyn didn't bother to answer. Ian wasn't a doctor, no answer she could give him, would supply him with the knowledge to make it right again. She had her own questions. Questions meant for someone else. Leaning forward to press her forehead against Daniel's shoulder, she closed her eyes and began to pray fervently. Tears burned down her face, and her lips moved silently. She felt someone hit her shoulder as they leaned past her, and over Daniel.

"Come *on*, boy!" Jim was muttering, his voice strained.

"Please, God…" Devlyn whispered desperately.

"*DANNY!*" Ian bellowed. "*YOU LEAVE WITHOUT PERMISSION AND SO HELP ME, I'LL--.*"

Suddenly Devlyn found herself yelling, her voice growing stronger with indignation, climbing to meet Ian's. "*DON'T TAKE HIM! DON'T--!*"

Daniel gasped, a sound so loud, it was as if he was drawing life itself back into his body.

Devlyn lifted her head, her eyes snapping open in the same instant Daniel's did. Their gazes locked.

Surprised, Ian started backward, slamming into Jim's shoulder, and knocking him out of balance. Jim stumbled, and Marley just managed to catch a hold of him, grabbing the arm of his jacket, before he fell. They watched in relief as Daniel rolled onto his side, coughing. For one paralyzing moment, no one seemed to be able to move. And then everybody did.

The first thing Daniel saw was Devlyn's face. The first thing he heard was his name climbing over itself, in a rush of voices. Then Devlyn was in his arms, hands fisted in his shirt, and Winchester was on top of him, drowning him with slobbery kisses. Daniel spotted his brother, standing beside the bed. Ian had his head tilted back towards the ceiling. His eyes closed, Ian gave a long grateful sigh, and then his gaze turned and met Daniel's. It wore a look Daniel knew well enough to put words to. *You ever try that again, and I'll kill you.* Daniel lifted a hand and Ian took it, clasping it hard in Conexus. Then he embraced Daniel in a death grip that nearly crushed him.

"Welcome back, kid," Jim suddenly said behind him, and he shook Daniel's shoulder roughly, as a pleased laugh rumbled in his throat.

It wasn't until everyone took a step back that Daniel noticed Ruby and Marley standing against the back wall together. Marley gave him a dipping nod and a pleased smile, and then with a parting salute to Ruby, she ducked out the door, her Weimaraner trailing at her heels. No one else seemed to notice her silent retreat. Ruby still hadn't moved, her eyes were down cast, trained on some spot on the floor. She looked shaken and teary. She gave a small sniff.

"Hey, Bee," Daniel said, with a gentle smile.

She looked up, storm grey eyes meeting his. For a long minute she just stared into them, and then in a sudden rush, hurried over. Carefully dancing around Ian, she threw herself at him.

"You idiot!" She said hugging him tightly. "You *stupid* idiot! I told you to watch yourself. I told you!"

She buried her head in his chest then, and nothing else she said after that was audible. Wrapping one arm carefully around her, Daniel reached out with his other hand and Devlyn's fingers curled around his. She leaned towards him and he pressed his forehead against hers.

He really wished he knew what was going on.

Then, as if some part of his brain had heard him, scenes from a dream came rushing back, in a blur of faces and colours. He blinked. One line seemed to stand out the clearest. *You went missing, Daniel.*

"I went missing?" he asked suddenly.

From close up he saw Devlyn give him a quizzical look. Ruby pulled back. Everyone was staring at him incredulously.

"What?" Daniel asked.

Ian stepped forward, clearing his throat gently. "Dan," he asked carefully, "what do you remember after taking Dev to work after church?"

Daniel took turns glancing between all their faces, trying to recall the gap they were implying, but all he managed to recover, were flashes of the same strange dream. He shook his head slightly.

"Nothing. I don't remember a thing."

"So you really don't remember anything?"

Daniel rolled his head over to look at his brother. "Just because everyone thinks it's a good idea that I don't sleep for a few good hours doesn't mean *you* can't. It's what everyone else is doing."

Ian was stretched out on his back, lying on his bed in the

Ay Motel. His feet were crossed at the ankles, and he was staring up at the ceiling with his fingers linked behind his head. The place was still a disaster. They'd been trying a hand at cleaning it, but at present it still looked like the Tasmanian Devil had gone tearing through it. Winchester was chewing heartily on a busted pillow in the corner of the room. Watching him, Daniel spun back and forth thoughtfully in the desk chair-- which miraculously had survived the room's ordeal, but for a broken wheel.

"I mean, this place isn't jarring any memories?" Ian asked. "You're not getting weird deja vu vibes?"

Daniel contemplated, his eyes scanning the disheveled room, taking in the torn carpets and abused drywall.

He shrugged. "Nope. Nothing."

Ian sat up. "You were gone for over two weeks, man, and you're drawing a *blank*?"

"Ruby thinks the potion that was given to me was a mind wiping drug."

Ian grunted unhappily.

"It makes sense," Daniel added.

"No, it doesn't," Ian snapped. "Why after everything they did, would they not want you to remember? Like come on, kidnapping is pretty severe for just pretending it never happened."

"I dunno, Ian," Daniel said exasperated. He felt worn out, like his body had run a marathon while he'd been unconscious. Everything ached. "Maybe they felt bad?"

Ian scowled disbelievingly in his direction. "It would be like you, to think the best of your attackers. That's kind of sick, dude. Almost as sick as those dreams you said you've been having."

Daniel kicked a piece of broken lamp across the floor. "You sure they're that far off?" he asked giving his brother a reproachful look. "Ruby filled me in on everything. Accusing her like that, Ian? Really?"

Ian looked away, setting his jaw. Then almost as soon as he'd adopted his brooding face, it lifted. His gaze had drifted out the window, and although Daniel couldn't see what he was staring at, it seemed to have done a good enough job of distracting him. Ian pushed up from the bed and immediately made for the door.

Daniel threw up his hands. "Ian," he said, irked that his

brother was running out on him now. But he went ignored. "*Ian.*"

The motel room door slammed shut, and Daniel sighed heavily, leaning back in his chair.

"Well if it isn't my disappearing and reappearing stalker."

Marley turned around to face Ian, brushing red strands of hair away from her mouth. It hadn't taken him long to notice her, as she'd paced in front of the motel room windows, hoping for one of them to be theirs. He was standing on a busted parking stop, squinting --or perhaps glaring-- into the receding sun, which was giving the parking lot a late day glow.

"I know when I'm needed," she told him.

Ian raised his eyebrows. "Do you?"

Marley felt her forehead crease. "Just listen, okay. I don't think this one's over. It doesn't sit right. Something about this whole thing is just-- off. It was all too planned, and yet so rash at the same time. I just have this feeling… like the Fifth Worlders still got an ace up their sleeve we haven't seen yet."

Ian stood quietly, his face thoughtful. His hands were shoved deep in his pockets. "I know," he said finally. "I've been thinking it too."

Marley nodded, his answer confirming her beliefs. "Just… don't let your guard down. I'm still keeping an eye open, and I suggest you do the same."

They stood in awkward silence for a long moment, something unexplainable hanging in the air between them.

"I just had to say it out loud," she admitted. "Get it out of my system." With a parting shrug she turned away, starting to stride back up the parking lot. She called over her shoulder, "I mean, you weren't exactly answering your phone."

"I… smashed it," Ian said.

Something about the admission caused Marley to stop and glance back, regarding him carefully. For a second she thought she saw his guard slip.

"Okay," she said, her eyes wandering his face "We'll pretend that doesn't need counseling."

Ian's blue eyes instantly looked away, cutting her off from any insight she might have read into him. "Considering the last phone call I got from you," he said slowly. "I don't think I ever want another one." He shook his head mournfully. "Ever."

Careful to keep her expression neutral, Marley pretended as if his words didn't both sting, and send her pride burning towards a witty come back. Instead, she settled for crossing her arms over her chest. "Right," she said flatly. "Well, watch your back. And have a nice life, Ian." And then she walked away without giving him a second glance.

Chapter Eighteen

Ian watched Daniel from across the table in Devlyn's apartment. His brother was shifting uncomfortably in his seat, every now and then rubbing the back of his neck, or rolling his shoulders.

"You good?" he asked.

Daniel's head cocked to the side slightly, like he was considering.

"Yeah," he said finally, giving an unconvincing laugh. "Still a little sore, I guess."

It was somewhat understandable. They had been hard at work the last couple of days, putting back together the motel room. They had had to redo the drywall completely for one of the walls, Daniel and Devlyn taking the opportunity to repaint the entire room. Ian had cleaned up shattered glass and helped Jim replace the front window, while Ruby had sent over new desk lamps, along with a fresh mattress. They'd hardly stopped, if you didn't count the paint fight that'd broken out. Daniel still had a streak of brown paint on his cheek, and one of Devlyn's blond curls had fallen victim. Ian could still see it sticking out of her loose ponytail as she cut avocados into a salad bowl at her counter. Ian had never been one for green, leafy food, but when it came accompanied with a home cooked meal of steak and potatoes, it was impossible to turn down. The smell was growing intoxicating as Devlyn flitted about her small kitchen humming tunelessly alongside the whirl of the stove fan. Ian noticed a paint handprint marked one of the back pockets of her jeans.

Across the table, Daniel suddenly hissed in a low breath, grabbing at his side.

"Dude, what are you? Eighty?" Ian asked, eyeing him warily.

Daniel just shook his head, his jaw clenched.

Devlyn pulled the potatoes out of the oven, and started piling the steaks high on a plate. Cutting off a small corner, she let it drop to the ground, where Winchester, normally, would have been panting at her heels. For once, however, the dog was nowhere in sight. Stretching back in his seat, Ian noticed their small companion skirting around the bottom of Daniel's chair. He seemed antsy, letting out anxious, intermitted whines.

Ian frowned.

Whatever had the dog on edge, was now prickling at the back of his neck, like it was contagious. He flickered another glance at his brother, as Devlyn moved to the table in front of him, placing dishes of food down. It was set and laid out fancy, with the silverware her grandmother had left her, positioned correctly beside each plate. Her grandmother had been the only relative still in contact with Devlyn before she passed away, and Ian could tell the old lady had tried to leave her granddaughter with as much as she could, even if the cutlery was now starting to blacken around the edges.

Ian hadn't even noticed Devlyn finding her seat beside Daniel-- until he heard the word grace.

"Grace?"

She gave him a disapproving look. "Yes, Ian, grace. Giving thanks for the food."

"I know what it is," he snapped.

"Good," she said, folding her arms with a small smile. "You say it then."

Ian scowled, turning to his brother for help, but Daniel was busy rubbing his forehead with one hand, and only offered up an encouraging half-smile.

Ian swore.

The resulting look he received from Devlyn suddenly had him bowing his head.

"I mean, the food looks great. Thank you for cows, and meat, and steak. Amen."

Ian expected some sort of criticizing comment from Devlyn for that, but surprisingly, she just smiled to herself and grabbed for the salad bowl.

The smile was forgotten almost immediately, as Daniel reached for his fork.

Ian had paid little attention to the action at first, as he stabbed for a steak-- until Daniel suddenly cried out and leapt to his feet, dropping the utensil. The swiftness of the movement upset his chair, knocking it over backwards.

Ian's eyes snapped up. "Whoa, whoa, hey!" he called,

startled, the words coming out in a rush.

Daniel's eyes were wide with fright, and as he reeled away from them, he tripped backwards over the chair. Winchester let out a startled bark, as Daniel crashed to the floor, his back slamming up against the lower kitchen cupboards. His shoulder blades smacked into the wood with an audibly painful thud, but it was his hand he nurtured, staring at it with a stunned expression, like it was something from outer space. He hissed in a pain-laced breath, as he repeatedly flexed his hand.

Devlyn stared with wide eyes, and Ian, too shocked and caught by surprise to know what to do, did the same.

Then a visible shudder passed through Daniel's body, and he gasped, hunching over.

Ian was out of his chair in an instant. He nearly tripped over Winchester on his way over. The dog was tearing around the apartment like he'd gone mad. Ian watched as the tracking dog made a skidding U-turn, and barreled back the way he came.

Something was very wrong.

Looking to his brother, he could tell that Daniel knew it too. Crouching down in front of him, Ian grasped his shoulders.

"What's going on with you, Dan?" he asked, his voice sounding about as desperate as he felt.

"I can't--." But Daniel's words were cut short as another shudder thundered its way through his frame.

Devlyn pushed her way in beside Ian, just as Daniel gave another gasp.

"What's happening?" she asked frantically, turning her pleading, dark blue eyes on Ian. She was begging for answers.

But he had none.

She grabbed Daniel's face in between her hands, pushing his now sweaty auburn hair away from his eyes.

"Look at me," she pleaded. He already was. His brown eyes always attuned to her every movement. "It's going to be okay, okay? We'll find out what's wrong. We'll--."

Then Ian felt it-- the bones of Daniel's shoulder break under his touch. He jerked his hand back, as his brother cried out in pain, his hoarse yell rising to fill the apartment. Something else snapped, and Ian jumped back at the same time Devlyn did, eyes wide. Daniel slid to the side, falling onto his hands and knees. His hair fell back over his face, and his fingertips tried to dig their way through the tiles.

Winchester bolted past again, this time skidding to a stop in front of Daniel. He barked frantically, prodded his master once with his nose, and then sank to his belly on the floor with a low whine.

Daniel expressed yet another wave of pain. This time his backbone visibly rippled, moving under the skin like an unwanted parasite. He collapsed fully to the floor, cheek against tile, convulsing, bones cracking.

That's when Devlyn screamed.

Tears trailing down her face, she crawled, trembling to his side, where she wrapped her arms around him, as if she could somehow hold him together. Keep him whole. Winchester pawed at Daniel and then tried to bury his snout under his shoulder. Daniel's face was lined with torment, his eyes a silent plea of "help, please help," but he was beyond voicing his agony anymore.

Ian felt cold.

Someone started banging persistently on the apartment door.

Devlyn turned on Ian. "What do we do?!"

He didn't answer. He just stared.

Daniel moaned, and Winchester mimicked the sound. The sickening, snapping, breaking noises continued. Daniel's eyes rolled up into the back of his head.

"Ian, *what do we do*?!"

Ian's brain suddenly snapped back into working order. His eyes moved frantically around the kitchen. Searching for something. *Anything*. Then he spotted Daniel's abandoned fork lying under the table.

He swallowed hard.

"The utensils." His voice was like a ghost.

She looked up at him with utter and bewildering disbelief. "*What?*"

"They're silver!" he suddenly bellowed, over the knocking that continued to drone on in the background.

"*And?!*"

Ian swore loudly, desperately hoping his hunch was wrong.

"Dev, get back," he said urgently.

213

She barely seemed to register his words, her eyes locked on Daniel. His arms were stretched out in front of him, veins pulling in his neck. He threw his head back.

"He's shifting! Get back, *now!*"

Panic filled her eyes, but she didn't move. Ian dove forward. Wrapping his arms around her waist, he rolled out of the way, sending them both sprawling across the kitchen floor. In the same moment, a ripping noise tore through the room.

Daniel split his skin. And where the rest of it had been agonizingly slow, this part was fast, so fast it was nearly impossible to catch.

He had changed.

In front of them, all four legs wobbling like a newborn giraffe, was a large, auburn wolf. Small interspersions of white marked the otherwise solid coat; his left ear, which was quivering and twitching uneasily with the other, and all four paws, as if he'd tread through white paint.

Winchester was barking excitedly, bounding around on the spot, and licking the wolf's muzzle.

Ian felt Devlyn go very quiet and very still in his arms, as if unable to comprehend what it all meant. Just how quickly everything had changed. Like an unexpected slap to the face. Ian let go of her and slid away, slowly getting to his feet. He felt suddenly cautious of the large animal in front of him.

"Danny?"

The wolf slowly turned to look at him, blinking as if to clear its vision.

Ian took a step forward, and it hastily backed up against the cupboards. Feeling cornered the wolf's ears flattened against its head, and the fur along its neck bristled. A low growl rumbled from deep in its throat.

Ian froze.

"Come on, man. You know who I am," he said hopefully. "You know me."

He took another step forward, and the wolf snarled, lips pulling back over its teeth. Ian was close enough to see its eyes now. Big and brown, and very much his brother's.

"You're in there," he said. His voice was forceful, willing it to be true. "I know it. So snap out of it. Fight the instincts, Dan.

You can do it. Shift back."

There was someone towering over Daniel. A threat. An enemy. Daniel lunged, giving a warning snap. What was he doing here? He didn't belong here. Something was wrong. The lights were too bright, there were too many voices, and too many sounds. Daniel's senses were alive and overly assaulted in this place.

The threat came back, his presence ever palpable. Too close. Too close. The voice grew. Too much. Daniel snapped again. He needed to escape. He didn't know where, and he didn't know how --but he needed to flee-- to run.

His surroundings suddenly snapped into perfect focus, crisp, clean, black and white.

The second one, the one behind the male was talking again. Making familiar sounds, but little sense.

"The fire escape. Use the fire escape."

Noise. So much noise.

"I'm not letting him out of here, Dev. We're not losing him again!"

There was more banging on the door and a muffled voice. "Miss Morrow? Miss Morrow, is everything all right?"

"Yes!" the female shouted, her voice high pitched, and Daniel winced. "I'm fine!"

Daniel could sense her vulnerability and her desperation, feel her sadness.

"Ian, help him!" she begged. Her eyes brimmed with wetness that rolled down her cheeks.

The male figure moved closer. Far too close.

Instinct took over and Daniel crouched, ready to lunge, to defend-- until his way was suddenly blocked.

The other dog stood in his path, no longer showing signs of devotion or submission. The Shepherd was now a pack leader, holding himself with an air of importance. The dog didn't growl or show aggression, just stood calm and firm, planted protectively between Daniel and the other figures. That was when Daniel realized, that somehow this dog had accepted these creatures into his pack. The figures belonged with the dog, they were his family, and he took care of them.

Daniel backed down. Even though he was far bigger and

215

could push a dominant level if he chose, he didn't, because this was something he finally understood, something he could sense, that made sense. The protectiveness, the willingness to put oneself on the line for the life of another. Somehow it was all... familiar.

Seeming to realize the attack was off, the tension in the room ebbed a notch. But Daniel felt exposed, outnumbered and packless, especially in claimed territory, and the moment their guards fell down-- he bolted.

Seizing the opportunity, he surged past them into the next room. Skidding on the slick floors, he crashed into a sofa, and then a side table, as he ran out of places to go, sending a lamp smashing to the floor behind him.

"Dan, it's okay," the female pleaded, and he could feel the tightness in the way she spoke. He was picking up on it, like it was contagious. It made him anxious, worried.

She took a step forward, and the male thrust an arm out to stop her, as Daniel careened into the TV stand. A picture toppled to the floor, narrowly missing his head. The glass shattered at Daniel's feet, and he sprang away from it, with unnatural speed.

"He can't stay here, Ian! He'll hurt himself!"

"And what do you think's going to happen out there?! This area's both a Fifth Worlder and Knocte hot zone now! "

Daniel overturned a potted plant, and it threw up soil all over the rug.

The muffled voice again, "Miss Morrow, what's all that racket? I'll call the police. You hear me? I'll call the police!"

Daniel felt the panic and nervousness spike in the room, like it was a palpable thing. There was silence for a blessed minute. And then, "The window. How do we get him through the window?"

The female looked around helplessly. "I don't know! Just open it."

The male moved to heft the window open, while the female continued to block the entrance to the kitchen. She now had a broom in one hand. Daniel could almost feel her resentment towards the object, even as she clutched it like a lifeline.

He paced the far wall uncertainly, where he'd retreated as much as he could from them both. If they moved too suddenly for his liking, or the dog got anywhere near, he barked fiercely in their direction. He felt trapped, caged. His ears stayed pinned back threateningly. He would give them trouble if they started it.

It seemed like ages, before they all backed off into the kitchen, and he could stop hugging the wall. Daniel dared to move forward, padding slowly and softly. He was cautious and watchful, but the moment he felt it, the cold hitting him, playing havoc with his fur, it was like he couldn't help himself. Through the window, the fresh air called to him, filled with the scent of trees, earth, and small animals. He felt his ears snap forward in joy. It was impossible to ignore. He leapt over the sill, and as he darted down the metal stairs, Daniel knew his escape was being watched. He felt the humans' eyes on him until the darkness of the night cloaked him from their sight and swallowed him whole.

You've reached Ruby. Leave a message.
Beep.
"Hey. It's Ian. I don't know why I'm doing this, but Dev kept insisting you needed to know. She would have told you herself but she's-- she's… well… yeah. But Dan" --there was a pause. A shuddering breath-- "Dan's umm… He's a lycanthrope. And you can thank your good for nothing Fifth World pieces of--."
Beep.

Ian was sitting alone on his bed in the Ay Motel, staring resentfully at the freshly painted wall across from him. Daniel and Devlyn had painted their names with a different colour in the top right corner, initialing their work of art. He'd left Winchester at Devlyn's, concerned about her being alone. In all honestly, he didn't really think it was a good idea for himself either.

He appeared placid on the outside, but on the inside it was taking every ounce of strength he had, to stop himself from smashing everything he could get his hands on. He'd had about ten fantasies in the last three minutes of completely re-trashing the motel room. He was pretty sure the lamps weren't going to survive the night.

He couldn't get the image of Devlyn out of his head. After Daniel had disappeared from sight, she'd wordlessly walked over to the couch and sat, wrapping her arms around herself protectively. Hunched over she'd cried quietly to herself. There wasn't a whole lot to say. They'd lost him. They'd both lost him. There was no fix in finding him and bringing him home. There was no longer a run and settle down option anymore. With the war against Fifth Worlders brewing-- his brother was the hunted.

Leaning forward Ian linked his fingers behind his neck, and fought hard to keep it all together. Then the door opened with a small creak, and Jim walked in, hands shoved deep in his pockets, face solemn. He sat beside Ian, lending his presence, and rubbed a hand over his tired, scrubby face. Once again nothing was said. There were just no words.

Daniel had found the park, the end of the city, and the start of the forest. His paws thundered over the terrain and his muscles leant him an everlasting strength. It was unlike anything he'd ever experienced before. This was right. This was how it should be. His pupils widened, taking in the moonlight, as his eyes searched through the darkness. Trees flew by in a blur, and his claws dug into the earth, propelling him forward. As he streaked through the forest, his tread was silent, the pads of his feet light on the foliage. The only sound was the sound of his breath, fogging in the cool night air ahead of him.

And then he smelt them. The wolves. The pack. Each with a scent more distinct than a name. He tensed and pushed himself harder, unsure of where he stood. But they fell in behind him, matching his strides and keeping pace. Then he understood. He felt it. Their acceptance. Their welcome. Not just *the* pack, but *his* pack. They were like a school of fish, when one member moved, they all felt it, the tiniest twitch and they all shifted as one.

A pale, cream coloured wolf pulled up at his flank, glowing eyes stealing weighted glances at him. There was something so familiar about the look, and about the wolf himself. Singling out the scent of the wolf individually-- it hit him. A scent more distinct than a name. And a name to go along with it.

Jack.

Daniel pulled up so suddenly that a wolf crashed into him from behind, and they were sent sprawling to the forest floor. But the blow was nothing in comparison to the onslaught of memories. His head pounded, as moment after moment of his life came rushing back.

218

His brother's face. Ruby's smile. Devlyn's lips. Jim's hearty laugh.

And he knew who he was.

Throwing his head back towards the starry sky, he let out such a howl, that it seemed to erupt from his very soul. The others came to a halt, circling back, pushing in around him. They too tilted their muzzles towards the moon, and lent him their voices. They knew his pain. Had felt what he felt. They cried out, when he cried.

He was Daniel Browning.

Dan.

Chapter Nineteen

"Drowning our sorrows are we?" Luke asked, taking the seat across from Ian.

Ian took another swig of his beer. Neither the drink, nor the familiar hum and stir of the Roadhouse, had been able to take the edge off the pit inside him.

"It's not funny," he growled. Luke sat silently, watching, the weight of his pitying eyes growing heavier and heavier, until Ian could hardly stand it. "What?" he snapped. "You want to say something, just say it."

"Is 'I told you so' too much?"

Ian felt his face cloud over. He shook his head. "Too soon, man," he warned.

But Luke seemed to have lost his patience. "There is no time for this nonsense, Ian. We cannot afford to keep waiting on you. This war is staring you in the face, and you need to make a decision. You are a big player, with more raw talent than ten Knoctes combined. We *need* that on our side. I will not underestimate their strength," he said firmly, and Ian knew he meant the Fifth Worlders. "Daniel made the mistake of trusting them, to an unfortunate end, but we can make it right. You can help us make it right. Please, brother. Join me."

For someone who always seemed so sure of himself, full of superiority, dignity and poise, there was an awful lot of pleading to be heard in Luke's voice.

"You're asking me," Ian said slowly. "to start a war against my own brother? In case you forgot, Luke, he's out there. He's one of those things, and I don't know where he is."

"That thing-- that creature Daniel turned into? You are going to tell me that, *that* is your brother? Did he even remember you? Know who you were?"

Ian downed the rest of his drink with a grimace.

"You have to accept it," Luke continued. "Your brother is gone, lost in his own mind."

"No," Ian said sharply. "He's in there. I know it."

"He will be nothing but the faint memory of the person he was."

Ian's eyes flashed. "I can pull him back," he said with assuredness. "I can draw him out. I've done it before."

"Ian, just--."

"I said, I can do it!" he shouted, pinning Luke with a cold glare that he knew, despite all calm appearances, never failed to rattle the man. Even when they were kids, it had been so. Luke may walk around with a self-bestowed importance, but there was a part of his old friend, Ian knew, that was scared of him. In Luke's eyes he was a wild card. A deadly one. One that was to be taken into serious account.

"Ian," Luke said patiently after a moment, pressing his hands together. "You are my friend and I care for you, but I am calling on this battle, and it is time to choose which side you are playing for. This war has begun."

Daniel's front legs stretched out ahead of him, his claws digging into the earth, as he lay whimpering into the fallen leaves. In his panic of realization, he had taken off from the pack, doing his best to lose them. Now his body shuddered and jerked. He could hear his bones breaking and reforming, the pain building until he could feel it behind his eyes. He was shifting. He was going to be human again. A twig snapped nearby, and he barely had time to register the scent of another wolf, before he no longer was one. He ripped out of his skin, the pain spiking to a high. He just caught a glimpse of a pair of glowing eyes, and had time to realize he hadn't lost all of the wolves, before darkness pulled him under.

"Hey!" A female voice said breaking through his consciousness. "Hey, come on, wake up."

Daniel peeled back his eyelids, his body feeling like it had been fed through a meat grinder. There was a girl sitting next to him. She had short, layered brown hair that hugged her face in a bob cut. It brought out the deep tan of her skin. Her eyes were so dark it was hard to pick out the pupil's until the light caught them. Resting beside where she sat, nudging his shoulder with her leg, was a small, neon blue, cloth bag. The name of a cell phone company was printed across it.

His face still pressed against the ground, Daniel let out a

heavy groan.

"Trust me, you're going to want to eat something, or you'll just waste away into those leaves."

Daniel propped himself onto his elbows, his limbs shaking unsteadily. He didn't feel quite solid in his skin yet, as his stomach continued to tie knots in itself. His dog tag necklace skimmed the ground beneath him.

"Why?" he asked. It was the only thing that seemed important. "Tell me why."

"Everyone wants to know why," she answered flatly. "It's always the same thing. Why me? I have a family, a life, a promising future. Now it's ruined, blah, blah, blah. I've heard the speech before, and you know what? I'm about done hearing it. Next time Luther can deal with this himself," she said frowning at the unknown and un-present Luther.

Daniel opened his mouth, whether to demand more answers, spew accusations, or let his anger burn, he would never know, because she immediately cut him off.

"Don't talk. Listen," she said putting up a hand. "I know you're experiencing this life altering reality at the moment, and the gears in your head are spinning a mile a minute, trying to cope and make sense of it all. I know. I've been there. Unfortunately, I really don't have time for it, because I need to get you up to speed. So, I guess that means it's your lucky day. You want story time? Well, here it is:

"The truth is, us Fifth Worlders were getting desperate. To the point that, even amongst rivaling groups, there was common talk of an oncoming war. A storm so great, it could leave us all in the dark forever. People panicked. Rumors flew around about which side was stronger. And I guess it was decided that the Browning brothers, and their renowned reputation tipped the scale in the wrong direction. Your brother duo needed to be broken up. A plan formed, a theory that if we could get to the younger, Scitor brother, we would rip the rug right out from under the older, Knocte one." She pointed at him. "You fall, Ian cracks. The end. We win.

"And that was all it took. Suddenly there was a resounding cry of 'Kill Daniel Browning!' flooding through every Fifth World network. It was presumed genius and everyone was on board.

"Then things started falling apart. Anytime someone got close, people died, or people changed their minds. Until, one day, a Scitor by the name of Jack gets changed into a lycanthrope, and finds himself accidentally running into a pack. My pack. He thinks he's got a better idea. 'Daniel Browning's different. He's the man with many faces. Have a chat. Get him on your side. He understands.' We started to believe him. But unfortunately, other Fifth World groups caught on to the same wavelength. And so started a new race. 'Find Daniel Browning. Secure him for your side.' Well, no Fifth World group was about to share, and my pack was done playing games. We weren't going to let anyone else get their paws on you-- our one hope. The man with all the connections, who likes to play from every side.

"So, here we are. Now, you can give me some indignant rant and take off pouting, but in the end, this is just how it is, and you need our protection."

Silence fell in between them for a moment and when Daniel finally spoke, his voice was low and deadly with a rage that boiled under his skin. "You know nothing of my brother, have no *idea* what he's capable of, or what he would have done, if you had succeeded in killing me. And you had no right to change me. *No* right to that kind of decision. I had agreed to help you!"

"And now you will," she said with a sudden flourish of her hands. "Just a little differently than you had originally planned. And we'll help you too."

"I can take care of myself, thanks," Daniel growled, forcing his aching body into a sitting position. "And you know what *I've* had about enough of? Your help."

She looked away from him with a sigh, and squinted into the fading sun. "Yeah, heard that one before too. You want to know what happens to all the wolves who strike out on their own? Try it their own way? They're dead."

Daniel said nothing, just stared down at his hands, shaking in his lap. He knew there was a valid point to what she was saying, but at the moment it wasn't the threat to his life he was worried about, so much as the emptiness to it. He was cut off, isolated from the most important people-- the people he loved.

"Ever thought it might have been on purpose?"

Her dark eyes flickered back to regard him.

"None of that," she said sharply. "We spent too much time on you, to let you even think about throwing it all away, and as your superior I have every right to smack some sense into you, if so required. Understand?"

Daniel blinked. "Superior?"

Her chin tilted up a notch. "Yes. I'm Jolie Temprin, the head female of the pack. Luther's your head male. You answer to us, and we'll both defend you with our lives, and put you in your place when you need it." Reaching over she retrieved a blue power drink and a candy bar from her bag, the kind with lots of peanuts and caramel. "So, here I am, looking after my pack, and trust me when I say this: you're going to want these."

Not waiting for a response she pitched them towards him one by one. He caught them against his chest.

Pulling out another power drink, Jolie cracked the seal and taking a deep pull, crossed her feet over at the ankles.

Daniel fingered the gifts longingly, his ravenous stomach as needy as ever, but his anger warded him off. As a wolf he could suppress the emotion, but human, it was suddenly too close to ignore. He didn't want to accept anything from her or her people. People who could un-regrettably cause so much pain. How many lives had they knowingly ruined? Enough for the process to become a routine and emotionless task.

"If it's poison you're worried about-- it's only in the bottom."

Daniel wasn't amused. Abruptly he dumped the bar and drink aside, turning instead to face her.

She gave him a stern, consequential look.

"I want to know," he said seriously, holding her gaze. "Who gave the order? To change me. Was it you?"

Something in his voice caused her disapproving expression to falter into a wary one, her eyes suddenly accusing, as she heard the underlining threat, and recognized it for what it was.

"I tell you, and you do something stupid," she said plainly.

"I've done my fair share of stupid, and I'm still here."

"I think," she said irritably, "you have your brother to thank for that. But what are you going to do, Daniel?" she asked. "Kill the person who altered the course of your life? Extract some sort of revenge? We both know that's not what you do, and you're not going to do it, so what choice do you have left? You can become a Knocte throw rug, or you can become a part of a family that cares for you."

"I have a family that cares for me," Daniel snapped. "I'm not looking for a new one."

She rolled her eyes, and recapped her drink. "Whatever." Rising to her feet, she brushed off her jeans. "This decision's yours. I just wanted you to know we'll be waiting for you."

She picked up her bag, hoisting it onto her shoulder, and began to walk away.

"Why'd you make me forget?" Daniel blurted suddenly, and she stopped in her tracks. Slowly, as if she'd rather not, she turned back around to face him. He thought he saw something flit across her face, before she managed to compose it into a neutral expression.

"It was just some faerie stuff we managed to get our hands on," she said. "Not my decision."

"Then who's was it?!"

She set her jaw and shook her head. "Look. The main reason you needed to forget was so that you *couldn't* put blame to any particular face. Call it what you want, a little insurance policy—whatever, but believe it or not, I have other engagements," she barked. "You're not the only member who needs taking care of, and you're not the only member I have to welcome into the pack either."

"You've changed more people?" Daniel said, his voice sounding horrified even by his own ears.

"One," she said firmly. "He's a doctor."

Daniel felt a sudden pang. A mix of indignation, and the realization that there never really was a solid way out of this life. No matter how far he could have pulled himself out, or how hard he could have strove to make something out of himself, he could still, very possibly, be sitting in the same exact position he was sitting in now. It could all be ripped away in one fleeting moment.

He fought the urge to scream all his frustrations at her. Instead he found himself saying, "That man worked hard to become what he was."

Jolie looked down at him with an unrelenting expression. "And now his efforts will be put to good use."

Daniel was about to say something else, when she threw a hand up.

"Just-- save it," she said sharply. "I don't have the time."

Then she spun on her heels and stalked off, muttering under her breath. Daniel thought he heard the word 'ungrateful', in her rantings. He watched her go with an expression of contempt, and two painful minutes later, he was a wolf again, her gifts to him laying forgotten on the forest floor.

Ruby pattered down the hall to Devlyn's apartment, searching for the right number, as she hugged her laptop to her chest. It had been two days, and she hadn't been able to get any work done since she'd heard about Daniel. Somehow the silence echoing around in her house seemed more permanent, more lonely than ever before. She sought company, any kind of company, but what she found as she neared apartment number two hundred and twenty-one, was unexpected-- even for Devlyn.

Ruby could hear music reverberating from inside, loud and overly demanding. It was death metal. Devlyn hated death metal. Ruby pushed her way into the apartment, grateful to find it unlocked, alarm off.

And froze in the doorway.

Her jaw hit the floor.

Nearly everything in the place was overturned, lying broken, or spilling out all over, looking exactly like a lycan had torn through it. There were scratch marks in the floor, and dog hair covering the furniture. But the most remarkable of all-- every wall, of every room Ruby could catch a glimpse of, was painted in a similar way.

Floor to ceiling wolves.

Wolves with glowing eyes, wolves with crouching figures, wolves prowling the forests of the walls. They were hiding in the shadows and baying triumphantly at the moon, an artistic phenomenon of which took a whole wall in and of itself, as full and bold as ever. Some lay quietly, and others bared their teeth, but most just watched, watched with their eerie eyes, so bright and utterly haunting.

Devlyn was standing at the counter, her arms covered in flour up to her elbows, as she rolled and molded dough with more

226

fervent efforts than were required for the job. Her blond curls were thrown up in a listless bun on the top of her head, and her clothes had that rumpled, disheveled look of being worn for more than one day in a row. Stacked on the table and beside her on the counter, were containers full of baking. Muffins, brownies, cookies, you name it. There were more than Ruby could count.

"Oh. Dear. Lord."

Her words went unheard, drowned out completely by the crashing coda of the current song. Devlyn, still completely oblivious to anything and everything, didn't even notice Ruby's appearance, until she'd rushed over and ripped the plug to the CD player out of the wall. The apartment fell into a ringing silence for a blessed moment, and then the sounds from the living room quickly rushed in to fill it. Ruby could hear both the TV and the treadmill running.

"Please tell me you haven't gone insane," Ruby begged, still clutching the CD player cord in one hand.

Devlyn blinked, then turned to look at her. "What are you doing here? I didn't buzz you in."

"Didn't have to," Ruby said, still a little cautiously. "I still have the key Dan loaned me."

"Oh," Devlyn said mildly, and then went back to kneading her dough.

Ruby didn't know what her friend was making now, but she did know it was entirely unneeded. "Your landlord is going to crap a brick."

Devlyn shrugged tense shoulders.

Ruby sighed, setting her laptop aside on a clean portion of counter. "Dev, I have news-- an update on Dan. It's why I came over, well that and the fact that I haven't been able to concentrate on even a morsel of--."

Suddenly an excited bark erupted from the living room.

From where she was standing, Ruby leaned back to peer into the living room. Winchester was running the treadmill at full tilt, his ears pricked forward towards the TV, which was set to the Animal Channel. A large cat was slinking across the screen. Winchester barked fiercely again.

"Why--? Why is Winchester *here*-- running on your treadmill?" she asked incredulously.

Devlyn, finally seeming to warm up to a conversation, left her dough. "Ian left him here for me, but after about two days of being cooped up, he got extremely bored. I wasn't really in the mood for any long walks so I… improvised."

"And what? Ian never came back for him?"

"Uh… no. No, not yet," Devlyn said seeming puzzled, her brow furrowing as if she was thinking for the first time, just how strange that really was. "Hope he's doing okay."

Ruby glanced uneasily back towards Devlyn, feeling uncomfortable as always around the subject of Ian. He wasn't the brother she'd come to talk about. She'd come here for other reasons. Grabbing Devlyn's wrist she led her over to the table where she righted a chair and motioned for her to sit.

"Dan came into himself. He remembers, Dev, and the pack accepted him," Ruby said when they were both seated, and Ruby had dusted off her chair as best she could.

Devlyn buried her forehead into the heels of her hands, but it was a sign of relief, tension leaving her shoulders. "Oh, thank God. Thank God, thank God, thank God."

Ruby cringed slightly. "But…"

Devlyn looked up sharply, echoing her, "But?"

"He's decided," she said exhaustedly, "not to join them. He's going to try and go it alone."

"Why?" Devlyn asked, horrified, her eyes growing rounder with concern again. "Why would he do that? There's a bunch of self-righteous Knoctes flailing guns around out there, who think they have something to prove to Luke."

"Let's face it, Dev," Ruby said. "The pack took everything from him. You, me… his brother. Any family he had left, any hope of the future he'd planned for-- gone. He's not going to give in so easily."

Devlyn nodded solemnly in understanding. Loose curls escaped her bun, and fell against her shoulders. "He's got to let it go first. He has to forgive them."

"We just need to talk to him, get a message to him somehow…"

Devlyn looked up at her. "How did you get this information, Ruby? Do you know anyone? Have any connections that could swing something like that?"

Ruby shook her head quickly. "The lycanthropes are a tight sect. They don't make a lot of friends on the outside."

"Then… how do you know any of this?"

"Marley told me…" Ruby answered.

Devlyn's eyebrows shot up. "And *she* has connections in the pack? She's a Knocte!"

"I don't know, okay?" Ruby said quickly, throwing her hands up. "I don't know how she finds out these things. The only things I do know lately are what she tells me."

Devlyn sighed, and rubbed her face with her hands, smearing a flour line across her cheek. "I can't keep doing this," she admitted. "I can't keep waiting around for answers. I have to go out and *do* something. The worst course of action is inaction."

"So, is that what you were doing, painting murals and making tens of thousands of batches of cookies?" Ruby asked. "Being in action?"

Devlyn frowned. "I dunno. Maybe. But lately I've been thinking about going back to work at the Roadhouse. We could use an inside man more than anything right now."

Ruby felt her brow knit with worry. "You'd have to be careful though. *Very* careful. Only God knows how dangerous that could be if Luke finds out what you're really doing."

Nodding, Devlyn leaned back in her chair, her expression growing distant again. "Only God knows…" she whispered to herself.

Chapter Twenty

Daniel was lying hidden under a fallen tree, ripping greedily at a rabbit carcass between his front paws. It wasn't easy being on his own. It seemed like he never stopped hunting, never stopped tracking his next meal. He was always watching his back, and keeping to the shadows. He had a sense that he was haunting the woods, rather than actually becoming any part of it. He felt rundown, unsettled, and more wolf in each moment than human.

Careful to consume every part of his meal he could, he turned away from it and sighed into the leaves. He could feel his stomach, semi-full at least, urging his body towards some much needed rest. He watched the forest around him suspiciously through half lidded eyes, until their weight became too much.

The instant his mind drifted, a small voice seemed to creep into his head. With every muscle that relaxed into sleep, it crescendoed into existence.

"Oh… that's it… I think… and-- yes! We're asleep!"

Daniel was laying on his back in a stretch of grass. He blinked up at the face hovering above him. He flexed his fingers. Human.

"Reid," he said, feeling less than thrilled at the man's appearance. The man had been haunting his dreams night after night, so readily, that for the last couple of days, Daniel had forgone sleep for more reasons than those necessary to his survival.

"I've been trying to get a hold of you, mate!"

"My head isn't a telephone, Reid," Daniel said with a sigh, sitting up and brushing grass from his hair.

"Well, it is for *me*-- if you remember what I am. I'm not doing any veterinarian, forest house calls now am I?"

"That's not funny," Daniel scowled.

"No," Reid agreed sitting himself down next to him. "You're right, Daniel. Your solo adventure is losing its charm. If you were a part of the pack, you wouldn't be wolfed out 24/7. You could actually walk around as yourself. You'd be protected."

Daniel gave him a hard look.

"It's a *good* thing," Reid assured him. "Brilliant, actually."

"Yeah, you've been saying that," Daniel said automatically.

"But I'm not so sure."

Reid adopted a rather uncharacteristic glare. "Have you taken *anything* I've showed you in the past seriously?"

"Uh…" In all honesty it was something he'd tried very hard to forget.

"You're the glue, the securing elastic band, the one keeping Ruby with her morals, and Ian from Luke. You're the reason Devlyn's agreed to go undercover for our side. We can't have our glue running around, in danger of getting himself killed, because he's 'not so sure'!"

"You're starting to sound like Jolie," Daniel accused. Then another aspect of the speech flickered through his head. "What was that about Dev?"

"Not all the lycanthropes were responsible for your change, mate," Reid said seriously, ignoring Daniel's last question. "Some of them are just like you, forced into a life they never asked for. They're good people. Are you going to punish them for the actions of their leaders? You can help them, Daniel. And you can let them help *you*."

Daniel looked around with a sigh, and came to realize, suddenly, that it was the lawn in front of Devlyn's apartment they sat on. The building loomed up beside them. He could imagine her face, happy, and alight, like the lantern in the painting over her door. He could see her leaning out the window, her blond curls hanging free past her shoulders, as she smiled and called down to him. His mind fell into the reverie so effortlessly, it was almost as if he couldn't help it. He seemed to be drinking more of the past lately than was healthy, but the uncharacteristic future he was faced with left him torn. There were too many choices to be made, and not enough knowledge to make them. Again he thought of Devlyn, and her ever-prevailing faith.

"You make it sound easy."

They sat in silence for a moment. A lone cricket started up to Daniel's left, and with an immediate thought he wiped it from existence. He'd just begun to ponder Reid's passing comment about Devlyn again, when the man distracted him.

"It might help to know that Miss Morrow and Miss Becker are both waiting for you to become a member."

Daniel couldn't leave the skepticism out of his voice. "And

how would you know that?" he scoffed.

The moment he said it-- he knew.

"Well…" Reid began, but Daniel turned on him.

"You've been inside their heads again haven't you?"

Reid looked like he very much wanted to disappear into the grass.

Daniel made a mental note not to let that happen.

"I… ah… well, maybe a little…" the man admitted sheepishly.

Daniel shot to his feet. "I told you to take a step back, man-- like ten! You get to snoop around my head, but the line draws there, understand. Some things just aren't meant to be looked at, or uncovered. And I think the category of private thought, falls under those headings."

"I'd say," Reid said unexpectedly. "I tapped into Luke's mind once." --he gave an induced shudder-- "and trust me when I say this, mate-- I'm scarred for life."

Daniel made a furious sound in the back of his throat, his eyes slitting. He didn't find it funny. Suddenly the cricket was back, a hundred more joining in the song, until the bushes nearby were humming with the noise, the sound climbing into a menacing number.

"This isn't a game," Daniel blurted. "We're not chess pieces you get to push around."

Reid's face grew serious again. "I know that," he said evenly. "It's like some six year old found the super glue, and pasted your stubborn Knight permanently to the board. Not so easily pushed around as you might think. You can only do so much in the subconscious-- watch, drop hints, dreams, anything else and they would know I'm there. And just *try* to get into your brother's brain, it's like trying to claw through a brick wall."

Daniel began to throw another rebuke, but Reid rushed on. "Listen, you just needed to know. Devlyn and Ruby, they just want you to have a little back up, that's all, some players on your side," Reid insisted. "*That's* what's important right now."

Daniel felt his anger go out of him. He felt tired and drawn. "I think it's time to go, Reid. Sorry, but I need my head person free every now and then. Just give me room to think, all right?"

With some effort, Daniel pulled at the landscape around

them with his mind, slowly ripping it down like wallpaper. He tried to image the fallen log he knew he was laying under, the feel of the leaves beneath him. He pictured having four legs again and that incredible sense of smell.

A familiar scent hit him, and he pushed his brain, straining for it. The scene plummeted into darkness, and Reid faded from sight, a look of displeasure on his face. The last thing Daniel remembered before waking up in the woods, was Reid calling after him:

"It's what they want, mate. You got to believe me! It's what they want!"

The forest came into clear black and white view in the next instant. Lifting his snout Daniel sought out the smell that'd drawn him out. Now that he was conscious again, he recognized it for what it was, or rather-- who it was.

Jack.

But he wasn't alone. Dozens of wolves, their distinct scents following them, seemed to press in around him. He let out a low warning growl, feeling his space invaded, and they halted in their advance.

Then slowly, one lone wolf stepped closer, pushing his black nose through the nearest shroud of foliage.

Daniel sprang to his feet defensively, his claws leaving grooves in the earth, but the other wolf stayed on the perimeter, watching him almost inquisitively, keeping at a respectful distance. Their gazes held steady on one another for a moment, and then the dark wolf suddenly tilted his head back and let out a short, night chilling howl. It seemed to sail clear through the canopy of trees above them, and towards the looming moon hanging in the sky. Daniel waited for the pack's response, but no one else lent their voices, although several pairs of glowing eyes were now watching attentively from the bush. The black wolf was watching him again too, waiting, expectant.

Then Daniel got it.

It was an invitation.

A second offer to join the pack. They hadn't given up on him.

Daniel had a flashback to the first night he'd shifted. He remembered running with the pack, falling into step almost naturally with them, picking up on the signals, and feeling their support when he cried out to the darkness. He felt frozen with the memory.

A pang of longing struck him.

Another wolf emerged from the bush, taking a stance of superiority at the black wolf's side, and Daniel found he could put a name to the she-wolf in front of him.

Jolie gave a small hopeful howl, and then watched him with her dark shining eyes. The black wolf touched the side of her face with his nose, and Daniel immediately knew him to be Luther, the head male. One of the hidden wolves --probably Jack-- gave a tentative, impatient yip of encouragement.

But Daniel couldn't forget why he'd felt the way he had that first night, why he'd called out into the darkness.

He remembered the familiar faces he'd seen, and had almost forgotten. Ian, Devlyn, Ruby, Jim…

Even his present form wasn't enough to squander the ache it left inside him, and without a sound he turned his back on the pack, and returned to his spot under the fallen log, the leaves still indented from his stay. He could feel their disappointment like a palpable thing, and slowly the glowing pairs of eyes melted back into the darkness of the forest, one by one. After a moment's pause, the head male and head female also turned away, leaving him to himself. To his thoughts.

Only then could he hear just how still the forest had become, the silence ringing in his ears. All other forms of life had fled with the previous onslaught of wolves, or continued to lay fearfully in quiet hiding. The emptiness was instantaneous. After so many nights alone, Daniel had to admit, stubbornness aside, that he craved the presence of the other wolves. A wolf was a pack animal, and no matter how much he denied that part of him, it didn't stop it from being true. He dug his claws into the ground and let out a small whine.

His conversation with Reid played over in his head, the parts about Devlyn and Ruby he continually circled back to. Were they worried? Did they really wish for him to join the pack that'd taken him from them? Was it the only option? *Was* he being overly reckless?

Could he forgive them?

Devlyn could. He knew she could. She gave forgiveness out like candy, because that's what her God did, forgave anyone who asked-- without question. It was just that easy. That. Easy. She was a better person than he'd ever be. It was why he loved her. And why he could come to believe that despite everything, she could still care, still want to protect him.

Daniel hadn't even realized what he was doing, until he found himself standing in front of the bushes where the wolves had disappeared, tilting his muzzle back towards the sky. A howl burst from his lungs, cutting through the silence like a knife. He pushed it to such a crescendo, it seemed to rattle the very leaves above him. For a long minute it was just him, his voice alone, and then-- there was an answer. Far away at first, but growing, until in the next moment, Luther was directly in front of him again, his appearance as soundless as ever. They stood so close their front paws nearly touched, Luther's deeper, huskier howl blending in with the piercing resonance of his own, in a chorus of acceptance and belonging. The pack erupted in the distance, their excited yips and barks springing forth to welcome him home.

Daniel was human again, his world suddenly, overwhelmingly visually dependent. The vibrant colors he'd gone so long without seeing, blinded him and gave him a headache. His senses were still acute, greater than any Innocent's, but his world no longer revolved around the distinct smells of everything around him. He did however, find himself staring at his hands and flexing his fingers a lot.

He was sitting across from Jack in a small food joint called Dig Dog Diner, occupying a particularly red booth. The diner was overflowing with lycans; nearly every customer in the place was a member of the pack. It was strange to be around them all like this-- human.

Everything seemed of little importance, however, to the laminated pages of the menu in his possession. He hadn't lifted his eyes off the thing, from the moment it had been placed in front of him. He was so beyond starving, there were no words.

"I'm craving a hamburger, like there's no freaken tomorrow," Daniel said as he continued his perusal of the menu. "Is that normal?"

"You're not even listening to me are you?" Jack asked, pushing his glasses back up the bridge of his nose.

"No," Daniel said honestly. "I'm thinking a double cheeseburger. Think I could get it without veggies?"

"Trust me, you want the Mega Mutt," Jack said reaching over to tap a picture of a plate, full to bursting with pancakes, sausages, bacon and eggs. "Shifting the first few times is like waking up with a massive hangover. The greasier the better. But as I was saying-- you came into yourself remarkably fast. It usually takes wolves a couple weeks to do what you did in a couple of hours."

"It was you," Daniel said, as he seriously considered Jack's suggestion. "It was like somehow the wolf scent, combined with the presence of someone I already knew, just made everything make sense. That little click was all I needed, and everything else came flooding back."

Now *that* had been a headache. The one he was nurturing at present had little to stand on in comparison.

"It took me near a week and a half to remember who I was," Jack muttered quietly to himself, as the waitress swung by to take their order. Remembering Carmen, Daniel avoided her gaze completely, as he ordered the Mega Mutt, and then handed over his menu.

He sat, watching the other members of the pack stab at their bacon and laugh until soda came out their nose. The place echoed with the sound of fork against plate, the squeak of skin against leather booths.

It was all so mundane; it was hard to imagine that the night before they'd been streaking through the forest together, a silent and deadly force.

Daniel had never been part of such a family. In the Knocte world his brother team up had been surreal beyond all else, but in this world, the Fifth World, the togetherness was as easy as breathing. Everything they did, they did as one.

The head male was the only member not present.

Luther, in person, was the tall dark type, with a sinister feel, and Daniel found he could catch a glimpse of the man if he stared out the window long enough. Their leader was nothing but a flitting shadow on the edge of the parking lot. He was a wolf doing what a leader did best-- guarding his flock.

"Well, well, well. Took you long enough, now didn't it?" came Jolie's voice, drawing Daniel's attention back into the diner and back to their table. "Bet you're thinking you shouldn't have refused that candy bar right about now."

She slid into the booth across from him. Jack was looking at her with a wide-eyed expression, like he never thought he'd see the day, when she would sit next to him and start up a conversation.

"I'm not thinking anything," Daniel said tersely, even though it was a lie. He'd begun calculating how long he thought their food would take, judging the time it took for different food types to come out to the other tables.

"So, it's too hungry for rational thought, then?" she smirked.

"Hey, I was doing fine," he shot back. "You know I was, otherwise you wouldn't have been so concerned I wouldn't join the pack. I mean, two invites, truly I'm honored. Sure, being on my own wasn't an ideal situation, but I survived all the same."

She leaned back in the seat and crossed her arms over her chest. "Up until now. But it was only a matter of time before a Knocte came poking around, especially with that brother of yours knowing so much about you. All he would have to do--."

"Before," Daniel cut in coldly, "you take that road, I suggest weighing the consequences."

She scowled so deeply her eyebrows furrowed into a 'V'. "Watch who you're talking to."

Daniel's hand clenched into a fist at his side. Where had all his patience gone? Ian was always throwing crap comments and superior condescension at him, and it'd never reached his last nerve like this. He felt completely ungrounded in the sea of new faces around him.

Jack read his expression and immediately threw himself into the conversation.

"I'm Jack," he said thrusting his hand in front of Jolie's face.

She turned, looking him over slowly from top to bottom. "Yeah," she said, her arms remaining crossed. "I know who you are."

Jack held his hand out awkwardly for another second, before pulling it away to scratch the back of his neck uneasily. He threw Daniel a shrug when she wasn't looking.

Suddenly the diner door was forcefully thrown open across the room.

Every head snapped up on the alert, the diner lapsing into instant silence. Luther strode through, his short, jet black hair sticking up at every angle, evidence he'd shifted only moments before hand. He held his shoulders straight in his black t-shirt, and his jeans rode so low on his hips, his boxers were showing. He looked furious. He gave a hard tug and forcefully pulled someone into the diner behind him. A small someone, with dark translucent hair, a flowing neon yellow shirt, and a pair of matching glittering heels. She looked up at Luther, an expression of terror written on her face.

"*Ruby?*" Daniel gaped in disbelief, but the diner had erupted into such a noise, that his words were instantly drowned out. He strained to hear what was being said.

"I didn't mean-- I just wanted to see…"she begged, shaking her head furiously from side to side.

Luther jerked her towards him, his face maliciously scowling down at her. His hand was wrapped so tightly around her upper arm, it was cutting off circulation.

"Shut up, fae!" he growled.

A shot of anger exploded in Daniel's chest.

"Hey!" he yelled across the diner, gaining several eyebrow raised stares.

Jolie slid down in her seat, looking extremely displeased. Mortified, as if he'd spoken out of turn. "You know her?" she hissed sideways at him.

Daniel rose firmly to his feet. "She's my best friend."

The moment he was standing, Ruby's gaze found him. Her eyes went wide.

"Dan!" she cried, so many emotions flitting across her face at once, it was hard to pick one. Surprise. Relief. Sadness. Anxiety. She reached out for him with her free hand, but Luther jerked her back.

"Let her go!" Daniel shouted jogging towards them. As he drew closer, he repeated himself again with a calm finality. "Let her go, she's with me."

Some of the diner's staff had started exchanging tense glances and worried looks between themselves. One of the waitresses was unknowingly pouring coffee onto the floor. Luther seemed to register this, and looking around at them, it was like he'd suddenly become aware of how much attention they'd drawn to themselves. Giving Daniel a dark look, he reluctantly dropped his hold, taking a grudging step back.

The moment Ruby was free, she threw herself at Daniel, clutching his shirt in a vice, and burying her face in his shoulder. He wrapped his arms protectively around her.

"What're you doing here, Bee?" he whispered against her ear.

She pulled away slightly to look at his face.

"I'm sorry! I'm so sorry!" she exclaimed, and started wiping the tears rolling down her cheeks impatiently away with her fingertips. "I heard you finally joined, but I was tired of going off other people's word. I thought I was going to lose it, if I didn't see it for myself. I can only hold myself and Dev together for so long, without *some* kind of proof."

Daniel felt his chest constrict at the mention of Devlyn's name. Ruby must have sensed the change too, because biting her lip her eyes flickered away nervously.

"How is she?" He asked. He couldn't help but ask.

"She's, umm…"

"Umm?"

Ruby glanced around them, at all the watching faces, and when she spoke again, her voice was pitched much lower. "Can we talk, Dan? Like really talk?"

He nodded.

"You might have to do something for me first though…"

"Anything," he promised.

"Get me out of here alive?"

Jolie saw them head towards the door and knew there was going to be a problem, the moment Luther stepped out to block their path. Daniel had one arm still wrapped around the faerie, and the moment Luther moved, Daniel positioned her slightly behind himself. It was the first time she saw the Daniel she'd heard about, and not the bitter, wounded puppy she'd been experiencing since he'd shifted.

She'd caught a glimpse of his caring characteristic before, in the field that day they let Jack talk to him, but since then, it seemed to have buried itself under a layer of disappointment and pain. That was-- until now. A face from the past, and everything he was, the person he was, turned on as if with a flick of a switch. She saw the stubborn protectiveness, the loyalty and the heart behind it. In that instant she knew this was what he needed. If they were going to get the Daniel Browning they'd bargained for, he needed this encounter.

Immediately she slid out of the booth, striding towards the diner's entrance, and the tense stand off waiting there.

"Don't get your breeches in a knot, Daniel," She muttered when she passed him.

She could feel the faerie watching her warily as she grabbed Luther's shirtsleeve and dragged him a few steps away from them.

"What are you doing?" she demanded of him in a harsh whisper.

"What am *I* doing?" Luther spat her question back at her. "Protecting the pack, Jo, what are *you* doing? We don't know who this faerie is, or what she'll do with the information of our whereabouts. We have no friendly relation with the fae."

"You want to talk about protecting the pack? Then let's talk about protecting the pack," Jolie snapped, "Just take a look at what I've been doing for the last two months, and *pay attention*. That boy" --she inclined her head discreetly in Daniel's direction-- "whether you like it or not, has his part to play. The faerie's not the threat we should be worrying about, she's a friend of Daniel's and nothing more."

"That can't--."

"It's *exactly* what we bargained for, what we wanted even, when we took him on. If Jack was the only Fair Child he knew, we wouldn't have had any competition securing him. But we managed it, we got him, and we *need* him." She gave him an impatient look. "Comprende?"

Luther's jaw was clenched, his scowl deeper. "Still, if you think I'm going to let--."

But Jolie hurriedly cut him off again. "I'll watch them."

"Jolie," he said slowly, impatiently. He knew she hated it when he used her full name.

"I said, I'll watch them!" she said irritably, and turned to snap in the direction of Daniel and the faerie. "You and you. Outside. Now."

Daniel didn't argue, as he moved past her, with the faerie in tow. She-- what had he called her? Ruby? --clenched his hand like a lifeline, following closely behind him. Her translucent hair swished with each step. Jolie gave Luther a quick warning look, before taking up the rear and following the two outside.

The chilly last summer breeze rustled past Jolie the moment she stepped outside, and she zipped her coat up to her chin, annoyed. She'd be warmer as a wolf, but she settled for leaning against the outside of the building instead.

She watched Daniel and Ruby plant themselves on the curb. They sat in silence for a moment, as if they weren't quite sure where to start. Ruby was huddled so close to him, Jolie was pretty sure she would have crawled onto Daniel's lap if she could have.

Then all at once, Ruby started talking. Maybe talking was the wrong word, more like spilling, and pouring everything out in a rush, as if she thought the earth would somehow deny her the time to speak it all. Jolie only caught snitches of it. She heard something about Daniel's brother Ian leaving a Winchester at somebody's house, and then about him breaking in days later to retrieve it without anyone's knowledge. There was a hushed bit about someone named Devlyn, where Daniel rubbed the back of his neck a lot, the broken, puppy dog look emerging. Ruby pulled out a phone and started scrolling through what looked to be her picture album for him. Handing the phone over, his eyes went wide.

"She *painted* that?" he choked out.

It sounded like a rhetorical question, but Ruby answered with a nod. "The whole apartment."

He sank his head in his hands, slowly shaking it back and forth, and muttered the name Dev over and over again. Something in the way he said it, the aching despair, sent a shiver down Jolie's spine. She was overly relieved when Jack interrupted, pushing his way outside, but he only delivered Daniel's food in a Styrofoam to-go container, and left again. Jolie caught his eye briefly, but he

241

immediately looked away, hurriedly shoving at the diner door to get back inside. To be expected, she didn't normally spend time with the lower ranks, and Luther had done the negotiations with Jack over Daniel's case. With a sigh, she turned back, about to settle in for another go round, when she saw Daniel offer the Styrofoam container to Ruby. Something flared up inside Jolie then, and she pushed off the wall.

"*You* should eat, Daniel," she chastised.

"I'll be fine, Jolie," Daniel muttered. "I'll hunt later."

"It's Jo," she said sharply. "And I think time's up here. Tinker Bell needs to run along." She gave Ruby a hard look. "Far away, if she knows what's good for her."

Daniel started to protest, when Ruby put a hand up to stop him. "It's okay," she said, getting to her feet. "She's probably right." The faerie girl glanced in Jolie's direction. "Thank you, for helping us." Then after a pause. "I'm Ruby by the way."

Jolie fought a grimace, as Ruby extended a hand in her direction. She wasn't sure why people kept trying to introduce themselves when she already knew who they were.

"I think," she said instead of complying to the handshake, "it would be a bad idea if you were seen poking around here again, Ruby. If we understand each other."

Ruby withdrew her hand seeming disappointed, but unsurprised, and Daniel gave a sigh that was somewhere in the middle ground of frustration and exasperation.

"I forgot to tell you she's allergic to handshakes," he said apologetically to Ruby. "And I'm not entirely sure manners are in her vocabulary either."

Trying not to be offended, Jolie watched the two share a small smile. Then Ruby reached out and tousled Daniel's richly, auburn tinted brown hair.

"We'll figure it out, okay?" Ruby said. "We'll think of something."

One quick embrace later and a "Bye, Bee" from Daniel, and Ruby hurried out of sight, shoes tapping on the asphalt.

Jolie immediately glanced over at Daniel, in an attempt to get a reading on his expression, but it was too overly placid to tell if the visit had left him lighter, or more troubled than before.

Chapter Twenty-One

Jim's study had transformed into a hurricane of string and papers. The papers varied both from newspaper clippings and articles printed from the web, to Ian's own scrawled writing and pages torn from reference books. Anything that hinted at wolf sightings, possible Knocte movements, or related to lycanthropy -- no matter how wild-- had made it onto the massive bulletin board behind Jim's old oak desk. They were stapled up hurriedly and haphazardly, blue string connecting wolf sightings, and red string following the Knoctes.

At the desk sat Ian, a large map of the surrounding area spread out across the surface in front of him, adorned with both his markings and coffee stains. A few other items also claimed the desk, an array of sharpies, Ian's handgun loaded with silver bullets, and a fifth of whiskey, new a couple hours ago, and now half gone.

Jim shook his head, watching Ian with deep concern, where he stood unnoticed in the doorway. The kid hadn't slept in what seemed like weeks, cramming his brain chock-full of dead ends during the day, and patrolling abandoned streets in his truck at night. The bags under his eyes had become black bruises, his expression growing more tired and drawn with each passing day. He was running himself into the ground trying to find his brother. Even now, as he took another swig of his drink, meshing his eyes shut, he was barely keeping himself from nodding off.

Jim was bone tired too, he'd exhausted his resources and means of persuasion in every way he could think of, but they were getting nowhere, and no one was willing to step up to the plate and help them.

His phone rang.

Quickly stepping out of the doorway, and back into the hall, he hit the answer key.

"Yeah," he barked, unable to keep the edge out of his voice.

"Sor-ry," came the reply, and he could practically hear the eye roll. "I didn't realize I'd reached the set of Grumpy Old Men."

"Who is this? And what is it you want?"

"It's your friendly neighbourhood Marley Shray, answering

the recruitment call I hear you put out awhile back for heroes."

He was surprised to hear from her. He hadn't seen her since the day Daniel woke up, and had figured she'd picked up a case and moved on.

"Forget heroes," he sighed wearily. "I would settle for a couple of decent folks at this point."

"Right," she said. "And how's that going?"

"About as well as my fifteen year old lawn mower," he grumbled. "No one's budging an inch from Luke's side. A bunch of brain washed monkeys…" he muttered under his breath.

"Well I'm budging. Just called to tell you that I'm looking too," she said earnestly, and Jim had never been so glad to hear anything in his life. "Any sign of Daniel?"

He scrubbed a hand over his whiskered face. "Not particularly… I guess Ruby caught sight of him a couple of weeks ago, but they've covered their tracks and disappeared long since then. I've been keeping my eyes peeled, watching the news, trying to think up a new angle to this whole thing."

"And Ian?" she inquired.

Jim heaved another sigh, this one running down to his very soul. He took a step, placing himself back into the frame of the doorway.

Ian had collapsed onto the desk, cheek against unforgiving wood, finally succumbing to the sleep he so desperately needed. Regrettably, Jim knew it wouldn't last nearly as long as the boy needed it to.

"Like death," he admitted. "It's like he's on autopilot. Doesn't sleep, hardly eats. His drinking…" he trailed off.

"You're worried," she stated, and by the sound of her voice, he wasn't the only one.

"Darn right I'm worried. He's in a dark place right now. Luke's planted a seed. A deadly one. And Ian's been running himself ragged trying not to believe it-- but I see its poison working. I'm starting to wonder if the search for Dan hasn't become some twisted outlet to prove Luke wrong and affirm what he's always believed."

"You don't really mean that."

He was quiet for a minute. "No," he admitted. "No, I suppose I don't. I just wish I had better luck reaching the kid, that's all."

He could hear thoughtful tapping on her end of the line. "Well, hang in there, Jim. We'll sort this out," she promised.

Wandering into the study, he shucked his jacket off, draping it carefully over his son's unconscious form.

"I sure hope to God that's true," he said fervently, softly as not to wake Ian, "'cause I don't think this old heart of mine can take much more of this."

Chapter Twenty-Two

Jolie fingered the police tape, as it twisted in the wind. It wound between the posts of a barbwire fence, running the perimeter of an acreage. The pack stood far enough away from the paint peeling country house that the investigators took very little notice of them. They weren't the only curious onlookers. Neighbours, concerned citizens, and newscasters alike were pushing at the boundaries, shouting, demanding answers, thrusting microphones and cameras into the faces of the police.

The sight stretched out in front of them all was gruesome.

Wolf bodies laid strewn across the front yard, dozens of bloody, matted corpses, with lifeless glassy eyes and sprawling tongues. There were a couple human bodies as well, bullet wounds tearing through their shirts, penetrating their chests. That was the real reason why the police were here-- the murders.

But Jolie knew better. The bodies were all connected. One of the same.

A lycanthrope pack taken down in cold blood.

No doubt the Government Division of the Supernatural had picked up on this, and wouldn't be far behind either.

She glanced over at Daniel, who stood at her right side, taking in the Knoctes' handiwork. His face was grim, lined with sorrow and furrowed with anger, his soft brown eyes, suddenly and incredibly dark. She could see his rage boiling under his usually calm surface.

He caught her looking.

"This has to stop," he said to her, his voice commanding it.

Luther had other ideas. "We need to leave," he said from her left, at almost the same time. "Get as far away from here as we can, go into hiding."

Daniel swung around, and she cursed him internally for his inability to follow orders.

"We're running?" he asked incredulously, though his tone was threatening.

Luther's dark, irritated eyes shifted towards him. "I won't let this happen to my pack," he said curtly.

Something in Daniel's eyes flared. "The reason this

happened was *because* they were running and hiding."

"They did a poor job of it," Luther stated. "I'll do better."

Daniel shook his head disbelievingly.

"What?" Luther snapped. They were downright icy with each other. "You got a better idea."

"Yeah," Daniel said immediately, the muscles in his shoulders tensing, as he turned squarely to face his head male. "I do. We team up-- with our own kind, with other Fair Children, and we create a front." His voice spiked in volume. "We don't *sit around* waiting for the moment when it's our turn to get picked off."

"This is about *our* survival!" Luther spat. "You're talking about a war!"

"It's about EVERYONE'S survival!" Daniel countered, his chest heaving, his anger spilling. "They're never going to stop! -- You have to get that! They want us dead." His eyes searched those of the other members. "All of us."

Luther took a threatening step forward, and Jolie threw up a hand to ward him off.

"He needs to be taught his place!" Luther snapped at her.

"Luther..." she said in exasperation.

"You changed me," Daniel surged on, his hands shaking, "for my help. I'm giving it to you! *Please*," he begged abruptly. "Take it!"

Luther glared at him for several beats.

"I don't take orders from you," he hissed finally. "No matter how 'inspiring' the speech." And then turning away, he addressed his masses. "Let's move! It isn't safe here!"

Several pairs of eyes, currently locked on Daniel, slid back to their leader, and they followed him out from the scene, hushed tones, and whispered comments carried along with them.

Daniel didn't move.

"Daniel," Jolie said harshly, when the rest were out of earshot. "You can't keep doing this. You have to go through me. He will *kill* you. Do you understand me? *This* is what has to stop. Just forget about all the rest, okay? And so help me-- *behave* yourself!"

Brown eyes burned into her. "That speech about me being the man with many faces. The one with all the connections you needed-- that was a load of bull wasn't it?"

"Don't be ridiculous, of course we want that… It's just--."

But Daniel cut her off, something she wouldn't have let any other member get away with. "If you wanted my help," he snapped, "really wanted it. Then you should have shook Ruby's hand when she offered it to you."

And with that, he turned his back on her, another foul up that usually didn't go unpunished, and stalked after the pack.

Standing at the stove, Jim dragged a lasagne from the oven. The news droned quietly in the background from an old black and white television set. It sat on the coffee ringed table, its rabbit ears stretching through the air.

At Jim's side, Winchester whined quietly, eyes never leaving the pasta dish in his hand. Rolling his eyes at the dog, who'd been fed his own meal not two minutes ago, Jim moved to the table, placing the food on a hot mat in front of Ian.

Ian stared at it blandly from his chair, his expression unreadable.

"I'm not hungry, Jim," he mumbled. He was poking at the prongs of his fork in agitation.

"I don't give a lick, son," Jim said dropping into the chair across from him, and pulling off his oven mitts. "Eat."

Ian set his fork down roughly. "Dan's still out there."

Jim glowered. "I'm not talking about calling off the search! You think you're the only one who wants to find him?" he asked rather harshly. "I'm talking about being in the sort of condition that might actually do your brother some good. You need to eat, sleep-- get your head on straight."

"I'll sleep when I'm dead," Ian deadpanned.

Jim let out a long breath, willing himself some patience. "Which will be sooner rather than later if you don't *eat something*."

He pointed at the food again, and with a scowl Ian began dishing it onto the plate in front of him.

Satisfied, Jim turned towards the TV-- and nearly fell off his chair. Quickly recovering himself he scrambled for the volume dial.

A news lady with stylishly curled hair, stood outside of an

old rundown farmhouse. "--wolf attack outside of city limits has police stunned at the unprecedented amount of deaths, and sends them wondering at, and investigating into the odd behaviour..."

But Jim wasn't listening to her words.

Because behind her, across the yard at the paralleled fence perimeter, stood an auburn haired, brown eyed boy of unmistakeable familiarity. He looked disapprovingly at the scene, his mouth in a hard line, standing with a group of others. One of them was playing with his cell phone, the light causing his eyes to glow in an inhumanly way.

"Ian?" Jim asked disbelievingly. "Are you seeing this?"

When he didn't receive an answer, Jim swung around-- finding Ian's chair empty, lasagne sitting untouched.

He was gone.

Winchester gone with him.

Pounding his fist against the table's surface, causing the silverware to dance, Jim swore loudly.

Chapter Twenty-Three

Luther's screwing everything up, Daniel thought, the chilly, misty dusk sending a shiver along his spine.

He was part of the hunting party that was trailing a male deer, his muscles propelling him eagerly through the woods after it. The silent woods, both calm and complex, towered up on either side of them, their canopies giving not a breath of movement in the absolute stillness of the coming night. Daniel watched the buck spring and weave around the tranquil trees, with a light-footed grace, that took a considerable amount of concentration to follow. It wasn't something the pack would normally have trouble managing, except Luther kept jumping the gun whenever they got close, making a sudden move and snapping at the animal's hind legs before they had the buck effectively flanked. He did it nearly every time, wanting credit for the take down, anxiously reaching for his glory moment.

Meanwhile, The pack was starving, and this time there wasn't a Dig Dog Diner, in fact there wasn't a restaurant around for miles. Ever since Luke's men had hit the pack nearby, Luther had commanded them into full retreat. They were far out in the forest now, a good hour away from any city, and they were low on supplies, on food especially.

Also among the hunting party were Jack and Jolie. And Jolie was furious. Daniel could practically feel the irritation and anger rolling off her in waves. She'd kept quiet so far, trying to keep focused on her task, but if Luther kept things up, she was going to explode at him, and another valuable food source would get away-- again. It was this realization that drove Daniel to a decision, and the next time Luther began to make a move, Daniel was ready.

The head male lurched away from the party, pushing himself in an attempt to out distance the rest, and Daniel immediately kicked it up a notch, responding to match his leader's heightened pace. Luther growled in agitation at him as they pulled ahead together, but Daniel adamantly ignored the warning, until he saw his opportunity.

Then he made his move.

Just as Luther made to snap in his direction, Daniel threw his shoulder into the head male, putting him right in the path of an oncoming tree. It was an enormous thing, too large to maneuver around at such short notice, and with a surprised yelp, Luther instantly dug his claws into the earth, putting the brakes on his advance. The head male skidded to a halt, his nose an inch away from the gigantic oak.

If he was human, Daniel would have laughed, instead he settled for giving voice to a howl of amusement. A couple brave members echoed the sound behind him, as they surged past their leader. Daniel could feel their relief like a palpable thing as they made an effort to catch up with him.

He didn't slow for them, instead tipped his head back and howled out enthusiastically, encouraging and urging them on, until they were nearly all at his flanks again, matching his strides. The buck made an abrupt right turn and the pack split into two. It was an amazing thing running like this, with the pack like a school of fish, understanding one another by the smallest of movements, a flick of an ear, the twitch of a tail. Daniel and a few of the fastest members took the wide side, pushing in closer until the deer was caught in a deadly sandwich, between the two halves of the hunting party. Daniel's breath clouded the air ahead of him, as he pushed in closer to the deer's hindquarters. When he was certain the buck had no room to suddenly dart away, he lunged, closing his jaws around the deer's hind leg. Struggling on three legs the animal quickly slowed, and the pack wasted no time in bringing it down. It toppled to the earth, its free legs thrashing to ward off its attackers. Daniel barked a warning to a younger wolf who was inching too close to the flailing hooves, and another member went for the throat.

Then it was all over.

Whooping howls rang out in victory, and Jolie sprang at him, a blur of dark fur knocking him over and nipping at his ears in her excitement. Then the whole pack erupted into playful chaos, lunging at one another, and rolling over in the grass. Seeing the celebration made Daniel feel happier than he'd been in a long time. He'd spent too many long nights running home and lurking around the Roadhouse, Devlyn's apartment, and the Ay Motel. He was always careful to make the journey back to the pack before the sun

251

rose in the morning, but the motel room continued to be vacant, and Daniel's concern was growing. There was a part of him, twisting his stomach into knots, that wondered if Ian had packed up and joined Luke. He kept deciding to believe in his brother, but the evidence was increasingly making it harder to do so.

Someone else pounced on him, and he'd just turned to tackle the wolf, when a shadow seemed to fall over them all. Luther stood, his human form lurking above them, his eyes a deadly blaze, as he took in the events around him.

"Everyone-- human! Now!" he yelled, his order bringing the hunting party into abrupt silence. Daniel saw a couple of annoyed glances being exchanged between certain wolves, and this only seemed to fuel the head male's anger. "You think we have time for games?" he barked. "Get this meat back to the pack before it spoils."

Daniel understood the necessity of the man's words, but couldn't help feeling the same un-desire, as he was sure the rest of the pack was feeling, to give himself over to the change and the world of agony between two forms. With a sigh, Daniel let the inevitable happen. He heard others doing the same as his body was shot through with pain. A minute later he was gasping for breath on his hands and knees. Luther kicked a shoe full of dirt in his direction, whispering harshly under his breath, "Don't test me, Browning."

Looking up at Luther, Daniel was surprised to find how unintimidated he was by the statement, and it was probably for the best, that Luther had moved on to engage the rest of the pack, before he laughed aloud into the leaves.

A hand grabbed his arm, in an attempt to hoist him up off the ground.

"You're an idiot," Jolie informed him as he let her tug him to his feet.

He brushed his hands off calmly on his wrinkled pants, and raised his eyebrows at her.

He watched her expression soften ever so slightly, and then she punched him lightly in the arm. "But thank you."

Daniel started, and she began to walk away, seemingly pleased by his off guard expression.

"Hold up," he shouted after her. "Did Jolie, the no

mannered head female just thank me?"

"It's Jo," she called back over her shoulder and then turned to face him, an almost smile twitching at her lips. "And don't get used to it."

They joined the rest.

Someone had already called for the truck they had stationed in the area. It was a beat up four-wheel drive, with chipping blue paint. It would be dwarfed next to Ian's truck, but it got the job done regardless.

A few minutes later, its clunking engine chugged the vehicle into view. It bounced over a tree root that stuck too high out of the ground, before it came to a stop. Daniel helped heft the animal onto the truck bed, supporting it with his shoulders. Once the game was properly secured, the pack piled into the cab and truck bed. It got to the point where there was only standing room. Someone slammed the tailgate closed and another member pounded the roof of the cab twice with his fist.

The truck lurched forward, and Daniel was pleased to find that he didn't feel the need to grab hold of anything. Every muscle in his body seemed attuned to the truck's movements, his supernatural balance something to marvel at. It was the same for the others around him. The ride had the sensation of surfing on a wave. The truck bounced over another tree root, and everyone flew a good foot off the ground before landing again. Daniel heard someone give an excited *whoop*, and watched others fist pump the air, screaming their exuberance. He singled out Jack from the cramped crowd, and they exchanged a smile. Then his friend tilted his head back and let out a joyous laugh. They were sent soaring over another bump. And Daniel couldn't help but do the same.

They reached the rest of the pack in a swarm of welcome. Daniel disconnected himself from the group, receiving a few pats on the back as he went, and trekked up the nearest hill, which loomed over them from one side. From the top he could see the whole scene. Families ran to embrace their providers, the nearly vanished sun sending its last sliver of light out in a red hue. Daniel felt a brief sense of contentment and satisfaction that he could bring smiles to the faces of the people below him, while also getting in a jab at the head male. The human exchanges below were a comforting sight, like an old friend. They'd been in the wilderness too long, and too long they'd been the animals they were only meant to be half of the time. He was starting to worry that if they stayed isolated, the wolves inside them would slowly start to eat away at their humanity.

Sitting with his arms resting on bent knees, Daniel watched Jack break away from the mayhem and make his way up the hill towards him. Jolie noticed his retreat and quickly disengaged to follow. Jack seemed to be pretending not to notice her tailing him, until they both came to stand beside him.

"Not tonight guys, okay?" Jolie said with disapproval.

Daniel exchanged a perplexed glance with Jack.

"I don't understand," Jack admitted.

"Oh, please," she said with a roll of her eyes. "Like you two weren't coming up here to slink off and disappear back into humanity, like you have every other night."

Surprised, Daniel turned to look at Jack, whose glasses were sliding down his nose as he returned a similar expression. True, Daniel had been taking off, had been for a while, but not once had Jack been with him. Where would Jack be disappearing to?

Neither one of them answered her, just sort of stared at places around her face.

She sighed heavily. "Well not tonight, all right? And do *not* get yourselves killed out there. If Luther ever found out that--."

"Wait," Daniel said suddenly. He could hear something. Something-- off. Something that didn't belong in the forest. Jolie frowned, and opened her mouth to continue anyway. "Just," he cut her off quickly, "listen."

She fell silent and the noise slowly, but audibly grew.

"I hear it," Jack said pensively.

Jolie's head cocked to the side slightly, and Daniel could tell she heard it too. She glanced around, surveying the perimeter. "What *is* that?"

Daniel shook his head trying to think. The rumbling, roaring sound was somehow very--.

Then it hit him.

He shot to his feet, catching both Jolie and Jack, who took a startled step back, off guard. It was an engine. Different than that of the rusting blue truck. This engine was the one he'd grown to think of as the background music to his childhood. The truck.

Ian had found them.

Daniel took off down the hill, his sneakers sliding on the loose soil. He heard Jolie and Jack pause for only a moment, before tearing after him. Daniel could see Luther at the bottom of the hill, he'd heard it, probably long before they had. Luther was jogging through the pack shouting orders, calling for everyone to shift, to run, a few to stand and fight. As Daniel reached the bottom, and the ground leveled out under his feet, wolves were already streaking past him, back the way he'd come. He tore his way through them, until he pulled up short in front of Luther.

Luther spun to face him, his voice stern, all business. "Are you with us?"

Such a simple question, with no easy answer. There were wolves in place around them, ready to fight, some still shifting. Ears twitched towards the sound of the engine.

Daniel looked at all the faces of the wolves around him, a few he'd come to recognize and know. The familiar engine's hum still rang in his own ears, a reminder of his true loyalties. Then he heard the truck come to a stop in the distance, and the engine cut off.

"I…," Daniel struggled for words, as Jolie and Jack caught up, skidding to a halt behind him.

Luther stared at him for a long minute, before shaking his head disdainfully and turning away.

"What's going on?" Jolie demanded.

Luther didn't answer, but he didn't need to. A member, still human, ran out of the woods, yelling and waving his arms for his head male's attention. He didn't have to be close, for them to hear what he was saying.

A Knocte. Armed. One. There was only one.

Luther nodded to the lycan, then turned to face his army. "Take him down," he said.

Daniel felt everything stop inside him.

"*No!*" he exploded.

"Daniel," Jolie said sharply behind him, grabbing his sleeve for his attention. "You don't have to be involved. Just stay out of it."

Daniel jerked his arm away. "You don't *get* it! It's Ian!" He

255

saw Jack's eyes grow large. "It's my *brother*!"

They stared at him. And then Jolie swore so loudly, that Jack flinched at her side.

Luther looked over at Daniel with unwavering determination. "He came for a fight, and it's what we're going to give him."

Then the leader inclined his head, just a tip of his chin, and to Daniel's horror the pack took off, heading in Ian's direction. Luther himself hunched over, his body trembling and shaking, trying to phase. And Daniel knew. He didn't have time for an agonizingly slow change. If he didn't shift before Luther, didn't reach his brother before the rest and put a stop to everything, more than one person was going to die tonight. After an evening that had finally come together, had finally started to feel right, the sudden situation felt like a cruel joke.

As the wolves vanished from sight into the trees, Daniel found himself concentrating, paying close attention to the little details of his transformation, unlike he ever had before. He felt the bones that wanted to snap and reform, the muscles that needed to tear in order to mend, and he pushed at them. He pushed towards the pain as hard as he could, until it over whelmed him, blinded him from everything else-- and then it happened. A loud snap. One second human and the next-- a wolf.

Just. Like. That.

It had happened so suddenly that his four legs felt like Jell-O beneath him. It had been a quick flash of intense pain like he'd never felt before, vanishing as suddenly as it'd appeared. It wasn't supposed to work like that. The contrast nearly sent his mind spinning into blackness, and he found himself grasping desperately to consciousness.

The three people around him had frozen, staring at him in disbelief, as he tried to find his bearings. He staggered to one side, nearly smacking into a tree. Jack stood, his jaw nearly touching the floor. Luther had stop shaking altogether, his brain shocked from its course of action, and Jolie, her arms once crossed now fell uselessly to her sides.

Then Daniel felt his mind jolt, a single name screaming at him through a hundred neuron connections.

Ian.

He sprang into motion, his wolf swiftness winning out over his disorientation, as the name brought clarity. He left Luther, Jolie, and Jack far behind, all still human. He hoped he'd earned himself enough time. The moss under the pads of his feet, like little soft springboards, pushed him onward. He became intensely attuned to all his senses. His ears pricked forward, and he could hear the others, smell their unique scents. Now he just had to catch them. He lifted his voice in an eerie howl. A battle cry lost between two sides as he moved, his strides eating the ground as he went.

Ahead, he could hear the pack slowing, hesitating. Despite their orders, they were uncertain. And then-- he could hear Ian.

"It's hard to hide, when your eyes glow like some first of July freak show!"

Daniel was going to kill him.

He was going to try and save his good for nothing life first-- but then he was going to kill him.

Ian's comment did not go over well. Daniel could hear low growling resonating from the wolves.

He sprang over a fallen log, and continued running.

Almost there.

"You enjoy destroying the lives of others? Huh? Just hate your lives so freaken much that you have to spread the joy. Well, I swear it! I promise you, I'll stand here and take on every single one of you before I let you rip apart another person's life like you did my brother's." Daniel's stride faltered a step. "You take everything that matters away like you're freaken God or something. You wanna tell me what the point of it was? So you could hide out here and shiver in fear. You're a bunch of cowards!" The growling amplified, rising into a fury. "You hear me? *You're all cowards!*"

Daniel swerved around two more trees, and then he was in view. His brother's fierce expression glowered down on them all, as he strode through the trees, growing closer to the hunched wolves with every step, Winchester trailing faithfully at his heels. There was a handgun in the waistband of Ian's jeans, but his hands were free for the moment. Such an act couldn't fool Daniel anymore though. He was close enough to see the details. He could see Ian's icy, always watchful eyes, slit to peer through the dusk. He saw his brother's fingers twitch. Ian could draw a gun faster than anyone Daniel had ever known.

Then Ian took one step too far, and Daniel watched a wolf crouch to spring, saw Ian notice him immediately, reaching for his gun.

Daniel tensed his muscles and leapt forward, bridging the remaining gap between them. He crashed into the wolf, knocking him to the side, a split second before the gun when off, the sound loud and echoing through the stillness of the forest, just missing them. A couple wolves yipped, a startled and uncertain sound, as Daniel sprang back to all fours. He could feel every pair of eyes on him, as he backed up, placing himself between them and his brother. Then he did something he knew that he was one hundred percent not allowed to do. He threw his muzzle into the air, and howled out the retreat call. He threw as much authority into it as he could, when he knew he held none. For a moment there was absolute silence, and then he saw the betrayal suddenly displayed on the faces around him, anger quickly burning into chaos. Wolves leapt at him, jaws open, and nails thrashing. Daniel threw one off, his teeth sinking into fur. He heard Ian's gun ring out again, and again. Yelps filled the air, followed by pitiful whining. Someone leapt on his back, another caught hold of his ear. He slashed someone across the face, and they backed away, but every time he wrenched a wolf off, another took its place. A set of teeth sank into his neck-- and then just as suddenly was gone. He was freed. Jerking his head up, he saw four or so wolves surrounding him, barring their teeth at the others. It looked like he'd managed to win some points with members of the pack after all.

He'd split this army in two.

And Ian hadn't slowed down.

Silver bullets still flew. To Ian there were still only two sides to this battle. The Knocte and the Fifth Worlders. And the Fifth Worlders were divided, turning on each other because Daniel had let it happen.

Out of the corner of his eye, he saw the head male and the head female suddenly appear on the scene, Jack behind them, all wolves. They regarded the mutiny for a fraction of a second, in which Luther met his stare. The message was clear enough: he was a dead wolf. Then they joined in, throwing themselves into the chaos, Luther taking down any member that'd gone astray.

Daniel needed to get Ian out of there.

Now.

He began picking his way through the battle. A wolf leapt at him, and Daniel retaliated. They tore at each other, Daniel trying not to lose ground in the process, until he had the wolf pinned into the leaves helplessly beneath him. He growled menacingly in his face. Ian was only a few feet away, reloading his gun. A wolf jumped Winchester and Ian spun, slapping the next load into place. He pegged the attacker right between the eyes, and the wolf fell in a heavy mound of fur. Then something else caught his attention, and Ian's gun arm swung around, training on the new target.

And there crouched Jolie, her deep brown coat nearly indistinguishable from the night. Her lips pulled back over pink gums, as she snarled her rage. Ian's mouth twitched up in a smirk, and Daniel knew what would come next.

He lost it.

Springing into his brother's view, he snarled pure murder at him, a flourish of anger burning words that Ian couldn't understand. His brother's gaze shifted, and the gun turned. In that instant Daniel realized he'd made a terrible mistake. He saw his brother's gaze, held with something Daniel had never before seen directed at himself. Something that made his blood run cold.

Night had almost completely fallen. He was just as indistinguishable as the rest, the white marking on his coat not enough to draw recognition from his brother. He was just another pair of glowing eyes in the darkness, and Ian wasn't looking at individual colours. They were all the same to him, thieves and murderers.

Ian pulled the trigger.

It had to have taken less than a second, but it felt like eternity, as Daniel threw himself out of the way-- but not fast enough. He felt the bullet bite into his leg, the silver sizzling against flesh like a red-hot poker. He collapsed to the ground, the bullet slowly eating its way through his upper thigh. The gun followed his movements, and Daniel threw everything he had into becoming human again. He howled, a mournful sound, turning into a yell, becoming lost under the sound of his own skin tearing.

As soon as he had fingers, Daniel clutched the grass, his eyes slammed shut, squeezing so hard against the burning in his leg, that it took a considerable amount of effort to pry them open again. He just managed to catch a glimpse of his brother's horrified, ashen face before there was suddenly a sea of wolves between them again. Hands grabbed his shoulders, and Daniel whipped around, finding himself face to face with Jack, his mint green eyes in hysterics.

"He shot you! I can't believe he actually shot you!"

"Jack..." Daniel gritted his teeth.

"Dan!" Ian's voice suddenly carried over to them, climbing over the sound of chaotic, unrestrained battle.

Jack looked over, making a sound very close to a growl. His body shuddered.

"Don't even,"--Daniel gasped, grabbing hold of the front of Jack's shirt-- "think about it." He bore his gaze into his friend's, trying to keep a steady expression. His leg stung something terrible, and he ground his teeth together, suddenly clutching at it. Jack pressed closer. "Get out of here!" he snapped at him.

"Jack, go. That's an order," Jolie said, materializing suddenly in front of them. She was human-- obviously, but she clearly felt naked without her teeth and claws in the heat of a battle, because she had in her possession a tree branch, and not a necessarily small one at that. Daniel vaguely wondered if she'd picked it off the ground, or ripped it right from the tree. He tried to sit up and she shoved him back down.

"Don't *move*!" she hissed at him. "Or that thing will eat its way through you ten times faster. I don't need you bleeding to death at my feet!"

Jack still hesitated, and Jolie took a threatening step towards him. "I'll club you over the head and *drag* you away, if that's what it takes, Jack!"

Jack gave her a stern look, pushed his glasses back up the bridge of his nose, and turned away, patting Daniel on the shoulder.

"Don't die," he said, and then was gone.

Daniel heard his name again, and Jolie's grip tightened on the branch.

"He comes anywhere near us again, and I'll kill him. Right where he stands." Her eyes told him she had every intention of doing just that.

"Jolie--," Daniel began when a smaller figure darted out of

the crowd towards them. Jolie adopted a wider stance, her fingers flexing over the tree branch. She looked more like a baseball player than a warrior, as the animal raced towards them. "No, don't! Don't," Daniel blurted the moment he recognized who it was. "It's my dog."

"Your *what?*" she barked, dropping a hasty glance at him, but Winchester was already on them.

He was no longer the vicious animal that had stood at Ian's side ready to fight and die for his master, he was the pet, excited to see his best friend who had been gone for far too long. His ears pricked forward, he rushed to nudge Daniel with his nose, his wet tongue against his face. When Daniel painfully managed to push the dog down, it was just in time to see Jolie's eyes grow wide, and then settle into a scowl at something stationed ahead of them. Following her gaze, he saw Ian part his way through the mayhem. Daniel tried to catch his brother's eye, tried to hold it long enough to convey some unspoken message, but Jolie stepped in front, blocking his immediate view.

He heard Ian's voice carry over to them, cold and deadly, like an ice storm in the thick of night. "Get out of the way." And with a groan Daniel dragged himself forward enough so he could see. Even from a distance he could tell Ian's handgun was trained on Jolie's chest, hovering at height with her heart-- and he knew his brother wouldn't miss.

"Jolie," Daniel immediately tried to say. It took more effort for his words to come out steady than he would have liked to admit. "Do what he says."

"Shut up, Daniel," she snapped at him, their conversation too low to carry over to Ian. "This is my job remember." Once again her hands tightened around the tree branch. What was she going to do? Throw it? This wasn't a fight meant for sticks and stones; it was a *gun* Ian held in his possession.

"I don't ask twice!" Ian called to her.

Daniel thought he could hear Jolie's teeth grind together. "And I don't listen to arrogant, murdering--!"

Ian's eyes narrowed. And Daniel panicked.

"Jo, *move!*" he screamed cutting her off.

"I protect this pack," she said without looking at him.
Screw that.

Ian's shot was lined up, his gaze trained. Daniel spun, kicking out with his good leg, connecting it with the back of Jolie's knees. Winchester gave a startled yelp, as her legs gave out under her, and she collapsed to the ground. She dropped the tree branch, her hands reaching out to catch her fall-- just as Ian fired. Daniel heard the bullet whiz by above their heads, and for all her bravado, he could hear Jolie gasp, her breathing heavy as her fingers curled around fistfuls of leaves. She turned to look at him, black eyes wide, her short dark hair clinging to her cheeks and lips. Then, her expression betraying whatever stupid move she was planning to make next.

Daniel wasn't going to let it happen.

His hands shot forward, catching her by surprise. He grabbed the front of her shirt and rolled, throwing her over himself, landing her somewhere behind him.

"Stay," he commanded without looking at her, already turning back to face his brother. He had to bite back the string of curse words that threatened to escape his lips, as his leg burned. It was a never-ending fire he couldn't put out, and he realized he must have left behind bloody handprints on Jolie's shirt.

Ian was just a few feet away, striding forward, his gun still in his hand. Daniel watched the metal glint in the rising moonlight. He didn't take his eyes off the weapon. He could feel himself frowning at it, silently cursing its very existence, until Ian was directly in front of him. Daniel tried to push himself up, but there was no need, as Ian dropped to his knees beside him.

"Danny," he said. He was a mess of wind blown, brass coloured hair, and rumpled clothing. Daniel couldn't pick out the dominant emotion on Ian's face. Relief. Regret. Exhaustion. In that moment he wasn't sure who had had a worse time floundering about on his own for the past few weeks, him or his brother. "I didn't mean--. I didn't *realize*--."

Ian pressed a hand against Daniel's wound, trying to stop the bleeding. In a cry of pain, Daniel jerked back sharply, his hand shooting out to grip his brother's arm. His fingers dug into the sleeve of Ian's jacket as he tried to stop him from searing the silver bullet farther into his leg. Winchester whined.

Ian looked wretched, his face a mask of torment that had nothing to do with the physical world, but Daniel was frowning, and he couldn't seem to help it. The sight of his brother had been like a weight he hadn't realized he'd been carrying lifted off his shoulders, but at the same time he kept seeing Ian's enraged features, shooting down pack member after pack member as he went. One of Reid's concocted dreams filled his mind, and he couldn't help being angry, couldn't stop seeing Luke's hand on his brother's shoulder, coaxing him, whispering lies-- and Ian buying it.

Daniel was just about to open his mouth and say something he knew he'd probably end up regretting, when there were howls, springing up behind them, refusing to be forgotten. Daniel could see Jolie's shadow in the foliage ahead of him, as she rose up, slowly, from somewhere behind him. Daniel hoped she was planning to head off the advance, stop them before another wave of violence threw the pack into yet more blood and madness. Unlike him, she was the head female, and they would heed whatever she had to say. Under his grip, Daniel felt his brother tense, his hard wired muscles ready to act, as his eyes slid up to follow Jolie's movements.

Daniel didn't think-- he just acted. He lurched forward, his teeth ground together against an expression of his torment, as his fingers coiled around Jolie's discarded weapon. The tree branch in his grasp, Ian barely had time to register the turn of events, before Daniel swung, bashing his brother over the head with the hunk of wood. He made sure to connect with the temporal lobe, and his brother slumped to the ground in front of him, unconscious. He let the branch drop from his fingers. Breathing hard, he raked a hand through his hair, causing it to stick up. He wasn't sure if he was more surprised by what he'd done, or that he'd been fast enough at it to catch his brother by surprise. He turned to regard the wolves, his chest still heaving in exertion. They stood in a semicircle of glowing eyes. Eyes that were shifting from Ian's still form, to Daniel himself. Jolie seemed to pick up on the thought wave as quickly as he did. Beside him, Winchester gave a low warning growl.

"Now everybody just wait a minute!" she commanded, arms stretched out in front of her, palms facing down in a 'be calm' gesture. "This is where the show ends for tonight."

Mutinous glances were exchanged throughout the pack. A

wolf, probably someone who'd lost a family member to Ian's blazing firearm, actually snarled at her. But that wasn't the real problem here, Daniel knew. The pack was under obligation to follow orders. The problem was-- their orders were conflicted. Jolie and Luther, whose presence had to be among them somewhere, were not singing the same song. The decision was left up to the masses. A wolf advanced, and suddenly a rather small, tan one leapt forward from the group to block the animal's path. Jack. He hadn't left after all, merely doubled back amongst the other members.

Scared for his friend, scared for all their lives, Daniel forced his brain into action. A strategy began to form in the case of another wave of attack. He started picking out weaknesses and injuries of any wolf he could see and filed them carefully away. He needed to keep them alive just long enough. He dug in Ian's jacket for his cell phone, glad his brother had remembered to buy a new one.

"I need you," Daniel whispered to Jolie between deep breaths, his mind still whirling unceasingly, "to make a call. I'll give you the number. Just make him come." She must have heard some sense in his voice, because she instantly stepped up behind him. He held the phone above his head for her.

"This better be a Scit of a good plan," she hissed back at him. "Things are about to get ugly again-- fast."

Chapter Twenty-Four

Jim hadn't been expecting a call. He'd hoped beyond hope in the last couple of weeks, to hear from either Browning brother. He'd left countless messages, but hadn't really expected a reply with the number of unanswered calls stacked up against him. He was fidgeting with his pen, clicking it in and out against the wooden desk of his cluttered home study. With a weary sigh he scrubbed a hand over his whiskered face, finding himself unable to concentrate on even the simplest of his paper work for the Ray Motel chain.

Then Ian's caller ID lit up the screen of his cell phone.

His heart pounded like thunder in his chest as he scrambled to flip it open.

"Ian," he answered almost breathlessly. He was surprised and yet not, when the voice on the other end of the line did not belong to Ian.

"Thank God, no," came a female's voice.

A coldness seemed to seep into his bones. "Where is he?" Jim demanded, his voice grisly with concern.

"With his brother-- though he shouldn't be," she said fairly irked, but her voice dropped, growing more serious with every word she spoke. "Listen, whoever you are, they're in trouble. Big trouble. If you ever owed them for anything, they need you right--."

Jim heard the urgentness she hadn't wanted to display, leak into her voice anyway, and he was out of his desk chair in an instant. It spun uselessly behind him as he stormed out the front door, nearly tripping on the porch steps, as he jogged towards the pickup, half hidden in the darkness of his graveled driveway. He'd forgotten a jacket entirely and the chilling night nipped through his button-down shirt, as he pulled the door open to the cab. He cut her off before she was even finished. "Just give me the co-ordinates," he urged, not looking to waste anymore time. "I don't have to owe them nuthin'. Tell me where my boys are."

There was a brief hesitation on the other end, and then some swearing as if she was frustrated with the question. But even before she told him "the forest," or Jack had somehow gotten a hold of the phone, and given the exact location, Jim had already heard the howls in the background, his headlights pointing in the right direction.

Jolie had never been so happy to see a stranger in her entire life. When the pickup rolled into view and the old man stepped out, Jolie felt a weight lifted off her shoulders. She glanced behind her briefly where Daniel, once more a wolf, still stood his ground over his brother. The German Shepherd was running guard back and forth in front of him, and Daniel's wounded hind leg was shaking so badly that it was only a matter of time before it collapsed under him. His coat was matted with blood, and his one white ear torn. He looked like a stray animal with a history of violence, but one look at the older man, and loving recognition seemed to replace any feral expression the fight had put into him. Those glowing, brown wolf eyes of his were instantly full, both grateful and relieved at the same time.

She couldn't help noticing the contrast to the way Luther was looking at her. He now stood just across from her, separated by only a few feet. His arms were crossed over his chest, his scowl deep, and his dark eyes hard. The majority of the pack stood behind him in complete uncertainty. She couldn't get the look of betrayal he'd worn out of her mind, when she'd stepped in between the chaos of the two sides, telling him flatly that if he wanted to kill Daniel's party he was going to have to go through her. There was hate in every line of Luther's face now, and Jolie shifted her gaze to look at the old man, where there was only a concern so raw it was almost just as painful to look at. He'd gotten out of his pickup, hands immediately held high to show he meant no harm. Luther's eyes snapped towards him.

"What business do you have here, Knocte?" he said, his voice hard and cold. "It's dangerous to step foot in territory that does not belong to you." At that last bit his eyes had slid to Ian's still form and Daniel's ears flattened against his head, a warning growl creeping up in his throat.

"I only want to take what's mine and go," the man replied.

"Nothing belongs to you here," Luther said curtly at the same time Jolie found herself saying, "Yes, take them."

Luther glared at her. "One's a traitor," he said to the man, though his eyes still rested on her, "and the other a trespasser. They are ours to punish as we see fit."

Suddenly Daniel's leg gave out and he staggered on three, fighting to stay upright. His body shuddered, but this time Jolie didn't think it was from the change. He let out a low whimper.

That seemed to spark a note of urgency in the new comer. "*I* will handle this," the man said, his voice rising into a yell. "*I* raised them-- not you. You don't know two craps about either of them, or what makes them tick. We have one enemy here, and it isn't you and it isn't us. It's Luke. And you're looking at the best team" --he gestured towards the brothers-- "to counteract something like that. If you want to stand a fighting chance, you'll *grow up, and start learning how to work together*. A side divided stands nothing against a side that is firm."

Luther's eyes flashed and he turned abruptly to face the man. "People died here tonight."

"I'm not condoning what was done, simply telling you it's not your responsibility to handle anymore."

"Knoctes," Luther muttered in anger, "always thinking they're the law. You--."

But Jolie couldn't be quiet anymore. "*Shut up, Luther*. He's right. Let the man take care of his own." she glanced over, making sure to catch his eye and hold it. "It's what we'd do. They're his family."

Luther mirrored her gaze for a long time, until it weighed heavily-- then it was almost as if she could physically see him swallow his pride.

"Fine," he said, the word like poison on his lips. "But Daniel is no longer a part of this pack. He no longer stands under our protection, and I suggest that any who dared follow him, leave as well, without returning." At that, his eyes moved just over Jolie's right shoulder where she knew Jack was standing, a mess of fair hair, his glasses sitting slightly askew on his face.

"Luther Collins. Are you asking me to step down from my position as head female?" Jolie asked, her head tilting slightly to the side in inquiry. She watched as his jaw clenched. He gave her a hard look, but in the end she knew his answer. Even after tonight he wouldn't dare turn his back on her.

"No," he said finally. And that was all he said. He turned

his back on them and made his way through the pack. They parted for him like the red sea as he moved through, then slowly one by one they turned to follow, until only a few were left behind. Jolie's shoulders dropped, relaxing in relief, as she turned around to face the party she'd stood for. The older man had already rushed forward towards the boys, the tracking dog instantly letting him through. Daniel gave a weary, labored sigh that seemed to rattle in his chest, and the man reached him just in time to catch the wolf, as he gave in and collapsed. Daniel fell heavily into the old man's arms.

Jolie heard the sound of laborious, enduring change behind her, where the remaining pack members stood. Then a tall man, with skin as dark as a shadow, was standing beside her, the German Shepherd eyeing him warily. She recognized him as the doctor who'd joined their ranks around the same time of Daniel's first change. He was rolling up his already wrinkled sleeves.

"I guess this is where I come in," he said studiously.

Daniel's world was a blur of sight and sound, and fractured bits and pieces. He had the vague sensation that he was drowning, as he wavered in and out of consciousness. One minute he was above the surface and the next he was below it all-- but neither place was silent. Above he could feel the fire in his leg, Jim's calming, husky voice in his ear, hands stroking his fur soothingly. Below, he saw only Reid, all sandy, blond hair and sea green eyes. His face was a sheen of sweat as if he worked very hard at something. He clutched at his temple with one hand, the other extended out in Daniel's direction. The scenes flashed back and forth so very suddenly that Daniel quickly lost track of the voices between them. They spun around him, mingling together until they were no longer comprehensible from one another.

"Hang in there, son," Jim's voice seemed to echo.

"--not a vet," someone was saying. "--shift."

"Get it out--!" he heard Jolie.

"Listen to--," came Reid.

"Shift!" Jack shouted.

"Daniel--."

"--have to--"

"Lift--."

"Dan--!"

"Stay--."

"--too deep."

"--awake!"

"Shift!"

"Shift!"

"Shift!"

He slipped under the surface again, and the last thing he remembered was Reid's form slamming him up against something hard, pressing a hand to either side of his head-- a scream, pain, and then-- blackness.

Chapter Twenty-Five

It was a long time before anything came back to him, and even then he knew he wasn't fully with it. He wandered a grassy expanse that had the sort of humming feeling to it he'd learned to associate with his subconscious. It wasn't until he really looked around, that he recognized the grassy expanse for what it was: Macy's Golf Course. Suddenly knowing where he was, he knew the only reason he'd be there. He spun, eyes searching-- and saw it. The truck was parked across the street with not one, but two figures lounging in the open truck bed. Squinting he tried to see clearer, but it wasn't until he'd strode closer that he could distinguish them. He froze, shocked as he looked into his own face. A perfect mirror image of himself, replaying a familiar scene, mouth cracked open in a wide smile as he laughed. He looked happy. Actually happy. And the reason sat beside him, eating ice cream right out of the container with a plastic spoon.

"Dev," he whispered unable to stop himself, her name both honey on his lips, and a void in his soul.

Suddenly as if she'd heard, she turned away from the other him, squinting through the fading light surrounding them. Recognition flashed across her face and she nearly dropped the bucket of ice cream into her lap, her surprise causing her deeply, dark blue eyes to go round under pale eyelashes. She stared at him for a long moment before turning back towards the other him, who she quickly discovered was carrying on without her, like the movie reel it was, the memory playing through without hesitation or delay. The other him talked into the silence, saying familiar things as if she were truly replying. Setting the ice cream aside, she gave the other him a long, sad look, before pushing forward and sliding off the truck bed. Her steps were almost reluctant as she made her way towards him. There was uncertainty in every line of her expression. Daniel didn't move, but stayed perfectly still, following her with his eyes as she came to a stop in front of him. Slowly, with trembling fingers she reached out, and then suddenly unsure-- drew back again.

"I- I don't... understand," she admitted, throwing one more glance over her shoulder towards the other him, still murmuring softly as if she was there.

"We're dreaming," Daniel said with more assurance than he felt. He was pretty sure she was dreaming at least. How he ended up here, he only had one guess.

"But," she said her head tilting to the side, her eyes trying to read his expression, every detail in his face, "this isn't possible. It can't be."

Daniel thought about every occurrence he'd ever had with Reid, and an actual smile tipped up the side of his mouth. "That hasn't been my experience."

That small, half-smile seemed to reassure her. She reached out again her feather like finger tips trailing from the corner of his mouth, down the line of his jaw. He closed his eyes, leaning into her touch.

"I miss you," she whispered, and Daniel couldn't hold back anymore. He reached out and drew her against him. Even in a dream her skin still smelt lightly of vanilla. "Tell me you're safe."

Daniel froze, his fingers pressed against her soft t-shirt. What was he supposed to tell her? That he'd burned nearly every bridge he'd made in the past couple of weeks in one night? That he'd passed out, probably from a combination of blood loss and adrenaline wear off?

"I'm-- I'm fine," he lied, less smoothly than he'd have liked to.

Her brow furrowed, her head tilting back to look up at him. "I can tell when you're lying Daniel Browning. Even when you're not lying badly."

"I'm sorry," he said, burying his head against her shoulder. She wrapped her arms around him, running her fingers up through his disarrayed hair. "But I don't have a good answer for you. Jim's with me, that's one thing I know though… and Ian."

"They're both with you?" she asked, and if he hadn't known better, he'd have thought there was jealousy in her voice. "Then they got you. They wouldn't let anything happen to you-- they wouldn't."

In his mind's eye Daniel saw Ian's unconscious form, drained of anger and worry lines, and Jim, hands in the air, pleading his case before an entirely bad tempered lycanthrope pack. He wasn't sure they had a whole lot of choice in the matter.

271

He was at the mercy of many hands. That, at least, he knew with certainty.

"There's so much I need to tell you," Devlyn continued. "Luke stopped trying to find your pack, but he's always watching in case someone sticks their neck out." Daniel nodded along grimly with this. "But he's going after the vampires next, Dan. He's already raided one clan. They came into the Roadhouse after... you should have seen them, laughing like it was all a joke. They told stories... It was horrible. It was all I could do not to blow up in their faces, scream until I couldn't scream anymore."

"What're you still doing at the Roadhouse?" Daniel asked in bemusement. "I thought you'd be out of that scene."

Devlyn shook her head slowly. "I thought someone would have told you," she said, her expression careful. "I'm playing the double agent. I make sure Ruby and the Fair Children have all the weapons and information they need to fight this war."

"From the Roadhouse?" Daniel asked, his jaw going slack. "*Dev*, if Luke gets any wind of this, any at all, that you're playing the double agent, it's game over for you. If he finds out you and I still have contact, or you and Ruby, he's not going to take you selling him out lightly. You can't do this. I can't *let* you do this."

"Dan," she said, ever patiently. "I can't sit on the sidelines forever. I have to do *something*. I won't stand idly by anymore. God calls us to action. He works *through us*. If I can help-- if I can save even one innocent life, it'll be worth it. He is with me."

"And you're so sure your God will protect you? You're not a Knocte Dev, and you can't beat that. God knows I've tried. Ian's pulled me out of so many situations that I wouldn't have been able to--." He cut himself off abruptly, suddenly aware he was giving information he shouldn't.

For once though, news of his close calls didn't send panic flashing through her eyes. Instead they seemed big in that moment, dark blue orbs full of a faith he didn't think he'd ever fully understand. "'Greater love has no one than this, that he lay down his life for his friends,'" she quoted. "You risk your life everyday, Dan. Are you really going to tell me I can't do the same? I may not be ready to leave this world, but I'm prepared. His will be done."

"I can't lose you, Dev. Anything else I can--."

She'd put her finger to his lips, stopping his speech. She

was watching him with a slight frown. Her hands moved up to his face, her thumb smoothing the lines on his forehead.

"You have to stop worrying, Dan," she told him, and stood on her tiptoes to press her lips against his temple. "It's going to kill you. I know. I've been there."

The word *kill* seemed to ring in his mind, and he felt something like a half sigh half groan leave his throat-- then his arms were around her, his head ducking down to take her mouth with his. She pressed closer, and for a moment he forgot it was merely a dream, that this was all just happening in their minds, because having her with him again was a dream come true if he ever believed in one. Her hands slid down his chest, passing over his tattoo, and his body shuddered, only his thin cotton shirt between her and his scars. His hands slipped into her hair, blond curls tangling around his fingers. His mouth explored hers, wandering over familiar territory, remembering every curve. He felt her smile against his mouth, as if she too was remembering every night they'd had together like this.

Then a sudden shrill beeping filled their world, and Devlyn let out a gasp, jumping backwards. She held her hands out in between them, her fingers disappearing at the tips. Her gaze snapped up to meet his in shock.

"What's happening?" she asked, the beeping amplifying steadily over her voice.

"It's your alarm, Dev," Daniel said, recognizing it. "You're waking up."

"Waking up...?" she repeated, and then looked back down at her hands, gone up to the elbows. "Dan!" she said panicked, and he reached out, his calloused fingers running down her cheek, tucking a curl behind her ear.

"It's okay, Dev," he murmured. He felt her relax slightly under his touch.

"Dan, I--."

But she was gone, his hand hovering in empty air. Slowly he lowered it to his side. "I love you too, Dev," he whispered, and then gave a heavy sigh. Slowly, he turned, shoving his hands into his jean pockets, to regard his scenery.

His eyes searched the green.

"Reid!" he called loudly. "I know you're out there

273

somewhere. Might as well join me."

There was a long pause, and then, "That depends on how mad you're going to be." The voice came from everywhere, and nowhere. Daniel craned his neck looking around, but found no one. He smiled.

"Come on," he said with a shake of his head, "for once I'm *asking* you to materialize your butt down here."

He blinked and Reid was suddenly standing in front of him, nervously wiping sweaty hands on his jeans.

"Look, I know you told me not to fish around in your grapefruits, but there was this string between your brains, you see, like a bridge, and all you needed was a little help getting across. I just thought you'd been through a lot--."

"Reid," Daniel said, gently trying to stop the man's ramblings.

"--and I've seen ties like that so rarely."

"Reid."

"I thought it had to mean something. It always does. I thought it would help... possibly."

"*Reid*," Daniel tried again, this time more sternly.

The man fell silent, his expression wary.

Daniel made an effort to soften his voice. "I'm not going to yell at you. I-- I'm sorry." That seemed to grab the Artifex's attention, Reid's sea green eyes flickering up to meet his, curious and perplexed. "I know you're just trying to help. That's all any of us are trying to do-- some in different ways than others," he amended, and then shrugged. He began pacing back and forth across the green of the golf course. "But I gave it all some thought."

Reid nodded in a quiet prompt.

"You were right. The more I look at it, the more I see it. We need each other, as much help as we can get our hands on. I saw what becomes of a divided army today-- or yesterday?"

"Yesterday," Reid said immediately.

Daniel laughed lightly, rubbing the back of his neck. "Glad one of us can keep track of time in here."

Reid's mouth tipped up with the hint of a smile. "I'm not the one unconscious, mate." Lifting his arm in front of his face he pulled his grey sweater sleeve back, revealing a rather expensive looking silver watch, the hands sleek, ticking over roman numerals. "Though you're due to wake up any moment now."

"You know," Daniel admitted, pushing his auburn hair out of his eyes, "you are good company sometimes."

"It's the accent," Reid said, as the scene around them began to give way, walls dripping, the colours of the artificial world around them running like paint. "Everybody loves the accent." He turned. "I should go."

Daniel found himself calling after him. "Hey, Reid." Reid glanced back, somewhat reluctantly, over his shoulder. "Thanks."

The Artifex seemed to sway in and out of focus like a mirage before him, but Daniel could still make out the man's pleased, but crooked smile. "Anytime, mate."

Then everything went black, his mind leaving Macy's Golf Course for the real world.

Having been grateful for the change of clothes on the nightstand, Daniel limped his way down Jim's familiar hallway. His leg still gave him some trouble, though he was pleasantly surprised to find it hurt a lot less than expected. His sock feet brushed over the ancient dark brown carpet, and his fingers trailed along the peeling, pale yellow wallpaper, only pausing for the pictures. They were pictures of himself and Ian when they were younger, the few Jim had managed to take without one of his fingers obscuring part of the frame. There was a side shot of them standing shoulder to shoulder, shotguns leveled at the same height, eyes fixed ahead, at some same point off picture.

In another, Daniel was sitting on the floor of the drawing room with his legs drawn up. Completely surrounded by books, he was grinning ear to ear. In the background behind him, Ian could be seen asleep, sprawled out on the worn, orange, striped couch. One of his arms hung over the edge; a book lay open on the floor where he'd dropped it.

The last on the wall, hanging slightly crooked, was of the two of them, arms slung around each other's shoulders. Their necklaces hung over their shirts, catching the room's light like flickering flames. Daniel straightened the picture; he couldn't have been more than ten in it. He backed away, turning the corner into the kitchen. Lingering in the entranceway, he leaned against its frame.

Jim was sitting at the table, an enormous, sturdy, dark wooden thing, older than dirt, and with more coffee cup rings than was possible to count. He was reading the morning newspaper, where it lay on the table to one side of his plate. He had a cup of coffee in one hand, and a fork in the other. He stabbed at his eggs almost subconsciously, his mind somewhere else, lost in whatever article he was reading. Winchester dozed under the table at his feet. The room still smelt like bacon. Daniel was relieved to see Jim there, sitting in the cream coloured kitchen, with the ugly green countertops like he had every morning Daniel had grown up in the house, but his mind was still on the first person he'd seen upon waking. In the room beside his, Ian had lain on the bed, still not awake, a hand resting limply on his chest.

"Ian's still unconscious?" Daniel asked, and Jim slowly raised his head, his reading glasses glinting in the hanging light above him. Winchester's head snapped up at his voice, his tail thumping a vigorous beat against the linoleum floor. Jim regarded him silently for a moment.

"Do you ever comb your hair these days?" he asked, finally speaking. "What kind of half-brain raised you anyways?"

"Jim…," Daniel said not comforted, and Jim took his glasses off, tossing them aside on the table.

"He's fine," Jim said, and rubbed his eyes. "I think it's just exhaustion more than anything now, and I can say this for lycans-- they heal a heck of a lot faster." He got up from his seat and went to the cupboard, pulling out a plate. He then moved to the stove, where he started piling bacon, and eggs, and hash browns high, until it nearly overflowed.

"They tore his shoulder," Daniel said, venturing into the room to stand behind the chair, opposite the one Jim had been inhabiting. "I couldn't stop it. I tried, I-- but they jumped us a second time while we were waiting for you to make the drive. If Jo hadn't stepped in the middle again…"

"We patched it up," Jim reassured. You couldn't have fended them all off, Dan, even with the help you had. I'd say Ian is darn well lucky to be walking out of this with just a banged up head and a torn shoulder."

"He's an idiot."

Jim placed the plate on the table in front of Daniel. "Agreed. Now, sit."

Pulling the chair back, Daniel dropped into it. Coming to his feet, Winchester ventured over to rest his head in Daniel's lap. He scratched the dog behind the ears, as Jim handed him a fork. Daniel stared at the mound of food in awe. He felt like he hadn't seen this much in a long, long while. "You sure made an awful lot of food, for being the only conscious person in this household," Daniel noted, his perspicacious nature leaking out.

Jim raised an eyebrow. "Says who?"

Daniel looked back down at his food, frowning in puzzlement, and then as if to clarify, the front door banged open. Winchester leapt in its direction and Daniel watched three people file into the house. A tall, dark skinned man, who wore a white button-down shirt, stepped in and hung his trilby hat on the coat rack. A girl, twelve at most, in jeans and a dark green cardigan, followed him timidly, patting down her wind blown hair. Behind them both-- Jack, who upon seeing him, kicked off his lime green sneakers and stormed into the kitchen.

"Daniel!" He exclaimed, and Daniel rose to meet him. Jack clasped his hand and pulled him in, slapping his back. "Look who's awake. How are you, my friend?"

"Well I'm walking, all things considered..."

"I think you have Wonder Doctor to thank for that," Jim said from his chair. The man behind Jack stepped forward then, extending a hand. The girl leaned around him to watch, her caramel hair falling over one shoulder. Winchester nuzzled at her hand.

"Dr. Carter Gakwin, at your service," the doctor said, smiling fondly. "And might I say it's a pleasure to meet you officially, when you're not bleeding to death under my care."

Daniel shook his hand, momentarily at a loss for words. "Yeah-- *yeah.* Thank you, by the way. I don't know what to say to--."

"We're even," Gakwin said firmly, waving away his attempts at gratitude.

Daniel blinked. "Even?"

"The wolf, the one you pushed out of your brother's line of fire" --Gakwin tapped his broad chest-- "It was me."

"You?" Daniel asked, surprised despite himself. "But…"

"I was stupid really, eager to prove myself. And well… I guess it just stands to prove I should stick to saving lives instead of trying to end them, albeit neither job is all that pretty."

Daniel smiled faintly. He'd never imagined that he'd be having a casual conversation with someone who both saved his life and attempted to murder his brother. He glanced down at the girl and she looked up at him blushing. Her eyes were so light brown they were more a cream colour. Something about her jarred his memory, and he started mentally flipping through his internal photo album of faces. In his travels, there'd been many.

"Wait, I know you," he said to her offhandedly. It took Gakwin a minute to realize Daniel hadn't been addressing him, while Daniel still silently mulling things over.

She was clearly from the pack, though it wasn't where Daniel had seen her before. She held his gaze, almost worriedly-- and then the right memory fell into place. He saw it all over again like it was happening for the first time.

He saw Ian kicking in the door to the Howler's residence, and them rushing inside. He saw the body of a woman on the floor being torn apart by a vampire, its eyes so washed out of all colour, it reflected the crazed mind of the creature. Daniel could hear, once again, her blood curdling screams filling the house, watched Ian throw himself at the vampire, and them rolling across the floor together. Daniel remembered rushing forward towards the woman, her bloodied fingers clutching at his shirt for only an instant before falling lifelessly away. He had checked her pulse and found nothing. Reaching out he had closed her eyes, and then looking up-- he'd seen her, the little girl. Her hands were clamped over her ears, and she sobbed uncontrollably in the corner of the room, her cream coloured eyes so big and round they consumed her face. She had been younger then. Daniel saw himself go over to her slowly, hold her against him and try to distract her from the noises of struggle, emanating from Ian and the creature behind them. He remembered whispering what reassurances he could give, placing himself as a solid barrier between her and the sight of her dead mother. He remembered the girl's tears soaking his t-shirt.

"Oh, this is Winn," Gakwin said, at the same time Daniel had found his voice and said, "You're the Howler's daughter."

Winn nodded mutely, but her eyes showed that she was pleased he remembered, despite the circumstances.

"What are you doing here?" Daniel asked gently. The last he remembered hearing, she was living with her aunt and uncle, her father never having been in the picture.

"Anyone who aligned themselves with you was thrown out of the pack, remember?" Gakwin said, misunderstanding his question.

Deciding to leave his discussion with Winn to a later date, Daniel fixated on the new problem facing them. "And now you have nowhere to go," he said despondently.

"We all came from somewhere before joining the pack, Daniel," Jack said. He had moved and was now surveying the food on the stove with extreme interest.

"Not all of us can go back," said Gakwin dismally. Winn sighed as if in agreement, and ran her hand through Winchester's fur.

"No one's kicking you out here," Jim remarked from his place at the table.

Daniel gave him an appreciative smile. "I think we both know we need to bury ourselves a little deeper than that. Luke knows I have connections here-- he'll be watching. Trust me, sooner or later someone's going to check in. It's not as safe as I'd like it," Daniel answered, and then shifted his gaze to the others. "And we'll have to keep shopping trips to a minimum as well, if we're going to lay low."

The three former pack members exchanged guilty looks.

"Told you he'd notice," Jim muttered triumphantly, and took a self-satisfied sip of coffee.

"Of course he noticed," Jack said, who now had a plate in his hand, and was weighing it down heavily. "Lycanthropes in clean, wrinkle free clothing? That's something I've yet to encounter," he pulled a fork out of a drawer and gestured with it. "Unless of course said clothes are fresh off a sales rack. It's not something that would have escaped my notice, and Daniel's as much of a Scit as I am."

Daniel smiled, glancing back at Gakwin. "Your shirt is pretty white pressed, dude."

Winn giggled, and straightened her new cardigan. Daniel

found himself staring at her. He didn't think he'd ever seen her with a smile on her face.

"It was necessary though, I assure you. We were looking rather like we were homeless," Jack said around a mouthful of egg.

"I had to borrow clothes from Jim just to walk around in public, mine were completely blood stained," Gakwin admitted.

"Sorry," Daniel said automatically, and then wondering why he was apologizing for nearly bleeding to death, looked away from Winn towards Jack. "And by the way, that's still a statement that's under scrutiny as being a fact."

"If you mean us being homeless, you're mistaken. You three may have nowhere to go back too, but I still have a house to my name. I wouldn't object to having it made into a secret headquarters of sorts. It would be every child's fantasy come to life."

"Will it have food?" Winn asked timidly. "You know… real food?"

Jack swallowed his latest bite and smiled. "As long as you're not a health food junky. Us geniuses run on Macaroni and Cheese, I'm afraid."

Winn seemed satisfied enough, though Gakwin's mouth tipped down slightly in disapproval.

"But that reminds me," Jack said, setting his plate on the counter momentarily to fish in his pocket. "Another thing us geniuses run on…" He tossed something in Daniel's direction, and he caught it out of the air reflexively. Glancing down, Daniel found himself holding a brand new, touch screen, cell phone, "technology," Jack said with a smile. Daniel felt the same kind of smile Ian would get every time he slid behind the wheel of his truck, find its way onto his face as he held the phone.

"Did you put it under--?" Daniel began to ask.

"An alias? Of course," Jack confirmed. "You are now John Muttson. A last name nearly as ironic as Winn's real one, I might add."

"How about--?"

"GPS? Not to worry, I took care of it. I can assure you, we are untraceable."

"Perfect," Daniel grinned and then looking around, noticed the rest of the room was staring at them. He shifted uncomfortably.

"Are you two speaking geek Pig Latin?" Jim blurted.

"Technically, neither of those are languages," Jack said, not all that helpfully. "Though geek could be considered a sort of jargon. It...," he said, and then let the sentence drop off, having caught the look Daniel was giving him.

Jim cleared his throat. "So what's the plan gang? We just going to lounge around in my kitchen for the rest of our lives?"

To Daniel's surprise, everyone turned to look at him. Silence filled the room for a minute and Winchester whined impatiently into it.

"Uh...," he said, desperately trying to come up with some course of action.

His mind spun, his clockwork, Scitor brain beginning to piece bits together one by one.

"We head over to Jack's," he started, "and then we keep doing what we have to. I'm going to keep taking cases." Jim looked about to say something at this, but Daniel pushed through, "I'm faster now, and stronger, I'm sure I'll manage." Jim muttered something about him limping, which Daniel ignored. "I want to off the bad seeds, and stop the negative publicity," Daniel insisted. "The more reasons Luke has, the more Knoctes he'll manage to convince. I'm going to try and cut that number down." He turned to the others. "Jack, Winn, Gakwin, I want you three to start making as many Fair Child friends as you can, especially vampires. They're next on Luke's hit list, and if we can get to them in time, and warn them, then we'll be sitting mighty pretty in their eyes. It's time we started trying to piece a decent army together."

"Wait a minute boy," Jim said. "How do you know the vampires are next?"

"I heard it from D-- someone," Daniel said quickly, catching himself. He knew right away, that no one in the room was about to believe he and Devlyn had shared a dream last night. None of them even knew of Reid's existence.

"And you're sure this person knows what they're talking about?" Gakwin questioned.

"Don't be absurd," Jack said suddenly, "He's right of course. I-I... heard it as well." He trailed off, everyone now staring at him.

"Fine," Jim said sourly, after a short silence. "Everyone

keep your secrets, just don't get yourselves killed trying to come by them. You hear?"

Solemn nods went around the room, Daniel once again thinking of Devlyn's situation. He knew everyone was itching to get going, to start things moving, but Jim wouldn't let them go without insisting that they sit and eat something first. Winn went over all too willingly, and Jack took the opportunity for seconds. Sitting on the counter, his leg swinging over the edge, he collected everyone's phones and started swapping contacts.

Daniel ate his fill quickly, some of his food already having gone cold, though he didn't care in the slightest. It sat like a welcomed weight in his empty stomach. Gakwin had taken a couple of plates as well, but Daniel couldn't help noticing everyone's eyes flickering uneasily towards the hallway. Daniel thought he felt their nervousness, Ian could walk through into the kitchen at any minute, and he too was beginning to think that one encounter with Ian and the pack had been one too many. They seemed greatly relieved when he pushed up from the table, and giving his thanks to Jim, headed for the door. They followed his lead, Winchester's disappointed whines trailing their retreat.

"Be careful out there," Jim ordered them, and then seeming to remember something, stalked off towards the pantry. He came back with an armful of power drinks and candy bars, evidently a parting gift from Jolie, and shoved them towards Jack, who muttered a short, "I'd nearly forgotten." before exiting the house.

With parting smiles and grateful remarks, the rest followed silently after him, Daniel limping in their wake. He'd just reached behind him to close the door, when Jim's voice stopped him.

"Dan," he said quietly, and something in his voice made Daniel look back over his shoulder at him. "Anything you'd be wanting me to tell your brother?"

Daniel stared at him, Winchester panting softly at his side. His hand still resting on the doorknob, Daniel realized there was a million things he wanted to say, some of them things he knew he shouldn't, but in the end all that ended up leaving him was, "I'm taking Winchester." And then whistling for the dog to join him, left the house, the door clicking firmly closed behind him.

Chapter Twenty-Six

A crow swooped over Ian's head, and he followed it with an ice-cold glare, despite it having been a few days, the argument he'd had with Jim still rang in his ears. It was like a broken record playing over and over again.

"Why I taught you to shoot a gun I'll never know!" Jim had shouted, his voice burning in anger the same way it was drowning in an unspeakable emotion. "You lost your head back there, Ian-- that was your brother you hit. Your brother! Knoctes can't afford to pull stunts like that! Do you even remember who you are anymore?!"

Ian remembered himself saying, just as equally angry, "You just let him walk out? Let him *leave*? After all this time we've been busting our butts trying to track him down again? Did you even bother to talk to him? Was he… you know…" Words had failed him at that moment, but squeezing his eyes shut briefly, he'd forced it out. "Was he normal? Like…"

"Himself?" Jim had provided then. "Of course he was. Perhaps you remember? Brown eyes, auburn hair, his brain an attic full of knowledge, his heart stretching an even greater distance than your idiocy."

It wasn't Jim's biting words that'd struck Ian most, it was the simple fact that while it seemed Jim had managed an entire conversation with Daniel, his brother hadn't bothered to say but one word to him during their encounter. Not once.

And now, Ian was in a worse mood than he'd ever been in. He walked the streets trying to suppress the guilt eating holes through his chest. Despite his best efforts though, it kept leaking through, and the irritability along with it. Another caw sounded above him, and a second crow swooped down, actually clipping Ian's shoulder with its talons, before flapping over to a nearby fence.

"Seriously?!" Ian yelled at it, as the bird tilted its head at an odd angle, regarding him with a beady black eye. It cawed again, the sound like mocking laughter, and rustled its feathers pleasurably. Ian had half a mind to shoot it. In fact, his hand was already halfway to the gun tucked in the waistband of his jeans, when someone screamed.

Gun instantly in hand, Ian's head snapped up, searching for the source of the sound.

"No, please!" the voice called again-- a man's. Ian instantly took off in its direction, following the sound of tormented cries. It was late enough that the street was nearly deserted, the only couple in sight, stood stationary on the sidewalk, looking around with concern for the source of the plea. Ian came up behind them without pause. Spotting his gun, they leapt hastily out of his path, the woman uttering a startled exclamation.

The voice continued. "No! *No!* Ahhh--."

It cut off just as Ian ducked into the nearest alleyway. It was dank, and his sneakers splashed through small pothole puddles recklessly in his haste. The smell of garbage assaulted his nose. He turned a corner around the back of an old restaurant, long since closed up for the night-- and saw him.

The victim lay dead; his body sprawled out awkwardly on the ground of the alleyway in front of him. The man's face had been completely bloodied, to the point where there was hardly anything left of it. Ian gave the scene a look of disgust, and noticed the big black crow sitting on the man's chest. It was twittering back and forth, pecking at the corpse almost gleefully.

"Stupid bird," Ian muttered.

"Careful," a voice said-- but Ian had already moved, spinning around, with his gun raised. He'd been waiting for an appearance, and had seen her movement reflected in a puddle, tipping him off, before she'd even spoken. "They are rather smart creatures."

Ian had no doubt, the woman before him could put any asylum inmate to shame. Her ink black hair was a frizzy, matted mess. Her equally dark eyes were wide in her thin face, and staring, hardly blinking as she regarded him. Her jeans were ripped and stained, and her baggy black shirt hung off one shoulder uncaringly. She spoke with a voice that was both dreamy and wondering, as if lost in time.

"Harbinger," Ian spat, realizing what she was. She could see through the eyes of her victims, intrude on their lives, their past, with just one touch she could read their future. Ian's jaw tightened, another thing realized, he'd faced her sort before, and guns were a completely useless defense. Still-- he wasn't putting it down.

"Young Knocte," she countered, and with each word her neck cocked at a more unnatural angle, as she continued to stare. "Such blue eyes. Fierce you are, aren't you little Knocte?"

"Little?" Ian scoffed. "Come on, give me some credit."

Her head cocked to the other side, and he half expected to hear it crack. "You cannot have walked this earth very long fledgling."

"Twenty-three," Ian snapped. "I'm twenty-three. Thanks for asking. And I promise all twenty-three years of my measly existence has taught me enough to damage the likes of you."

"Such short lives the human race leads," she said dreamily. "So little time. Yet quite the mark it's left on you already, little Knocte." She seemed to peer harder at him. "So hardened for one so young."

"Yes, and all your years of time have worked absolute wonders for you," Ian remarked dryly. A second crow cawed loudly, as it glided down on black wings to land beside the first.

"What an interesting child you are. I'd very much like to read your future." She took a step towards him, and Ian's grip tightened on his gun. Another crow swooped past, this one nestling itself on the alley fence.

"Sorry, crazy lady-- hands off."

"One touch," she insisted, and took another step forward. Without blinking Ian emptied two shots into her chest. She jerked backwards with each one, her dazed eyes flaring. Ian watched as her hands curled rigidly at her sides, a sound escaping her lips, like the screech of a crow.

And in the next minute-- Ian's vision was obscured.

The birds dive-bombed him on command, and he saw only feathers and slashing claws. More joined as he threw his hands up instinctively to protect his face. Beaks flashed, and pain bloomed along his arms and forehead where they made contact, as he tried to beat them away. A loud cackling laugh echoed in front of him, and he swung blindly. There was a loud sound of flapping wings, and then she was suddenly behind him, grasping him by his jacket.

She threw him across the alley, like he weighed nothing. He crashed into a pile of crates stacked near the restaurant's back door, and the wood splintered under him as he landed. One of the jagged ended pieces pierced his leg, and he felt blood starting to soak his jeans. Ian tried to push himself to his feet, but another blow leveled him on his back again. His gun was sent clattering to the ground far out of his reach. With a groan he blinked, and found he could see her now, the birds backing off to give her room. They circled above menacingly, and she lashed out again.

This time he was ready. He reacted, his hand snapping up to catch her wrist, but her free hand slid under the collar of his shirt, pressing into his chest just under his collarbone. He cried out as her skin seared against his own, the smell of his own flesh burning filled his senses. He watched her eyes glaze over, his future an overpowering drug to her. She let out another screech, but this time Ian found he could make out words, through the suddenly hoarse and gravely voice.

"Ian," she said, with the cruel pleasure of having drawn out his name. But then the pleasure seemed to freeze on her face. Cocking her head at its unnatural bird-like angle she pressed her hand harder against his skin. Ian's protest was lost somewhere between a cry of pain and a moan of agony. "Curious. What a deep, dark, empty future you have here, little Knocte."

Using as much will power as he could muster, Ian forced himself to focus. Using his free hand he began trying to reach, his fingers just coming short of a shattered crate.

"You cause suffering to the ones who love you. Put them through great pain," the Harbinger continued. "And they will leave you. Yes, death will claim them. Or they'll disappear from your presence, never to be heard from again. That brother of yours-- you don't think he'll last long do you? Yes. Yes, I see. He'll die. Die like the rest of them. Over nothing but a lost cause."

Fury surged through every muscle in Ian's body.

"SHUT UP!" he gasped out, somehow managing the strength to get his hand around her throat, and throw her off him.

She cried out a terrible, surprised sound, as she rolled, coming up in a crouch. Her dark hair stuck to her face with the wetness of puddle water, and clung to the eyelashes framing her glossy, crazed eyes. She sprang at him a second time, in the same moment he pulled himself across the gap separating him and his weapon of choice. Fingers curling around a broken shard of wood,

Ian retched it free from the busted crate, just in time to whirl around and meet her attack head on.

"See this coming, *witch*!" The moment she was on him, he thrust the makeshift stake through her heart. Her eyes flew wide, seeming to gain clarity for the first time their whole meeting. Ian glared right into them and wretched the stake deeper with a sharp twist, his lip curling in an angry snarl.

"You...?" she said in mild disbelief, and then collapsed, dead weight on top of him.

Shoving her corpse to the side, Ian lay breathing heavily, his blood steadily staining the alley beneath him.

Chapter Twenty-Seven

Marley was trying desperately to ignore him, as she sat in the Roadhouse, a book propped open on the table in front of her, and Lady lounging near her feet. Ian had sat down, three tables over, covered in blood and muck, looking very much as if someone had bound and dragged him behind a horse for a good couple of miles. It was hard not to notice, when he had sank into his chair and started throwing back drink after drink though. She was fairly sure the entire place was aware of his appearance actually, from the moment he'd stepped through the front doors.

Ian Browning was the kind of person whose presence alone could fill a room, though he seemed completely unaware of it. His entrance hadn't been anything grand, on the contrary, he'd stumbled in ungracefully and limped his way up to the mahogany bar for his first drink. Marley had been sincerely sorry Devlyn wasn't working that night. She would have taken one look at him and launched into a heated lecture.

The girl running the bar now, however, had looked completely terrified from the moment she'd caught sight of him. Knoctes didn't normally stroll into public places looking like they'd wrestled a semi truck, even if it was a Knocte home base. Unless, of course, they were planning to bust out bragging about some sort of high achievement, but Ian wasn't the type for campfire stories, she knew. He was just, well-- Ian.

Marley tried to stay immersed in her book, working hard to pretend she wasn't aware of Ian's deadened expression, staring without really seeing, at some point ahead of him. It almost worked, until Ian ordered another drink, and the waitress, too intimidated to cut him off, hurried away on command.

It was when the waitress was about to pass her, on way back over to his table that Marley snapped her book shut and got abruptly to her feet. Lady's head jerked up from the floor, and the waitress blinked, looking surprised as Marley stood blocking her path. She plucked the drink neatly off the girl's tray, and waved her away. That was when she went over, Lady following close by, and threw herself into the seat across from Ian. She smacked the heavy bottomed glass of booze down on the table in between them.

His eyes focused on her, though no expression adopted itself onto his face. They stared one another down for a long minute, and then slowly Ian started reaching for the glass.

Marley snatched it back immediately, leaning back in her chair. She examined the liquid as she swirled it around the glass thoughtfully.

"What is this?" she asked. She sniffed it, and then took a sip. Scotch? Really? "I prefer bourbon myself."

"What do you want Marley?" he asked dryly, his arm was still resting on the table where he'd stopped reaching.

"Someone has to stick up for your liver," she said haughtily, though it got no reaction out of him. He just stared at her blandly. She couldn't help wondering how drunk he really was. "You look like death by the way."

Up close she could see the damage more clearly. His leg was hastily bandaged over his ripped jeans, his skin was split above his left eyebrow, and red angry scratches marred his forehead and arms where he'd pushed up his sleeves. The wounds hadn't been cleaned, and his brass coloured hair still had blood crusted in it. His face had gotten thinner, his sharp features more prominent, as were the dark circles under his eyes. He looked fatigued beyond recognition. She had no idea how he was upright at all. It was as if she was watching someone drown in front of her, without the means to save them. Somewhere under all that ice, Ian was drowning.

"I've been busy."

"Uh huh. I can see that. You thought you'd come in here and drink yourself into oblivion? You're not a machine, Ian. You're flesh and blood. You need sleep and food-- real food. These are things people usually have to remind a five year old of."

"Last I checked, that's not your problem. None of this is your problem."

Setting the glass down heavily, Marley stared at him for a long moment, saw the tired, angry lines of his face, and felt the sting of his words from their last conversation. *Considering the last phone call I got from you. I don't think I ever want another one. Ever.*

"Fine," she said coldly, and started to get to her feet, when she suddenly thought better of it. She felt his anger seep into her, poisoning her system like a contagion, and her fist smashed down on the table top, spilling a large portion of the drink, before she could stop herself. Lady howled discontentedly, but to his credit, Ian didn't even flinch, and if he was surprised, he didn't show it. He was the master of the poker face, as he slowly shifted his blue eyes, his steel gaze drifting over to regard her curiously.

"No! You know what? This *is* my problem now," she barked. She sensed she was making a spectacle of herself, but couldn't stop. "I know what side of this war I'm on! Between Jim, J--, Ruby, and you. My mind's been long since made up. How about you, Ian? Had any epiphanies lately?"

Ian's eyes flickered away from her for a second, to scan their surroundings. Marley realized she had to be drawing some unwanted attention, their conversation nearing blasphemy to most ears in the room. She felt the eyes of other Knoctes resting on them, and dropped her voice to a harsh whisper.

"You're the only Knocte in existence that can send fear shivering down Luke's spine with one look. I know it. He knows it. Everyone knows it. It's time *you* do. I know Luke's pled his case," she said, and leaned across the table so their faces where just inches apart, "so hear mine. Get out of here. Listen to Jim. Go find your brother. Beg forgiveness for that stupid stunt I heard you pulled, and I mean *grovel* if you have to." She pulled away, and sank back into her seat. "You can't sit there and tell me you wouldn't do everything in your power to protect your brother. Lie if you want-- but no one's going to buy it. It's like you're two sides of the same coin. That's why you're going to fight with us. That's why our side's going to win."

Ian was quiet for a long minute, and then very adamantly he said, "No Knocte is getting anywhere *near* Dan."

She heard the furious undertone in his voice, and found herself grateful for the shadow of life it put back into him. Despite how irritated he could make her, she found her lips lifting in a slight smile. "Yeah. I thought not."

He looked at her then, for what felt like the first time. There was something enigmatic about his expression, but it only lasted a split second, because in the next instant, a face poked its way in between their line of sight.

"Hello? Hi, there!"

Marley turned to regard the man regretfully. He was very short, even by her standards, with muddy brown hair, and an over enthusiastic smile, she half felt inclined to slap off his face. Ian didn't so much as acknowledge the man's presence. He instead stole the opportunity to reach forward, finally snatching the glass off the table. He threw back what was left of its contents without so much as a wince, before Marley could stop him.

She scowled disapprovingly at him.

"The name's Thomas," the man continued, apparently immune to their indifference. "I'm new to the area, and I'm looking for a job. I heard the unfortunate news about your Scitor…" He was staring directly at Ian now, who'd turned to ice in his chair at the allusion to his brother. "If you're in the market, I would be pleased to offer you my services."

Ian whipped around to face him so fast, the man --Thomas-- nearly yelped as he staggered backwards a few steps. *What did you say?"* Ian demanded.

Thomas seemed completely taken aback by the reaction, and had a hard time finding his words. He began stammering uncontrollably. "I-I was just saying--."

But Marley couldn't stand it anymore, she wasn't sure Thomas knew quite the level in which he was in over his head. Ian was on the edge of his seat, his breathing heavy, eyes like piercing daggers. His tensed muscles made little white scars stand out along his skin.

"Oh, trust me," she quickly cut in, addressing the Scit. "You do *not* want to repeat that." She turned on Ian, hoping to give Thomas time to run, or at least gain a decent enough head start, when a round of laughter exploded from a nearby table, and Ian's attention, as much as it ever was, was lost to the new distraction.

"I wouldn't have believed it myself, if I hadn't seen it with my own eyes," came a Knocte's voice, carrying over to where they sat. He was one of three sitting around the table. "A lycan I tell you, with glowing brown eyes and white feet, carrying a shotgun 'round in its mouth, like some twisted game of fetch or something. The Fifth Worlders must finally be understanding their days are numbered."

Thomas took the opportunity to melt back into the scenery of the crowded Roadhouse. Ian's eyes flickered his way briefly, though he made no move to follow.

"Were you sure you could handle that one, Jerry?" one of the other Knoctes jeered in return, and erupted in another fit of laughter. "Or did he manage to shoot back without any opposable thumbs?"

Ian's chair creaked under him as he leaned in closer to listen. Marley couldn't see the first Knocte's face, he was seated with his back facing her, but when he spoke again, she thought his voice sounded a little sheepish. "It was such a sight you see, I very nearly laughed outright at it. He had a dog following him around too, just a regular old domestic mutt. It took me a minute before I even thought to reach for my gun."

Something said, triggered Ian, and he was suddenly out of his chair, his long strides eating the distance between him and the other Knoctes. He moved with an amount of grace, entirely surprising for the amount of alcohol in his system.

"Must be nice," the third Knocte commented, unaware of any approaching danger, and raised his beer mug in the air slightly, "finding free weapons lying out in the forest like that."

"It wasn't even in the forest!" the Knocte called Jerry exclaimed, "I was just walking around down near-- Hey!"

Ian had reached the table, not pausing for pleasantries; he'd taken hold of Jerry by the lapels of his jacket and hoisted him out of his seat. Marley swore under her breath, at the same time the other Knoctes around the table voiced their surprise. Ian thrust his victim up against the nearest wall, and held him there.

"Did you shoot at my brother?!" Ian demanded in a voice so deadly, Marley thought the man would drop dead from the sheer amount of poison in it. "Did you?!"

"No! I-- well, I-- yeah." Seeing the look on Ian's face he sped up his speech. "But I missed!"

Regardless, Ian's fist connected with Jerry's face, and Marley leapt out of her seat, Lady instantly scrambling to follow. She felt panic. Knoctes didn't turn on Knoctes; it was an unwritten law, an absolute law. Knoctes were seen as brothers and sisters of battle, and an assault on one meant turning your back on family. Ian's actions would not be taken lightly. Sure enough, the other two Knoctes jumped Ian, trying to gain hold enough to restrain him. Ian threw an elbow over his shoulder, connecting it perfectly

292

with the nose of one of the Knoctes, who staggered back, his face immediately covered in blood. The other grabbed Ian's shirt, dragging him back enough to free Jerry, who took off in a mad, tripping, dash towards the nearest exit, but it wasn't without its price. Ian abruptly spun on his remaining attacker, the Knocte blocked his first hit, but Ian's next sent him flying into the nearest table. Ian then ripped a knife out of his shoe, and sent it cartwheeling through the air after Jerry. It pinned the man to the wall by his shirtsleeve.

But a circle had formed around Ian, other Knoctes now joining together to block him in. Ian spun slowly around regarding each one personally, his expression practically begging them to try something, but they were either too shocked, or too frightened to engage him further. Marley shoved a Knocte unceremoniously aside as she broke through the circle, skidding to a halt in front of Ian, who's eyes flashed in excitement at having a willing target, before he realized who it was.

"Ian," she said meaningfully, and stared him down for a moment. She was completely aware of all the curious eyes on them, when a voice broke through the silence.

"What is the meaning of this, Ian?" It was Luke, the crowd parting for their leader with an air of respect that made Marley want to gag. Then a Knocte Marley suddenly recognized, from his spiked dark hair, down to the hideous green shirt that had always been his favorite, appeared on Luke's right.

Her blood went ice-cold.

He took notice of her immediately, his face flashing with recognition, and comic surprise.

"Marley?" he couldn't seem to help speaking, though Luke was now looking down at him with a somewhat disapproving expression.

Forcing herself to move, Marley made a point of standing at Ian's side. "Andy," she said coldly back, though she considered even her acknowledgement of him an incredible privilege.

"What are you *doing*?!" Andy demanded stepping forward. Marley had to will herself not to step back in revulsion. Her chin jerked up higher instead. "Do you have any idea how long I've been looking for you? It's been *two years*! Your brother--."

"Don't," Marley snapped. Now, she was nearly shaking

with anger. If Ian was at all confused by the sudden turn of events, he didn't give any inclination of it. She felt his quiet restlessness beside her, the same as ever.

"How very touching," Luke suddenly spoke again, purposefully interrupting. His condescending eyes rested on her for a moment before shifting back over to Ian. "You have made a serious offence against a brother, Ian."

Ian seemed to weigh his words, and for a brief moment, Marley wasn't sure he'd say anything at all.

"He's not my brother," Ian said bluntly, earning a few mouth gaping stares of disbelief. Marley wasn't sure whether Ian had finally come to some sort of realization, or whether it was the alcohol talking, but in any case, his voice rang clear. "And neither are you, Luke. You won't ever be! When have you been the one to stand and fight by my side? No, my brother, my *real* brother, the one running for his life because of you, is the only person I'd consider worthy of such a title. He'd give his life for me, as surely as I'd die for him. But you wouldn't understand that, would you? You never did. Even when we were kids."

Some carefully concealed emotion flashed in Luke's eyes for a second. "You have chosen then?" His voice sounded stressed. "You are turning your back on this family?"

Ian's gaze was like ice. "You attacked mine first."

And there it was again-- that hint of disbelief on Luke's face, and Marley saw whatever friendship they previously had between them.

Then his expression turned hard, and it was all gone. "You are an enemy in our midst then. You leave me little choice."

Marley's heart beat wildly against her chest, as every Knocte within shooting distance, pulled a gun on Ian.

"No," she whispered.

A few Knoctes hesitated, shock the only thing registering on their faces, but as if he was waiting for such a move, Ian had his handgun out of the waistband of his jeans, and aimed in perfect line with Luke's head.

"I only need one!" Ian warned every one of them, his voice booming through the building, demanding authority. "And I promise you: I'm faster and I won't miss."

No one moved. They didn't want their leader dead, but

Marley couldn't help noticing that no one lined up to take the bullet for Luke either. It was still every Knocte for himself, even if they did share a common cause. And the threat they faced was perfectly valid. Ian was a more accomplished Knocte than any other in the room. His battered and bloodied figure seemed only to stand as proof of his reputation, and she knew his wounded appearance hadn't come across as weakness, as she might have worried, but instead seemed to promise the danger within him. It was almost fact; Luke would hit the ground before he would. She certainly believed it, with him slightly drunk or not. Even now she saw Ian's eyes moving around the place, accessing who's fingers were playing more prominently over their triggers.

Marley drew her own gun and moved behind him, covering his blind spots. She caught a glimpse of Andy's horrified face and would have felt self-satisfaction, if the threat of death wasn't hanging over her head. With the draw of her weapon, Lady growled promptly and a few tracking dogs echoed the warning.

"What would you have me do, Ian?" Luke asked placidly, though Marley wondered briefly whether he would start sweating through that stupid overcoat of his at any minute.

"I'm leaving," Ian barked.

"*We're* leaving," Marley corrected him, calling to Luke. "And we'll walk you out."

Ian didn't remove his gaze from his old friend, but she saw him give a curt nod from her periphery. Luke raised his eyebrows, and Ian took it as the threat it was. There was not an ounce of underestimation in the room.

"Don't try it," Ian warned and took a step forward. "Let's go, nice and slow."

Marley was careful to shadow his movement.

It was Andy who blocked their path.

Ian hardly blinked. He saw Andy as the minimal threat he was, and his gun remained trained on its target, but Marley couldn't help swinging hers around. She made sure not to move out from behind Ian, but she aimed out the shot just over his shoulder.

"Marley!" Andy exclaimed in desperation, his eyes on her weapon. "You can't be serious!"

And now it was her turn to raise her eyebrows in a

challenging fashion. "I think you know from experience-- I am."

"We can--."

"*We?*" Marley spat back at him in disbelief. There would never be a 'we' when it came to the two of them. She let out a high cruel laugh that made a few people glance at her, as if she'd gone mad. She felt half mad. Every cell in her body wanting to do something stupid, wanted to pull the trigger of her gun.

But Ian's voice suddenly brought her back.

"Marley." Just one stern word. He didn't look her way. Didn't dare take his eyes off Luke or the Knoctes, but his free hand was suddenly stretched out behind him. The gesture was both an offer, as much as it was a silent question.

Are you with me?

She wasn't sure if he even cared either way, but he couldn't look over his shoulder to check, and he needed to know.

Oh, I'm with you.

Refocusing, she swung back around to cover his back, her eyes flitting back and forth, keeping careful watch of their surroundings again. Her gun still held in front of her, she made sure to look at Andy one last time, as she reached out with her own free hand to take Ian's, her fingers curling around his.

"Let's get a move on, handsome," she said over her shoulder, and Ian didn't hesitate. One step after another he moved forward, until his gun was against Luke's temple, and the leader was walking with them. The whole time Ian's hand, warm and calloused in hers, guided her as she walked backwards, covering their retreat. She kept expecting to hear a shot ring out, to feel Ian collapse in front of her, his hand slipping away, and have all hope lost.

But it never came.

The only sound to follow them was the click of Lady's nails on the wooden floor.

Chapter Twenty-Eight

The moment they exited the Roadhouse, Ian dropped her hand, and shoved Luke roughly away from him, gun still trained on the man's movements. Marley swiveled hers on the startled guard, motioning for him to retreat back the way they'd come. It wasn't until he was out of sight, that she breathed for what seemed like the first time since Ian had left his seat at the table.

"You kill me, and I become a martyr," Luke stated. "The cause will just grow stronger."

Ian said nothing, just clicked the safety back on his gun, and shoved it into the waistband of his jeans.

Luke gave a pleasant smile. "You see, brother--." But he didn't get any further.

Ian's fist slammed into his face, so hard, and so fast, that Luke didn't even see it coming until he was flat on his back on the porch. Then Ian turned his back and strode away without saying a word.

Marley scrambled off the Roadhouse porch after him, into the parking lot. "You're crazy, you know that?!" she bellowed at him. Her red hair blew into her face and she swatted it away impatiently. "Insane! You could have gotten us killed! When I said '*pick a side*,' I didn't mean--!"

But Ian wasn't listening. He had made it to his truck, and was now leaning against it like it was the only thing keeping him standing. His bandaged leg trembled, as his hand fished in his pocket, pulling out his keys.

"Oh, I don't think so," Marley muttered to herself and stormed over to him. "Give me those," she demanded curtly.

Ian tried to ignore her, reaching over to unlock the driver's side door, but she slid herself in his way, blocking the attempt. "I don't care how steady your shooting arm was back there, or how high a threshold you've built against alcohol poisoning-- you're still too drunk and injured to drive."

"I'm not leaving the truck here," Ian mumbled, and Marley could practically see the adrenaline wearing off, see him slipping back into the same deadened state she'd found him in. She was beginning to think there were only two sides to Ian Browning--

emptiness and anger.

"I didn't realize you had the thing on a leash."

Ian said nothing, just stared at her, like if she knew anything at all about him, she would already have known that.

He wasn't going anywhere without the truck.

"Boys and their toys," she muttered. Then sighed. "I'll drive it."

"No."

"There are two options here, Ian," she said bluntly. "and a Roadhouse brimming with angry Knoctes, capable of changing their minds at any second now."

"Then move," Ian growled.

"It's cute," Marley said thrusting her hand out between them for the keys, "that you think I'm joking."

They glared each other down for a long moment, in which Lady barked impatiently, and Ian's leg nearly gave out under him. He grabbed the edge of the truck bed to steady himself, and taking the opportunity Marley wrenched the keys out of his grasp. She swung around to unlock the door, and he made a move as if to stop her, when the Roadhouse door suddenly banged open. Ian froze, his eyes narrowing, as Marley managed to pull the truck door open. Lady launched herself into the vehicle ahead of her as she hoisted herself into the driver's seat.

"Get in!" she barked at Ian.

One of the Knoctes attempted to reach into the inside pocket of his jacket, when a warning bullet ploughed into the siding of the Roadhouse next to his head, Ian's gun suddenly in his hand again. Even injured, he still managed to move fast. Marley's eyes trailed him as he made his way around to the other side of the truck, and pulled himself into the passenger seat next to her. The moment he was in, she slammed the truck into reverse. The Knocte yelled profanities, as the gravel protested under the tires and they lurched backwards. From the corner of her eye she saw Ian's hand gripping the window ledge, his knuckles white with the strain of not being in control. She didn't push the truck forward into drive until they'd well cleared the reaches of the parking lot. The engine roared and she almost laughed in giddy approval of the sound, something she didn't do often.

As the truck barreled down the road, carrying them to

safety, it took her a couple of minutes to register Ian's continual and eerie silence. Marley began to feel that chilling, hair-raising feeling she got when she was always around him, prickle at the back of her neck. His calloused fingers constantly twitched around the window frame, and just when she thought he was closer to passing out than ever opening his mouth, his voice slit the silence.

"I've killed us all."

"What?" Marley spat so fast, she realized she'd just been waiting for him to say something.

"I lost my head. Again. I should of stuck with Luke," he said quietly, his eyes staring through the windshield in front of him. He spared a glance down at his injured leg, grit his teeth and looked back up. "I made it personal now. I screwed up."

"Shut up," Marley snapped. "No, you didn't."

"You don't get it," Ian said turning to look at her. "I've thought about it. I would've only fought with him under certain conditions. I could've protected Dan, ensured certain people's safety."

Marley wanted to smack him, and hard. "Don't be *stupid!* That's exactly what Luke would've wanted. He would have dangled them over you, his own little insurance policy that Ian Browning stays on a leash." She paused. "He's more cunning than you give him credit for."

"Luke--."

"I know what Luke is," Marley said impatiently. "And I get that you grew up with him. But for the sake of everyone else, why don't you *take your freaken blinders off*. You're clouding your judgment dwelling on the past like that."

Ian said nothing at first. She heard him give something like a pained grunt, and had to resist the urge to glance his way.

"I only dwell on what's important," he said finally, his voice sounded softer, a little strained even. "The rest is dead weight, you put it on a shelf in the back of your mind, and you forget it's there."

"And how's that tactic working out for you?" she asked, feeling the acid in her own voice.

"A lot better than yours," he said evenly, his voice mirroring her tone. "Don't think I didn't notice. Andy? You're running, Marley. I don't know what he did, or why, but you may as well be on the Fair Child side just to spite the guy."

Marley slammed on the brakes. The tires squealed, Lady yelped in surprise, and Ian nearly went through the windshield. He hadn't expected it. She knew she'd caught him off guard, when his face actually connected with the dashboard. He exclaimed something fowl as Marley turned on him. She almost felt satisfied as she watched him dab at his forehead with the palm of his hand.

"Let's make something clear, shall we? Out of the two of us *I'm* the one sitting beside the wishy-washy, indecisive nut bag, who can't remember to put his seatbelt on, never mind which side of the war he's on, and you really want to talk motives? You? If Daniel wasn't a lycan right now, are you really going to tell me we'd be in this truck together? At this moment? No. Of course not. I'd be in my car, alone somewhere, imagining you and Luke side by side, wondering who I thought I was that I could stop it all, and how I was ever going to make it out of the whole thing alive."

She'd spoke so fast she needed a minute to catch her breath. She gasped, leaning back against the seat and pushed red strands of unruly hair away from her face. Her other hand held the steering wheel in such a vice her nail beds ached. She could feel Lady's nose prodding the back of her seat uneasily, seeking reassurance.

The truck cab grew quiet, and when Ian continued to say nothing, she couldn't resist stealing a glance in his direction.

His face was stony, pale, like no amount of confession had left any withstanding impact.

"Rule number one," he said slowly, deadly, "don't ever pull a move like that in my truck again, or you *will* wish you were alone and you'd never met me--."

"I already wish I'd never met you," Marley muttered. She could stare down her enemies with a condescending smirk, laugh at their attempts in battle even. So why did Ian Browning, sitting in the passenger seat of his own truck, smelling of alcohol and blood, make her want to both tear him a new one, and disappear into the leather of her own seat at the same time.

"Rule number two," he continued as if he hadn't heard her. "Try *not* to-- get-- us-- killed." She was about to cut him off for a second time, when he spoke over her forcefully. "Rule number three: just shut up and drive."

300

They fell into silence again, one that stayed with them for the rest of the drive. Marley fixed her eyes straight ahead, watching the road, not daring to look at him.

It wasn't until she pulled the truck up in front of the busted parking stop, and jammed it into park, that she addressed him again.

"There you go. Happy? Home at Motel Madness. Want to call me a cab now?" When he didn't answer, she sighed. In her mind's eye, she thought she could almost see his sullen look, the small crease in his brow. Still not talking to her… "Look. I'm sorry I compromised the stupid truck, all right? But seriously, what are we? Ten years--?"

Her words dropped away as she looked over and saw Ian slumped against the passenger window, his head tilted back at an uncomfortable looking angle. His injured leg, long as it was, was stretched out in front of him. One of his hands hung limply beside it, covered in his blood.

It was like a blow to the system. Marley said something unladylike, sudden panic twisting her stomach, as she launched herself at Ian. The seatbelt caught her, snapping her backwards and she swore even more profusely, as she struggled to free herself from it. Sensing her anxiety Lady began barking uneasily.

"Son of a--!" she exclaimed, but then it came free and she forgot about it entirely. Scrambling up beside Ian she grabbed his face in both of her hands, twisting it to face her. His complexion was pale with blood loss. He didn't stir. Her fingers slid down to his neck checking for a pulse, which she was immediately relieved to find.

"All right," she said repeating it slowly in an attempt to calm herself. "All right."

She raked shaking hands through her knotted hair.

Stop the blood flow, and then get him inside. Right. Okay.

She got out of the vehicle, Lady leaping after her, and swung around to the passenger side to get a better access point. Throwing the door open, she took one look at his leg, grimaced, and set to work. Ripping off the blood soaked bandage, she replaced it with a fresh one she found in a first aid kit, which lay strewn apart and littering the back seat of the truck, exactly where Ian had apparently left it.

The hardest part was removing him from the seat. She slung his arm around her shoulders in an attempt to drag him to the motel room door, but carrying Ian's six-foot-four and well filled out frame proved a lot heavier than she'd anticipated. They both ended up hitting the asphalt roughly and feeling like cursing all over again, Marley leaned over him, already feeling guilty for what she was about to do.

"Please don't kill me," she whispered, as Lady leaned in to lick his face, and then drawing her hand back, slapped him full across the face. The sharp sound seemed to echo across the parking lot. At first he didn't react. Then he moaned. "A little help here, handsome?" she asked. He didn't open his eyes, but even a semi-conscious Ian was better than an Ian as sheer dead weight.

The second time, she managed to get him on his feet enough to lead him inside, elated to find the door unlocked. Lady dashed inside ahead of them, as Marley fought to get him over to the closest bed. She intended to dump him there, but she saw the busted lamp --shattered on the floor in front of her like the rib cage of a dead carcass-- too late. She attempted to side step the mess, and losing her hold on Ian, went for shoving him in the right direction, as she tried to dance out of harm's way.

But Ian had other ideas. The moment he started to fall, his eyes suddenly snapped open. Out of reaction he grabbed the first thing in his path-- her, and dragged her down with him. His back hit the bed, at the same time her arms did, bracing themselves above his shoulders. His hands flew immediately to her hips to catch her-- and they both froze. Ian's eyes shifted from her face, down to his hands, and then back again.

And Marley looked too. She saw the tousled brass hair curling from sweat around his temple, the curve of his neck, the blood smeared high across his cheekbone, the scar that ran along his jawline. Everything. For a brief moment, she could tell he was caught off guard, even confused, his sharp blue eyes inquisitive, but then they flickered, his lips curving into an amused smile instead.

"Well this is tempting."

And just like that-- the spell broke.

"Oh, for the love of--," Marley exclaimed, shoving herself away from him, but as she sat up-- she saw it. A red handprint

302

branded into the skin beneath his collarbone. Feeling shock, she reached out to yank the neckline of his shirt down without thinking. "A Harbinger *got* you?"

Ian's expression grew cloudy, but he said nothing. He was good at that. Saying nothing.

"Is this what your whole doomsday speech was about back there?"

"She saw things…"

Marley's hand fisted in the collar of his black t-shirt. "Yeah, your future right?" She rolled her eyes. "A Harbinger's talent is about as useful as a starfish with antlers. They see your future as it stands in the present moment, but you make a different choice, change your mind but once, and *bam* completely different future."

"They've been known to get it right."

"Uh huh," she said sarcastically, "and I'm so sure that this morning you were planning on making decisions that would lead you into a motel room with me."

His smile was almost genuine. "I suppose I forgot to tell her I have a stalker."

"No. What you forgot to tell *me* was that you were slowly dying off in the seat beside me."

"What? This?" Ian asked, pulling his re-bandaged leg up. Marley noted, feeling pleased with herself, that it appeared to be holding. "It takes more than a giant splinter to the leg, to bring me down."

Images of Ian that night suddenly came back to Marley. She could see his recklessness and his fearlessness, in the way he'd faced down Luke. In the moments when she'd felt like he had nothing left in him, he'd pulled out the will of dozens. He had an all consuming and deadly passion for his loyalties to those he loved, the likes of which she'd seen only glimpses of in other Knoctes. In their strange world Ian was the moon to everyone else's stars.

But Ian *was* the life, Marley realized. The life of Knoctes. All sharp lines, thin scars and hard expressions. Somehow she knew it didn't matter what condition circumstances found him in, every time the life called for him-- he would give it more than it bargained for.

"You know," Marley said with a small smile. "I might actually believe you."

Ian woke to the sound of his cell phone's shrill ringing. He was still getting used to the sound of the new contraption. He groaned, rolled over, and threw a pillow over his head, willing it to stop. His head pounded. And his leg throbbed. After about five rings the sound died, and he'd just started to relax again, when it started up for a second round. With an irritated noise he pulled himself into a sitting position and glanced around the motel room. The bathroom door was open; he could see the mirror, still fogged up with steam. The fan was going.

"Marley?"

He received no answer. She'd crashed on Daniel's bed last night-- but she was gone. He frowned to himself as the phone kept ringing, and then impatiently patting himself down, he retrieved it from his pocket. He was still wearing his clothes from last night.

"What?" Ian snapped. He swung his legs off the bed, his bare feet touching the cool floor, though he didn't remember taking his shoes off. His elbows rested on his knees, as he scrubbed his hand over his face. He needed a shave.

"It's good to hear your voice too, Ian."

"Dev," He said suddenly sitting up straighter. "Everything's okay right? You're keeping your head down?"

He sensed her hesitation. "Sort of…"

"What's 'sort of' supposed to mean?" he demanded, unease sweeping over him at her words.

He heard her let out a small breath on the other end. "We might have a slight problem."

"Right," Ian said getting to his feet. He held back a grunt as his leg protested. His free hand reached out to clasp the headboard. "Cause we can really use more of those."

"It might be nothing," she admitted. "I'm probably just overreacting."

Ian wandered the room, trying to work out the stiffness of his injury-- and nearly stepped on the smashed lamp. There was a piece of paper now resting on top of the mess.

"Just rip the Band Aid off, Dev." Ian said, stooping to pick it up. "What's wrong?"

It was a note.

This is a hazard. Clean it up.
--Marley Shray

He smiled wryly down at it, then tossed it aside onto the
bed.

"It's Luke. He's here at the Roadhouse, and he's not happy.
I heard about what you did... saw his face. And I'm proud of you,
but I think he's starting to question the allegiance of others he
thought he trusted. He started asking questions today." In that
moment she sounded more sad than worried. "About inventory of
weapons. And other things."

Ian pulled his phone away from his ear for a second, to
check the time on it. It was two in the afternoon. He cursed himself
inwardly for nearly sleeping the day away. "You think he knows?"

"I really don't know, Ian," she said tiredly. "I only know
what I just told you."

Ian blew out a heavy breath and stared at the wall in front
of him. There was a little crack in the plaster that spider webbed
out from the roof, unrelenting evidence from the night when Daniel
had been attacked and taken. If he couldn't be with his brother
now, the least he could do was make sure the love of his life was
kept safe.

"I'm recalling you then."

"I'm not a malfunctioning toy, Ian."

"Close enough," he said. "I know you wanted to do this.
But your cover's blown, and there's nothing but danger for you
now. I know Luke. If he suspects something, he'll be watching
your every move, up until the moment you slip up."

"I really think I can still--."

"Dev," Ian said sharply. "Listen to me. Get out of there
now."

"I can't just walk out in the middle of my shift without
completely giving myself away." She sounded desperate. "Have
you found Dan? Is there anyway I can talk to him?"

Ian decided to ignore that last question. "You're talking on
the phone in the middle of your shift," he noted.

"That's different," she argued quietly. "I'm in the

305

bathroom."

"Is there a window?"

"Not one any human can fit through," she said ruefully. "Ian…"

"No," Ian stopped her. "I haven't found him, all right? But don't start giving up on me."

"I don't give up," Devlyn said quickly, indignantly. "But I'm not delusional either."

For a long minute neither of them said anything, Ian listening to the sound of her gentle breathing on the other end of the line with increased worry.

"I'm coming to get you," he said suddenly. "I'll hide who I am. Kidnap you or something."

"Ian, that's a horrible idea."

And she was right, of course. This was when they needed Daniel. The one who came up with all the plans. The *good* plans.

But they didn't have him now.

"I don't care. You're talking to me. And reckless is all I got."

Chapter Twenty-Nine

"Take one more step and you'll be the wine to my main course."

Daniel froze, slowly raising his hands in the air. He stood on a crumbling sidewalk of a lonely district of town, as a vampire rounded on him. Her dark brown hair hit her shoulders straight and flat, resting there almost buoyantly. Her bleached hazel eyes regarded him with a look of mixed curiosity and wariness. He didn't miss the way she fingered something along the inside pocket of her jacket, or the way the red hues of dusk reflected almost blindingly off her pale skin.

"I just want to talk." Daniel said slowly. "That's it."

She didn't remove her hand from her jacket pocket, and Daniel was glad he'd left Winchester at Jack's place. In this situation, the less he looked like a Knocte-- the better.

"Why?" she asked.

He noted the skepticism in her voice. "My name's Daniel. I don't know if--."

"Yes, Churchill," she cut him off, impatiently. "I remember. Water dragon nearly ripped your pretty face off. That doesn't answer the question."

"You saved me that day. Do you also remember that?"

She eyed him silently, an inquisitive frown etching her face. "Yeah, so?"

"What's your name?"

"Audrey," she answered automatically, and then looked as if she wished she hadn't. He could tell the question had caught her off guard.

"Audrey," Daniel repeated. "Can we walk?" He indicated the street ahead of them, with a sweep of his arm.

He saw her stiffen at the movement, and for a second he thought she was going to refuse. "That's a dangerous thing to do these days," she said instead, sounding indignant, "walk."

"I agree," he affirmed, and then turning his back, started up the street. At first there was nothing. Then he was pleased to hear the soft sound of footsteps behind him.

"Don't play games with me, lycan," she said stiffly,

moving up to walk at his side.

Daniel looked sideways at her. Her eyes were darting about their surroundings suspiciously, her shoulders tense and her footsteps light.

"Yeah. Lycan." His voice was bitter. He wanted to laugh. A kind of laugh that was mirthless and dark. "It seems like I had more than vampire problems to attend with."

Now she looked over at him. Pale eyes both large and prying in her round face. She was reading him, he knew, deciding whether or not he was worth her time to trust. It was times like these, in which trust could be a scary concept, a rare thing to give.

In the end, she spoke. "How much do you know?"

"I know I went from being a target to being recruited."

She nodded slowly. "That was the line of thought. I changed my mind when I met you, tried to convince others. They eventually wanted you as one of us."

"But the lycans beat you." Daniel stated.

"We're vampires," she shrugged, like that explained everything. "Mostly we lie, we wait. Then when the right opportunity comes-- we act. Lycanthropes don't. They're more... outgoing and destructive beings. They went all --break in and smash stuff-- crazy. So, yeah. They reached you first."

"I still don't remember any of that," Daniel muttered more to himself than to her.

She smiled grimly. "So why are you following me out in the open, for the whole Knocte population to potentially see?" Even as she said it, her eyes did another wary sweep of their surroundings.

"I'm the one recruiting now, I guess."

"Ah. Irony then."

Daniel turned so he was walking backwards in front of her. His remarkable sense of balance preventing him from tripping up on the rough surface of the sidewalk. He looked straight into her face as he spoke.

"Luke's coming for your kind next. But we're all still in danger, there's no denying that. You could use some help. So could we. And we have one advantage-- Knoctes work alone. All's good and well when they speak of a similar cause to stand for, but when they actually try and fight by one another's side... it doesn't always work to their favor. It falls apart. Us? We can lend one another our strength. Knoctes? They just get in each other's way."

She gave him a look. "But not for you and Ian. I've seen it. You're different."

"Yes," Daniel said evenly. "We're different."

"And is he on our side?" she asked carefully, curiously.

"That--." But she would never find out what he was going to say, for in that moment, a vehicle flew around the street corner, bathing them in the intensity of its headlights.

Wait until it was dark. That had been Devlyn's last words of advice to Ian before she'd hung up. Wait for the darkness. Like it was some cloak of invisibility that would shield and aid him. But Ian had never been afraid of the dark. Never understood the difference between light and dark. Nothing really changed after all did it? He had driven through all hours on the clock, slept through all hours. The difference had never really been important.

Until now.

Until his brother's deep brown eyes reflected in his headlights, like some cornered animal's.

How many nights had he driven the streets, coffee the only thing lending his muscles the strength to hold the steering wheel, while he searched for his brother, aimlessly and tirelessly? How many days had he wasted away at the desk of Jim's study, staring at his relentlessly tangled web wall, wishing for the spelling spider from that pig movie to simply swing down and letter it out for him one by one? And now, out of nowhere, Daniel stood not ten feet away from him, glowing eyes wide with alarm. Ian felt paralyzed in his seat. It was a remarkable coincidence. Though Devlyn would argue there was no such thing.

There was someone with him, whirling around to face the truck, someone with skin so pale it reflected the headlights in a rather blinding fashion, and sent his hands itching for a shotgun. As if sensing his thoughts, she pulled a dagger from the inside pocket of her jacket. The metal shone in the rising moonlight, but with one sweeping motion, Daniel shoved her behind him.

"Go!" Ian heard Daniel shout at her over the roar of the truck's engine.

"But--."

"Go!" he interrupted her again, with urgency. He pulled a piece of paper from his pocket, and folded it into her hand, already beginning to tremble. The muscles on his shoulders jumped and rippled. She took a startled look at him and stepped back.

"I'll be in touch," she called to him as she retreated. A tinge of fear licked at her voice. With a last glare at the truck, she spun, disappearing into the shadows, leaving Daniel standing alone.

"Ian!" Daniel yelled, his familiar voice tearing through Ian like a physical pain. It was the first thing his brother had said to him in what felt like a long time, and it hurt to hear it laced with such anger and hate.

"Danny…" Ian whispered in answer, but the sound was easily drowned out.

Then there was a deafening crack, an explosion of skin and fur, and his brother was gone, a wolf bolting away through the night. Ian didn't think-- just reacted. His foot slammed against the gas peddle. The truck lurched forward, and he swung it around to follow the streak of auburn coat. He would not lose him. He would not lose his brother again.

He lost track of how long he chased Daniel, the engine of the truck roaring its perseverance, as he barreled after a flash of eyes or a flitting auburn tail. The sun had disappeared completely, ducking out behind the horizon. A couple times he thought he lost him, dashed hope nearly choking him as it caught in his throat, but he tore over sidewalks, and through parks relentlessly, until he picked him out from the darkness again. His tires squealed against asphalt, and slipped on grass. He tightened his grip on the steering wheel, his knuckles turning white, his eyes penetrating the scene in front of him.

Then his brother disappeared around the corner of a more upstanding area of town, where clean cut siding met gleaming windows and stone on front facing garages. The lights that spilled out from inside the homes, lit the street like candlelight, as the truck bounced over a manhole. Ian took the turn sharper than he would have liked-- and came face to face with Daniel, eyes so bright and blinding, even as he slammed on the brakes, he knew he wouldn't be able to stop in time. The tires protested as Daniel stood braced on four legs, ears pinned back, his sides heaving with exertion. Just when Ian lost sight of him over the dashboard, his heart frozen in his chest, something crashed onto the hood. He swerved to the side coming to a stop in the entrance of an alleyway. Breathing heavily, he faced down a wolf, its nose an inch from the windshield, menacing eyes glowing brown like molten earth, seemed to tear a new one right through his soul. His brother's stance was for balance, his legs slightly splayed over the hood, white paws stained grey with street grime. For a moment, it was all Ian could do to stare over the wheel at his brother. It wasn't until he felt like he could safely breath again, that he threw the door open.

"Easy," Ian murmured, his hands by his shoulders in plain view. "I'm not here to pick a fight." The wolf gave a disbelieving growl, lips pulling back over teeth. "Can I please talk to the version of you without a tail?"

If a wolf could give a condemning look, Ian was sure he received one. And then with a loud crack, that seemed to snap every bone in his body at once, the creature was his brother again, sliding off the front of the truck and away from him. Daniel's jeans and white t-shirt were rumpled, his hair windblown across his forehead, but he was every bit as Ian remembered him. A sight for sore eyes, though he'd never seen a faster shift, and it nearly brought him up short.

"Where do your clothes go while you're a wolf?"

Daniel's eyebrows lifted, easing the force of his scowl. "Is that really what you want to talk about?" His voice was carefully flat, drained of emotion.

"What? You wanted to talk about the weather? --Hey. Don't look at me like that. I'm still your brother."

Daniel looked skeptical. "The brother I know," he said, his voice straining for calm. Ian could hear the anger layered beneath, "would never harm an innocent being."

Ian knew he meant the pack.

"They attacked me first you know…" Then when Daniel's face turned mutinous he quickly backtracked. "A mistake, all right? It was a mistake. You were gone… And I-I lost my head."

"I'm not looking for excuses, Ian."

"Oh, come on! Tell me you wouldn't have gone bat crap crazy if it had been me, if I was the one ripped from your life, and you watched everything I'd worked for fall to ash."

"I'm still working for the same cause, you know. I'm just in it for the long haul now."

"So you are," Ian agreed. "And I need your help."

Daniel laughed out loud. "My help... right..." With a shake of his head, he turned his back on Ian, and began walking away down the street, calling over his shoulder, "Everyone wants my help these days-- until I decide to give it. Then suddenly I'm crazy. I'm suddenly just a couple dozen cats away from the nut house. So, no. I won't help. You'll just have to trust that I'm doing what I can."

"Even if it's about Dev?" Ian asked of his brother's retreating figure.

Daniel stopped short. Spun around. "What about Dev?"

"She's in trouble," Ian answered honestly. He hated how his voice came out unsteady.

Daniel's eyes flashed, and for a moment, Ian saw the wolf beneath.

"Please." He extended his hand in an offer of Conexus. "I need you, brother."

Daniel barely looked at him. He was heading straight for the passenger side door of the truck, with his hands jammed in his jean pockets. "Get in."

Chapter Thirty

Ruby was at the Roadhouse. On all accounts it was the stupidest thing she'd ever done-- but it didn't matter. No one was looking at her.

Because for once, there was something worse than a Fifth Worlder treading on their sacred ground.

The Roadhouse was on fire.

The flames stretched towards the sky, casting dancing shadows over the frantic crowd of Knoctes. Shouts rang out, climbing over each other in every direction, engulfing Ruby in their fear.

"Water! Someone--!"

"--still inside?"

"Luke--."

"--911!"

"Where's--?"

The whole building was crackling like kindling. The smoke poured out in an inky cloak, streaking through windows, creeping out from under the door, twisting with the flames, light and dark in the suddenly red-lit sky. She stood mesmerized by the flames, afraid to venture forwards, refusing to turn and run.

Then strong arms grabbed her from behind, lifting her off her feet.

She screamed, trying to struggle free.

"Ruby! *Bee!* It's me!" She froze. She would recognize that voice anywhere.

Daniel set her down at a safer distance from the Roadhouse, and she spun around to face him, clutching his arms so fiercely, she was sure she was leaving nail marks. He didn't seem to notice.

"Where's Dev?" they both demanded of each other at the same time. And then stared horrified at one another. She saw his young, handsome face etched with lines far beyond his years. It gave him the ruggedness of a Knocte, though it was his eyes, soft and brown, and suddenly scared that gave him the gentle boyish look that could melt people's very insides.

"Don't panic," came Ian's voice over Daniel's shoulder, and Ruby shrank back from it reflexively. Now Daniel was the one clutching her arms. "I'm sure she's around here. Who knows? Maybe this fire is a good thing. Maybe she lit it."

"She wouldn't do that," her and Daniel both replied immediately.

Ian frowned in their direction. "What is this? 'Talk at the same time day?'" Then his glance lifted, taking in the Roadhouse again. "Does make for a good distraction though." He said it almost flippantly, but Ruby could tell he cared more than he let on. His normally chilling eyes reflected the fire, orbs of blue flames in his face. His hands were held a little too rigidly at his sides, his expression somewhat contorted, looked tortured like he was the one burning from the inside out, not the building.

Something was terribly wrong. Ruby could feel it, like a knife twisting in her gut.

Then Daniel's phone rang.

She saw lycanthropy in the speed in which he answered it.

His shoulders sagged. "Dev," he breathed. "Thank God." He paused, listening, and then his face turned a deathly pale colour. "What...? Dev, what are you--? Where are you?"

"Dan?" Ian said warily, circling closer to them. But the phone had slipped from Daniel's fingers, colliding with the grass on the perimeter of the parking lot. Understanding flashed in Ian's eyes, but he reached for his brother too late, and Daniel was gone, a near blur headed straight for the Roadhouse.

"No!" Ruby exploded, leaping forward. But Ian reacted faster, shoving her backwards and out of his way, as he tore after his brother. She hit the ground roughly, hair spilling over her shoulders, palms smearing with dirt. She turned her head, just catching a glimpse of Daniel as he threw his shoulder against the Roadhouse door. It collapsed inward with a bang and a burst of flames. Panicking she fumbled for the cell phone, wondering how on earth Devlyn had gotten the number, but when she held the phone up to her ear, there was no longer anyone on the other end.

The roar of the flames was deafening, the heat intense. Daniel's sleeve caught fire, and he ripped it away without looking back, already feeling the burn start to heal, his skin mending itself in a way only a Fifth Worlder's could.

"Dev!" he called, and then choked on the smoke.

Staggering he caught himself against a wall, trying to see through squinted eyes. He could see the bar he had to get past, on fire like everything else. Coughing, he backed up, his steps testing the weakened floorboards. He watched, finding a gap in the flames. Then lurching into a run, he threw himself over it. He collided with the ground on the other side, his shoulder breaking the fall, as he rolled out of it. He caught up a breath, and forced himself to his feet, his lungs feeling heavy, as he maneuvered his way down the hall.

"Dev!" he cried again. "*Dev!* Where are you?"

Then, faint and horrified, a single door down: "Dan?"

He swung himself in front of the door. It was the weapons room, enormous and vaulted. "Hold on! I'll get you out!"

He grabbed the handle-- and his hand burned, though it hadn't yet grown hot to the touch. He jerked it back with a choice word.

Silver.

The weapons room was laden with silver, a precaution that had once been meant to protect.

"No!" Devlyn screamed. "Dan, go back! Go back!"

"I'm not leaving you here!" He yelled back at her, and then gritting his teeth, he grabbed the handle again, this time trying to turn it as he forced his shoulder into it. It didn't budge. He cried out in pain, and dropped his hold, stumbling back. He stared at the door terrified. She was an arm's length away, and he couldn't get to her.

Couldn't get to her.

"You have to! You don't have a choice. Dan, listen to me-- you have to."

He hurled himself against the door.

This time using his whole body. But it was like trying to convince a rock into becoming pliable. He heard Devlyn's surprised intake of breath, as the door jerked under his weight. She called out his name from what seemed like a long distance away.

He threw himself at the door again. His heart pounded in his ears, loud enough that it threatened to bring the whole place collapsing in on them.

"I love you. I love you." Her voice. Thick and strangled. "But go."

And again.

She was pleading with him, her voice choked with tears, breaking with sobs. She begged him over and over, her hands smacking against the door from the other side, emphasizing his name, demanding to be heard.

But he wouldn't. He would never go.

"I'm not going to let you die with me!" she cried.

But death, dying here, in this building with her, was better than any scenario where he walked away. He could never forgive himself. Wouldn't be able to live with that kind of guilt. It would crush him more thoroughly than any licking flames, or strangling smoke. How could she not understand that? To leave was to die. In more creative ways than the mere physical.

He lost count of how many times he connected with door. A sound, something more animal-like than human, was grating its way out of his throat, rumbling in his chest. He could smell his own flesh burning, feel his shirt searing into his skin.

Then a voice rang through the pressing smoke. "Danny!"

Ian.

Daniel saw hope and called out for it.

"Help me!" Daniel begged, his voice unrecognizable, rising to a scream. *"Ian,* HELP ME!"

His brother appeared at his side, charcoal smeared across his cheek, eyes wild. He took in the scene for all of a second, a second that felt like far too long to Daniel, and then the next time he attempted to break the door down, Ian lent his weight. They both crashed against it a second time, gasping in heavy breaths of air. They're attempts quickly became weak, the thick acrid smoke scorching its way down their throats with every exerted breath. A section of the roof gave away, crashing to the floor inches away from where they stood, sending up a pluming pillar of ash. They coughed.

"Ian!" Devlyn cried, switching tactics. Her voice was raspy, weak, but still fierce. "It's useless! Get Dan out of here! GET HIM OUT OF HERE!"

Ian stopped, and glanced up at the ceiling. It was going to come down, crash down on their heads and bury them all alive. Unless he did something. Because it was all up to him. Him, still with a partially injured leg, throbbing out pain with its continuous use.

Anyone who looked at Daniel would have been able to tell, with one glace, that he wasn't going anywhere. He hadn't stopped. There where sickening red welts all down his right side, but his eyes were crazed, unwilling to give up, unwilling to believe it was all over.

"Dan," Ian said quietly. "I'm sorry. I'm so sorry. But we have to go."

And suddenly it was like they weren't in the Roadhouse anymore, but in their parents' house again, with Daniel's hands curled in their mother's nightgown, as she stared ahead with lifeless eyes. Daniel, a boy again, tears streaming down his cheeks, his mop of auburn hair clinging to his face. And Ian. Himself. Begging for his brother to leave, to come with him.

Daniel faltered, his hands catching himself against the door. The sound the connection made was sickening. His palms smoked, but he just stared at them.

"Dan!" Ian called in alarm, and grabbed his shoulder, jerking him back. The moment Daniel took a forced step away from the door, he whirled around. Ian felt even before he saw, his brother's fist connecting with his face. He stumbled back, bringing a hand to his jaw, and stared at his brother. There was nothing but betrayal written in Daniel's features. "Are you--?" Ian started, but it was as far as he got.

There was a loud crack. His eyes snapped to the ceiling. A large beam tore from the roof, tumbling to the floor above their heads, a crackling blaze.

Ian dove, tackling his brother out of the way. And only half succeeding. The beam caught Daniel on the way down, and when they hit the floor, his auburn hair was already darkening with blood. Ian watched him groan, his eyes fluttering shut. The last word to leave his lips, before losing consciousness was Devlyn's name.

Ian cursed.

"Dan! *Please! DAN!*" He could hear Devlyn. The words frantic, but the delivery sluggish, and he snapped back into action.

Ian fisted his hands in his brother's shirt, refusing to check for a pulse. He wasn't dead. He wasn't. And hefted him onto his shoulders in a sort of fireman's carry, grunting under the added weight. His muscles burned with lack of oxygen.

"I got him!" Ian called reassurance to her. "Dev…" He stopped. What could he possibly say? There were no proper words.

But she seemed to understand. "It's okay. It's okay." He wasn't sure who she was convincing. "'Though He slay me, yet will I trust Him.'"

Devlyn couldn't hear Ian anymore. Just the fire's roar, the building's giving. Everywhere the sound of death, of destruction.

Yet she wasn't alone.

Leaning against the wall, her breaths too deep, drawing on nothing, she tried to preserve the sound of Daniel's voice in her mind. Her hands rested uselessly at her sides, her head tilted back.

"Why, God?" she wept. She could feel Him. His presence, sending trembles up her spine. She was afraid. So afraid. "What is it you have planned for me, that I hadn't pictured for myself?"

Her answer came in a voice. As soft and gentle as a caress. *Do not fear, my child, for I am with you.*

And words rushed into her mind. Reassuring words. She played them over and over in her mind for as long as she could, drinking them like water.

A loud crash interrupted. Heat and white light rushed in to meet her. She closed her eyes. Surrendering.

And then.

The world was gone.

Ian collapsed outside with Daniel, one hand still clutching his brother's shirt, who now lay beside him under the blackened sky. He propped himself up on his elbows, gagging, coughing ash from his lungs. His dog tag necklace slipped free from the collar of his black t-shirt, swinging freely beneath him. He saw the shadow it cast, a cross fluttering along the ground. Something else caught his eyes and he glanced up.

Luke.

The man leaned against a car, calmly watching Ian, his brown eyes so different from Daniel's. Dark. Alight with a twisted amusement. A cold excitement. His overcoat hung from him, barely a thread out of place. In his hand he held a pocket watch.

And it was as if Ian could hear it from where he was. Ticking. Keeping time. Marking what was past and would never be again. As Ian stared, a cruel smile tipped up the side of Luke's mouth.

He would kill him. If it was the last thing Ian did, he would kill him. Sweat rolled from Ian's forehead, stinging his eyes, as Luke slammed the watch shut. His job completed.

The world blurred from Ian's sight, Luke with it.

The ticking ceased.

Chapter Thirty-One

"Ian. Ian, wake up."

Ian's eyes snapped open. The first thing he saw was the colour green, a dark intense green.

"Marley," he muttered, and then groaned. His insides felt like he'd breathed in saw dust all night long. "What are you doing here? Where am I?"

Her green eyes blinked. She seemed irritated with his questions. He was laying on a bed, that much he knew, and she was leaning over him, her red hair nearly skimming his nose, as it fell over her shoulders.

"Ruby called me. We're at Jim's. And we got a problem."

Ian closed his eyes again. He didn't want to think about problems. Maybe if he fell back asleep, they would all go away. "Add it to the list."

"Daniel's awake," she said flatly, ignoring the comment. "He's wolfed out. And he knows Devlyn's dead."

Memory rushed back.

Ian shot upright so fast, their foreheads nearly smacked together.

The Roadhouse. Flames. Devlyn.

"Yeah," she said, snapping back away from him, avoiding the collision. "That's what I thought."

But Ian hardly heard her, already making his way to the door. He paused for a second, leaning against the frame as a wave of dizziness swept over him, and then forced his way down the hall. He sensed without looking, Marley silently following him. Her footsteps were nothing but a light brushing against carpet.

"Jim!" Ian bellowed.

"Drawing room," Marley supplied from behind him at the same time he heard Jim's voice call: "We're in here, son."

The drawing room was rather crowded. Ian didn't know what he'd been expecting, but it hadn't been that. He recognized Jack, his fair hair standing out, his inquisitive light green eyes shifting to look in his direction, almost like he was looking through him.

But there were others.

A tall dark man, and a little girl with caramel coloured hair-
- who promptly leapt away from him, as if he were a rattlesnake
that'd slithered into her path. Winchester was there too, barely in
control of himself as he danced at Jim's side. Jim himself stood
directly in front of Ian, blocking the entrance. And Daniel, an
auburn wolf, still shuddering between the miss matched furniture,
stood on the coffee table. His sides heaved, and his claws dug
furrows into the table's surface, little shavings of wood curling
away in rings. The windows behind him backlit the scene, carving
out his dark silhouette.

"Danny," Ian said gently, side stepping Jim. "We tried.
Brother, we tried. We did everything we could've."

Daniel's eyes snapped towards him. Ian didn't realize he'd
been expecting accusation in them, until there wasn't any. For
whatever reason, that made the situation that much more dooming,
because it meant Daniel was blaming himself. Only himself.

Oh, no, no, no, little brother…

"Don't do this," Ian said, and was shocked at the amount of
pleading he heard in his own voice.

Daniel's eyes flashed. And before anyone could stop him,
he spun, his claws digging into the table. Ian wasn't the only one
who shouted his brother's name, as Daniel launched himself at the
nearest window. Ian took an immediate step after him, and felt
Marley grab his shoulder from behind, stopping him short as the
glass shattered on impact. Everyone flinched at the sound. Jack
threw his arms up to shield his face. They heard Daniel hit the
ground outside, and Ian shoved Marley off him, about to throw
himself after his brother.

But Jim was there, catching hold of the back of his shirt, as
the wolf streaked away. Ian tried to pull himself free. The seams of
his shirt started to give under the strain, stretching out of shape,
and Jim threw his other arm around him, clutching his shoulders in
restraint.

"Let him go, Ian!" Jim grunted, his voice rough, desperate.
"He needs to deal with this on his own terms. Let him go."

Chapter Thirty-Two

All Daniel knew was running. The sound of his pace, the steady rhythm of paws against earth, his own laboured breathing. The faster he ran, the more exhausted he became, and the more exhausted he became, the less he was able to think. Though his feet carried him, thought did not guide them. He ran blind, only knowing that civilization was left far behind. Trees replaced buildings.

Then there was someone beside him. Dark fur. Dark eyes. Jolie. She growled and he pushed harder, unwilling to let recognition infiltrate the numbness he was beginning to feel, spreading over him like a welcomed shield. It wasn't until she whined sharply that he was forced to take notice. Jolie didn't whine. Then he recognized where he was. Though he hadn't been paying attention some instinct had drawn him towards company. Drawn him towards the pack. He dug his claws in, grinding to a stop so fast, that Jolie shot past him.

But it was too late.

"I told you not to come back here." Luther's voice was like a shot of ice to Daniel's system.

He turned to face the man. Luther stood, his hands crossed over his broad chest, black hair plastered to his forehead with wetness. When had it started raining?

So what? He wanted to shout, but as a wolf it was only an angry thought. A low growl resonated in his throat.

"You're a declared enemy," Luther continued. "Bad move."

Daniel's growl escalated into a snarl.

"Here's your cue for a motivational speech. We all know you're so good at them," another voice jeered, and Luther chuckled. Suddenly pack members stepped out from behind nearby trees, enclosing him in a ring. Some looked troubled. Others had eyes lit with excitement, a hungry anticipation for a fight. He spotted Jolie, now human, as she pushed her way into the circle.

"Luther, knock if off!" She barked. Her cheeks burned red with anger.

"He came here of his own doing, Jo. He wanted this."

"No!" she screamed, but even as she said it, Daniel knew what Luther said was true. Devlyn was dead, this war needed soldiers, and he found himself, suddenly, and very willing, to gamble his life away.

Luther ignored her, hardly spared her a glance, and Daniel knew nothing Jolie said was going to be enough to stop him this time. "You and me" he shouted to Daniel through the rain, "till there's only one left standing!"

For a moment there was silence, and then Jolie stalked her way towards Luther, her short, soaked hair sticking out at odd angles. "You promised!" she yelled accusation. "You promised me!"

When she reached him she grabbed for his arm, but he jerked it back, and shoved her hard and readily to the ground. She fell flat on her back in the mud and decaying leaves. Her eyes were wide, disbelieving. They met Daniel's and he gazed back, giving her a meaningfully look. She shook her head frantically, knowing what came next, but he didn't listen. Tipping his head back he howled his acceptance. He would take Luther's challenge.

Luther smiled. A spreading, wicked grin.

Jolie shot to her feet.

"No!' she yelled again. "He'll kill you, Daniel. He'll *kill* you!"

Let him try.

He howled again. Louder. He wasn't about to change his mind. He was also positive there hadn't really been a choice to begin with.

Luther turned to Jolie, and Daniel saw the man's distrust in her, reflected in his eyes. She believed Luther would win, but there would be no auguring the fact that she wasn't in his corner anymore.

"Restrain her!" Luther ordered just as she lurched forward. Three pairs of hands shot out to hold her back, clamping around her arms, her shoulders. Things had changed in the pack too, there wasn't any doubt of that. There was only one leader in charge now, standing tall at the head of the circle. Jolie struggled against the other pack members, shouting futile orders, and icing them with choice curse words. She shook all over, her body trembling.

But she wasn't the only one.

323

Luther fell to his knees, his body slowly breaking. Daniel watched him writhe in agony, determined that he would see it again. His tail swished behind him anxious and impatient. Luther slapped his hand against the ground as if to force the shift, but it was another couple minutes before a black wolf stood before Daniel. Luther stood tall for a wolf, packing muscle power he didn't have as a man. Perhaps that's what his human ego translated over as.

They circled each other, ears pricked forward, alert. Daniel kept his distance, taking the opportunity to size his opponent. Luther was both big and experienced in battle as a wolf. He also knew Daniel's previous injury-- the gunshot to the leg. It would be a certain target, and a disadvantage Daniel would have to defend against. His recent burns were another factor to contend with, but the main target would ultimately be the throat.

He'd just started to wonder what advantages were his, when Luther lunged. He reacted, ducking to the side. He went for the legs like he would with any prey he hunted, but Luther was too fast, catching a hold of his ear. Daniel reared up trying to shake him loose, and they clashed, balanced on their hind legs, teeth going for one another's throats, nails thrashing. Daniel felt gashes open up along his neck and sides, felt the warmth of blood spill free, matting in his fur. Crimson with auburn. He could hear Jolie screaming at him, as they tore at each other, but the words were incoherent, lost among their angry snarls. Their battle travelled, first Daniel retreating when Luther found the upper hand, then Luther, when the situation reversed. The ring around them spread and contracted in accordance, the wolf spectators growling their encouragement, howling for blood. Daniel felt his teeth graze Luther's face one instant, and in the next, he felt pain of his own bloom to life from his side. He sprang forward, his nails opening Luther's flank, his teeth finding the scruff of his neck.

Then somewhere on the periphery came the distinct, ripping, tearing sound of the change. Growls escalated, and then Jolie howled in pain. Without thinking, Daniel turned to look for her, and Luther immediately ducked out of his hold.

That was also when Luther's teeth found his injured leg.

Daniel felt himself go down, his leg collapsing under him. Luther dragged him a short distance, and then lunged, his jaws snapping in Daniel's face. Daniel's front legs shot forward, only just keeping the black wolf at bay. He tried to roll in an attempt to regain his feet, but Luther continued to attack. Just waiting for an opportunity. An opening.

And Daniel thought about giving it to him.

He just had to stop struggling, and it would all be over. Maybe he'd see Devlyn again. Or his parents. Maybe he'd be left to float in a deep black nothingness. He'd welcome that too. No pain. No feeling of a dark hole in his chest, like his heart had been ripped out through his ribs. None of it. No anger.

Because, oh, he was so angry.

Luke's face flashed in his mind, and suddenly it was like a time bomb going off.

Images flooded him. Devlyn spreading colours. A paintbrush sticking out of a back pocket. A high, cruel laugh. Yellow lilies. A dead bird. Sprinklers. A slowly spinning wine glass. Hands lifted towards a church ceiling. Lifeless, glassy eyes. Cookie dough. A dream. A phone call.

Fire.

Screaming.

And then Daniel was screaming. Screaming as he exploded. Both inwardly and outwardly.

He was no longer a wolf. The change was instant, a sudden, loud crack.

Luther jumped back involuntarily, and then realizing the mistake leapt forward again.

But Daniel knew his advantage. He had two forms to fight in. Luther only had time for one. He kicked out, using his human legs, and Luther's own momentum to send the wolf flying over his head.

Daniel used the time he gained to roll into a crouch. He pulled the knife he always carried out of his sock, flicking the blade out in a swift movement. It wasn't silver. But it would do. Luther stumbled to his feet across from him. His lips peeled back over his teeth in a fierce snarl, but Daniel saw something in his eyes that hadn't been there before.

Fear.

They resized each other for a split second, and then they both moved. Luther sprang, sharp teeth out, but Daniel knocked him aside with the blow of an elbow to the face, and sunk the knife in above his shoulder blade, jerking it free just as fast, and as smoothly as it had gone in.

Luther howled, spinning as if to counter, but with a crack, and the soft thud of knife hitting dirt, Daniel's attack came first. His jaws sank into Luther's hide.

Crack.

A knife to the side.

Crack.

Teeth tearing into his throat.

Crack.

A blade between the ribs

Luther slumped to the ground. Blood poured from his nose, his wounds. Daniel, his hand still tight on the hilt of the knife, slick with blood, leaned over him. Suddenly, the only sound was his heavy breathing, his chest heaving up and down under his shirt, and Luther's ragged inhalations. Their surroundings were incredibly, and deathly silent. Jolie wasn't struggling with her captors anymore. In fact, they were barely barricading her, their stances slack, and their glowing eyes wide.

"I'm not a murderer," Daniel half spat, half whispered, though everyone could hear him. "I'm not you. And I'm not Luke." Luther whimpered, and Daniel straightened. "So fix yourself up," he said, wiping his blade clean on his jeans. "And start running."

Luther's black body shuddered against the earth. His eyes blinked, and it was a long time before they opened again, but he would heal. All it would take was enough time.

Daniel turned away, pushing soaked auburn strands of hair out of his eyes, and strode forward. Even though he limped with each step, wolves still stumbled over themselves to make room for him.

"He's yours to patch up," he called over his shoulder to them. "Or yours to leave behind."

He kept walking, leaving the choice theirs. By all rights, he was their head male now, but he would not lead a people who didn't wish to follow. Jolie caught up with him first, human once again. She grabbed his arm and draped it over her shoulders, taking some of his weight.

"You should have killed him," she said outright, her voice heated. "And then used him as a toothpick."

Daniel ignored the comment. "What'd he promise you?" he asked instead.

Jolie looked sideways at him. They took a couple more steps. "I stay his head female, and you live."

Daniel said nothing to that, and by the time they passed the next wave of trees, more had joined them. Daniel found himself doing a quick count.

But there were too many.

Far too many to count. Even some of the ones who'd called out hatred and thrown jeers were present.

They walked together, everyone grouped as a single pack of dishevelled, wrinkly clothed humans, and followed him into town.

"Ian," Jim said gently, straightening his blue and white striped button-down shirt, as he exited the funeral home. Taking the stairs down to the sidewalk hastily, he tried to catch up with the boy. But Ian was strides ahead of him, and not slowing down any. "Ian. *Son.*"

Ian froze. Then spun around so fast, Jim nearly tripped on the last stair.

"I can't do this, Jim." Ian clasped his hands together behind his head, and paced along the sidewalk. "I mean, they're talking about coffins and urns."

Jim watched Ian with a compassion that broke his heart. These days there weren't very many pieces left, because when his kids broke-- he broke too. "I know it's hard, son. But these decisions have to be made."

"Yeah, well, not by me they don't," Ian mumbled. His voice was bitter, sad, and with his next pace he seemed to snap. "They didn't even find anything! Nothing! They tore the rubble apart. She's just... gone."

The boy stopped, and they stared at each other for a long moment, Ian's blue eyes wide, begging for answers. It made him look like a little boy again.

"I always told you," Jim started and then had to press his lips tightly together before he could continue, "to do your job, and

327

to give it your all. And I meant it. But when it comes down to it," his voice grew soft, "you can't save everybody. People die, Ian. This time it was someone we knew."

"Fine," Ian snapped. "So what if it's Dan next, huh? Or you? Or me?" He shook his head and turned away.

Jim said nothing. What Ian was suggesting was something he didn't think about. His heart may break because of Ian and Daniel, but without them-- he didn't have one. Ian shoved his hands in his jean pockets and squinted into the sun. He'd tried to dress up, also wearing a collared button-down shirt, though his was black. Somehow, despite the attempt, he still came off as looking casual.

"I'll tell you this though," Ian continued. "If I go down. Luke goes with me."

And suddenly Jim could see just how fragile their lives really were. How easily more than just Devlyn could slip away from them.

"Have you ever thought of holding on to what we *do* have?!" He hadn't meant to shout, but his fear continued to burn with anger. "The faster you and that brother of yours figure that out, the better off we'll all be. Because what *will* kill this family, is if you two go around throwing away the good that's left in it."

Ian shook his head, and turning his back, began to walk away again.

"Ian!" Jim called after him, though he already knew it was useless.

"I just," Ian yelled over his shoulder, and then the rest of his sentence was barely audible for his mumbling, "need to go for a drive."

Chapter Thirty-Three

Ian merged onto the nearest highway and didn't stop, Winchester whining softly in the passenger seat next to him. He drove the rest of the day and well into the night, following white and yellow lines. It was his way of out distancing the clutter building up in his mind. But by the time the daylight abandoned him, and the clouds rolled in, dumping rain, the clutter had caught up. His mind echoed. He could hear the Harbinger's voice repeating itself like the rhythm of the windshield wipers. *And they will leave you. Yes, death will claim them. Or they'll disappear from your presence, never to be heard from again.* She'd cursed him with her words. But Daniel and himself had been cursed long before that, and everyone they'd come to know seemed to share in their misfortune.

A memory, falling from the bookshelf of his mind came next.

Ian was eleven again, sitting on a dirty curb of a forgotten street, the shotgun resting in his lap. He'd used it so often lately, practicing with whatever he could, cans, signs, crates, that it felt like an extension of his body. An obsession to keep him sane.

He stared at the ground, his head in his hands. The legs of his jeans were permanently stained brownish grey with street filth, and his stomach rumbled loudly, slowly eating itself from the inside out.

He was angry, defeated, in pain, and ready to give up.

Running away from their adoptive parents' houses seemed like the best option on the table at the time, but now they were faced with starvation. They'd lived on the food they'd jacked from the cupboards of Daniel's family, but it'd long since run out. He'd tried his hand at shooting a few critters, pigeons and magpies mostly, but hadn't known what to do with them when he had succeeded. It had also been several weeks since they had a shower. And they smelled.

The only thing they did have was each other. And the truck. It was a roof over their heads. That was something at least. Ian had made sure to smear the licence plate so readily with mud, that it was unreadable. They also continued to keep to the shadows,

only driving at night when they wouldn't be seen, and only if it was
absolutely necessary. The truck itself, as well as an elementary
grade driver, was anything but inconspicuous.

Recently, however, they'd run clean out of gas. And
options.

Maybe it was time they turned themselves in.

"Hello?" It was a soft voice that broke through Ian's
thoughts. He hadn't heard her approach, and startled, he leapt to
his feet, swinging the shotgun around.

The girl threw up her hands, immediately jumping back.
She had dark blue eyes the colour of dusk, and springy blond curls
for hair.

He lowered the gun.

"Go away," he told her, and resumed his position on the
curb.

She didn't. "Do you need help?"

"What?" he asked, turning to look in her direction again.

"You're a Knocte, aren't you?"

"No," he mumbled, confused. Knocte?

She didn't seem to hear him. "I help Knoctes. Actually my
mom and dad do…" she admitted. "But I'm practicing!"

"You're what?"

"Practicing to help Knoctes."

"What?"

She frowned at him. "Is that all you can say?"

"No," he said rudely, his empty stomach making him feel
grouchy.

She huffed out a determined breath, and sat herself down
beside him. He could see she'd drawn patterns all over her arm
with a pen. He wondered if he should warn her about 'ink
poisoning'.

"So do you?" she asked.

"What?!"

"Need help!"

He wanted to yell 'no' in her face, and tell her to go away
again, but even at eleven he knew a lifeline when he saw one.

He closed his eyes. "Yes…" he admitted with a sigh.

"Really?!" Her eyes lit up, and she actually clapped her
hands. "We usually only give people guns and stuff… But I can

bring you food if you want. Just don't tell my mom and dad. They got mad last time I brought someone home. They said he wasn't actually a Knocte. Said it's too dangerous for me. But I can do it! I want to practice."

"I won't tell," he mumbled assurance.

"And when they're not home you could use our shower too. You smell bad," she informed him. He nodded and stood up. She jumped to her feet beside him, and moved to block his path. "You could come now if you want. They're not there now."

"Why are you letting us?"

Suddenly she was the one who looked confused. "Mom says it's our job. And church says W.W.J.D."

"What's that?"

She laughed like she thought it was funny he didn't know such a thing. "What would Jesus do?!" she told him.

"Oh..."

"Well come on then," she said, and reached for his hand as she started forward, but Ian moved away. She looked back at him. "Aren't you coming?" She sounded worried.

"We have to bring my brother too."

Her eyes got wide again. "Another Knocte?!"

"No," Ian said quickly. There was that word again. It seemed important, yet it meant nothing to him.

She only thought about it for a second. "Oh, that's all right still, I guess."

Good, Ian thought, and without another word, started walking towards the truck. She followed a few steps behind, seeming to bounce as she walked. He led her for a block, and then they crossed the street. The black paint of the truck reflected the streetlights, and their own images as they grew closer. Ian rapped on the driver's side window, and a few seconds later Daniel's scruffy head appeared to fill it. He unlocked it and pushed the door open.

"You took a really long--." His words cut off as he spotted the girl. His mouth hung slightly open, and his eyes grew round, astounded, like he thought she was some kind of angel. Ian kind of understood though, besides their mother, she was about the closest thing to an angel they'd ever seen.

"This is Dan," Ian told her.

She smiled up at him. "Hi, Dan. I'm Devlyn."

The windshield wipers continued to beat away the wetness of the storm. But Ian didn't move to wipe the wetness from his face, as the tears cut trails down his skin.

Chapter Thirty-Four

The cemetery marked the end of town on the north side. On one side of the short, black iron fence that surrounded the headstones, was the road to the heart of town, on the other side sat the trees of the forest. Ian stood by Devlyn's grave, lost in the crowd of other guests. The fresh smell of wet grass was so strong from the shower the night before, that if she were alive, Devlyn would have stood outside all day just to breathe it in. But it was cold, and the way the weather was heading, the rain wouldn't be rain for much longer. Devlyn's Pastor stood at the foot of her grave, leaning on a cane. He was dressed in a suit, a Bible in one hand that Ian could tell had been sought out and found useful many a time. The man grieved. He kept his voice steady as he read, but there was a sadness in it they all knew well. While he grieved, however, he was not broken, not consumed by it. The man believed it was not the end, but a new chapter he would eventually become a part of himself when his own time came. Ian wished he could say the same, as he listened to the man's words.

"'Let not your hearts be troubled,'" he was saying, his old finger skimming down the well-loved page of the fourteenth chapter of John. "'Believe in God; believe also in me. In my Father's house are many rooms. If it were not so, would I have told you that I go to prepare a place for you? And if I go and prepare a place for you, I will come again and will take you to myself, that where I am you may be also. And you know the way to where I am going.'"

And a more haunting one from Isaiah.

"'Good people pass away; the godly often die before their time. But no one seems to care or wonder why. No one seems to understand that God is protecting them from the evil to come. For those who follow godly paths will rest in peace when they die.'"

Ian couldn't help wondering why the man had chosen that one, as the Pastor flipped through a few pages and continued on. He also couldn't help wondering at the amount of Knoctes who'd turned out. There were many, and he knew only a couple of them by name. Jim stood at his side, Winchester at their feet, his head resting on Ian's foot. Marley was with Ruby, positioned across the semi-circle of people from them. Lady sat panting softly, and Ruby looked too utterly worn to care that she was surrounded by Knoctes who'd kill her on any other occasion. The funeral had brought on a temporary peace, but Ian wondered if she could feel the tension as she stared at the ground and fiddled with the end of her neon pink scarf. Beside her, Marley was staring intently at the Pastor. She was wearing her heeled, knee-high leather boots, and her beat up, old leather jacket, like she always did. The shirt underneath was green, matching the colour of her eyes, and the grass. Her arms were folded over her chest, her fingers drumming against her arm. Then, as if she sensed him staring, she turned to look at him. Her face was grim, but she acknowledged him with a dip of her head.

He gave no response, looking away instead to focus on the other Knoctes-- the ones he didn't know, and suspected didn't know Devlyn as well as they claimed. He could deduce as much, because they wore black. Anyone who knew anything about Devlyn wouldn't dare wear black to her funeral. Ian himself was wearing the brightest, bluest t-shirt he owned. Even the Pastor wore a bright yellow tie and shirt under his suit jacket, making him look a little like a thin bumblebee.

But despite the black, some did appear sincere, even sad, wiping their eyes when they thought no one was looking. The majority looked guilty. They didn't grieve like the rest, just stood with a sort of pained expression on their faces, like they didn't have the right to be sad. It had been their leader, after all, who was responsible for the event.

How many were simply there as Luke's spies?

When the Pastor finished, closing his Bible with a small sigh, the guests gradually formed circles, discussing the tragedy, swapping condolences. Ian spotted Marley and Ruby heading in their direction, and both him and Jim moved to help close the distance.

"I thought he'd be here," Ruby said, when they were close enough, and Lady and Winchester were sniffing each other in recognition. Her eyes were red, and even though she didn't let on, they all knew whom she meant. Daniel.

"He's here," Jim said.

And Ian knew it too. With a sigh that clouded the air in front of him, he shifted his weight, and glanced toward the trees.

"We just can't see him," he added.

Ruby looked to the forest perimeter, her expression both longing and sceptical. Marley noticed it too. She rolled her eyes.

"Here," she said. "I'll prove it to you." Cupping her hands over her mouth, she gave her best impression of a howl. Lady and Winchester's heads both whirled around in her direction.

And they weren't the only ones. Everywhere people stopped talking mid-conversation and turned to look. A few kids pointed and giggled. And strange as it may be, Ian felt the beginnings of a smile tug at the sides of his mouth.

At first there was only silence from the forest. And then an answering howl pierced through the cold. The dogs yipped back, their tails colliding with each other's in excitement.

"That's not Dan," Ian said immediately, and then was taken aback by himself for realizing he knew such a thing.

"It's Jack," Marley informed.

Then let's try it again.

Ian didn't know what possessed him, maybe it was the longing you got at funerals not to be alone, or the desire to do something crazy that trumped the aching sadness, but he threw his head back, and in an imitation of Marley, sent out his own howl.

The answer was immediate this time. Before he'd even finished, a high, resonating sound had sprung up to join it. Winchester went nuts.

Marley actually laughed. Reaching over, she clapped Ian on the shoulder, cutting his howl off mid-stream.

"That our boy?" Jim asked, watching them.

"That's him," Ian nodded, feeling relieved.

Ruby smiled through watery eyes, reaching down to scratch Winchester behind the ears, and though they all felt slightly better, the rest of the guests looked somewhat worse for wear. Frightened eyes and disturbed expressions watched the edge of the forest. A few began to shuffle off towards their vehicles. But as he glanced through the crowd, Ian spotted a man watching them. He was wearing black, a sharp suit that Ian would have bet any money concealed a gun in the jacket's inside pocket, but when the man reached inside it was his cell phone he pulled out instead, punching in a number.

"We might be getting company," Ian warned. Marley

moved to his side and followed his gaze. Then scowled.

"You know there's something just wrong about crashing a funeral," Jim grumbled.

No one disagreed with him.

When Luke stepped out of the car, it wasn't until all the Innocent population had cleared the scene. He had at least a dozen men with him, stepping out of Jeeps and various trucks, Andy being one of them. When he got closer, picking his way carefully through the headstones, some of the black clad Knoctes from the funeral joined his ranks.

"Luke," Ian acknowledged first. "Your face healed nicely."

Luke stopped a few feet in front of them. "Ian," he countered. "Still keeping good company I see."

Ian felt Marley stiffen beside him, and he could have sworn her green eyes grew a shade darker. Andy kept trying to catch her gaze, running his hand uneasily through his crisped, spiked hair, but she was studiously avoiding looking in his direction.

"This is a place of remembrance and respect, Luke," Jim warned him.

"I have no respect for traitors."

Before anyone could give an answer to that, the standoff grew one person larger.

"*You have no right to be here!*"

Ian whipped around just in time to see Daniel vault himself over the black fence that cut in front of the forest. Winchester jerked to his feet, and Ian had to snap for him to stay.

Daniel's auburn hair was unkempt, his arms, neck and face bore new marks, and his eyes were wild. He looked crazy. Maybe he was crazy. Ian's mouth went dry.

"Ah, Daniel," Luke said with a smile. "It appears my sources were correct then."

Ian wanted to tell him where his sources could go. And as he pondered creative places, Daniel caught up with them. The moment Luke was within his reach, he made to launch himself. Immediately, Ian, Jim, Ruby and Marley all jumped forward to restrain him, grabbing at his shirt, his arm, his shoulder, anything they could. Three of Luke's men moved to stand in front of him.

"Hiding behind walls now, Luke?" Ian barked, his voice

strained as his brother struggled under his grip. "You were always a coward."

Something in Luke's eyes glinted, and he waved his bodyguards away impatiently. "I'm not here to participate in verbal banter, though you make it hard." he said sharply, and brushed unseen dirt from the sleeve of his overcoat. "I came to make you an offer."

"Why would we take anything from you?" Ian demanded.

"Because, compared to mine, your veggie platter is short a couple sticks of celery."

"All right." Jim stepped forward, his voice impatient. "I'll play. What is it you're wanting?"

"Your broccoli."

Marley shifted in irritation. Her arms dropped to her sides in a show of exasperation. "Can we drop the metaphor, please?"

"Daniel and Ruby," Luke said immediately. Daniel's struggling abruptly halted, and Ruby's hands fell from his arm. "Hand them over. No buts. No questions asked. And I will *forgive*."--he said the word like it held a lot of weight coming from him-- "this little temper tantrum parade, you all call a resistance."

Ian started laughing. Uncontrollably. He couldn't help it. From beside him he heard Marley mutter, "Unbelievable," and Lady yipped like she agreed.

Ian tilted his head back toward the sky, trying to find some resolve, but he was still laughing when he looked back down at Luke. "And if we refuse?" he forced out.

"Then this scene turns bloody really fast."

"Fine," Ian said after a minute. "You can have the faerie."

Jim cuffed him on the back of the head, at the same time Marley's heeled boot found his foot.

"Ow," he complained.

Luke wasn't amused. "It is a generous offer," he said, and he didn't mean Ian's.

"Luke," Ian levelled with him, "how long have we known each other, man?"

When Luke didn't answer right away, Daniel answered for him.

"Ten years," he said, but even those two words burned with his anger. His chest expanded rapidly, and his shoulders shook as they moved up and down in time with his every breath.

"And in what period of that time," Ian asked, with an uneasy side-glance at his brother. "Would I have ever taken that deal?"

"There is a first for everything," Luke replied.

"Not this. Never this."

"Being sentimental is a sign of weakness," Luke observed.

Ian was about to reply something classy, something along the lines of '*Eat me*' when Daniel suddenly spoke over him.

"What makes you so sure you're one up on us?" He stepped forward, and Ian grabbed the back of his shirt again.

Ian could see the way Luke's men looked at them then, at the party of seven, including the dogs that stood before them. Some exchanged amused glances with one another. A few laughed.

Luke arced an eyebrow. "The numbers are a bit unbalanced. Would you not agree?"

Daniel didn't hesitate. "I agree," he said, and then his voice rose to a shout, "*Jolie!*"

"*What?*" came the answer from the tree line behind them. A short girl, with bobbed, deep brown hair and dark eyes, strode towards the fence. "It's Jo!"

Luke contemplated her approach, as she jumped the fence and stalked in their direction. "I am frightened. Truly, I am."

"You should be," Jolie remarked. She was close enough now to have heard the remark. "I brought friends, Numb Nuts."

Ian watched as everywhere people and wolves alike unfolded themselves from behind trees, dropping out of branches, or sliding from the shadows. The ones who were human carried weapons, anything from shotguns to wooden boards with nails sticking out of them, while the others, the wolves, had their weapons already built in. Teeth gleamed, ears pulled back, and claws ground into the earth.

"Leave!" one of them shouted in Luke's direction.

"Or we'll do it for you!" another added.

The wolves lent their say in feral barks, and Luke narrowed his eyes with displeasure at the scene. Marley saw it as a threat and bending down, pulled a pocket pistol from her boot. Andy tracked the movement carefully, raising his eyebrows.

Ian wanted to punch him in the face.

"Are we doing this, Luke?" Daniel asked, spreading his arms wide. Layered with cockiness and anger, it was something Ian himself would say. It was somehow disturbing to hear it come from his little brother.

"Indeed, we will," Luke said with caution. "In time." Ian knew that was Luke talk for retreating with his tail between his legs, and he felt his shoulders relax. "But I promise you, that though we have seen your army, you have not seen the half of ours. So here is your last chance," he warned. "Hand them over."

Jolie stepped forward, shoving Ruby carelessly aside as she did, so she was right next to Daniel. "You really are dumber than you look. Maybe if I remove all the contractions from my speech, people will mistake me for a genius too."

Behind them the pack hollered and howled their agreement, beating either the ground or the trees with their weapons. Winchester and Lady joined in.

"So be it," Luke stated, and then Ian felt his attention shift towards him. "I am disappointed, Ian."

"Yeah, well," Ian said, shoving his hands in his pockets and staring Luke down. He didn't know what Luke saw in his face, but his old friend actually took a step back, "that makes two of us."

Shaking his head, Luke turned away, his party with him. Ian, Daniel, Jim, Marley, Ruby, Jolie and the pack all watched them go. Though they felt relieved, no one dared to celebrate, and when they lost track of the retreating car engines, Ian rounded on them.

"I need a minute with my brother."

Daniel's eyes snapped over to look at him, his expression now impassive, like Luke's sudden absence had drained his ability for emotion. Ian got it though. Anger was a safe emotion, simple in its ways. It burned inside of you, made you feel alive. Grief was nothing like that. It was hollow, empty. Riddling holes and deep chasms. With grief nothing could be changed, one could only keep on, and with time hope it faded. And if Daniel couldn't have anger, and the grief was closing in, it was much safer to try and feel nothing at all.

"Who taught you those manners?" Jim rebuked. "'Cause I know it wasn't me. A thank-you's in order, don't you think?"

Ian tore his gaze from Daniel, glancing over at the lycan

named Jolie. Her dark eyes regarded him, and she cocked her head to the side, waiting.

"Yeah, thanks…" he muttered half-heartedly in her general direction. "Whoever you are."

She was silent for a second, and then: "It'll do," she decided, though with a scowl, and then whirled around and disappeared with the pack as quickly as she'd appeared.

Ian didn't bother watching her go.

"Jim," he appealed again.

Jim sighed. "Oh, all right." He turned to Ruby and Marley. "Come on gals, it's time we be heading home."

At first Ian didn't think they'd leave. Marley was watching him as closely, and as warily, as Ruby was watching Daniel. But Daniel hadn't noticed. He'd looked back to watch the pack disintegrate once again into the trees, and his eyes had found Devlyn's grave. Now he just stared.

"Please," Ian said to Marley, his voice low, begging. After a moment she nodded, and followed Jim back towards the parking lot. She didn't say a word as she passed by him, but reached out to pat his shoulder. Ruby and Lady trailed behind her. Ruby somewhat reluctantly.

When they were alone, Ian turned to his brother, but Daniel was already halfway to Devlyn's grave, his steps so supernaturally light, that Ian didn't think he'd ever get used to his brother's new smooth and silent tread. With a heavy sigh, Ian followed him.

They read the epitaph over together, Daniel kneeling in front, and Ian standing behind him.

DEVLYN MORROW
IN THE ARMS OF HER KING

And a couple of spaces down, under the dates:

A PICTURE COMPLETED

Ian put a hand on his brother's shoulder. "Danny," he said gently. "You look like you went ten rounds with a rock slide. What's going through your head?"

Daniel was silent for a moment, then: "That night," he said finally, "how did she get my phone number?"

Ian hadn't thought about it. And he didn't have an answer.

Daniel didn't wait for one anyway.

"She said…" he began, and had to try again. "She told

me…"

"She was trapped," Ian finished for him. "I know."

"No!" Daniel suddenly exploded, and shot to his feet. Ian dropped his hand, taking a startled step back. "She told me she was *sorry*! Like this was her fault! But it wasn't. It was mine. I knew what she was doing! I should have been watching her! Taking better care-- I should have been--." He choked, and then slowly, before Ian's eyes, all the anger and all the numbness slipped away. It left nothing but the broken shell of a man. Tears spilled down Daniel's face.

Ian stared with wide eyes, frozen, watching Daniel shake in a way that had nothing to do with lycanthropy. He couldn't move for one very long minute. It wasn't until Daniel almost collapsed, that Ian stepped forward. He caught his brother against him, and didn't let go as his brother gasped into his shoulder like he was six years old again. Daniel's fingers dug painfully into his back.

"It's okay, Danny," he promised, though it wasn't. In fact, it was probably the biggest lie he'd ever told him, but sometimes all people needed to hear was the possibility that the world could be right again. "It's going to be okay."

Audrey looked out a window twelve stories up, to a sight she never wanted to see. Circling below were the tiny forms of Knoctes. She wished she could squish them like the ants they appeared, but things didn't work that way. A pity, really. Their vehicles were parked in a ring around the long since closed down hotel. On the inside it was a mouldy, rotted out piece of crap, with as many hiding spaces as vermin, but she'd thought it'd be the perfect place for them to squat. Unfortunately she'd been wrong. She dropped the moth eaten curtain and stepped away from the window. She started pacing her own circle around the nearly empty room-- nothing but a bug-ridden mattress and a nightstand with no drawers. She found her hand slipping into her pocket, and not for the first time, did her fingers brush the piece of paper there.

Most of the clan would turn on her for even considering allying with a bunch of lycanthropes, but it'd reached the point where she had to choose between pride-- and death. And sadly, a large chunk of their sect would choose the former. She closed her eyes and tilted her head back.

"What do I do? What do I do?" she whispered to no one in particular.

Somewhere down on the street a shot went off.

Her eyes flew open.

She heard the sound of people beginning to panic throughout the hotel. Swearing loudly, she burst through the door of her room and into the hallway.

"Rob!" she shouted to a scrawny boy with greasy hair, who had originally been standing guard at her door, and was now halfway down the hall. He froze, turning to face her with wide, frightened eyes. The coward. "I need your phone," she commanded.

"My--?" He seemed confused at her request; to him it didn't fit with their current situation. "Are you kidding me?!"

"Robert," she said flatly. "Your phone."

He looked at her like she was crazy, and then looked around for support. When he found none, he fished the device from his pocket and threw it at her. She caught it out of the air.

"Take it," he said already backing up again. "I'm outta here."

"Where are you going?" she demanded, but he turned and ran. "You won't make it far!" she yelled as he rounded a corner out of sight. She heard the sound of his boots on the stairs a couple seconds later. "Moron."

She looked at the phone in her hand. Then with a sigh she pulled the piece of paper out and dialled the number.

"Who is this?" he answered half-heartedly.

"Your Twilight connection. Remember when I said I'd be in touch?"

"Yeah. I do." his voice sounded rough.

"Well this is me," she said ruefully, "being in touch. You were right, all right? We do need your help. I should kick myself for even asking, but if you're not too busy-- now would be an excellent opportunity."

Chapter Thirty-Five

"It's been awhile for this place," Jim remarked. He was standing on the shore of a lake, surrounded by mountains and pine trees as far as the eye could see. There was one dock floating on the cold glacier water, a couple of canoes tied securely to it. Loons were fluttering and crying out on the glassy sheet of water, paddling in wide circles.

"Do you like it? Your father used to take you here, didn't he? For camping trips."

Jim spun around. Standing suddenly next to him was a thin man with sandy blond hair and eyes green like the sea.

'What--? How did you--?" Jim sputtered. Then the scene around them glitched for a second, moving out of shape like bad TV reception. Jim gave the place another look. "Oh, I get it," he said, catching on. "I'm dreaming aren't I?"

The man smiled a crooked smile and moved forward. The pebbles of the shore shifted under his feet as he did. "Quite right, mate, you are."

"Well that explains why I'm here. But it doesn't explain you."

"I'm here on a little errand."

"Oh, are you now?" Jim muttered sarcastically.

"Yeah," the man said, stopping directly in front of him. "Sort of."

Then he raised his hand above his head and snapped his fingers.

It felt like the floor dropped out from beneath Jim's feet, the scene rushing away, and in the next instant they stood together on a dark street. Jim stumbled and had to regain his footing. Breathing heavily, he slowly took everything in, from the dim streetlight, to the bricked walls of the buildings around them.

"Where are we?" he demanded.

The man, standing perfectly straight and comfortable beside him, gave him a sideways glance. "You don't remember?"

Suddenly a piercing scream tore through the night.

"What in the--." But Jim cut himself off as a kid ran directly through him, one second behind him, the next in front, exactly as if he was some sort of ghost. He felt his midriff in astonishment. Ahead the kid paused at the corner of the street, and Jim got a better look. He carried a shotgun, the grips on it old and worn with use. His brass hair shone under the streetlamp. "Ian?" Jim said disbelievingly.

"Yup," the man confirmed. "A little more innocent and a little less surly, but yeah."

There was another scream and younger Ian's head jerked in the direction. He disappeared into the next alley. Jim stared after him. The boy couldn't have been more than eleven or twelve. The man beside him started forward, and Jim took the cue, breaking into a jog after the boy.

He turned the corner to a standoff.

There was a woman pinned in the corner by a younger man, his back facing them. She looked roughed up, her hands held in the air as if to protect her face.

"Let her go!" Ian shouted. He had the shotgun up, levelled with the man's head. He had both eyes trained on his target. The end of the shotgun rested snugly against his shoulder, and his legs stood apart in a solid stance, ready for the recoil. Even then he'd known how to handle a weapon.

The offender turned away from the woman, a sharp movement, too fast to be normal. His eyes glowed in the darkness.

"Oh, Ian…" Jim breathed and stepped forward.

"You can't do anything, mate," the man beside him informed. "It's just a scene running its course."

"Are you one of those things?" Ian asked angrily, his hands tightening on the gun.

The offender chuckled darkly. "That depends what you mean," he said, and then fell to the ground on his hands and knees. His body began shaking violently. The woman gasped, and seizing her opportunity, darted past him, her very high heels clacking loudly on the pavement as she ran by Ian and onto the street. She didn't stop, and didn't look back.

But Ian glanced up from the sight on his gun. He looked confused.

"Get out of there, boy," Jim couldn't help muttering an anxious warning. He was staring at the shotgun. "You brought the wrong tool for the problem."

But it was too late. There was a terrible ripping, breaking sound, and the man was a wolf. The animal was a deep grey colour with fur bristling at its neck, teeth bared, and a malicious pair of glowing eyes.

Ian fumbled to regain his aim and opened fire. The creature jerked back from the rounds, annoyed as if brushing off a few ants found crawling along its person, and howled a fierce revenge. Ignoring the pelt of rapid fire, it crouched to spring.

"I remember this..." Jim realized aloud. He knew he watched with wide eyes, and he also knew what would happen next.

"That's about right." The man next to him smiled.

And right on cue Jim rounded the corner into view. Another Jim. A younger version of himself, back when his hair had been a light brown colour instead of the salt and pepper mix it was now.

The wolf connected with Ian and they both hit the ground, the shotgun the only thing between the wolf's teeth and the boy's neck.

Only years of experience allowed the younger Jim not to hesitate or freeze up with the shock of the sudden scene he'd stumbled upon. Reaching into his sock, he pulled a knife free and threw it. Jim watched his throw for a second time as it flew through the air and lodged itself in the wolf's side. It was silver, and hissed on contact with the skin. The animal gave a feral cry and tried to shake it loose, yelping and dancing when it didn't free easy. The younger Jim hooked his arms under Ian's armpits and dragged him back to a safer distance. The boy's legs kicked at the ground, the heels of his worn sneakers helping to propel him backwards and out of harm's way.

"Ian!" came a small cry.

The younger Jim gave a start as a kid with brown eyes, brown eyes that would always belong to him no matter what age, ran headlong into the alley. Daniel was carrying a gun, but in the way a person did when they were seven and had only seen people do it on TV.

Laced with the pain of a burning knife stuck hilt deep or not, Daniel had gained the attention of the lycanthrope. Spinning on the sudden and new presence helping to outnumber him, the wolf lashed out-- and the other Jim moved without thinking. He

345

ripped the gun from Daniel's hands, and slipping his finger in against the trigger, fired. The shot pegged the creature in the forehead, and it collapsed to the ground, a heavy heap of fur in front of them all.

They all stared at it for a long moment, until everyone had caught their breath.

Younger Jim looked down at the gun in his hand. "This has silver bullets in it. Where did you get this?"

But the boys weren't listening to him. "What is it?" Ian asked, getting to his feet and venturing towards the corpse. "It's not like the other one." Daniel followed in his wake almost naturally, looking over his older brother's shoulder.

"I think a werewolf," Daniel mused. "You should read the books that Dev gave me." Ian turned to him and made a face.

"I think 'lycanthrope' is the term you'd be looking for," Younger Jim informed, coming up behind both of them. They spun to face him and stepped back, leaving a wary distance between him and them. "You boys shouldn't be out here. What were you thinking taking cases on your own so early?"

But they weren't satisfied. They exchanged a look.

"Is there more?" Daniel asked suddenly. Ian nodded beside him.

"More?" Younger Jim asked, stumped. He stared between them. "What do you mean?"

"Of that," Ian clarified, pointing to the dead wolf. "Or the other, fast one, but that looks normal."

"What? Vampires? Faeries? Shifters? The works?"

With every thing he listed their eyes grew bigger.

"All those?" Daniel said in wonder, his mouth dropping open. "For real?"

"You mean to tell me," Younger Jim said in astonishment, "you've been out here flailing guns around and you don't even know what it is you're *up against*?!"

They shared another look.

"You know a lot," Daniel observed.

"Of course I do! I've been doing this for--," he began, when he chose to cut himself off. "But why am I telling you this? I should be getting you kids home. Come on, I'll give you a ride. And I think I'll need to have a little talk with your parents."

He'd meant it to sound threatening, but they just blinked up at him.

"We don't have any," Ian told him stiffly.

"Mom and dad are gone now," Daniel added, his curious expression quickly falling into a sad one.

Younger Jim stared down at their dejected postures. Daniel was looking at his feet, pushing a rock around with the toe of his shoe. Ian was also avoiding any eye contact.

"No parents, huh?" he said sympathetically. "Happens to a lot of us. Well, where are you staying? Who's looking after you boys?"

"Nobody," Ian said defensively. "We take care of ourselves."

"Dev helps us," Daniel whispered to his brother like he thought Ian had forgotten.

"And we live in our truck," Ian added, shoving his hands in his pockets. "Just us."

"In a *truck*?"

Jim saw the white expression on his own face and remembered how he'd seen them for the first time then. Their small, too thin frames. How their stained and ripped clothes seemed more to hang around them than actually fit. The way their skin was marked with bruises and small cuts. How they seemed to gravitate towards one another, always hovering within the other's space. Ian looked worn, tired. Daniel's features carried a somewhat haunted expression.

"I parked it over there," Ian continued, when Younger Jim said nothing else and continued to stare. The boy pointed just down and across the street. Younger Jim followed his finger and saw the truck's big black frame lurking in the shadows. How they'd acquired such a thing, he couldn't begin to guess.

"A little young to be driving don't you think?" Younger Jim wondered aloud.

Ian said nothing.

"He's good at it now," Daniel said helpfully.

"No cop on the planet is ever buying that one," Younger Jim muttered.

He couldn't believe they'd lasted this long. He looked at them again, at the shotgun dangling from Ian's hand, and the way

Daniel's hair fell into his eyes, unbothered to brush it away. He sighed. Scarcely believed what he was about to say, until he said it. "I guess this means you're coming home with me then."

"End scene," the man beside Jim said suddenly, and snapped his fingers. Jim barely paid attention to him until the scene dropped out from under him, and Ian and Daniel fell away. The moment his feet hit the sandy shore by the lake again, Jim turned on him.

"Who are you? How'd you know about all that?" Jim barked.

"Name's Reid. And from *you* mostly, mate. A little from Ian at the beginning. That took some work I'll tell you. I've been piecing that bit together for awhile now."

"Why would you do a thing like that?"

"In case they ever needed your help again." Reid's sea green eyes looked worried. "And now they do."

"Be honest with me," Jim said. "Am I crazy?"

Reid smiled crookedly again. "No, mate. Daniel used to think the same. Maybe you can finally convince one another you're not."

"Where is he?"

"Thought you'd never ask."

Chapter Thirty-Six

"Wow, standing out in the open. Not my choice of strategies-- but count me in."

Ian turned along with Daniel, Jack, and whom he'd since learned were Winn and Gakwin, to see Marley striding towards them. For someone who was worried about concealment, her intentions couldn't have been clearer. Her bright red hair was tied back in a tight knot that made her seem of a higher authority, and hanging from her waist was a weapons belt, decked out with knives and guns of every metal and bullet. She still wore her worn leather jacket and the high boots that hugged her calves, however. Lady could also be seen trotting along at her side. Some things never changed.

"Hey, Stalker," Ian greeted.

She stopped in front of them, putting her hands on her hips, and smiled. "Oh, hey, Handsome."

She wasn't alone. Coming into view behind her, stalked Jim.

He looked ticked. "Do I look like the man you get to leave behind? I'm fighting this battle with you, you morons."

"How'd you know?" Ian asked, looking between them.

"Jack," Marley answered, her green eyes shifting to lock with Jack's light green ones, where he stood at Daniel's side. Everyone turned to look at him curiously.

"It's evident we're in need of her assistance," he sniffed defensively, and pushed his glasses back up the bridge of his nose.

"Yeah? Well, I dreamt about it," Jim cut in with his answer. "A man calling himself Reid crawled into my noggin and started preaching to the choir."

Daniel gave a start, spinning back around to face him. The old, grey duffle bag slung over his shoulder nearly took out Ian as he did, and he had to lean back abruptly to avoid it.

"Yeah," Jim said knowingly at Daniel's reaction. "You ain't crazy."

"Am I missing something?" Ian raised his eyebrows. From the corner of his eye he saw Marley press her lips together, trying to fight a smile, and also, he suspected, some sort of remark.

"Later, Ian," Daniel dismissed. "Bigger fish remember?"

"Yeah, about the bigger fish," Marley said, eyeing the ramshackle, old hotel across the street from where they all stood on an adjacent sidewalk. "Wouldn't a cloak and dagger approach be more effective? Infiltrate from the inside? You know-- element of surprise and all that."

"It's quiet," Daniel noted.

"Suspiciously so," Jack added.

"Which means either they've come and gone…" Daniel continued, which Ian didn't believe for a second. There were too many vehicles parked along the street and in nearby alleyways for a hotel that was no longer in business, and probably hadn't been for near a decade.

"Or they already know we're here," Gakwin finished for him. He rolled up the sleeves of his white button-down shirt. The man always managed to look sharp, despite any wrinkles lycanthropy placed in his clothing. He already had a new trilby hat. He was also quickly growing impatient. They'd been through the run down before Marley and Jim had shown up, and were currently wasting time debriefing them.

Jim understood. "So what's the plan team?"

"You mean besides don't die?" Ian said helpfully, and earned himself a sharp look.

Daniel stepped forward. "I already have my pack running a perimeter, so once we're in, anyone leaving the area has to go through them."

Marley nodded knowingly. "We met them on the way in. Charming little beasties they are."

Daniel ignored that.

"We just got to get past the windows," he said and everyone turned towards the building. It loomed up above them, old red brick patched with thickly framed, dark windows. Nearly every pane of glass was shattered, and the ones that remained were heavily caked with dirt. A rusted sign hung from the corner of the building proclaiming the word HOTEL, the letters stacked on top of one another in a vertical display. It looked as if it had glowed at one point in time and maybe even spun.

"Classy," Marley noted. "So how do we get past?"

"A look out. Some weapons. And a prayer they only

brought shotguns," Daniel answered grimly.

"And who's our lucky look out?" Ian asked mildly. He pulled a knife from his pocket and began testing it against his thumb.

Daniel's gaze shifted down towards Winn, who had before then, been contently listening in, and her creamy brown eyes went wide in her soft face.

"Me?" she asked sounding alarmed.

"Will you do this for us?" Daniel asked gently.

But she wasn't buying it. She shook her head, butterscotch waves of hair floating around her face as she did. "I want to go with you."

Daniel, Jack, and Gakwin all made sounds of protest at the same time.

"You're not going in that building," Gakwin added firmly, when she scowled at them all.

"Definitely not," Daniel confirmed.

She crossed her arms over her chest stubbornly.

Rolling his eyes, Ian tucked the knife away. "Not that I'm not enjoying this touching moment," he said turning on Winn, "but listen up kid. No one wants to bust out the 'life isn't fair' speech, so just take it like a champ, all right? You want to help? They offered you a job. *Take* it."

He tried to ignore Jim's hypocritical stare. He wasn't going to mention that by the time he was her age he'd already had several notches on his belt, and had flung himself into several situations he hadn't been remotely prepared for.

But it didn't matter, he wasn't even sure she'd taken in any of his words. The moment he'd addressed her, she'd stared at him terrified, her face slowly going white.

Gakwin stepped forward and placed a protective hand on her shoulder. "Why don't you back off a little, okay?"

Ian glared down at him. "Shouldn't you be on my side with this one?"

"Hey, hey, hey," Daniel warned, and swiftly stepped in between them, though Ian noticed he was only looking at him as he said it.

"We're supposed to be playing nice, remember?" Jim reminded them all.

"Nice," Marley repeated with a scoff, "right. Maybe if we took the testosterone levels down a notch boys." She stepped forward, moving past both Ian and his brother to crouch at eye level with Winn, her arms resting on her legs. "Let's find you a good hiding spot, all right?" she said firmly. "Just howl if anything pops out of any windows. One howl if it's on the right side, two if it's left. A long one if it's high, and short if it's low. You got that?"

Winn's lips moved silently for a moment, repeating her words, and then she nodded.

"Good," Marley said. She straightened and grabbed the girl's hand, towing her away without a backwards glance at the rest of them.

*   *   *

"Hey, guys!" Ian shouted over the sound of pelting bullets. Marley glanced over at him. He, Jim and his brother were held up behind a car, using it as a shield. Gakwin had gone to the surrounding pack to recruit help, and Marley had found her own vehicle to hide behind with Jack. "'The Look Out' plan? --Yeah, it sucks!"

Understatement.

"What's the howl supposed to be for Knocte in every single window anyway?" Ian asked, leaning out to look at her, and then swearing loudly when a bullet ricocheted of the hood of their vehicle. Daniel grabbed his brother's shoulder and forced him back.

"His commentary isn't of much help, is it?" Jack muttered beside her.

Marley sighed. Winn's tired, now meaningless howl, continued to fill the street as a continuum, and Marley's long legs ached from crouching for so long. She understood Ian's restless, and irritated attitude, as she reloaded her revolver, popping open the cylinder, slapping out the spent rounds, and using her speed loader to punch in the next round. "He's right though."

Jack wasn't the only one muttering.

"Screw this," Ian continued to grumble, and then turned on his brother, his voice rising to a yell. "Has lycanthropy fried all your Scit brain cells?! I thought you were the one with all the

352

ingenious plans!"

"Ian," Jim reproached.

"I am!" Daniel yelled back. "The look out wasn't the plan."

"Oh, really?" Ian shouted irritably, as another wave of bullets collided against their vehicles, the metallic pinging sounds nearly drowning him out. "Would you care to enlighten the rest of us as to what exactly the *real* plan is then?!"

"Step one," Daniel rattled off, sparing a glare for his brother, "remove Winn from inevitable battle. We couldn't leave her behind, because she simply would have followed us. She's too curious for her own good. I suspect that her state as a lycanthrope is evidence enough of that. Step two," he continued as if step one needed no further explanation, "send Gakwin for reinforcements."

"And now?" Ian demanded impatiently. He checked over his shoulder and then spun, firing a couple of retaliating shots, before ducking down again. When he had successfully averted their attention, Marley popped up to take her turn. Panicked, Jack caught hold of her jacket, trying to force her back down.

"Step three," she heard Daniel answer, as a bullet bounced off the roof of the car and she hurriedly dropped back down. There were more than just shotguns out there. The younger Browning brother reached for his duffle, unzipping it hastily, and pulling out a gun Marley couldn't help taking a second glance at. It was clearly a sniper rifle. Long, elegant, and promisingly deadly.

Ian's eyes lit up, and he nearly cooed over it. "I like step three," he admitted.

Daniel handed it over with a brief smile. "Yeah," he said, pushing his hair out of his eyes, and causing it to stick straight up, "I thought you might." Then his brown eyes fell on her, and flickered to Jim. "We cover him, got it?"

Jim nodded.

Marley gave him a salute. "You're the boss, Boss."

Ian slowly straightened, settling the gun stand on the roof of the car, and becoming an immediate target the moment he did. Marley watched several of the barrels set in the windows swivel to adjust.

Daniel leaned over the trunk, at the same time Jim did over the hood, and opened fire.

"I got right side!" Daniel called.

"Center!" Jim shouted.

Marley didn't argue, showering the first Knocte to her left who'd re-adjust his aim, with a flourish of bullet fire.

Then had to reprimand herself.

She shouldn't panic. Panic meant over shooting, and over shooting meant empty cartridges and precious time lost to reloading. To her right Ian tucked the butt of the gun against his shoulder and leaned into the sight. She heard him take deep breaths, exhaling loudly, trying to calm his heartbeat. She trained her attention on each one, using them as if her own to do the same. She felt her pulse lowering. *Accuracy* she told herself, *not quantity*. Quantity was the reason the bad guys in the movies could shoot rounds at a time, and miss the good guys with every single shot.

She smiled as her next shot caught her target in the shoulder, the Knocte disappearing from the window. She was still too far away to make decent shots-- but that's what Ian was for.

Ian's rifle fired and the gun took its first victim. The Knocte slumped over onto the sill and his shotgun toppled from the third story, crashing into the weed eaten pavement below. She laughed with excited approval, as his shots joined theirs, never once missing, as she fired another round of well-placed shots. Pausing to reload she glanced at him, but Ian wasn't nearly as elated, his face was set like a stone as he took another breath and squeezed the trigger. One more of Luke's men fell, this time plummeting completely from the window, hitting the ground with a sickening thud, and an ugly mess. Jack gagged beside her, his eyes trained on the twisted shape.

Then Ian cried out. Staggered back.

"*Ian!*" she found herself yelling with Daniel and Jim. The sleeve of his shirt was torn.

"Fine." He hissed in a breath. "Just grazed." Without another word, or glance in any of their directions, he leaned back into his weapon. She could already see blood trailing its way down the muscles of his arm.

She looked away. Squeezed her eyes shut for a second.

Then, "Jack!" she barked, unable to help herself. "Please, God-- just *fire something*." She wasn't sure whom she was begging. Him or God.

He was still crouched behind the vehicle. They'd given him

a gun, but he wasn't even touching it. It sat discarded at his side. He looked up as she addressed him, cringing with every shot fired. He looked like he wanted to plug his ears.

"I'm unpractised with firearms," he said regretfully, and then stared down at the pistol as if a rat had curled up next to him.

"I don't care!" she yelled at him in between shots. "Time to" --another shot-- "get practiced!" A bullet whizzed by her ear and she ducked, allowing herself a second to catch her breath. Her heart was hammering again. "Just watch out for us," she ordered, her gaze darting to the brothers.

Daniel was murmuring target locations to his brother in a steady stream while pulling off his own shots, and Ian was obeying every suggestion without question, never once looking up. Jim was busy trying to cover them both, and Winchester was parked at their feet, not once moving. Despite the noise, he waited for orders, his eager eyes shifting between his masters. His ears twitched in different directions.

At her side, Jack had resumed his muttering. "Point and shoot," he was musing, examining the weapon like a curious science project. "It can't be all that difficult…"

Lady whined and nudged her leg.

"Shh," she reprimanded the Weimaraner harshly. Jack thought it was meant for him and immediately clamped his mouth shut.

Well, good.

She spotted a Knocte, one of the last ones, leaning out of a window for a better shot, and fired, catching his windowsill and blinding him with the debris. The rest had already started turning away, retreating back into the building.

A howl rang out. One that didn't belong to Winn, and Marley saw Ian look up. Daniel nodded to his brother, and with one last scan of the windows, Ian pulled his gun up. He returned it to the duffle his brother now held open.

"Jack," Marley said, calling for his attention. She tucked the revolver back in her jacket, freeing up her hands. "We're moving."

Jack looked up from the pistol in his hand, just as a stream of his fellow lycans flew past them, some human, some wolves, all bolting headlong for the hotel. There were dozens of them, following dozens. All different coat colours, different shades of glowing eyes. Daniel slung his duffle over his shoulder and he, Jim, and Ian melted into the advance. Winchester, so small compared to the rest, streaked behind them.

"Come on," Marley said, grabbing Jack's arm and hauling him after her, as she followed suit. Lady leapt forward, following her at a steady trot.

The only thing that kept her tethered to the threesome's whereabouts amongst the sea of lycans, was Ian's height. He was a good head taller than the rest. She ran after him, towing Jack in her wake, her weapons belt weighing heavily on her hips. She was so fixed on not losing them, that it surprised her when Jack wrenched his arm away and grabbed her shoulder.

"Above," he panted. "Window."

Marley's eyes snapped up. And there was the Knocte she remembered clipping in the shoulder earlier. His shirt was soaked through with blood, and he was clearly too hurt to retreat with his allies. He must have known he was dying, must have known no one would be coming for him, the 'Knoctes work alone' slogan still firmly in place, because he was trying for a last ditch attempt at some payback. He hung on the sill, allowing it to support his weight for him, as his gun drifted over the crowd, searching. She ducked lower, reaching in her jacket for her own weapon-- when the Knocte's gun suddenly stopped.

She knew whom it was pointing at, even before she looked.

Because his height was also a problem.

"Ian!" She yelled, pulling out her gun.

But she was too late.

He swung around in her direction, his blue eyes finding her in the crowd, piercing her with question, at the same time the shot fired. She heard herself scream at him from somewhere distant, watched his eyes go wide at the sound, knowing what it meant. Saw Jim reach for his son.

He was too late.

But Daniel wasn't.

She wasn't even sure he'd known where the threat was coming from. Only whom it was for. And that was enough. The moment she'd called his brother's name, Daniel had thrown himself in front of Ian.

The impact jerked him backwards, and he fell, slamming into Ian. Marley lost sight of them both as they hit the ground together. She shoved the thinning crowd of people and wolves roughly out of the way, following Jim's stunned face, and Ian's voice.

"Danny! *Danny!*"

Another shot went off as she reached Ian's side and crouched down next to him, but this time it was the Knocte who fell. She didn't see who got him. It didn't matter.

Ian had collected his brother into his arms, but Daniel was still, his eyes half open, staring blankly up at them. Winchester seemed to sense something was wrong, letting out a low whine that caught Lady's attention. Ian looked frantic. His hands shook as he clutched his brother's shirt, his gaze flitting over Daniel, taking it all in, but not yet believing it. She reached out to put a hand on his shoulder, just as Jim dropped to his knees next to them, swearing softly.

Jack suddenly appeared behind them.

"He's not dead," he assured, and Marley realized she'd left him behind.

And as if he'd heard, Daniel suddenly coughed. He made a choking noise, and lifting his head, examined the shotgun damage to his chest. With a groan he dropped his head back against Ian.

"Ow," he said, and coughed again.

They all stared down at him, trying to come to their own realizations.

"Lycan," Jim breathed first, "right. I must say it does come in mighty handy sometimes."

"Not silver," Daniel confirmed, his voice grisly, and attempted to sit up again. When Ian tried to help, he pushed his brother away. "Just go. I'll heal."

Ian's anxiety quickly dropped away into anger. Marley could tell by his face, that it was one order he would never follow.

"Not on your life," he growled, and threw his brother's arm around his shoulders, hoisting him none too gently onto his feet. Marley hastily stepped back out of their way, and nearly ran into Jack.

"Careful, boy," Jim cautioned Ian, as Daniel gasped, clutching at his chest with his free hand.

"We need to get inside," Jack reminded. "They'll be waiting for Daniel."

Ian froze. "Why?"

Daniel sighed and urged his brother forward; Ian complied to helping him, but didn't let the subject go.

"Why, him?"

Jack looked to Ian with confusion, following in the brothers' wake, just as Jim did. Marley moved after them, her eyes trained on the windows above.

"Daniel," Jack said. "You didn't tell them."

Daniel closed his eyes briefly. "No."

"Tell us what?" Jim and Ian both demanded at once.

"He's the head male. The top dog, if you will. The pack leader," Jack supplied.

"*What?*" they chorused. Ian screeched to a halt, but Jack waved them on persistently.

"You mean that scene at the grave yard… that wasn't just a 'we're your pack and we've got your back, brah' moment?" Ian asked, his eyes searching his brother's carefully neutral expression.

"No," Daniel admitted. "I asked them to come."

Jim was concerned with other matters. "How'd you do it? What was the challenge?" When Daniel remained silent he prompted, "*Dan.*"

"It was just a little fight," Daniel muttered. Marley noticed how he was already walking straighter, his breaths less ragged.

Jack snorted. "A little fight? Is that really what you'd call it, Daniel? I wouldn't."

Daniel shot him a look that said clearly '*shut up.*'

Jim looked angry again. "When will you boys learn that playing with fire doesn't make you brave, it just gets you dead?"

At the word fire, Daniel's usually gentle brown eyes darkened remarkably, and by the word dead, they were all at the front doors, and he'd freed his arm from around his brother's shoulders. They all stood behind him, watching his back as he faced the doors, his shoulder's rising and falling as he took a heavy breath.

Jim looked apologetic, and Ian's face was hard-edged and grim.

Then Daniel threw the doors open, and walked through as if

he hadn't sustained an injury at all.

A garble of noise rushed forth to meet them the moment he did. They followed behind him, and then froze, as all conversations simultaneously died, every pair of glowing eyes, human and wolf, turning to look at them. The doors slammed shut loudly behind Marley, and she had to force herself not to flinch. The lycans were perched on old abandoned, probably infested, lobby chairs, leaning against cobwebbed windowsills, and camped out on the grime-covered floors. There were bodies too, vampire ones, fairly old. A Knocte's handy work, left headless and crumbling. A few lycans even lounged against them, like they were just another piece of busted furniture.

"Okay," Ian muttered, so only their immediate party could hear. "I'm officially weirded out."

"Nice of you to join us," a voice rang out over his. A girl both dark in hair and eyes, laid across what must have once been the front desk. Her shorts were jean cut-offs, her t-shirt a faded and wrinkled black. Both her arms were stretched up above her, her legs dangling off the far right side. Her head swivelled to regard them. "Your team's got to keep up, Dan. We can't always wait for you."

She said it like it happened all the time, like they always fought side by side with Knoctes and were often held up by them. No mention of their contributions seemed important either. Marley crossed her arms tightly, and glared at the girl. Noticing, Dark Eyes chuckled, rolling to her side, and propping her head up with one hand.

"That's enough, Jo," Daniel cut in curtly, when she seemed about to say more. "We're running short of time, and every minute counts now." Gakwin, still wearing the hat Marley couldn't help admiring, nodded to him in agreement from the far wall. "Everyone, phones out," Daniel ordered. "Group with people and swap contacts. Then each group cover a level. Keep in touch with one another. No one gets left behind, you hear me? Jack and Jim will be covering the lobby." He glanced back at them. "Watch for Knoctes, and watch for us. If we find survivors we'll send them down to you. Make sure they reach the pack members stationed on the perimeter safely."

"You got it, kid. We'll do our best," Jim nodded, and then

359

scanned his home base.

"All right," Daniel said in finality, and the lycanthropes understood the dismissal, moving to do as ordered. Some more willingly than others. "Ian, Marley," he added for them, "with me."

They ended up on the ninth story, staring down the row of grimy doors. The numbers, which originally hung on them, now slanted to one side, hung upside-down, or were simply and altogether missing. The carpeted hallway itself was stained. Water most likely, but who could know for sure?

"What do you think the chances are we walk down the hall and nothing jumps out at us?" Marley asked.

The brothers answered her at the same time, their similar tones melting together. "Zero."

"Right," she said with a sigh, "weapons out then."

Daniel let a knife slip free from the sleeve of his shirt, sliding neatly into his hand. Ian pulled a handgun from the inside pocket of his jacket. Marley selected her own blade from the collection at her waist. The long one. Her favorite. She examined it briefly, her green eyes reflecting back at her.

Ian stepped forward first, Winchester following, and led the advance directly into the center, where he stopped. Glancing around, he looked somewhat bored, but Marley could see the way his eyes, though calm, took everything in, his fingers playing over his gun with familiarity.

"Well, so far so--." He never finished-- the doors bursting open on each side, Knoctes flooding out to fill the hall, battle cries mingling with curse words. Marley dove under the first shotgun blast, sliding across the floor towards her attacker. She took him out at the knees with a fluid slash, and when he fell, she promptly connected her knee to his face for good measure. Booted steps behind her, and Lady's growl, made her whirl around. Ripping a smaller dagger from her belt, she threw, imbedding it in the woman's stomach. All it took was a shove to bring her down the rest of the way, her brown hair spilling beneath her as she hit the floor.

Then hard arms seized Marley from behind, a knife pressing against her throat. He had hold of her blade hand. Unfortunate. But not unfixable. Lady circled anxiously, but didn't interfere, as Marley's heeled boot found the Knocte's foot. She seized his wrist with her free hand, preventing herself damage, as he protested, and then threw her head back, smashing it into his nose. His hold slackened, and she was able to wretch her blade arm free, swinging it up to thrust it through his neck. She jerked it back roughly, and he crumpled to ground behind her, making wet choking noises.

For a second she had room to breathe, and she spotted Ian and Daniel.

It almost made her forget where she was.

They fought as one person. All fluid movement and predicted outcomes, picking up where the other left off. She watched Daniel slam his hands over a Knocte's ears, screwing his balance, before shoving his knee into the man's chest. As the Knocte hunched over, Daniel slammed his knife into the guy's back, who then stumbled past him, where Ian, appearing consumed with his own battle, found time to rip the blade free, and toss Daniel his own gun in return. Daniel pegged a Knocte clear through the forehead with it, and then threw a shoulder into the next one, forcing the woman toward his brother. Ian jammed the knife between her ribs, then ducked as Daniel ploughed a bullet into a man fast coming up behind him. Winchester dashed around them, creating a small perimeter, deterring attackers from bombarding the brothers all at once.

It was like watching an intricate dance. And in that moment, more than any before, she saw their bond, how deeply they understood each other. They knew exactly what the other would do, even before they knew themselves, knew what they needed, and how to get it to them in a quick, efficient way. It was mesmerizing. A fist shot. A moan. Another fluent swapping of weapons, this time over their shoulders. A gunshot. A disarming-- the blade immediately handed off to the other, then tossed, cartwheeling with undeniable aim at a target.

A noise. Behind her.

She spun. Then realizing it was too late to make a counter attack, hit the ground. The shot missed, ploughing through the wall behind her, but in the next instant, a hand fisted in her hair, hauling her to her feet. She grabbed for the barrel of his shotgun, forcing it away from her. He released her hair, but took the opportunity to use the weapon as a bar, slamming it lengthwise against her chest, pinning her to the peeling, wallpapered wall. He caught her wrist, twisting it until, with a sound of protest, her blade hit the ground. His body played too, pressing tightly against her to prevent any unarmed assaults. Lady attacked his pant leg, but he kicked the dog away, his boot connecting with her snout. The dog yelped.

He leaned in. "Oh, this is going to be fun," he smirked, his hazel eyes gleaming. His breath smelt like coffee and something sour. He pressed the gun into her harder, constricting her breathing. She drove her heel into his foot like she did the other, but he didn't react nearly as much. His eyes flashed, and removing a hand he struck her across the face.

A mistake.

The hit stung, and she tasted blood in her mouth, but it was what she was looking for. She shoved the loose end of the gun up abruptly, forcing it away, and connecting it with his chin. She only had a second before he'd gain control again, and rushed to jump on her slight advantage. Finally having some space, she swung her knee back and drove it hard into his groin. Low blow, but so be it. When he dropped a couple of inches in height, she slammed her hand into his throat, and then shoved him backwards. He writhed on the floor, and she reached for her fallen blade. The moment he tried to regain his footing, she was ready for him, driving the blade home.

He gasped, and she jerked his head close to her. "You're right," she whispered, "that was fun." Then she pulled her weapon free and let him drop to the dank carpet at her feet.

She looked up. Ian and Daniel were standing amongst a pile of bodies. The battle finished. Daniel looked around himself with a regrettable expression on his face, his lips pressed in a tight line. He patted Winchester's head, as the dog panted at his side.

Ian was going through the fallen's pockets.

Triumphantly, he pulled out a small wad of twenties, and held it up for his brother to see. Ian's eyebrows lifted, pleased. Daniel shook his head dismally in acknowledgement, then caught Marley's gaze.

"You good?" he asked. She realized she was flexing her jaw, pressing on it with a hand, where she'd been hit. Ian paused to look up at her.

"Fine," she said roughly, then glanced away from them, wiping the sweat from her forehead with the back of her sleeve. At her feet Lady was rubbing her nose against the carpet, pawing at it with displeasure.

Marley crouched down in front of the dog, aware of the brothers' scrutiny, and grabbed Lady's muzzle. She examined the damage from side to side. "She'll be fine too," she deduced, after a moment. Winchester trotted over and licked the other dog's snout helpfully.

"Oh, you better be fixed," Marley scolded him.

"Sadly," Ian remarked.

Daniel rolled his eyes. "Let's check the rooms," he prompted.

They did. Without much success. At least until they reached the third from last door. It was locked. Or perhaps rusted shut. You could make your guess.

"That's not a red flag at all," Daniel noted sarcastically.

Ian made a face of agreement. Then abruptly kicked the door in.

Dust plumed as it left its hinges and connected with the floor. The room was dark, and Ian saw Daniel's eyes adjust, flaring brighter. He forced himself not to react.

"Marley, guard the door," Daniel ordered, looking to their victims, sprawled dead or unconscious on the floor. "Take care of anyone who wakes up." Then he stepped through the door. Winchester leaped after him, Ian following.

Ian didn't make it two steps when a light flared on, and a voice called out. "It's about time! I--." Then the man cut himself off with a curse, his eyes flitted between him and Daniel.

The man was in his early thirties, sitting in a torn armchair. His chestnut hair was trimmed short, and his face a five o'clock shadow. There was a scratched table beside him, a flashlight sat aimed at the ceiling, and sitting on the floor at his feet, placed in between his knees was a girl. Ian immediately recognized her from Churchill. The dragon. The dock. The Knocte had a shotgun to the back of her head. Straight, brown hair skimmed her shoulders, her pale, hazel eyes looked to Daniel.

But that little scene wasn't their biggest problem.

Because she wasn't the only one. The rest of the room was filled with vampires, all sitting on the floor. Men, women, children, arms hugging their legs. They stared silently at him and Daniel, their eyes judging whether or not their situation had improved or worsened. Ian could feel his brother's tension beside him like a taut wire, his eyes taking in the captives in front of him.

Ian strode further into the room, twirling his handgun around his finger. Everyone's eyes followed him.

"What?" he threw the question to the Knocte. "Not who you were expecting? Thought your little allies would come back to your rescue? " He stopped and stared at the man. "Well guess again. We took good care of them." His eyes swept to the captives, reading their mood. Hope mixed with fear. "All of them."

"Screw off," The Knocte snarled.

"They wouldn't have come for you anyway," Daniel said moving to Ian's side. "Knoctes don't operate that way-- even if they are working together." He nodded to the man. "You have to know that nothing's really changed."

"Really?" the man snorted disbelievingly. "I didn't sign up for this crap!" His shotgun pressed harder against the back of the girl's neck, and she stiffened. "Waist deep in Fifth World filth," --a muscle in Daniel's jaw twitched at his words-- "*and* pep talks. Well I guess it's just my lucky day," he droned sarcastically, then leaned back in his seat and stared at the ceiling in protest. "*Come. On.*"

"To you?" Ian asked. Sometimes he just couldn't help himself. "Keep dreaming, pal."

Daniel moved into the man's view. "You want off the train? Fine. I'll open the emergency door."

The man's head dropped back down to look at him. "And what, in that cracked head of yours, is that supposed to mean?"

"It means," Daniel said, and gestured to the girl. "You let her go. We let you go. I can make that happen."

"Or I could just use her as a shield and drag her along with me. Then I still got her. I'm free. And I come out on top."

Ian laughed. Again, couldn't help it.

"Oh, brilliant." He turned to his brother. "This guy's a freaken genius! Dragging a vampire hostage down to a bunch of lycanthropes and expecting them to care. Can't see how that could go wrong." He looked back at the Knocte. "Buddy, they don't lose sleep over the loss of one vampire, they care about killing the Knoctes who try to kill them, all right? To be honest, I'm surprised you kept things controlled here." He wandered closer, till his shoulders, although taller, lined up with his brother's. "It's like, what? Thirty lives to one? I'd have thought you would've been swamped by now. Kudos. Really."

"She's the leader, Ian" Daniel said stiffly. "They won't pull a move that might get her killed."

"Ah," he said and looked at the girl, "the leader." Her face was an emotionless mask, but her fingers twitched unconsciously. "And who spilled that little secret to the Knocte network?" He turned to regard the others of her kind. "One of you, right? I bet it was. Got caught maybe? By a Knocte who went all 'take me to your leader' on you?"

"Him," Daniel said suddenly, sounding surprised with his own conclusion, and pointed out a kid with long greasy hair that hung in his face.

"You're crazy," the kid snapped.

"And they speak!" Ian announced.

"Next time try glaring with hatred like everyone else, and not studiously avoiding eye contact with the accuser," Daniel suggested. "It stamps 'guilty' on your forehead."

"Yeah, it was him," the Knocte confirmed. "Just wave a gun around, and he caves like bats in the daylight."

The witty remark on Ian's tongue was suddenly pushed from his mind with the sound of gunshots. They all glanced towards the door. Marley was framed in its entranceway. She'd opened fire at a target just out of their sight, Lady barking furiously at her side. She ducked from returning fire.

Would this day never end?

"Looks like you were wrong," the Knocte grinned. "Someone came for me after all."

"Or for us," Ian noted, forcing himself to remain calm. "They could have come for us. Sadly, we're not everyone's favorite band of weirdoes." He glanced towards the shattered window. At the fire escape that lay just beyond it. Thinking fast, he pointed in its direction dramatically, though there was nothing to see, but a satisfying exit. "I know those guys did."

365

The Knocte couldn't help himself. He looked. Leaning forward in his chair, his gun dropped slightly.

Stupid.

Faster than he thought he could, Ian brought his handgun up and fired. The shot caught the Knocte straight in the head, and he slumped forward. The girl skittered out from underneath his weight.

"Lesson one," Ian muttered to himself, already on the move. He followed after his brother, Daniel already heading towards the window. "Never underestimate the old 'what's that?' distraction."

Daniel wrenched it open, unleashing dirt into the air, and glanced out of it either way. "Fire escape's clear," he announced. He tucked his knife away, and set aside the duffle.

Ian waved impatiently at the clan. "Let's go, let's go," he urged, Marley's shots consistently ringing in his ears. "We haven't got all day, people."

Winchester skirted around them, rounding everyone up. They stood in line, and Daniel started helping them out the window one at a time, murmuring reassurances and directions. The clan leader stood at his side, surveying his work, lending words of her own.

Ian stood facing the door. Marley and her combaters had travelled out of sight. Only their shadows danced on the walls. "Faster, Dan," he pled.

Daniel glanced at him. His murmurs increased in pace.

Ian felt torn between barging into the hall to assist Marley, and staying to guard the room and his brother from any threat that might slip past. Leaving Daniel alone with a clan of vampires wasn't high on his favourite's list either.

He hoped Marley could hold her own.

The shots outside the door died off around the same time Daniel rushed the last few people through the window. Ian overheard the clan leader say something about adding Daniel's number to her speed dial, and then with a quick swoop in, kissed him on the cheek, before ducking out the window.

Normally, Ian would have been all over that with a remark, but as Daniel returned to his side, retrieving the duffle, and snaking the Knocte's shotgun as he did, his face was a hard mask. Now was not the time for joking. Ian stayed silent as they made towards the door together. They paused, each flanking a side of its frame, then without the need to count, simultaneously swung around, guns up.

They met no resistance at either end. The hall deserted, except for the fight's casualties lying on either side. Anyone of them could have been Marley's recent target.

Ian had just begun to lower his gun and venture forward for a better look, when Winchester suddenly erupted in a bark and sprinting past them, headed in the opposite direction. Looking up, he exchanged a glance with his brother.

"Follow him," Daniel decided.

Ian didn't argue. The dead would stay dead, that much he knew for sure.

Cautiously they tailed the German Shepherd. The dog cocked an ear and let another bark go. This time there came an answer, Lady keening a response. Ian felt a chill move through him, and gripping his gun, stepped up the pace. Winchester took the hint and loped on ahead of them.
"Marley!" Ian called, and with a couple more paces, Ian could hear Lady more prominently, letting out a continuous stream of whines. Winchester cut left, disappearing into one of the last rooms of the hall, and Ian followed.

The moment he barged into the room, shoving the partly closed door aside, he froze. Daniel nearly ran into him, shouldering him aside, when he didn't move.

"Marley?" Ian asked.

She didn't answer him. Propped up against the wall, her expression was pinched with pain, her breathing too fast, hissing between her clenched teeth. Her red hair had almost all fallen from its elastic, cascading down the back of her neck, and plastering itself to her face, getting caught in her eyelashes. Both her hands were pressed to her abdomen, trying to force pressure onto a leaking wound. Her shirt was already soaking through, blood oozing between her fingers.

Daniel moved, dropping his shotgun, and crouched down in front of her.

"Ian, I need your help," he said, his voice a forced calm. Daniel shouldered his jacket off, and tossed it at him. Ian caught it automatically, snapping into action. He moved to her other side as

Daniel drew his t-shirt over his head. He folded it, as small and as thick as he could, and then held out his hand to Ian. "Yours."

Ian didn't hesitate, automatically mimicking his brother's action. He tossed Daniel his shirt.

"Get her belt."

Ian reached around her waist, unclipped it, and laid it aside. His brother placed his t-shirt over her hands and she slid them out from under it, her fingers shaking.

Ian understood what he was trying to do. "I'm going to sit you up and away from the wall, okay?"

She looked at him, their eyes locking. For a minute she just gazed, then without looking away, bobbed a trembling nod. He draped her arm around his shoulders, and parking himself beside her, let her lean against him, as Daniel worked. Daniel snaked Ian's shirt around her torso, in a process of securing his own in place as a makeshift bandage. Ian searched his brother's face, looked for clues as to how bad it really was, but Daniel's face was a determined mask of stone, sternly set and giving away nothing.

With a necessary jerk, Daniel pulled the knot tight. Marley gave a small cry, and then struggled to settle her breathing. Her forehead pressed against Ian's neck, and swallowing hard, he held a comforting hand to the back of her head. He could smell her shampoo, a sort of honey oat smell. In front of them, Lady was vibrating on the spot, her body jerking with non-stop anxiety. Winchester was sitting quietly, licking his lips nervously, and giving hopeful thuds of his tail.

Daniel emptied Marley's belt and used it as a second secure over the t-shirts, and then began collecting weapons of necessity and packing them into their duffle. He packed their jackets too.

"We need to get her out of here," Daniel ordered. "Now."

"On your feet," Ian warned her. "Ready?"

She grit her teeth, nodding. "Yeah."

He hoisted her to her feet, as gently as possible, but she still gasped, her body shuddering in pain and shock.

"Easy," he murmured, his arm slipping around her waist to offer additional support. "Push it to the back of your mind."

She smiled through her pain, but it was more like a grimace. "Easy for you to say, Handsome."

They exited the room, the dogs following, weaving in

between bodies. They took it slow, but as they reached the stairs, Ian was forced to take over completely, stooping to sweep her feet out from under her. She rested heavily in his arms. Daniel went first, gun ready, making their way. Ian tried to move with exceptional care. He had her cradled against his chest, her head tucked under his chin, but he could tell his every movement hurt her. Her breath hitching, even under his grace.

As they reached the lobby, Jim was alone, noticing them with sudden alarm. He looked like he'd been through his own trial. There was a large cut on his arm, and his nose was still partially bleeding.

"What happened?" Jim demanded.

Ian just shook his head.

"We found a group of vamps." Daniel supplied, "got them out a window. Marley held off the stream of Knoctes."

"Where's Jack?" Marley croaked.

Jim's concerned gaze dropped back to her. "On the move," he said ruefully. "The Knoctes won the fight on eleven and forced their way down. Like you, the lower levels weren't ready for the second wave. The Knoctes ended up escaping out the front here." he wiped his nose on his sleeve with a sigh. "Jack and a few others from the pack went after them, but there's more of them than we thought," he said regretfully. "Even with the perimeter, our group is going to need some help."

Ian watched his brother's brain trigger into Scit mode. "I'll shoot out a warning text," he said, already pulling out his phone. He ran a hand through his tousled hair, and looked up at them, concern in his brown eyes. "We need to go."

They all moved toward the door as one, Daniel's fingers flying over the keys of his cell. It wasn't until they reached the street that Marley spoke up.

"Stop," she croaked against his chest. "You need to stop."

They all paused. Daniel didn't look up from his phone, his brow set in a furrow.

"Let's be serious," she mumbled. "You can't carry me into a battle and expect to be able to defend yourself. I'm dead weight to you. You have to leave me behind."

Daniel immediately glanced up, and Ian exchanged a look with him.

"Now, look here--," Jim started, but Daniel interrupted, understanding instantly what would need to be done.

"I'll stay."

"No," Ian said automatically. Though he was unwilling to admit to it, having Marley curled and rendered helpless in his arms, lacking any sort of 'raising Cain' attitude-- scared him. Scared him deeply. "The pack needs you. I got this."

Chapter Thirty-Seven

"Ian," she protested softly.

But it was like she wasn't there. Daniel nodded grimly to him, set the duffle on the trunk of the nearest car, a black Toyota, and started rummaging through it. The tires on the vehicle were slashed, the hood popped up, still sitting erect. With one glance Ian could tell it wasn't going anywhere, and looking around-- neither were the others. He wasn't sure which side was responsible, but no one was escaping easily tonight. He felt grateful his truck was parked a safe distance away. In that one small fact, he could find comfort.

"Dan." Marley said his name a little louder, and he looked up briefly. "Don't tell Jack, okay?" She swallowed. Her eyes pleaded for a promise from him. "He needs his head in the game."

Daniel paused his searching, regarded her for a second, and then nodded to himself. He found the tool he was looking for and set it aside on the trunk. He left both the jackets too.

"Good luck," he said, zipping up the bag and tucking his phone away. "I'll send help back as soon as I can. Promise." Then in the next second Daniel had turned with Jim and took off running, leaving them behind. Winchester looked between him and Daniel with quick, jerky movements, let out a high yip, and booked it after his brother.

Ian watched them go for as long as he could allow, then set Marley down gently, nestling her close enough so she could lean against the shredded tire of the car.

Uneasy as ever, Lady circled around her, tail drooping.

"You should be with them," Marley insisted between gasps. She wasn't looking at him though, her eyes following her Weimaraner.

"Shuddup," Ian muttered, deadpan, and reached for the tool. A tire iron. "I'm done with 'leave me' speeches." He weighed the object in his palm, curled his fingers around it like he would a bat. "You heard Dan," he continued. "No one gets left behind." Then as an after thought. "Cover your eyes."

Not bothering to check whether or not she complied, he took a deep breath. Swung.

371

The driver's side window shattered on impact, raining down on the street around them. Lady barked, startled.

"No one gets left behind," Marley reiterated with a scoff, as he brushed away shards. Her hands had found their way to her wound again. "What is this? Disney?"

Reaching inside the car, Ian flipped the locks. He pulled himself back, giving her a stern look. He felt the weight of glass in his hair. "Does this look like Disney to you?"

She stared at him with tired, green eyes, a moment too long perhaps. Then relented. "I suppose not."

He shook his head mournfully, and hoisted the door open.

"What are you doing?" she asked.

He crouched down in front of her, his sneakers crunching on fragmented glass as he moved. His hands dangled off his knees.

"Getting us out of the way," he answered. "And out of the elements."

She lifted a hand to touch his face then, her fingers placed just under his jaw, her thumb brushing his cheek.

"You're sweet, Ian. But please," she begged, "let's be realistic." Her lower lip trembled suddenly, and she bit down on it. "I'm a goner." Her eyes sought his. "And you don't have to sit through it, like some babysitter of death. You don't need to be afraid to leave me."

Ian searched her face. Her eyes watered in pain, and her skin tone was an eerily pale colour, but she still managed to put up a façade of stubbornness. At first glance, maybe it would stand, but at a second it was easy to see how terrified she really was.

He refused to process her words. He removed her hand from his face, holding it between both of his.

"I'm going to move you, again." He looked straight into her eyes as he said it, so she would see his absolute resolve on the matter. "It's going to hurt."

She disregarded his comment. "Don't be an idiot."

Ian gave a mirthless smile, as he grabbed the jackets off the trunk, fitting one around her shoulders, and draping the other over her like a blanket. "Sue me."

He looped his arms under her knees and shoulders, and lifted. It took some manoeuvring, but he eventually got them both settled into the car. His back pressed against the opposite backseat door, his legs stretched out across the seat in front of him. Marley sat nestled between them, her back resting against his chest. Lady joined the huddle, and parked herself between Marley's legs. Ian had to hook his heel into the door handle to close their entry door behind them.

"This is what we're going to do," Ian said over the wheezing sound that was her fight to regain breath. "We talk. You listen to my voice, and you answer with full sentences. I don't care how hard it is. And you *do not* fall asleep. Do you understand?"

She nodded.

"Marley," he prompted meaningfully.

"I understand," she snapped.

Ian felt himself sigh. "All right," he affirmed. "Good." Then he strove to find a topic of conversation.

"I figured out the big mystery. And even though he hasn't said anything about it, I can tell Dan has too."

Her answer was a carefully controlled exhale of breath. "What mystery?"

"The 'who's your Scit' mystery," he said. "It's Jack isn't it? And he's in love with you."

"He thinks he's in love with me," she corrected.

"There's a difference?"

"Yes," she assured him, and her voice left no room for argument. "I don't claim to know what love is, Ian. But from personal experience-- I know what it's not. And it's not infatuation."

"I wouldn't know," Ian admitted though he wasn't sure why he'd done so. Talking-- he guessed.

Marley made a disbelieving sound. "Oh, please."

He frowned. "What's that supposed to mean?"

"I've seen women trip over themselves in your presence."

"Doubtful."

"Fathomable," she countered. "And you can't argue about knowing women with a woman."

Ian leaned his head back against the windowpane, feeling exasperated. This wasn't the course of action he'd planned for the conversation. He heard Lady give a soft sigh, and inch a little more onto her master's lap.

When he glanced down again, Marley's eyelids were

drooping. Her long eyelashes slowly fluttering closed.

"*Hey,*" he chastised, suddenly sitting straighter. Lady retreated back, and Marley moaned with his movement. "Come on," he insisted, "you got to promise to stay with me, Marley. I'm not giving up on you."

"Let's not make promises we can't keep, all right?" Her smile was slow, sad. "I never expected to walk out of this thing in one piece, anyway."

"You can't think like that."

"I teamed up with the freaken Browning brothers," she mused like he wasn't one of the title. "I asked for a world of thinking like that. A handful of Knoctes against the entire population? *That's* what I signed up for."

"Better a handful. It beats a world of crap out of being alone."

She fell silent for a moment, until Ian grew worried. He turned, pressing his forehead to her temple.

"Marley," he prompted, over the strain in his voice.

"Alone is safer," she managed. "You fight your own battles, and no one else has to get hurt."

"My brother's battles are my battles," he said vehemently. "That won't ever change. We take it day by day. We kick the crap out of whatever life throws at us. And we always do it together."

"So I've noticed," she confessed. "No one will deny you and your brother as a hurricane force, Ian. But hurricane forces leave collateral damage."

"You're not collateral damage," he promised.

"Agree to disagree then," she sighed. "So… do I qualify for my dying wish yet?"

"No," he snapped.

She ignored him. "Find my brother--"

"Marley," he tried to interrupt sharply.

"--and tell him he's a douche bag."

"Marley, listen to me…"

"I want him to know I hated him until the day I died. Feel free to punch him if you feel so inclined."

"I'M NOT GOING TO LET YOU DIE!"

"Shh," she scolded. "And after everything-- I think I deserve to speak my peace."

Ian took a deep breath, dug deep for control. "Aren't dying wishes supposed to be fruity nonsense. 'Tell this person goodbye and that I love them,' or 'tell me a story,' 'sing me a song.'"

She gave a phantom of a smile. "If I'd asked you to 'sing me a song,'" she mimicked his voice, "would you of?"

"No."

"There you go then."

They sat in silence for a minute, until he sensed Marley drifting again.

"You have to have a better wish than me flattening your brother."

"Not really," she said, and gazed up at him. "Though you could take out Andy too if you liked."

He stared right back, reassured by her green eyes.

"Fine," she said after a long minute, and a sigh. "How's this?"

At first her words confused him. But then her right hand slipped free of the jacket surrounding her, and came up, moving to the back of his neck, curling through his hair. He felt his eyes widen, and then without warning she pulled him down, their mouths connecting.

The kiss was stiff. Ridged with his shock. Lips moving in a sort of robotic response. But then, when his brain remained off-line, some urge seemed to kick in, and he leaned into her, his mouth softening.

He felt her gasp, felt her hand trail from his hair around to his face, and down his jawline, felt her heart hammering in her chest, pumping her blood faster.

That was when his brain suddenly clicked back in.

He swore internally.

Her left hand had moved up to joined her other one, at the same moment he jerked himself away. They both froze, staring at it.

It was covered in her blood.

Ian pulled the concealing jacket back with one swift movement, revealing her makeshift bandages to be soaked through. She saw it too. Squeezing her eyes shut, she tilted her head back against him. An uneven breath, that was probably meant to be steadying, left her lips, as her hand dropped back over her wound, adding pressure that wouldn't be enough. Ian sensed her trying to settle her heartbeat.

It felt like there was something stuck in his throat.

Wordlessly he slid his hand over hers, adding his own pressure. She let out an uncharacteristically soft whimper, her pinched face turning into his chest.

"Just hold on," he cajoled, and pressed his forehead against her clammy one. "Don't you go giving up on me."

Please, please, don't let me be too late... Ruby's thoughts echoed frantically through her head, as she raced towards the old hotel, translucent hair streaking behind her. She had had to ditch her car to slip through the fight unnoticed, and now her feet pounded relentlessly over asphalt, her shoulder bag slapping against her side. She nearly stumbled to a halt when she reached the street in front of the old, brick building, her eyes flitting around.

Daniel said they'd be here.

They had to be here.

He was worried. Even over the phone, she could tell. He'd desperately tried to keep her out of this battle she knew-- and had failed. She felt angry. Not because he'd failed, but because he'd tried to pretend this wasn't her fight to begin with.

They needed her. Her. Just a Scit/Knocte loving faerie, with no wings, no pixy dust, and a small talent with organics.

She turned a three-sixty, barely spotting the tint of brass hair from one of the cars.

Ian.

She sprinted to the Toyota, only just noticing the scattered glass in time to slow her pace, and begin picking her way safely through it. She could see them both now. Ian bare-chested, stretched out across the back seat, his arms wrapped around Marley, where she lay curled up against him. His lips were moving in a steady stream of words Ruby couldn't hear, and Marley was watching him with a barely comprehensive look, one both drowsy and quickly fading. She was beyond the point of speech.

The moment Ruby could reach the handle of the backseat door, she threw it open. Ian's eyes immediately jumped from Marley to her, where she stood panting in front of them. Lady, who she hadn't noticed before, sprang to her feet with a gentle bark.

Ian was scowling. "What're you doing here?" he demanded.

"Daniel sent me," she gasped, "to help. He told me to tell you," --another gasp-- "that someone named Gakwin is still otherwise engaged-- and you're to play nice."

"I don't know how to play nice," he warned.

"What happened?" she rasped.

"Shot."

"Show me," Ruby beseeched him. "Please."

She watched his blue, chilling eyes, hard set, and tried to plead with her own. Unlike some of the Fifth World population, it wasn't her eyes that gave away what she was, and she'd never been more grateful for that, than in this moment.

Tentatively she moved forward.

And the taut wire suddenly snapped.

"Don't touch her!"

Ruby retreated on instinct, but her inner hero wouldn't let her back down, not this time, wouldn't let her whither under the heated glare of Ian Browning. Daniel wasn't here to swing in for the rescue, and someone's life was on the line. She had to do this one on her own.

"Ian!" she exclaimed suddenly in frustration, her gel nails digging into the door handle, the only thing keeping her standing. "You have to just trust me on this one, okay? Trust me, or she's going to die!"

"I won't let it happen!" he snarled. "Lay off, Tinker Bell."

"It's happening, Ian!" she begged earnestly, tacking his name to the end of her plea, in the same way she'd always heard Daniel do it. "Please, Ian" --there was his name again-- "I can help." But his name was harsh on her lips. Bitter. Lacking the easy familiarity Daniel's always held.

Well there was a reason for that.

And suddenly she was very angry.

"LOOK AT ME!" she gasped out, and her sudden change in tone, caused him to do just that. "Have I ever hurt Dan?!" she screamed the question at him. The question she'd been wanting to hurl at him for as long as she could remember. "Have I?!"

The answer was no. And it would always be no. He had to

know that. Somewhere deep down, where the Knocte ingrained part of him didn't reach, he had to know it.

She took a deep breath. Tried again. "Please, let me see."

Ian's cold eyes lingered on her for another moment, and then without blinking, or changing his expression, slowly and gently pulled the concealing jacket back.

It was a mess.

Suppressing a shudder, Ruby set into action with trembling hands, swinging her shoulder bag around, and diligently digging through it. She found the bottle she was looking for, and up ending a tablet onto her palm, held it up for Ian to see.

"Make her take this."

He snatched it from her immediately, eyeing it over like some unwanted and venomous insect. "What is it?"

Ruby was already searching her bag for anything else useful. "Pain medication," she answered distractedly, adding another vile to her lap.

His fist tightened around it. "No. With the pain gone, she'll slip away."

"It won't be gone," she said regretfully. "Not all of it."

His eyes narrowed, hesitating.

"It has to be now," she prompted him both gently and sternly. *Now or never. Your choice.*

He closed his eyes briefly like he was letting resolve wash through him, and then using long fingers, tilted Marley's head back, and did as she'd asked him.

She nodded her approval. "Do you have a knife?"

He snorted in derision.

"Okay, good… I'll need you to get the bullet out."

He stared. "You're joking."

"You've done it for Dan before," she murmured. "He's told me."

"I have."

Now it was her turn to stare.

He caved, wordlessly pulling the knife from his waistband. They both looked it over, and Ruby realized by his expression that she wasn't the only one who wished it was suddenly thinner and longer than it currently was.

"You got some sort of magic faerie potion to close this

when I'm done?"

She gave another nod.

He sighed and set his jaw. "All right then."

With gentle, blood caked hands, he deftly peeled her shirt up to the top of her rib cage. Setting the knife tip to her wound, he started his work.

Marley's eyes widened, blinking more rapidly than before. She let out an anguished moan, and Ruby, feeling herself shiver, watched as Ian's eyes darkened.

She hugged herself. "Hurry," she pleaded.

He shot her a dark look, but a minute later he had the bullet in his bloody palm.

Knowing what she had to do, Ruby reached for the knife in his hand. She caught the handle, but he didn't let go.

"I need it," she said in way of explanation.

With a frustrated noise, and a nervous glance down at Marley, he dropped his hold.

Ruby held the knife in one hand, taking a couple deep breaths, and then leaning over Marley, she slid the knife across the length of her palm. Ian's eyes widened in horror, his hand shooting out to catch her wrist and force her hand away, up into the air. Blood started trailing its way down her arm, over his fingers.

His eyes were blue fire. "*What are you doing?!* It'll make her a faerie! It'll turn her!"

"It won't!" she yelled back. "It goes against every faerie law for me to tell you that-- but it won't."

He looked suddenly confused.

"Trust me." She was begging again. "Please."

Suddenly he jerked her wrist back down, his hold tightening as he moved her hand over Marley. A drop of blood fell into the wound, and Marley's lips parted in a gasp.

"Hold her down," Ruby urged ruefully. "It's going to hurt."

Then she squeezed her hand into a fist.

Marley screamed. The blood connecting with her wound. Her body bucking and arching upwards. Ruby felt Ian let go of her wrist, his arms locking around Marley, his lips pressing against her ear, frantically murmuring things lost in her screams.

The bullet wound bubbled, and Ruby felt her eyes well up with tears as Marley's torment continued to fill the car. They escaped down her cheeks, but she didn't stop until the wound had settled, and Marley's screams subsided into panting whimpers.

Then with shaking hands, she reached for the vile, the one she'd dug out of her bag earlier. She was breathing heavily she realized, and so was Ian, his chest rising and falling at a more than regular rate. They exchanged a worn look, and she poured the contents of the vile onto the wound and pushed the two sides of the bullet hole together. It took a minute, but it sealed shut.

"What is that?" Ian demanded, or perhaps wondered aloud. It was always hard to tell with him.

Ruby shook her head. "A lot of things. Took me awhile to get it right. Don't worry," she added hastily, "it won't hurt anything, and it will keep the wound closed."

She took gauze, a bandage, and ace wrap out of her shoulder bag next, three things she'd thought to pick up at a drug store on the way over. She folded the gauze carefully, and pressed it over the wound. She secured it with the bandage, as Ian took the ace wrap from her and started circling it snugly around Marley's torso. He tied the end and cut it loose with the knife she'd set aside.

They stared down at Marley's ashen features, their work completed. Ruby picked up what was left of the bandages and started to wrap her hand.

"She'll be okay," Ian tried to convince himself. Then dipping his head down closer to Marley, "You're okay."

"She still lost a lot of blood," Ruby noted. "She needs a hospital."

"Dan will have my truck," Ian sighed. "So I guess we keep her awake until the cavalry arrives."

Marley could only see the blurred outlines of the two people with her. She could hear their voices too, but the sounds melted and ran together, incomprehensible slurring as far as she was concerned. What kept her grounded, with the here and now, was the ever-present *thud thud* of the heartbeat beneath her ear. It had sped up, slowed down, and was now pulsing away at a steady and comforting rhythm. She tried to strain closer to it, but her body was sluggish, weak, and unwilling to follow her desired commands. If she was going to die, she would die to that sound she hoped, even as her own faded away.

She was only vaguely aware of the intrusion of other people. Only taking true notice to the mayhem when the thudding sound was suddenly gone, and the warmth it provided along with it.

No...

Her last thought before movement had her spiralling into blackness.

Chapter Thirty-Eight

"Marley…"

The clear sound glided towards her over a sea of black.

"Marley…"

I'm here, she thought back at it.

"Will you squeeze my hand for me?"

Pressure. And suddenly she found her body, her eyes popping open.

Blinking a couple more times, everything, blurry at first, started to slowly settle into focus.

Jack hovered over her, his light green eyes alight with relief.

Feeling groggy and confused, she searched past him. Puke green walls, sterile white tiled floors, a hanging curtain, and a bed with plastic railings. She was in a hospital.

And not alone.

Jack wasn't the only one present. Jim and Daniel both lounged in matching and equally green upholstered chairs. Jim looked tired, sore, and worn out, his plaid shirt only half buttoned. Daniel's lip was split, his left eye darkened since the last time she'd seen him, but still the gentle, warm, brown colour she remembered. Ruby perched in the windowsill, staring at the floor, or perhaps at her blindingly bright yellow heels. In the doorway behind them all, Ian leaned against the frame, his arms crossed over his chest, every muscle in his body looking tense and uptight. His face was both impassive, and careful, his eyes as intense as always. He wore a pair of dark jeans and a fresh, linen shirt, the same as his brother. His brass hair was wet like he'd just taken a shower. Her eyes dropped to his hands. Blood free.

"Welcome back," Jack said with a smile, and everyone looked round. Five pairs of eyes on her.

"How you feeling, kid?" Jim asked, his voice soft.

She did a quick once over.

"Stiff. Sore," she answered honestly, her voice rough from disuse. From the corner of her eye she thought she saw Ian's mouth curve down with disapproval. "Mainly tired."

She tried to sit up, and Jack pushed her back down, shaking

his mop of blond hair.

"It would be best if you took it slow."

"Better words were never spoken."

A woman wearing floral nursing scrubs stood in the doorway. She must have side stepped her way around Ian, because he hadn't moved. She gave him an appreciative look from the corner of her eye, her cheeks reddening slightly.

He didn't seem to notice.

"I'm sorry, but visiting hours have come to a close," she added.

"She just woke up," Daniel frowned, and the woman turned towards him. Her brown hair was pulled back tightly in a bun, but taking in the sight of him, and having Ian's chilling eyes suddenly shift towards her, she tucked an invisible stray lock behind her ear, looking suddenly uncomfortable.

The poor girl.

She wasn't used to the effect the Browning brothers could have on people.

The nurse cleared her throat. "Now that she's awake," she said with sudden and new conviction, pausing to nod in Marley's direction, "we need to take a few tests, and then it really is best if everyone lets her get some rest."

Jim stood first, and Marley watched as he swiped at the wrinkles in his jeans. "All right, that's our cue folks." He nodded in her direction. "Good to have you back with us, kid."

"We'll visit again," Daniel promised, standing next and giving her a reassuring smile. It didn't touch his eyes, and she wondered briefly if he'd felt any of the smiles he gave lately. Glancing at Ian, she saw her thoughts echoed in the concerned expression he was giving his brother.

Ruby shot her own fretful look at Daniel, before darting over to Marley's bedside. Squeezing her way in around Jack, she gave her a delicate hug.

Jack took her hand in his. "I have Lady, not to worry," he said, lifting and kissing the back of it, careful to avoid the IV.

She wanted to roll her eyes at him and the over gallant gesture, but found her gaze flitting towards the doorframe instead. It was empty-- Ian having unceremoniously departed.

She sighed inwardly, and the rest followed him, nodding

and waving their goodbyes, leaving her alone with the nurse.

The truck flew over the patched strip of road on the drive back.

"She's lucky. I admit I wasn't sure she'd make it," Daniel remarked, his voice rough.

Ian only gave him a curt nod, his eyes locked dead ahead. The truck cab lapsed into silence, and Ian knew both their minds were beginning to run to places they shouldn't.

Ian's disobediently running through comparisons. A younger Daniel with their dying mother, the older version with a dying Devlyn. His brother smaller and wounded, unresponsive in the backseat. Marley drifting away against his chest, his questions and ramblings going unanswered in both scenarios.

Death. Pain. This was their life. Both then and now.

Daniel was staring at the beads swinging from the rear-view mirror, his brown eyes never once leaving them, until they were almost at the Ay Motel, then something inside him seemed to snap, and he ripped them suddenly and unceremoniously from their perch.

Startled, Ian shot him a look, alternating glances between his brother and the road. The beads were pooled in Daniel's palm, dangling through the gaps between his fingers. He shifted them through his grip, feeling them, weighing them, and then as Ian pulled up to room thirty-three, shoved them deep into his jean's pocket. The truck had barely stopped when Daniel threw the door open, and got out.

Ian didn't move, the truck idling beneath him.

His brother seemed to debate with himself for a moment, and then with a sigh, Daniel leaned back in. "You coming?"

"I'm going to get a burger," Ian said without looking at him.

Daniel stared at him for the span of several seconds, and then shook his head slightly. "Right," he said, his face impassive, though his voice understanding. "Suit yourself."

The passenger door closed, and Ian reversed. He just caught sight of Winchester greeting his brother at the door, as he pulled away.

But he wasn't going to a burger joint.

He didn't know where he was going.

He was just doing what he always did, when he felt restless and his brain wouldn't shut off.

Drive.

Daniel exhaled a long breath as he entered the motel room, scratching Winchester behind the ears. He moved to the far side of his bed, and dug through his duffle bag of clothes for his familiar faded sweater, Ian's headlights retreating from the adjacent wall. Retrieving the item, Daniel threw it on, partially zipped it, and flipped the hood up, before stalking over to the desk and sinking heavily into the old swivel chair. Winchester followed, sinking to the ground and camping out at his feet.

He fished the string of beads from his pocket, looking them over once more. The ache inside him grew, his own internal monster, shredding him from the inside out. Dark thoughts he knew he couldn't allow himself to get lost in filled his mind.

It's your fault!

You should have been there!

Where were you when she needed you?

You should have protected her!

He tossed the beads aside hastily, firing up the laptop. There was an email sitting in his inbox.

Begging for a distraction he clicked it open.

This is only the beginning. Don't stop fighting. Never stop fighting for what is good.

With you,
DEEM

Marley woke in the middle of the night, momentarily forgetting where she was before it all slotted back into place.

Hospital.

Right.

She twisted, suddenly uncomfortable, realizing rather glumly, that the pain medication was wearing off-- and she was shivering. She made a valiant attempt at hiking the covers higher over her shoulders, but they were firmly tucked in around her.

She hated hospitals.

They even smelt bad, like anaesthesia and sterilizers. This one sure did.

But suddenly it was another smell that caught her attention. Something that didn't belong. Something both sharp and sweet. She jerked her head up, making the room spin for a few seconds-- and there he was. Parked in one of the green visitor's chairs beside her, his head rested on the edge of her bed, pillowed in his arms. His brass hair was lit up, catching the moonlight through the window. His eyes were closed in sleep, his breathing even.

"What...?" she whispered, but he didn't stir. She didn't even know how he'd gotten in the room, though her suspicions leaned towards the window. It would explain the chill in the air.

It was weird seeing him like this-- asleep. Not passed out drunk asleep, just an honest to goodness peaceful rest. His expression was relaxed, free of worry, guilt, and whatever else ate at his soul all the time. It made him look younger, more boyish like his brother, his hard lines softened.

And for once she allowed herself to let go of her own baggage and feel the same. Young, carefree, like the twenty-one year old girl she should have been.

Of its own accord, her hand stretched forward, resting itself lightly against the top of his head. She let her fingers run through the short strands of his hair, her thumb gingerly smoothing them away from his temple.

He didn't take notice, lost to sleep, but she still felt comforted by him, his presence seeming to fill the room like it always did.

Outside this building things were more wrong than they were right, she knew, tail spinning out of control, and there would be more battles to come. She'd barely scraped her way through the last one, but at the present moment-- she didn't care.

Feeling remarkably at ease, she allowed her mind to drift away, letting sleep once again claim her.

Acknowledgements

Thank-you God; all the nights I laid awake praying for inspiration, you always came through. A special thank-you to Bobbi-Lee's Art Studio for the gorgeous cover art. A thank-you as well to all whom believed in this endeavour, family, friends, and co-workers alike. Thanks to Cheryl Reynolds, Monique Chapman, Jean Read, and Josie Reynolds for their keen eyes, and help assisting me in my self-editing journey. And last, but most definitely not least, to the cast and crew behind my TV obsession: *Supernatural.* You have shown me the bond between brothers, and taught me what it means to be family. For that I will always be thankful.

About the Author

Leah J. V. Reynolds grew up in the small town of Coalhurst, Alberta, Canada. She is currently attending the University of Lethbridge for a combined degree in English and Education.